An Uncommon HONEYMOON

D0456432

Also by Susan Mann

A Covert Affair

The Librarian and the Spy

Published by Kensington Publishing Corporation

An Uncommon HONEYMOON

SUSAN MANN

To Robyn,

Susan Mann

ZEBRA BOOKS
KENSINGTON PUBLISHING CORP.

http://www.kensingtonbooks.com

ZEBRA BOOKS are published by

Kensington Publishing Corp.
119 West 40th Street
New York, NY 10018

First Printing: January 2018
ISBN-13: 978-1-4201-4332-4
ISBN-10: 1-4201-4332-8

eISBN-13: 978-1-4201-4335-5
eISBN-10: 1-4201-4335-2

10 9 8 7 6 5 4 3 2 1

Printed in the United States of America

For all who are stronger than they know

Acknowledgments

I'd like to take this opportunity to thank you all for reading the adventures of a librarian and her spy. It is my joy to write them.

I must thank my husband and science advisor, Ken. His ability to help me hammer away at my out-there ideas until they sound remotely plausible is indispensable. As always, I'm indebted to my brilliant and insightful editor at Kensington Publishing, Esi Sogah. She unfailingly knows exactly what my stories need to make them better. Thank you, too, to the entire Kensington team, who are a fantastic group of people. I'm so blessed to get to work with them. This also goes for my agent, Rena Rossner of the Deborah Harris Agency, who I also have the privilege of calling my friend. She is simply the best.

Finally, thank you to my daughter, parents, family, and friends for their unwavering support.

Chapter One

The bottom of Quinn Ellington's unbuttoned white lab coat fluttered behind her like a superhero's cape as she strode along the corridor of a Frankfurt pharmaceutical research facility. James Anderson kept pace beside her, his matching lab coat equally billowy. The aluminum briefcase hanging from his hand sporadically brushed against her thigh.

Dr. Dieter Ziegler and his assistant had joined a meeting in the conference room at the end of the hallway a moment before. That meant she and James had thirty minutes to slip into Ziegler's office, steal the vials from his safe, and sneak out without being noticed.

No problem.

Quinn dipped her chin and adjusted her black-rimmed glasses, shielding her face from the woman passing them from the other direction.

"You want to do something next weekend?" James asked when the woman was out of earshot.

She smiled at his attempt to keep her loose during her first mission as a full-fledged CIA undercover operative. "I can't."

"Why not?"

"I've got a wedding to go to."

"Blow it off."

"I can't. I kinda have to be there."

"Why?"

"I'm the bride." Their pace slowed as they neared Dr. Ziegler's office.

"You know, now that you mention it, I have a wedding to be at, too."

"Yeah? That's weird. I wonder if it's the same one. Is it in California?"

James held the ID badge he'd liberated from an unsuspecting senior scientist in front of the electronic lock. When the red light turned green, he pushed in the door and held it open. Quinn swept past him into a small front office. "As a matter of fact, it is. A beautiful church in Redondo Beach."

A brass nameplate placed at the front edge of the desk informed them Sabine Müller was the name of Ziegler's assistant.

"Mine, too. Maybe I'll see you there," Quinn said. She tried the knob on the door leading to the inner office. Locked. She slipped the lock pick set from the pocket of her lab coat and zipped open the case.

She took two implements and slid the wiry ends into the lock.

"How about you meet me at the front of the sanctuary, say four-fifteen or so?" James asked.

"I can do that. I hope you don't mind, but my dad will be with me. Fair warning. He'll be armed."

"No need for a shotgun. I'll be there of my own free will."

One of the tumblers in the lock gave way. "Nah, it'll just be his sidearm under his tux jacket. You know how Marines are."

"I do," he said. "I'll be armed, too, by the way."

"Me, too. I picked up a pretty thigh holster for the occasion. It's white and lacey. You'll like it."

She smiled at his rumbling growl.

"All right, you two. That's enough," she heard the long-suffering voice of Darius Sampson say through the communication device in her ear. "You keep it up and I'm gonna hurl all over this van full of expensive surveillance equipment. I'll tell Meyers to send you the bill."

"Okay, okay. We don't want any hurling," James said.

"What are you two doing anyway, going on an op so close to your wedding? Sounds crazy to me."

"The wedding has totally consumed my life the last two months. I needed a break before someone tossed me in a rubber room and threw away the key," Quinn said.

"Hard to argue with that, I guess," Darius replied.

"I'm sorry I wasn't able to help you more with all the planning," James said. "Living in Moscow made it difficult."

"It's okay. My mom was a huge help. I'm glad your stint there is over."

The lock gave way and she cracked open the door.

"We're in," Quinn said as she and James stepped into Ziegler's office. The door clicked closed behind them.

"Roger that," Darius said. "Ziegler and his assistant are still in the meeting."

Quinn took a quick survey of the room. The large office was well appointed with its massive wooden desk, leather couch, and bar with bottles of various types of liquor on the shelves behind it. One of the perks to being the company's chief research officer, she supposed. Ziegler may have occupied a corner office, but its location didn't mean it was meticulously kept. The desk was cluttered with stacks of scientific journals, papers, and files. Not one more book could have been wedged into the overstuffed bookcases. As much as the librarian in Quinn was drawn to examine and straighten those books, she resisted. She wasn't there for that.

James handed her the metal briefcase and headed for the

desk. He inserted a flash drive into Ziegler's computer and began to type.

Quinn went straight for the painting of a tranquil lake setting located on the wall above the sofa. She set the briefcase on one cushion and stepped up onto the other. Reaching out, she slid the painting mounted on rails to one side to reveal a wall safe.

From her lab coat pocket, she removed her smartphone and a thin cable. She plugged one end of the cable into her phone and the other into a port next to the keypad on the face of the safe. With a tap on the screen, she launched the CIA-developed app that would provide her with the digital key.

While the app ran, she took a small, flat plastic box with Ziegler's fingerprint on a thin piece of latex from her other pocket and opened it. She placed the latex on the pad of her thumb and breathed on it several times to moisten it.

Her phone chimed and displayed the six-digit passcode. She pressed her thumb to the biometric scanner and punched the code into the keypad.

The safe started to beep.

Crap.

Was it supposed to do that?

"Babe? I might have set off—" The beeps ceased and she heard a soft click. She released a relieved breath. "Never mind. We're good," she said and swung the safe's door open.

Inside, a half dozen glass vials of emerald-colored liquid were precisely arranged on a shelf. "Why is the evil stuff always green?"

"That mandate is clearly stated in section thirty-seven of the League of Evil Scientists Handbook," James replied, his eyes never leaving the computer screen. "I'm sure Ziegler checked to make sure the color of his psychotropic agent was regulation."

Quinn grinned as she lifted one of the vials from the safe

and carefully secured it in the slot cut in the gray foam lining of the briefcase. "I bet he did. He wouldn't want to get kicked out of the League of Evil Scientists for such a heinous violation." She repeated her actions and secured another vial. "Almost done?"

"Yeah. I uploaded the Trojan horse onto his system already. I only need a couple more minutes to finish copying the restricted data files."

"Uh, guys?" Darius said. The tightness in his voice snapped Quinn to attention. "You may not have a couple of minutes. Ziegler and his assistant just left the conference room."

"What?" she said with a frown. "He's not supposed to be out of there for at least another twenty minutes."

"I dunno. No one else has left. Even the CEO is still there. Hang on. Maybe they're not . . ." After pause, Darius said, "They're on their way to you."

"Copy." Under his breath, James grumbled, "Dammit."

Adrenaline flooded Quinn's system. Moving quickly, she snatched the last two vials in each hand and jammed them into the foam. She slapped the briefcase shut and snapped the fasteners.

Quinn closed the safe, removed the phone cable, and slid the painting back in place. She leaped from the couch, grabbed the briefcase's handle, and looked at James. His blue eyes were slightly wild as he urged on the computer. "Come on, come on, come on."

"Forget it. We gotta go."

"Done!" James yanked out the flash drive and sprang to his feet.

The urgency in Darius's voice sliced through her. "Too late. They'll see you if you come out now."

"Maybe we can chance it and tell them we were waiting for him but decided to leave," Quinn said.

James shook his head. "This is a restricted floor. We're not even supposed to be here."

"Crap. You're right." She looked at the bar and then at James. "Do we hide or shoot our way out?"

"Make a decision, guys," Darius said. "They're almost there."

James grabbed Quinn's hand and pulled her behind the bar. "We hide. Let's hope they came back to get something for the meeting and will leave again right away. If not, we tranq them and take off." Crouched behind the bar, they balanced on the balls of their feet, removed their tranquilizer pistols from their ankle holsters, and held them at the ready.

"They're about to open the outer door," Darius said.

Quinn strained to hear clues as to exactly where Ziegler and Sabine were. She heard their muffled voices through the wall between the two offices. If James was right and they had come back for something related to the meeting, was it was inside Ziegler's office? If so, he would go to unlock the door any second. She hoped she hadn't left any evidence that the lock had been picked. Otherwise, trouble would come their way fast. She swallowed and tightened her grip on her pistol.

She flinched when she heard what sounded like a body slamming against the door. The knob rattled, but the door remained closed. There was another loud thump.

James glanced at Quinn in confusion. She shrugged in response.

The doorknob turned and the door flew open. Ziegler murmured in a low tone, prompting a giggle from Sabine. Heavy breathing punctuated throaty moans.

Oh.

God.

No.

No, no, no.

Quinn's blue eyes rounded and she looked at James. He wrinkled his nose in reply.

She heard two clunks on the floor, which she assumed was Sabine kicking off her shoes. A white lab coat arced through the air and draped over the bar.

Ziegler spoke in an urgent growl.

Sabine's response was breathy and pleading.

For a fleeting moment, Quinn considered turning the tranquilizer gun on herself.

Air gusted from the couch cushions with a *fwoomp*, indicating the amorous couple had crashed onto the leather couch.

It sounded like a wrestling match had broken out.

Quinn grimaced when Sabine expelled a prolonged, guttural groan.

At the unmistakable clap of a hand slapping flesh, Ziegler blurted, "*Ach! Ja!*" With each smack, the level of his lusty enthusiasm rose.

Quinn bit her lip and struggled to keep the giggles at bay.

James's face relaxed into a grin.

The movements on the couch turned rhythmic.

A boisterous duet of ardent and sustained ecstasy filled the room.

Quinn grimaced and squeezed her eyes shut.

When the exclamations subsided and all she heard was ragged breathing, Quinn dared to open her eyes and peek at James.

He winked and shot her a crooked smile, which quickly faded. The eyes boring into hers turned intense and probing.

She held his gaze and gave him a sharp nod. Time to focus.

Quinn concentrated on the sounds coming from Ziegler and Sabine. Neither spoke as they rose from the sofa. Clothes were straightened and the lab coat disappeared from atop the bar.

One sound Quinn hoped not to hear was Ziegler settling in behind his desk. If that happened, they could be stuck behind the bar for who knew how long. Would they have to tranquilize him and his assistant to escape after all?

As Ziegler and Sabine moved about the room, Quinn kept her stare zeroed in on the open end of the bar. If either came around to pour drinks, she would drop them.

To her great relief, Ziegler didn't take a seat at his desk, nor did either step behind the bar. The door between offices opened and shut. Quinn blew out a long, slow breath.

"They're on their way back to the conference room," Darius said after the outer door closed with a clunk. "You two okay?"

"Yeah, we're fine," James said.

"What happened? I couldn't hear anything through your comms."

"We were witness to what would best be described as a quickie," Quinn said.

Darius snickered. "I wondered. They looked pretty happy coming out of that office."

James and Quinn stood and hurried out from behind the bar. "Get us out of here and we'll describe every awkward detail for you later," James said.

"Nah. I'm good." After a beat, Darius said, "The hall is clear. You're good to go."

"Copy," James said, holstering his pistol. Quinn did the same.

Seconds later, they were through the front office and out the door. Once in the hallway, they turned and retraced their steps.

They were halfway to the elevator when Darius said, "Security guard incoming from the corridor up ahead."

"Is there a bathroom or janitor's closet we can duck into?" Quinn asked.

"Nothing close enough," Darius said. "If you hurry, you can get into the stairwell next to the elevator before he turns the corner. Try not to look too obvious, though. You don't want to catch the eye of the security people watching these feeds."

Quinn practically jogged to keep pace with James when his stride lengthened. He arrived at the door first and shoved it open. Quinn caught a flash of a gray uniform as she swept past James and started down the stairs.

The sound of their pounding feet echoed off the concrete walls of the cavernous stairwell. They descended one floor and had three more to go when they heard the metal door bang closed.

"He's after you. Step on it," Darius said.

"*Halt!*" a voice boomed from above.

When James leapt over the steps two at a time, so did she. Since she was short, it wasn't an easy feat. "I feel like a mountain goat," she said between panted breaths.

They tore past the door with a 1 painted on it.

"One more floor," James said. "Darius, we need the van out front."

"On it."

"*Halt! Jetzt!*" the voice shouted.

Quinn launched over the last three steps and stuck her landing next to the door that exited to the ground floor.

She stooped, took her tranquilizer pistol from its holster, and slipped it into her lab coat pocket. James did the same.

Shoulder against the door, she held the handle and looked in James's face. "Ready?"

"Ready."

Quinn yanked open the door. They left the stairwell and kept their steps measured down the short corridor and into the lobby.

Her eyes darted about, surveying the area. Two security

guards stationed on either side of the exit scanned faces as people left the building.

Quinn slipped her hand into her pocket and wrapped her fingers around the pistol's grip. She looked through the glass doors. No sign of the van. "Darius?"

"Almost there," Darius said. She heard the blast of a car horn. "Move it, ya jerk!"

James glanced around. "Hurry up, buddy."

"*Halt!*"

Quinn looked over her shoulder. The guard from the stairwell sprinted toward them, pistol in hand. He did not look happy.

She withdrew her pistol, whirled around, and fired.

At the sound of the gunshot, shrieks broke out. People dove for cover.

The security guard stumbled forward, his face registering shock. He dropped to his knees and collapsed facedown on the marble floor.

Next to her, James fired off two shots. She spun around and watched the two guards by the door drop.

Quinn and James sprinted past the unconscious men and burst through the front doors, leaving chaos in their wake.

To their left, a black van took a turn at an impressive clip. Two of its tires nearly lifted off the ground.

They darted across the cement courtyard and arrived at the edge of the parking lot at the same time the van screeched to a stop.

James jerked open the back door. Quinn flung the briefcase into the back of the van and dove in after it. James hauled himself up behind her. "Go!" he shouted and slammed the door.

The van's violent acceleration sent Quinn tumbling backward. She crashed into James, pinning him against the back. He wrapped her in his arms and kissed the side of her head.

Trembling from the river of adrenaline coursing through her veins, she had no intention of moving. "Well, that was exciting."

"It was," he replied. "If we can handle that, our wedding will be a breeze."

Chapter Two

Quinn rifled through the clothes piled in her suitcase. Where had she put those blasted things?

The chiming phone in her pocket interrupted her frantic search. She huffed a breath to stop the rising panic and checked the screen. A soft smile formed when she saw the photo of James smiling back at her.

She put the phone to her ear. "Hey."

"Hey. I want to apologize for how awkward it got with my parents tonight. Ever since my mom left and opened that oxygen bar in Arizona, my dad has a hard time being in the same room with her. He's still bitter."

"Well, it hasn't been that long. I'm sure her showing up at the rehearsal dinner with her new boyfriend didn't help matters. How are you? Are you okay?"

He sighed. "I guess. I just wish she'd left Xander in Sedona. Him being here just adds to the drama. Mom and Kelsey are already hardly speaking to each other."

Quinn had noticed the strain between James's mother and younger sister. She wasn't about to mention it now, though.

As if trying to shake off his melancholy, he sounded more upbeat when he said, "Just so you know, you made a good impression on Mom. She said you're lovely and charming and I am lucky to be marrying you."

"Well, duh," she said, teasing him. "Seriously, though, that's sweet of her to say. I hope I get a chance to get to know her better. Meeting your future mother-in-law for the first time the day before the wedding isn't optimal."

"No, it's not. But with you in training at the Farm and me in Moscow, it couldn't be helped. We were lucky to squeeze in time with my dad and Kelsey in Colorado after we got engaged and before I left." James's father, Steven, was a corporate lawyer in Denver.

"True. Speaking of parents, I saw my dad had you cornered. You kinda looked like you were about to be devoured by a grizzly bear."

James breathed a quiet laugh. "That's about right."

"What did he say?"

"He said he was proud to have me as a son-in-law and if we ever needed anything, we could come to him."

"That doesn't sound so bad."

"No, it was a nice thing to say. But then he gave me this eagle-eyed stare and said in this bone-chilling way, 'If you ever hurt Quincy, you'll answer to me.'"

"Oh boy. Sorry about that," she said ruefully. "He's a little overprotective."

"No worries. I get it. You're his only daughter. I told him he'd have to wait until you got through with me first."

She laughed. "I bet he appreciated that."

"I think he did. He smirked a little, like, 'Yeah, that's my girl, all right.' And then your mom came over and told him your grandfather needed to talk to him."

"Grandpa to the rescue." Her grandfather, a longtime member of the CIA and the man who had recruited her into the agency, never missed a thing.

"Like a superhero. After your dad left, your mom assured me his bark is worse than his bite."

"It's true. Just don't tell anyone at Pendleton. He has a reputation to uphold."

"My lips are sealed." Shifting gears, he asked, "How are you? Ready for tomorrow?"

"So ready." Quinn's hotel room door opened and Nicole Park Baldwin, her best friend, matron of honor, and room-mate for the night walked in. She acknowledged Nicole with a quick wave and said to James, "I'm kinda freaking out, though. I can't find the earrings I was planning on wearing tomorrow. Grandma wore them when she and Grandpa got married."

Nicole shook her head and rolled her eyes. She walked to the nightstand, picked up a small red box, and flipped open the top. Holding it out for Quinn to see, she said, "You mean these?"

With an embarrassed smile, Quinn answered, "Um, yeah. Those."

Nicole snapped the box closed and returned it to the nightstand. "That's it. You've officially lost it. Time for us to find you something to do."

"But it's late and—"

"It's not that late. Tell James good night and you'll see him tomorrow."

Quinn shot her a defiant look. "Who said I'm talking to James?"

Nicole's response was a flat stare.

"Okay, fine. I'm talking to James."

"Who you left at the rehearsal dinner an hour ago," Nicole stated.

"You'd better do what she says," James said, amusement coloring his voice.

From the determined look on Nicole's face, Quinn knew it was pointless to argue. "You're right," she said to James. "What are you going to do?"

"Madison and Monroe said something about taking me down to the bar for a drink."

"Oh boy." Her twin brothers were always up to something.

"Don't worry. I won't let Fred and George lead me astray."

She grinned. Their shared love of all things Harry Potter made her incredibly happy. "Good. I'll see you tomorrow."

"Can't wait. I love you. Good night."

"I love you, too. Good night."

She'd barely ended the call when Nicole said, "Come on. Let's go."

Quinn stood firm and crossed her arms over her chest. "I'm not going anywhere with you until you promise me we're not going pole dancing again. You talked me into those lessons for my bachelorette party. Once was enough."

"You should keep it up. You're a natural. I bet James would love to install a pole in your apartment." Nicole smirked when Quinn snorted. "And relax, would you? There's a fro-yo place not far from here."

Quinn cast a wary glance. "Frozen yogurt?" She looked over at the clock. "I guess we could go and get back before it gets too late."

"Exactly." Quinn caught her purse when Nicole tossed it at her. "Let's go."

A few minutes later, they were in Nicole's car, driving along the streets of Los Angeles, crowded with people ready to blow off some steam on a Friday night.

Quinn didn't say anything when Nicole drove past the first yogurt place. When they sailed past a second, she spoke up. "Is there some special fro-yo shop we're going to? Because we've already passed a couple."

Nicole peeked over at her and then looked out the windshield again. "We're not going for fro-yo."

"What? Where the hell are you taking me?" When Nicole

didn't answer immediately, Quinn's annoyance was obvious when she said, "This isn't funny, Nic. I'm getting married tomorrow. Take me back to the hotel."

Nicole continued to drive, unfazed. "I'm fully aware you're getting married tomorrow. Trust me. I understand exactly how you feel. Nervous. Excited. Jumpy. I went through the same thing myself less than a year ago. Remember?"

Quinn did recall the day, even through the fog of disappointment, when she'd been convinced James was about to break up with her. He'd proposed to her instead. "Yeah, I remember." And Nicole described exactly how Quinn felt: nervous, excited, and jumpy.

"And to get you through the rest of this evening without going completely bonkers, we're going to go to a karaoke place—"

"Nic—"

Nicole held up her hand. "Just for a little while, to take your mind off the wedding. Because, come on. It's consumed your brain every waking minute for, like, the past month, right?"

Other than when she and James had been in Ziegler's office during the op the week before, what Nicole said was true. "Okay, yeah." Quinn huffed a laugh and confessed, "Not just when I'm awake. Last night, I dreamed I was driving myself to the ceremony and I couldn't find the church. I drove all over in a complete panic."

"See? Your brain needs this. It'll be fun."

The idea of not stressing about the wedding even for an hour or two was enticing. Quinn side-eyed her friend. "If we end up in jail, I'm never speaking to you again."

Nicole laughed. "No jail time. I promise. And you've gone to karaoke with me before. Not once has it ended in incarceration."

"True. Okay. I'm in, but just as a spectator."

"Good," Nicole said as she wheeled the car into the strip mall parking lot. "Because we're here."

Quinn got out and looked at the illuminated sign above the door that led into the unassuming bar tucked between a dry cleaner and nail salon. "You've got to be kidding. Sing and Swig?"

"Give it a chance. We're librarians. We don't judge a book by its cover."

Quinn closed the car door and noted the darkened windows featuring a Coors beer neon sign. "Yes, we do and you know it."

"Okay, bad example." Nicole's car chirped when she set the alarm. "If it's a total dive, say the word and we'll leave and go get fro-yo for real. Deal?"

"Deal."

Quinn opened the door and was smacked in the face by a wall of sound. Every voice in the bar sang along with the man on the small stage sporting a beer gut and male pattern baldness. He pumped his fist in the air as he wailed the chorus of "Livin' on a Prayer."

As the crowd continued to sing along with the Bon Jovi wannabe, Quinn and Nicole meandered through the dark, crowded room to one of the few empty tables. "Gonna grab a couple of drinks for us. Be right back," Nicole said.

"Just get me a bottle of water," Quinn called out to Nicole's retreating form. "She's not going to bring me water," she mumbled as she sat.

Quinn clapped for the man who'd just finished his inspired version of the rock classic while she inspected the room. It was unremarkable, with posters advertising various brands of beer tacked to the walls. And despite the fact any calendar would indicate it was the waning days of May, colored Christmas lights were strung along the walls. Lyrics scrolled on a large monitor attached to the wall behind the stage. As her recent training had drilled her to do, she also took note of the exits in the room.

The crowd was comprised mostly of professionals looking to start their weekends off with a bang. The largest single group was one of eight women, all in their mid to late twenties, crammed around two tables pushed together. Quinn and Nicole could have joined them and not appeared out of place. Three of the young women squealed and bounded to the stage when it was their turn. They launched into an enthusiastic rendition of "Shake It Off."

Quinn tapped her foot to the beat and smiled when the women flicked their hands in the air as if literally shaking it off. Her smile turned to a scowl, though, when Nicole walked toward their table. In each hand, she carried a shot glass filled with pale amber liquid. A lime wedge had been placed atop the salt-coated rim of each glass.

"I hope both of those tequila shots are for you and the water is mine," Quinn said, eyeing the plastic bottle clamped between Nicole's upper arm and rib cage.

As she sat, Nicole set one of the glasses in front of Quinn. Quinn opened her mouth to protest, but Nicole cut her off before she could utter a word.

"I know. You don't want to be hungover the day of your wedding. You know I won't let that happen. One shot. That's all I ask. It'll take the edge off." Nicole set the bottle on table. "Drink all the water you want after that."

A blanket of nerves had covered her for days. Having it lift, if only for a little while, was tempting. "I guess one shot won't hurt." The second she uttered those words, she hoped they wouldn't end up in the Words You Regretted Saying Hall of Fame. In one swift movement, she picked up the glass, downed the tequila in one gulp, and bit the lime. She slammed the glass on the table, shuddered, and squeezed her eyes shut as the tequila burned its way down her throat.

The fire in her chest rapidly spread and warmed her to her fingertips. She opened her eyes and grinned at Nicole.

Her friend nodded in approval. "Better?"

Quinn rolled her shoulders. The knots that had been there for months untangled. "Better."

Nicole slid the glass in front of her across the table. "If one is good, two is better." When Quinn squinted at her, Nicole gave her a passive look. "I shouldn't drink it anyway. I'm driving."

Quinn considered her friend for a moment. "Last one," she said and slammed back the shot. Her toes began to tingle. "Get me a couple more, would you?"

"I don't think so," Nicole said with a frown. "I promised you no hangover."

Quinn cracked the top on the water bottle, tipped it back, and took several long pulls. "Good, because that was a test. You passed."

"Gee, thanks for the vote of confidence, Q."

"You're welcome. And as a reward, I'll go up there and sing something."

Nicole's mouth dropped open in shock.

"But only if you go with me, since you're the karaoke maven."

"Deal," Nicole answered without hesitation and leaped from her chair. As Nicole made a beeline for the DJ, Quinn felt like she should worry that she had no say in what they would be singing in front of a large group of strangers. The thing was, she had a hard time caring. She'd learned long ago when it came to hanging out with Nicole, it was best to go with the flow.

The prim smile and glint in Nicole's eyes told Quinn her friend was extremely pleased with herself.

"What did you do?" Quinn asked.

"Trust me. I picked the perfect song."

"I'm beginning to regret my moment of spontaneity." The

number of cringe-worthy ditties Nicole could choose from was stomach churning. "I refuse to bark my way through 'Who Let the Dogs Out?'"

"Won't have to." Nicole smirked. "You know how to do the Macarena, right?"

Quinn pushed back her chair and started to roll onto her feet. "I'm outta here."

Laughing, Nicole grabbed her hand and tugged her back into her seat. "I'm just kidding. You're getting married tomorrow. It's perfect."

"Now I'm curious."

Nicole's response was an inscrutable smile.

As they waited their turn, they watched and cheered for the parade of singers who took the stage. Some were surprisingly good. Some couldn't to carry a tune if their lives depended on it and didn't give a furry rat's behind. And they were awesome.

The only performance that gave Quinn pause was when one of the well-dressed guys at the table next to them performed "Blurred Lines." He preened. He strutted. He smiled and winked.

Quinn leaned over to Nicole. "If I thought he was kidding around, I *might* give him a little slack. But he's just a prick, isn't he?"

"Oh, for sure. He's a complete douchenozzle."

He finished his song and returned to his seat. Quinn rolled her eyes when she overheard him say, "I crushed it. I'm the best by far tonight."

Quinn and Nicole were next. As Nicole towed Quinn onto the stage, Quinn expected her nerves to overtake her and send her scurrying back to her seat. They didn't. Instead, she felt a little giddy. It was then she realized the tequila shots had taken hold.

Like the karaoke aficionado she was, Nicole snatched

a microphone and announced, "My girl here is getting married tomorrow."

Cheers and hoots erupted from the crowd. Quinn grinned and gave them a little wave.

"She really loves him—"

"Awww," the crowd cooed in one voice.

"And they're gonna get married." Nicole paused and beamed at Quinn. "So they're going to the chapel of love." Nicole began to sing "Chapel of Love," changing the pronouns on the fly as appropriate.

The crowd cheered when Quinn joined in. It wasn't long before the entire room sang along each time the chorus rolled around.

Emboldened by the enthusiasm in the room, Quinn bopped and shimmied alongside Nicole as they sang together.

The song came to a close. Quinn and Nicole bowed to thunderous applause and shouts of "Congratulations!" and "Happy wedding!"

They bounded off the stage and slapped high fives with complete strangers on the way back to their seats.

Quinn flopped in her chair. Hot and perspiring, she gulped the rest of her water. "I need more," she said to Nicole and wiggled the empty. "You want one?"

"Yeah."

Quinn went to the bar while two young men made their way to the stage for their turn in the limelight. After receiving the bottles and the bartender's congratulations, she returned to the table and tossed one of the bottles to Nicole.

Once Quinn was sitting again, Nicole twisted in her chair to face Quinn and tipped her head toward her. Her eyes flashed with aggravation. "The prick next to us is such a condescending crapweasel. I just heard him say the huge response we got was because you're getting married and not our singing."

"I hate to tell you this, Nic, but he might be right." At

Nicole's fierce frown, she quickly backtracked by adding, "*My* singing, anyway."

She immediately regretted giving the man the benefit of the doubt when she overheard him say, "I don't know why any guy would get married in the first place. Why would I want a woman telling me what to do all the time? Besides, I can have any woman I want without all the nagging. I'm a stallion." Heat crawled up Quinn's neck and flamed hot on her cheeks when he snorted a derisive laugh and said, "Five bucks says the loser she's marrying is totally whipped."

Nicole's pique vanished with one look at Quinn's face. "Q," she said in a warning tone. "He's not worth the breath."

Quinn eased her clenched jaw and exhaled. "You're right. I don't need to waste my energy on a troll."

The opening guitar riffs of "(Don't Fear) The Reaper" filled the room. She forgot her annoyance with The Prick when someone shouted, "More cowbell!" One of the guys on stage yelled back, "If you say so!" He lifted the front of his shirt and revealed the cowbell and drumstick stuffed in the waistband of his jeans. He whipped them out and whacked the bell in time with the song. The crowd roared in approval.

The cowbell rang throughout the entire song, including the instrumental interludes when it should have been silent. No one cared. By the end of the song, everyone bobbed their heads to the beat.

The two men took deep bows as they received a rousing ovation. Even after they stepped down and returned to their seats, the room still buzzed with energy as the next singer, one of the women from the large group, took the stage.

She took the microphone in her hand and bowed her head.

The murmurs of anticipation rolling through the bar fell silent when soft, languid notes from a piano drifted from the speakers.

Quinn was drawn in by the rich, soulful alto who sang of a final night together before a breakup. When she sang the haunting chorus of "I Can't Make You Love Me," there was a palpable ache in the woman's voice. Not once did she consult the monitor as she sang. The words flowed from her soul.

Witnessing such raw emotion had Quinn blinking back tears. Glancing around, she saw she wasn't the only one affected. The singer's friends swiped fingers across damp cheeks. Some in the room lowered their gazes, unwilling to intrude upon a moment of gut-wrenching pain and vulnerability.

Only the creep next to Quinn and Nicole seemed to be immune to the spell the young woman cast over the room. He huffed and crossed his arms over his chest and squirmed in his chair. When Quinn saw Nicole's head turn toward The Prick, Quinn was sure he'd received a laser-like glare capable of burning a hole in his skull.

Quinn tried to block all that out and focus her attention on the woman on stage.

The singer lifted her head and poignantly sang her acceptance of her circumstance. In the morning, she would do the right thing. In her subtle movements, she stood a little straighter and her shoulders squared. With increasing power in her voice, she declared to her friends, to herself, and to the world she was moving on.

The final notes faded and the room fell silent. Spellbound, no one seemed to know what to do. Wearing a wistful smile, the young woman set the microphone down and stepped off the stage. One of her friends began to clap. Everyone in the room, save one, sprang to their feet and applauded her bravery and resolve.

The young woman received hugs from each of her friends, and when she sat, the rest of the room did as well.

It took a moment, but the constriction of Quinn's throat loosened so she could speak again. She looked at Nicole, who was clearly battling a swell of emotions. "That was heart-breaking," Quinn said. "It makes me realize how lucky I am to have a man who I know loves me as much as I love him."

"I know. Me too," Nicole replied. "She was just so incredible though. It about ripped my heart out."

The Prick had apparently been eavesdropping. He guffawed and muttered, "Sure. It's all about her."

Nicole bristled. With a dangerously arched eyebrow, she twisted in her chair and faced him. "Excuse me?"

"No wonder he didn't love her. She's trying to make it all about her."

Quinn rolled her eyes at the guy's gargantuan case of projection.

"Dude," his friend said to him. "Let it go."

"Look, you asshat," Nicole spat. "The girl's clearly going through some stuff. Give her a break and shut the hell up."

"Nic," Quinn said in a cautionary tone.

Nicole leaned back when he rolled forward toward her. "All you bitches are the same," he said. For the first time, Quinn noticed how his eyes didn't fully focus on anything. The guy was blitzed. "You're always bossing us men around and then complaining to your friends about how terrible we are. I'm not gonna take it anymore. So you shut the hell up, bitch." He shoved Nicole on the shoulder.

Nicole jumped from her chair, her hands balled into fists. "Don't you dare touch me," she said in a scary calm voice. Quinn was on her feet in a split second.

"See?" he said, swaying a little now that he was standing, too. "There you go, telling me what to do." He shoved her again. Nicole sprawled back into her chair.

Furious at the way he was treating her best friend, Quinn stepped right in front of him. He was at least a foot taller than her. She wanted to get in his grill, but having to stand on a chair didn't exactly scream intimidation. "Step off and never lay a hand on a woman like that ever again."

"Who's gonna stop me?" He stretched to his full height and sneered down at her. "You? You're gonna stop me from doing this?" He raised his hand to give her a push.

She clamped her right hand over his wrist, gripped his thumb with the other, and rotated the hand under his arm. When it forced him to bend over, she pivoted and put him in an armlock.

"Ow! Let me go, you crazy bitch!"

"Watch your mouth."

He grunted in pain when she torqued on his wrist. "You're gonna bust my arm."

"You're lucky I didn't knee you in the junk, too," Quinn said in an even tone.

Slack-jawed, Nicole gaped at her.

Quinn moved her shoulder and said, "I took a self-defense class." It was true. She just didn't mention it was at the CIA.

Her captive reached his free hand around and tried to claw at her. She cranked harder on his wrist and pushed up on his elbow with her other hand. From her own experience with the hold, she knew searing pain was radiating up and down his entire arm. He whimpered in distress.

By the time a bartender arrived, all eyes were on them. He slung a towel over his shoulder and surveyed the situation. Fighting off a smile, he asked, "What seems to be the problem?"

"He's had a little too much to drink and wasn't nice to my friend," Quinn said.

The bartender looked to The Prick's friend. "I think it's best you take him home."

He stood and tossed some money on the table. "Sorry."

Quinn released the arm, but was fully prepared to put him on his back if he made any kind of aggressive move.

He took a couple steps back and rubbed his wrist. Glaring at her, he asked, "What are you? Some kind of cop or something?"

"She's not a cop." Nicole stood and, in a voice brimming with pride, said, "She's a librarian."

Chapter Three

Quinn pressed her palms against the front of the beaded bodice of her wedding dress to make some slack at the back. She hoped it would make it a bit easier for her mother, Marie, to fasten the two dozen cloth-covered buttons.

"Halfway there," her mother said.

Since she would be immobile for a couple more minutes, Quinn figured she might as well put the time to good use. "Kelsey?" she called over to James's sister, who was sitting on a sofa in the bride's room of the church in Redondo Beach where James and Quinn were about to be married. "Could you do me a huge favor?"

Kelsey came over to her. "Sure. What's up?" James and Kelsey shared the same easy smile, but with her brunette hair and green eyes, she took after their father. James, on the other hand, had his mother's dark blond hair and blue eyes.

"With everything going on the last few days, I haven't had a chance to give James my wedding present. Could you bring it to him? I'm hoping he'll wear them today."

"Of course." Kelsey's eyes sparkled with mischief when she tipped her head closer to Quinn's and lowered her voice. "It's not a man thong, is it? That's not something I need to know about my brother."

Quinn grinned. "How'd you guess?"

Kelsey grimaced like she'd caught a whiff of skunk. From the first moment Quinn had met Kelsey, she'd known they would always have fun together. It was unclear how often that would be, though, given Kelsey was heading into her fourth year of veterinary school at Colorado State. Quinn and James were thrilled she was able to get enough time off from school to be a part of the wedding as one of Quinn's bridesmaids.

In the mirror, Quinn caught her mom fighting off a smile as she worked another button. To Kelsey, she said, "Just kidding. It's a pair of Ferrari cuff links."

Kelsey bounced on her toes. "He's such a car guy. He'll love them."

"I think so, too. They're in my bag over there," she said, indicating its location with a tip of her head.

Kelsey dug through the bag and took out a small box wrapped in silver paper. She held it up. "Is this it?"

"Yup."

"I'll be back." She was across the room and out the door in a flash.

"Where's Nicole?" Marie asked.

"She went off to hang out with Brian for a few minutes."

"While we're alone, I want to talk to you about something," Marie said.

Quinn squinted at her in the mirror. "Um, Mom? We had *the talk* when I was in middle school."

"Oh, for Pete's sake, honey, not *that*," Marie said, her cheeks now pink. "I mean about *marriage*."

"Oh," she said and gave her mother a sheepish smile.

Marie continued to work the buttons. "It's all sunshine and rainbows for you and James right now, as it should be. But there will be times when it's like a hurricane hit you. That's when you hang on to each other for dear life." Her mother raised her gaze and gave Quinn a pointed look in the mirror's reflection. "Given what you two do for a living, you might be doing it literally, too."

Quinn swallowed and nodded. Of her immediate family, only her parents and grandparents knew she and James were covert operatives for the CIA. Not even her five brothers knew.

"Good. Another thing. James isn't a mind reader. Don't make him guess what you're feeling. Talk to him when something he's said or done bothers you."

"Okay."

"And when hurtful things are said, you'll need to say either, 'I'm sorry. Forgive me' or 'I forgive you.'" Marie fastened the top button, blew out a breath, and said, "There." She stepped around, stood in front of Quinn, and gave her a wry smile. "Your dad and I usually end up saying both to each other after an argument."

Quinn smiled.

"And last but not least, say, 'I love you' every single day."

"You've done that?"

"I have."

"What about when Dad was deployed and you weren't even in the same hemisphere?"

"I said it anyway, even if I couldn't say it directly to him. That's when I needed to say it the most. It helped me stay connected to him, especially when he was away."

Quinn hugged Marie and blinked at the tears welling in her eyes. "Thanks, Mom. For everything."

"You're welcome, sweetie. Dad and I are so proud of you. James is a good man and we know you two will be deliriously happy." Marie released her from their embrace. She swiped a thumb across Quinn's now wet cheeks. "Stephanie made a good call on using the waterproof mascara on you." Quinn would be forever grateful to her sister-in-law for her wizard-like makeup skills.

"Yeah. Totally necessary." Noting the way her mother's eyes glistened as well, she added, "I hope you used it, too."

"I've needed it every day for the past week," Marie answered with a quiet laugh and ran a fingertip under each eye.

The door burst open and in rushed Quinn's six-year-old niece and flower girl, Bailey. Isabelle, another sister-in-law and Bailey's mother, trailed her.

When Quinn turned around, Bailey skidded to a stop. The little girl gawped at her, goggle-eyed.

Quinn glanced down at her dress, fearing a horrible stain had spontaneously erupted on the front of it.

"Aunt Quinn," Bailey said in an awe-filled voice. "You look like a princess."

A smile bloomed. Quinn usually disliked wearing dresses. But this one was different. The moment she'd tried it on at the bridal shop, she'd known it was the one. With its sweetheart neckline and full A-line skirt, she really did feel like a princess. "Thank you, sweetie." Bailey looked precious in her little white frock with the navy blue sash that matched the bridesmaids' dresses. "So do you."

Bailey beamed up at her.

"How are the guys doing?" Marie asked Isabelle.

Before she could answer, Bailey's brow furrowed. "Uncle Madison looks funny with his hair combed."

"Wow," Quinn said with a smirk. "He combed his hair? It *is* a big day."

Bailey nodded somberly.

Quinn didn't have room to tease. Her blond hair was in a loose bun at her neck. Buns were anathema to her, the tiresome librarian stereotype she usually eschewed. But in the case of her wedding, she'd made an exception. She was glad she had. It was stunning and sophisticated.

"The guys are all dressed and ready to go," Isabelle said.

"James looks fantastic, by the way. But you already knew that even though you haven't seen him yet."

Quinn's heart hammered. James was indeed handsome. Her sisters-in-law had gleefully shot her surreptitious "OK" signs upon their seeing him for the first time. But more than that, he was sweet and smart and brave and sexy and funny. And she marveled at the fact that in a couple hours, she'd be married to him. "I can imagine. Still, I can hardly wait to see him."

The door opened again. Nicole and Kelsey walked in together, laughing. Kelsey carried a present in her hand.

"What?" Quinn asked, sounding suspicious.

"Don't be paranoid," Nicole said, still laughing. "Kelsey was just telling me what's going on in the groom's room."

"Let's say my usually unflappable brother is wearing a hole in the carpet."

Quinn's stomach flipped. "He's that nervous? Is he about to bolt?" She knew James loved her and wanted to marry her. In her mind, it was never in question. But even a spy who fearlessly dodged bullets on a regular basis wasn't necessarily immune from a last-minute case of cold feet.

"Oh God, no," she said. "Yeah, he's nervous, but he's more excited than anything else. He kept checking his watch and saying how he couldn't wait to see you."

Quinn started to breathe again.

"Trust me. I know my brother," she said. "The only way he's leaving here is with you."

Kelsey's words were like a soothing salve. The tension in Quinn's shoulders seeped away.

"And apparently your brothers are teasing him to keep him loose," Nicole added.

"Great. If he does take off, I can blame my knucklehead brothers," Quinn said with a mixture of sarcasm, affection, and relief.

"He loved the cuff links, by the way," Kelsey said. "He

got this big goofy grin on his face the second he saw them. He couldn't put them on fast enough."

Quinn pictured the scene in her mind. "I'm glad."

Kelsey held out the gift in her hand. "James gave this to me to give to you."

Quinn didn't need to touch it to know it was a hardcover book. She took it from Kelsey, but hesitated, unsure if it was something she should open in front of everyone.

As if reading her mind, Kelsey winked and nodded her encouragement. "Go ahead."

She tore off the paper, revealing what she had been sure it was, a hardback book. The title on the dust jacket read, *When the Hammer Falls.* She recognized James's handwriting on the yellow note stuck to the front of the book. It read: *"I figured you'd need something to read on the plane, so I picked up the most recent Edward Walker novel for you."* MI6 superspy Edward Walker was one of her favorite fictional characters of all time. *"I hope you don't mind if there's a little writing on the title page."* She flipped open the book and let out a squeak when she saw the scrawling signature of the book's author, Kendrick Smalley.

"He got me a signed copy of the latest Edward Walker novel."

"Oh, sweetie, that's wonderful," Marie said. "Your grandfather will be so envious." It was he who had instilled in Quinn a love of spy novels in the first place.

"And James wrote notes to you?" Isabelle asked.

"Mm-hmm."

"They're too frickin' cute," Nicole said to Kelsey under her breath.

"I know, right?" Kelsey answered.

As Isabelle noted, another yellow stickie was stuck next to the autograph. One corner of Quinn's mouth lifted as she read it to herself. *Pages 146–147 are like an awkward middle school dance compared to what we'll be doing tonight. Just saying.*

She didn't care if every eye in the room was on her. She had to know. She turned to page 146. *Made you look*, the note attached to the page read.

Her smile grew. "Smarty-pants," she whispered. She heard Nicole and Kelsey snort, but chose to ignore them.

She skimmed the passage, which vividly detailed a torrid sex scene between Edward Walker and a character named Octavia. By the time she reached the bottom of page 147, her brain had shuddered to a stop. Not because of the words she'd read, but because of James's promise that Edward and Octavia's tryst would pale in comparison to what was in store for their wedding night.

"Quinn? Quinn!" Her mother's voice sliced through the haze. "Are you okay?"

Coming out of her trance, Quinn blinked several times and cleared her throat. "I'm great." She snapped the book closed. "Let's get this party started."

Chapter Four

Sunlight streamed through the stained-glass windows, dappling Quinn's dress with vibrant reds, blues, yellows, and greens. She stood next to her father, Robert, one hand holding a bouquet of white roses and the other tucked in the crook of his arm. Mrs. Wilkerson, the church's wedding coordinator and a cross between the Good Witch of the South and General Patton, quietly yet efficiently lined up the bridesmaids in front of Quinn. Bailey and Quinn's nephews and ring bearers, Hunter and Wyatt, were positioned directly in front of her. While Bailey stood still, the cousins poked at each other with their satin pillows.

The strains of Bach's "Jesu, Joy of Man's Desiring" wafted through the open double doors leading into the sanctuary. Marie, escorted by Quinn's brother George, disappeared through the doorway, and began their walk down the long center aisle.

In her life, Quinn's heart had never pounded harder than it did at that moment. And that included the times she'd been shot at. She sucked a deep breath in through her nose and gusted the air out through parted lips.

Robert covered her hand at his elbow with his. "You okay, kiddo?" he asked in a quiet voice.

"Yeah. I'm just super nervous. All those people looking at me. What if I screw up?"

The music changed to the piece played at every wedding Quinn had ever been to, known to the world as "Pachelbel's Canon." Quinn and her father remained off to the side while the rest of the wedding party took their positions at the sanctuary's entrance.

"So what if you do? What's the worst that can happen?" her father asked.

Kelsey started down the aisle.

"People will laugh, I guess. I might throw up."

Robert shook his head. "You're not going to throw up. And so what if people chuckle a little? Something always goes haywire at a wedding."

Stephanie entered the sanctuary.

"Great," Quinn said. "I'm gonna end up on YouTube as 'Epic Bridal Fail.'"

"Not necessarily. James might screw up and he'll end up on YouTube."

"Dad," Quinn said with a smile and bumped him with her shoulder.

Mrs. Wilkerson sent Isabelle on her way. Only Nicole and the kids were left. It was almost time.

"Say something goes sideways," Robert said. "When all is said and done, will you still be married?"

The question took her aback. In her fugue of nerves, she'd lost sight of what the wedding was all about. It wasn't a show put on for the people inside the church. It was about her and James promising to spend the rest of their lives together. "Yeah, I will."

Nicole stepped into the sanctuary and out of view.

"That's all that matters, isn't it?" Robert said and squeezed her hand.

"You're right. It is." Still, she hoped the ceremony would go okay.

Every concern flew out of her mind when five-year-old Hunter turned and sprinted toward her, leaving his cousins and the wedding coordinator behind. He slid to a stop in front of her and looked up. "Aunt Quinn, I gotta go potty."

"Right now?" she asked, dangerously close to freaking out. She was supposed to be walking down the aisle in less than a minute. "You can't hold it until after the ceremony?"

He hopped from foot to foot. "No."

Mrs. Wilkerson hustled over. "Either he goes down the aisle right now or I take him to the bathroom after you go in. He'll have to stay out here in the narthex with me during the ceremony."

Hunter looked from Quinn to the wedding coordinator and back to his aunt. His eyes rounded with panic. "I don't wanna do that."

By now, Bailey and Wyatt had wandered over and joined the confab.

"You won't have to," Quinn said. "I'm not going anywhere until you get back." She took the pillow from him and handed it to Bailey. To her father, she said, "Grandpa, can you take Hunter to the bathroom?"

"You bet." He scooped the boy up and as he carried him off, said, "Come on, Marine. Let's hit the head."

Over the music coming from the sanctuary, Quinn could hear murmurs and rustling from the guests. She could imagine what everyone was thinking. To her surprise, rather than losing it, her nerves began to dissipate. Her wedding had glitched and it wasn't the end of the world.

Four-year-old Wyatt looked horrified. "Aunt Quinn? Why is Grandpa gonna hit Hunter's head?"

Quinn chuckled and squatted down to his and Bailey's level. "He's not going to hit Hunter's head. It's what sailors and Marines say when they use the bathroom."

Bailey's nose wrinkled while Wyatt stared hard at Quinn.

Behind his brown eyes, she could practically see his brain churning on this new bit of information.

"I thought your mommies took you to the bathroom only a little while ago," Quinn said.

Both children's chins lowered, and guilty looks passed between them.

Quinn knew those looks. She'd been a part of many sibling conspiracies. "What?"

Wyatt dropped his gaze to the floor and dug the toe of his shoe into the carpet. "Hunter told us not to tell."

"It's okay," Quinn said. She straightened his little bow tie. "I promise not to tell anyone else, except for Uncle James. He should get to know what the hold-up was, right? It's his wedding, too."

The solemnity on Bailey's face had Quinn fighting off giggles when she looked up and said, "Hunter snuck another juice box after we all went potty, even though Mommy and Aunt Stephanie told us not to drink any more."

"Ah." Quinn glanced up at Mrs. Wilkerson, who was unsuccessfully biting back a smile. Looking at her niece and nephew again, she said, "Maybe from now on he'll listen to his mommy."

From the noises coming from the sanctuary, Quinn knew anxiety was continuing to build.

"Shall I announce the procession will resume in a few minutes?" Mrs. Wilkerson asked. "It's better than leaving everyone wondering."

Quinn peeked over her shoulder. There was still no sign of her dad and Hunter. "It is. Please do."

Mrs. Wilkerson hurried off.

Between the return of Quinn's jangling nerves and the contrite and morose looks on Bailey and Wyatt's faces, she needed to lighten things up for all their sakes. "At least Hunter could tell us he had to go. Can you imagine what might have happened if we had Pot Roast be a ring bearer, too, like Great-Grandpa wanted?" Her grandfather had made the suggestion in jest, of course. Quinn had shot down the idea, saying she couldn't take the chance of being upstaged by the slobbery, albeit adorable, English bulldog.

Bailey clapped her hand over her mouth and giggled. "If he had to go, he might have lifted his leg and tinkled on the end of a pew," she said through her fingers.

Wyatt shrieked with laughter and hopped up and down. "Or pooped in the aisle!"

"Shhh!" Quinn said, laughing now, too. It was too late. From the snickers coming from inside the sanctuary, many had heard him. At least the little guy's outburst had helped cut the tension.

Riding piggyback, Hunter bounced as Robert jogged toward them. Her father stopped, swung Hunter around, and set him on his feet. "We're good to go."

Quinn tucked the front of Hunter's shirt in and smoothed a hand over the clump of hair sticking out on one side. "Ready?"

He nodded, and Bailey handed the pillow back to her cousin.

"Good. Go over to Mrs. Wilkerson and remember, no running down the aisle, okay?"

Three heads bobbed. Then, as one, they turned and ran to where Mrs. Wilkerson stood at the entrance to the sanctuary. A wave of "awwws" and quiet laughter from the guests rolled through the doorway at the children's sudden and rather comical reappearance.

Quinn stood and took her father's arm again, grateful for his steadying strength.

Once the kids were successfully on their way, Mrs. Wilkerson closed the doors and motioned for Quinn and Robert to take their place.

Everything turned strange and dreamlike as Robert led her into position.

"Pachelbel's Canon" ended, and after several beats of silence, the bright, stately notes of "Trumpet Voluntary" filled the church.

This was it.

Robert threw back his shoulders and peered down at her. "You ready?"

She gazed into his eyes. In them, she saw love and pride tempered by a hint of melancholy. Emotion swelled in her chest. "Oorah, Daddy."

His smile was soft when he winked and said, "Oorah, honey."

The doors opened.

Upon catching Robert and Quinn in their sweet father/daughter moment, there was another round of "awwws" from the guests.

As she looked forward, the sea of smiling faces all around her faded away. She only saw one.

James's eyes lit up the moment he saw her. She returned his brilliant grin with one of her own. In his black tuxedo and with the way his thick, wavy hair was combed just so, he had never been more handsome. He was truly swoon-worthy.

Robert and Quinn started the slow walk toward her groom. As they did, she watched James's smile crack and saw the raw emotion on his face.

Nose burning and eyes prickling with tears, she struggled to maintain her composure.

Quinn and her father reached the altar and came to a stop.

James's smile returned in full force when his gaze dropped to the necklace she wore. It was a simple gold chain with a small pendant of an eagle with outstretched wings. It had been his first Christmas gift to her.

James glanced down at his necktie, looked back at her, and waggled one eyebrow.

Catching his hint, she studied the tie. It wasn't the white one she'd expected him to wear. Instead, he wore the Lamborghini tie she'd given him that same Christmas. He'd told her once he only wore it on special occasions. She was glad to know their wedding day qualified. She grinned at him and moved an eyebrow. She understood.

Quinn dragged her gaze away from James and focused on the minister in front of them when he, in a mellifluous voice, began to speak.

Vows were made. Gold bands were exchanged. A kiss was shared. And they were married.

Chapter Five

As violins played the opening passage of Etta James's "At Last," James led Quinn to the center of the dance floor and drew her to him. Her hand gripped in his and pressed to his chest, his cheek rested against the side of her head. She melted against him as they began to slowly sway in time to the song.

"What do you say, Mrs. Anderson? You ready to blow this Popsicle stand?"

"I am. Doing all the traditional reception stuff has been fun, though, hasn't it?" She leaned back and shot him a wicked smile. "I especially enjoyed it when we fed each other cake." The smoldering look he'd given her when he'd put her finger in his mouth and sucked off the frosting—to hoots and hollers of the delighted guests—had her knees buckling.

"That was pretty great, although I gotta say my favorite was removing your garter," he said with a wolfish grin.

A shiver rolled through when she recalled the feeling of his hand unhurriedly running up her thigh. "Yeah," she croaked. She cleared her throat and tried again. "That, um, yeah. That was pretty good, too."

They fell silent and danced, with Quinn's head resting on his chest.

"I'm a little disappointed, though," James said a moment later. "You're not wearing the lacy holster you told me about."

She picked up her head and looked into his face. "I do have two thighs, you know." She smirked when she felt him jolt. Piling it on, she added, "And your hands are gonna have to travel a little higher."

The hand on her back pressed her body hard against his. "We need to get out of here." The same urgency in his voice stirred in her.

"We really do. Besides, next up in the parade of traditions is the wedding night."

There was a gleam in his eye when he said, "And we don't want to break with tradition."

"No, we don't."

The song ended and they kissed, the sound of the applause of their friends and relatives enveloping them. Mindful of the fact they were still in public, they kept their kiss brief. Fueled by their flirtations, however, it packed a serious wallop.

Hand in hand, James and Quinn left the dance floor and started their good-byes.

"The day James came to the library and I saw you two together, I knew he was the one for you," Nicole said as she squeezed Quinn in a tight hug. "Even if you didn't know it yet."

"You were right. Thanks for being the charter member of the James and Quinn Fan Club."

Nicole laughed. "You're welcome, Q."

"I love you," Quinn said, her throat taut with emotion.

"I love you, too." Nicole released her and gave James a hug. "You keep my girl happy." It wasn't a suggestion. It was a command.

"I will. Always," he said with equal seriousness. He

straightened and his tone lightened. "I'm looking forward to keeping up with my husbandly duties."

Nicole's eyes glinted with approval. "Then my work here is done."

"Thanks, James," Brian said as they shook hands after Quinn had hugged her friend's husband.

"You're welcome. And thank you." Something passed between the two men Quinn didn't understand.

As they walked toward James's family, Quinn said, "What was that about?"

"What?"

"You and Brian are up to something."

He kissed her cheek. "Don't be paranoid." When she side-eyed him, hard, he sighed. "Trust me."

She always trusted him. Placated, she answered, "Okay."

They said their good-byes to James's family. Quinn noted, in addition to the palpable tension between his divorced parents, James's grandparents didn't appear to be too thrilled with their daughter's recent life choices either. Going forward, when it came to James's family, Quinn's game plan was simple. She'd support her husband and keep her head down.

When James and Quinn joined her family to say their farewells, Monroe shook James's hand and said, "George and John have to put their kids to bed, but the rest of us, like me and Madison and Tom and Nicole and Brian and Kelsey, are going for drinks at the bar. You should come hang out with us for a while."

Quinn shot her brother a sour look. "You're kidding, right?"

"Nah, it'll be fun," Madison said and clapped James on the back.

"Ignore your brothers," Marie said, pushing between the twins and pulling Quinn into an embrace. "You and James go. Have a wonderful honeymoon and give us a call when you get back."

"We will." She hugged her mother tighter. "Thanks for everything."

Marie rubbed Quinn's back. "You're welcome, honey."

Quinn slipped her arms around her father and held him tight. "Thanks, Dad. You and Mom are the best."

"Anything for our little girl," Robert said gruffly and kissed the top of her head.

She stepped back and swiped at the sudden tears streaking down her cheeks. Through blurred vision, she watched her husband and father shake hands. When the two men she loved most in the world did one of those awkward, back-slapping man hugs, a watery chuckle burbled up.

Finally, they went to say good-bye to Quinn's grandparents. After kissing her grandmother's cheek, she said to her grandfather, "Thank you for sending James to the library."

His blue eyes twinkled. "You're welcome, angel."

"You couldn't have known this would happen," James said.

"Well . . ." His voice trailed off.

"Oh, Chester," Grandma said and gave him an exasperated look. "He didn't know," she said to James. "Although once he told me what he was up to, we both had a feeling something good could come of it."

James took Quinn's hand and threaded their fingers together. "Best assignment ever."

Quinn smiled at her husband.

"Okay, you two." Grandma flicked her hands at them. "Shoo."

"You don't have to tell me twice," James said.

"Bye." Quinn gave her parents a little wave while James tugged her away. He snatched his tuxedo jacket from the back of his chair and, with his hand still clasping hers, strode out into the hotel lobby.

Quinn veered for the bank of elevators that would take them to their room. To her surprise, James kept walking straight for the front entrance of the hotel. "Change of plans," he said and gently pulled her along.

"What are you up to?"

They went through the front door. Parked in the valet drop-off area was the black town car that had ferried them from the church to the nearby hotel where the reception had taken place. The driver, who had been standing next to the car waiting for them, opened the back door. He nodded crisply and said, "Mrs. Anderson. Mr. Anderson."

Quinn raised an eyebrow at James in question.

His response was a slanted smile and a sweeping hand toward the open car door.

She narrowed her eyes at him and then smiled, secretly pleased by this unexpected twist. She slid into the backseat, and once she'd wrangled the long skirt of her dress, James bounced in next to her. The door closed with a solid *thunk*. Seconds later, the car glided away and turned onto the street.

"If we're on our way to meet with a contact, you're sleeping on the couch tonight," she teased.

"I guess it's lucky for me we're not." He loosened his tie and unbuttoned the button at his throat. "Lucky for you, too," he added with a lascivious grin.

She snickered and playfully slapped the side of his leg with the back of her hand.

"There's someplace we need to go," he said without elaboration.

"You do realize we could be alone in our room right now."

The interior of the car was dim, but she could still see earnestness on his face. "I'm hoping you'll think it's worth the wait."

Quinn rested her palm on his cheek, leaned over, and kissed him. "I'm sure I will," she murmured and kissed him again. Without their lips breaking contact, he shifted, slid his arm around her waist, and rolled into her. They were nearly horizontal and kissing each other hungrily by the time the town car made a series of sharp turns and came to a stop.

James lifted his head and grumbled, "I'm seriously questioning my earlier thought process." He pulled Quinn upright. "I'm pretty sure I'm a complete idiot."

"No, you're not. If you went to all this trouble, I'm sure it'll be worth it." She looked out the window and grinned. "An In-N-Out drive-thru?"

"To commemorate our first date."

"Hmm. I seem to recall at the time you made a point of saying it wasn't a date."

"Yes, and you will also recall I admitted the next day I was kidding myself about how I felt about you. And I asked you to go out with me that very night."

She remembered. It was the night that had changed her life forever. She pecked his lips with hers. "Good point. I'll allow it."

"Plus, I thought we might be hungry after the reception. Did you eat any of the dinner?"

"I ate a few bites." Her brow furrowed. "I think it was chicken."

"See?"

"Now that you mention it, I'm starving."

"Me, too." He reached across her and pressed a button on the door panel. The window slid down with a whir. "Double-Double, fries, and a chocolate shake?"

"Obviously," she said in a lighthearted tone.

His pleased grin warmed her.

When they pulled even with the speaker, James placed their order. The car crept forward and stopped at the window.

The teenager in the red apron and white shirt looked dumbfounded when he opened the window and saw Quinn, resplendent in her wedding dress, smiling at him. "Hi," she said and held the money out as if it weren't one of the most unexpected things ever.

"Hi." His voice was filled with awe. He took the proffered twenty-dollar bill and, seconds later, said, "Here's your change. Your food will be ready in a minute."

"Thank you," she said brightly. She handed James the cash and giggled. "I don't think he's blinked once since we pulled up."

"He's blindsided by how beautiful you are."

"You're sweet." She gave him a soft kiss that swiftly turned scorching. "And unbelievably sexy."

A throat cleared behind her. She twisted around.

"Your food." The worker passed two drinks and a white bag across the gap. "Ketchup?"

James bent over and peered out the window. "Yes, please."

He stared at James, somehow more stunned than he was before. But at least he was blinking again. The guy shook himself from his stupor, grabbed some ketchup packets, and dropped them in Quinn's outstretched hand.

Now that they had everything, James waved and said, "Thanks."

The young man raised a hand hesitantly and intoned by rote, "Have a nice evening."

"You can count on it," came James's enthusiastic reply.

"Wow," Quinn heard the young man say in reverence as the town car pulled away.

She put up the window while James took a Double-Double from the bag. The aroma filling the car made her mouth water. Eating at In-N-Out was one of the things she missed most now that she lived in Virginia. "I think you're his hero," she said, taking the burger from his hand.

"As well I should be. I just got to marry you, didn't I?"

"Flattery and Double-Doubles will get you everywhere, Mr. Anderson." She took a huge bite of her cheeseburger. At its gloriousness, her eyelids fluttered and she released a deep, satisfied groan.

"I'm not sure my fragile male psyche can handle it if I don't elicit at the very least a similar response from you later." James bit into his Double-Double and grunted in approval.

She swallowed and sipped her milkshake. "Trust me. You have nothing to worry about."

He grabbed some French fries from the paper tray, swiped them through the blob of ketchup he'd squirted from the plastic packet, and held them in front of her mouth.

Her lips grazed his fingertips when she bit into the clump of fries. After he popped the ends of the fries in his mouth, Quinn took his hand and licked the salt from his fingers. His breath hitched in his chest when she kissed his open palm.

"Um, yeah," he said with a shiver. "Neither do you."

She smiled at him and took another bite of her cheese-burger. It gave her immense satisfaction to know she could rattle his cage as much as he did hers.

After they'd demolished their burgers and fries, Quinn's eyebrows knit together when she glanced out the window. "We should be near the hotel." When she saw the name of the street they'd crossed, she grew more confused. "We're near UCLA." They were twenty miles from where they'd started. She'd been so distracted by James and the food, the world beyond the interior of the car had become irrelevant.

"I know. It's okay. We're not going back to the hotel in Redondo."

"What? Why?"

"We're going to a different one. I didn't want to stay in the same place with everyone else. It seemed weird."

"Why didn't you tell me?"

"I'm sorry. I guess I should have. I wanted it to be a surprise, something just for us. Only Brian knows where we'll be. And he won't spill unless it's an absolute emergency. As a thank-you for keeping my secret, I gave him the key to the honeymoon suite."

"So that's what you two were up to. Nicole will be thrilled. And I do like the idea of being off everyone's radar." They had spent a lot of time with a lot of people over the last few days.

"Exactly. It's just you and me. Besides, who knows what Madison and Monroe might have cooked up to mess with our wedding night?"

"I know better than anyone what kind of goofballs those two are, but I don't think they'd do something like that. I mean, they're thirty years old." Seeing his dubious expression, she sighed. "You're right. Chronologically, they're thirty, but there are times they have the maturity of a couple of twelve-year-olds."

"And they may not have planned anything. I didn't want to take the chance of the phone ringing every ten minutes or walking into a room crammed with balloons or . . ."

"Squeaky toys stuffed under the mattress."

"Yeah."

"Good call," she said.

They relaxed until the car turned into the driveway and stopped at the front entrance of a luxury hotel. A valet opened her door. "Good evening and congratulations."

"Thank you," she said and smiled.

James bolted from the car, ran around the back to her side, and helped her out. While she straightened her dress, James spoke to the driver hauling their luggage from the trunk. "See you back here tomorrow at noon."

"Yes, sir."

Quinn took James's elbow, and the newlyweds entered the posh lobby. She tried to ignore the stares from the handful of people as they walked toward the front desk. She couldn't blame them for rubbernecking. She would have, too.

It wasn't long before they entered their room, the bellhop

trailing behind them. He set their bags on the floor, and once James tipped him, he barely made a sound as he discreetly slipped from the room and closed the door.

The first thing Quinn did was step out of her heels. She hummed a happy sigh. Next, the bobby pins came out. She raked her fingers through her freed mane.

James shrugged off his tuxedo jacket and tossed it over the back of a chair. As he worked to remove a cuff link, he dipped his head toward the bottle partially submerged in a silver ice bucket. "Do you want some champagne?"

Her dress rustled as she moved to stand in front of him. "Here, let me." She deftly flipped the little bar on the back of the cuff link and pushed it through the hole with her thumb. She set it on the table and took his other wrist. "I'm good right now, but you should have some if you want. I'd like to wash off all this makeup first." After removing the second cuff link, she worked the buttons of his vest. "But before I do that, I need to get out of this dress." She couldn't keep the coy smile from her lips when she said in a matter-of-fact tone, "I can't reach the buttons down the back, so I'm gonna need you to undo them."

Her gaze flicked to his face.

Her smile widened at the gleam in his eyes. "Anything for my wife."

She unfastened the last button, removed his vest, and tossed it away. Her hands ran over his chest and slid under his suspenders. "Anything?" She pushed the straps over his broad shoulders and ran her hands over his muscled arms.

His eyes never left her face as she pulled the end of his necktie through the knot and leisurely drew it from under his collar. He swallowed, his Adam's apple bobbing up and down. "Anything," he said in a strangled whisper.

He took the tie from her and flung it away. "Your turn."

She slowly spun until her back was to him.

A chill raced up her spine when his knuckles grazed her skin as he fidgeted with the top button.

With each button he loosened, his hands moved a little lower. The pressure inside her built. By the time he reached the small of her back, the air around them crackled with electricity.

From behind, his hands slithered under the bodice and skimmed over her belly. The dress slipped over her hips and fell to the floor. A pool of white lace covered her feet.

Her hands rested on his forearms curled around her waist. His taut muscles twitched under her palms. She closed her eyes and hummed with pleasure when he pressed his lips to the top of her bare shoulder. Like a slow burn, he took his time, leaving one sensual kiss after another as he made his way toward her neck.

Not wanting him to stop, she tilted her head to the side. His arms tightened around her, crushing her against his flat abdomen. Her legs almost gave out when he dragged his parted lips over her neck. His hot breath scorched her skin.

She couldn't take it anymore. He was driving her out of her mind. She turned around, hauled his face to hers with her hands, and crushed her lips to his. He released a low, throaty moan when she slipped her tongue into his open mouth. They kissed each other ravenously, the skin of her bare back sizzling under his splayed hands.

She tugged at his shirt until it was free of his waistband. One hand roamed his bare back while the other gripped his firm butt. The feel of his hard body under her touch nearly sent her into orbit. She kissed him deeper and harder.

James broke the kiss and slid his mouth to her throat. "You make me crazy."

She fumbled with the button of his trousers. "And you have too many clothes on."

He peeled his unbuttoned shirt off over his head and

blindly tossed it away. It landed on the bucket of entirely ignored champagne.

While James yanked off his shoes, removed his ankle holster, and ripped off his trousers, Quinn went to one side of the giant bed and flung back the covers. Pillows arced through the air.

She clambered onto the bed at the same time James launched over the end of it. She bounced when he belly flopped onto the mattress next to her.

Side-by-side, he levered onto an elbow and settled a hand on her hip. She cupped his face in her hands and drew him to her. They shared a kiss so passionate, so enflaming, so arousing, she was about to incinerate where she lay. She needed him. Bad.

His hands and lips were like magic, driving her closer to the edge. A mind-blowing shock wave rolled through her when they came together. Sparks exploded in her vision as she cried out and arched against him as he thrust into her. Spent, he collapsed on top of her.

He rolled off, but kept her firmly in his arms. Within a few minutes, his breathing turned deep and regular.

Supremely contented, Quinn burrowed further into her sleeping husband's embrace. Her meandering thoughts before she joined him in slumber were of her mother's words. Sure, married life wouldn't always be rainbows and sunshine. But so far, with double cheeseburgers, a luxury hotel room, and teeth-rattling sex, it was off to a really, *really* great start.

Chapter Six

Quinn awoke in the same tangled mess of arms, legs, and sheets she and James had fallen asleep in the night before. Blinking against the morning light flooding the bedroom, she breathed deeply. Warm, sultry air drifting in through an open window filled her lungs. She held her breath for a few seconds and then silently released it so as not to wake her sleeping husband.

In no hurry to get out of bed, she closed her eyes and dozed until James stirred. He yawned and heaved a contented sigh. His arms tightened around her, and he pulled her closer and kissed her cheek. "Good morning." His voice had a rumbling and raspy quality from lack of use. He rolled onto his back and rubbed an eye with the back of his hand.

Turning on her side, Quinn draped her arm over his chest and rested her thigh across his abdomen. If she tried to get any closer, she'd end up on top of him, which was in no way a bad thing. She tilted her face up toward his. "Good morning. How'd you sleep?" With her lips so close to his jaw, she seized the opportunity and kissed it.

"Best night's sleep ever." The thumb of his hand on her thigh brushed back and forth over her skin. He closed his eyes again. "I've never been this relaxed in my entire life."

She smiled. "I'll take that as a compliment."

"There's not a word in any language that can do justice in describing your ability to relax me." He opened an eye and peered down at her. "How about you? How'd you sleep?"

"Take my ability to relax you and triple it. That's what you do to me."

"So you slept like the dead."

"Basically, yeah."

The corners of his lips twitched. "I'd strut around like a peacock to celebrate my prowess, but I don't want to get out of bed."

"I'm torn. I'd love to watch you preen, but I don't want you to get out of bed either," she said and nipped his chin with her teeth. This precipitated an enthusiastic, giggle-filled tussle that left them sweaty and panting.

Some time later, Quinn picked up the hanging thread of their conversation. "What should we do today?"

"Are you saying we should actually get out of bed?" he said in mock surprise. "I'm not sure how I feel about that."

She chuckled. "It is a conundrum. But did we fly all the way to Turks and Caicos Islands to stay in bed for a week and a half?"

"I fail to see a problem with that plan," he said, trying to suppress a smile. "It worked really well for us all day yesterday."

An involuntary hum escaped when she thought back on the first full day of their Caribbean honeymoon. They'd done nothing but eat, drink, talk, nap, and make love. "It was the perfect day, wasn't it?" She flipped onto her stomach and propped herself up on her elbows. "I withdraw my original question."

He sighed. "No, you're right. We should take advantage of being here. How about this? Why don't we go down to the beach in a little while? That will give housekeeping a chance to come by our room and I'll get to watch everyone admire my smoking-hot wife in her bikini."

She shot him a wicked smile. "Not when all eyes will be on you in your Speedo."

"Which I would totally rock," he deadpanned. "Sadly, though, my Speedo didn't make the trip. You'll have to settle for regular swim trunks."

"I dunno," she said, eying him. Bare-chested and propped back against his pillow with his hand behind his head, he was all sorts of sexy. And the way the rumpled sheets only partially covered his lower half, it was all too much. She was only human after all. She crawled on top of him, stretched out, and gave him a long, languid kiss. A shiver racked him when she gently caught his earlobe between her teeth and tongue. "I prefer you with no trunks at all."

They made it to the beach. Eventually.

Quinn glanced up from her menu and raised her gaze to the canopy of palm fronds above their heads. Through the web of thin green leaves, she noted the sky had turned indigo as darkness began to fall.

Their table was in the outdoor section of The Grove restaurant situated amongst spotlight-bathed palm trees. The glowing candles and white tablecloths gave it an elegant yet casual feel. Reggae music played softly in the background. It was the perfect Caribbean setting.

"What'll it be?" James asked, looking at her from across the table. "Surf or surf?"

She snickered and scanned the menu. While there were a few dishes featuring meat of the land-dwelling variety, most were aquatic. "You know, I'm thinking surf. Should I have the salmon or the conch?" Her nose wrinkled. "I'm not sure about the conch, though. Did you see what came out of that shell down at the beach today? *Really* big. *Really* slimy."

"Hey, you were ready to eat goat eyeballs when we were in India. Now you're gonna let a giant mollusk gross you out?" His head cocked to one side. "Gastropod?"

Quinn whipped her phone from her pocket and did a quick search. "Actually it's both. All gastropods are mollusks, but not all mollusks are gastropods." As she put her phone away, she said, "Thus endeth the marine biology lesson."

He shot her an affectionate smile. "I love how being married to a librarian means my questions will never go unanswered."

"Ah. So that's why you married me. For my reference skills."

"Well, you do have *other* skills I appreciate." He raised his glass and sipped his wine, failing to hide his lopsided grin.

Her eyes twinkled with mischief. "Yes. I can catalog with the best of them."

"Yes, that's exactly what I'm talking about." He returned his glass to the table. "Cataloging."

"Well, if *that's* what you want to call it." Smiling at his quiet laughter, she closed her menu and set it on the table. "I'm going with the salmon."

"And I'm gonna live on the edge and try the conch ravioli."

A roar of raucous laughter boomed from a table at Quinn's four o'clock. She peered over her shoulder to check out the rowdy bunch. It was a table of six—three men and three women. One of the men was red faced, and not in the "spent time in the strong, tropical sun" way. The guy was well lubricated. Noting the number of bottles and glasses populating the table, she had the feeling the volume from that particular group was only going to increase as the evening wore on.

When one of the other men occupying the table looked directly at her and smiled, she gasped. She recognized him. The chiseled jaw, the thick black hair, and those emerald-green eyes were unmistakable. Her head snapped around. Wide-eyed, she leaned toward James and hissed, "One of the guys at that noisy table over there? It's Rhys Townsend."

His eyes darted toward the party of interest and back to her. "Who?"

"Rhys Townsend. He plays Edward Walker in the movies. They just finished filming *Destination Khartoum*."

"He must be here on vacation. I'm sure he's exhausted after all of those fake shootouts and pretend car chases."

She smirked. "Don't be snarky. Not everyone can be you." She peeked over her shoulder again. The gaze of Rhys Townsend hadn't left her.

Her head whipped around again. Busted.

"You should go over and talk to him," James said.

Her mouth went Sahara desert dry. "Really? You think?"

"Why not? You're a huge fan and this is probably the only chance you'll ever have to talk to him."

"What do I say?"

"I'm a big fan? Edward Walker is my favorite character ever?" His eyebrows rose with inspiration. "I know. Have him autograph the novel in your purse."

"But he didn't write it. He just plays the main character in the movies."

James gave her a flat stare. "You mean to tell me if you had a Harry Potter book with you and you saw Daniel Radcliffe sitting at a nearby table, you wouldn't ask him to sign it?"

"Good point." She retrieved her purse from the floor and fished out the paperback and a pen. "You want to come with me?"

"Nah. You're the fan. I'll stay here to keep our server from thinking we've abandoned our table."

"You're not worried about me talking to a good-looking movie star?" she teased.

"Not to sound too cocky, but I'm sure you'll come back to me. You weren't exactly calling out Rhys Townsend's name a little while ago."

Her face flushed hot when visions of her and James in the shower together before dinner flashed in her mind. Water streaming over his wide chest and down his hard, flat abs. Soapy hands gliding over wet skin . . . His name had indeed echoed off the shower tile. Repeatedly.

She sucked in air through her nose, blinked, and shook her head. "Yeah," she drawled. "I'll definitely be back." To soothe her cottonmouth, she downed three swigs of water before pushing back her chair. She rolled to her feet and held her bag across the table. "Hold this please." It contained, among other things, her Baby Glock.

He took it and set it on his lap. "Married three days and I'm already the guy holding his wife's purse."

"I promise to give you a proper thank you later," she said in a husky tone.

His gaze burned into her, igniting a fire inside. "I'm looking forward to it."

She was tempted to skip everything, haul him back to their room, and ravish him. Only her growling stomach and the promise of a delicious dinner kept her from doing just that. "Be back in a minute," she said and headed for Rhys Townsend's table.

When she reached it, she stopped and stared into that familiar and handsome face.

He smiled at her expectantly.

Her tongue felt two sizes too big for her mouth. "Hi, Mr. Townsend," she said haltingly. "I, um, I really love your Edward Walker movies. I've seen them all a bunch of times.

My favorite is *The Shogun Sword,* where you, I mean Edward Walker, had to fight that Samurai wannabe, Takeharu Shimizu, on that rickety bridge over that gorge." A moment ago, she could barely speak. Now it was nothing but verbal vomiting. "It wasn't even in the book, but it was so gripping. The whole thing made my palms all sweaty. I can't wait to see the next movie." Her mind kept going and so did her mouth. "Did you know that many consider the deepest gorge in the world to be the Kali Gandaki Gorge in the Himalayas? It all depends on how you measure it."

She willed herself to stop and internally cringed now that she'd finally turned off the word spigot.

"It's always nice to meet a fan," Rhys Townsend said smoothly. His dazzling smile showed off a set of perfectly straight teeth. Their whiteness in contrast to his tanned face nearly blinded her. His British accent wasn't as refined as his movie alter ego's, but his baritone voice was just as rich.

She relaxed now that Townsend hadn't called security to drag her away. "I'm sorry you caught me staring. I'm usually more polite." She gave the other members of the party a tentative smile.

The three women were clone-like in appearance. They were in their mid-twenties and blond, and wore too much makeup. In unison, they glanced up and gave Quinn the once-over. Apparently, she was found lacking since they turned away and tipped their heads together in private conversation.

"S'all right," the red-faced man said in a volume greater than necessary. "Happens all the time." He pointed at Townsend with his drink. Some of the amber liquid sloshed over the rim of the glass and splashed onto the tablecloth. "Right, Rhys?"

She internally rolled her eyes. Of course the most obnoxious person at the table was an American.

From a distance, Quinn had estimated the inebriated guy

was the same age as Rhys Townsend, about forty or so. Up close, she now realized he was closer to her and James's ages, late twenties. Based on the way he seemed to be actively pickling his liver, she wondered if he would even reach forty.

He looked vaguely familiar to her, but she couldn't quite put her finger on from where. Maybe he was Rhys's fellow actor. He had the looks for it. Whatever his claim to fame, with his preppy clothes, four-hundred-dollar haircut, and massive watch forged from a solid gold ingot, the man oozed affluence.

"That it does," Rhys answered.

Quinn turned the paperback around so Rhys could see the cover. "I was wondering if you could autograph my book. I know it hasn't been made into a movie, but it is an Edward Walker story."

"Ah, yes. *The Leopard's Claw*," Rhys said and took the book and pen from Quinn. "Don't mention this to anyone, but it's being considered for the next Walker movie." He clicked the pen and opened to the title page.

"I hope they choose it," Quinn said. "I haven't finished it, but Takudzwa Marufu is a great villain."

"I'll be sure to cast your vote with the producers on your behalf," Rhys said with a smile. Pen poised on the page and ready to scribe, he looked up and asked, "What's your name?"

She answered, and while Rhys signed the title page, her gaze flicked to the third man at the table. He was a mountain of a man with an intimidating mien and massive, tattoo-covered arms bulging under a tight, black T-shirt. A two-by-four cracked over his bald head would snap in half like a matchstick. The bodyguard, she surmised.

"There you are, Quinn," Rhys said and returned to her the now signed book and pen.

"You wanna sit with us?" the red-faced man asked, gazing at her with rheumy eyes.

Before Quinn could decline, Rhys threw a glance in James's direction. "I don't think she does, Gibson. Her dining partner appears keen for her to rejoin him." To Quinn, he asked, "Boyfriend?"

Quinn tossed a look over her shoulder at James. His expression was amiable enough, but she noted the sharpness in his eyes. He wouldn't fully relax until she was safely back with him. "Husband. We're on our honeymoon." Addressing Rhys again, she said, "Thank you for the autograph."

"You're welcome. Happy honeymooning."

"Thank you." Quinn turned on her heel and hurried back to her table.

"How'd it go?" James passed her bag over to her. "I ordered for you, by the way."

"Thanks. Rhys Townsend is really nice." She stuffed the book and pen in her purse and set it on the floor between her feet. "He didn't even bat an eye when I started rambling about the deepest gorge in the world." She took a deep drink from her wineglass.

James smiled affectionately and said, "Which is . . ."

"You know me so well," she said before relaying to him the information. "The younger guy with Townsend was blitzed." Her nose crinkled when she scowled and shook her head. "I feel like I've seen him somewhere before, like I should know him."

"I know what you mean," he said. "Did you catch a name?"

"Townsend called him Gibson."

James took piece of garlic bread from the basket and tore it in half. "Gibson," he said quietly, clearly mulling over the name in his mind. A few seconds later, he set the uneaten bread on a plate and looked up at her. "I think I know."

He took his phone and tapped at the screen with his

thumbs. A half a minute later, he nodded, shifted his weight onto one hip, and returned the phone to his pocket.

She waited for him to convey his findings.

He picked up bread, took a bite, and chewed deliberately. The twinkle in his eye told her he was merrily yanking her chain.

"Care to share?" she asked.

He swallowed. "What's it worth to ya?"

She bit back a smile. He was so damn charming. "I might ask you the same question." An eyebrow arched defiantly.

"Withholding sex already?"

She tried to keep a straight face, but failed miserably. "I can't even tease about that. The very idea makes me ill." After a sip of wine, she said, "Okay, here's the deal. Tell me what you know and I'll give you a back massage as soon as we get back to our room."

He squinted and scratched his cheek. "You have to use massage oil."

"Of course."

"*Hot* massage oil."

"It'd be wrong if it wasn't." Her heart rate spiked just thinking about straddling her husband, her hands gliding over his slicked-up skin.

"Naked."

"I assumed you would be."

"No. Both of us. Naked."

Her stomach fluttered. "Deal."

He beamed at her. "You're not very good at this negotiating thing. You never even countered my offers."

"That's because your offers *were* my counteroffers." She took another sip of wine and set the goblet on the table. "You know what?" He leaned in when she lowered her voice and said, "I don't even care who the sloshed guy is anymore. I just want to go back to our hotel. I'm ready to live up to my end of the bargain."

He ran his tongue over his lips. "I wonder if we could get—" His words were cut off when their server arrived with their dinners.

Set before them were plates laden with food. Quinn breathed deeply and filled her nose with a mélange of mouth-watering aromas. She forked a bite of salmon drenched in a lemon butter caper sauce into in her mouth and purred. It was simply divine. She snatched a piece of garlic bread and broke it in half. "If it's okay with you, I'll give you that back rub after we finish dinner."

"That's fine," he said before stuffing his mouth with ravioli. "We need to eat to keep up our strength."

"I like how you think." She bit into the bread and hummed with pleasure at the intense flavor.

"And since I know you're good for that massage, I'll give you the intel on Rhys's friend. His name is Gibson Honeycutt the Fourth. His great-grandfather was a real estate tycoon. The family is worth a gazillion dollars." He shoveled in another forkful of pasta. "Also, his dad, Gibson Honeycutt the Third, is a senator."

"Right. I remember now. He's the senator's son who had a fling with that reality TV star. He got her pregnant and it turned messy when he left her for another woman. My guess is one of the women over there *is* that other woman." A corner of her upper lip lifted into a tiny sneer. "Although, for all we know, she might be the *newest* other woman."

"Yeah. He seems like a real charmer," James said wryly.

Quinn pushed the less than gallant Gibson Honeycutt IV from her mind and changed the subject. "What do you want to do tomorrow? Snorkel? Take a boat out? Lie on the sand like beached whales?"

His head cocked to one side. "You know? I'm having a hard time thinking about anything beyond you fulfilling your part of our deal tonight."

"Yeah." Her imagination—and her autonomic nervous

system—kicked into overdrive. "Maybe we should ask for the check."

"You don't mind skipping dessert? I hear they have some incredible coconut pie here."

She slid her foot from her sandal and stroked his shin with her toes. "Maybe we can get it to go."

They got it to go.

Chapter Seven

Quinn had never been inside a casino until that evening. A librarian's pay never had her swimming in pools of cash like Scrooge McDuck. She loved her job and the income kept her housed, clothed, and fed, but not much else. So the idea of taking her hard-earned money and likely losing it playing games of chance had always been a nonstarter for her. She was better off playing Go Fish with Bailey.

She did have experience playing card games, though. Her brothers had taught her how to play Texas Hold'em when she was younger. Of course, her rambunctious brothers were never content to play for meager plastic poker chips. That wasn't "full contact" enough for them, so they invented something called "Bathroom Poker." The player who lost the hand had to drink a glass of water. The diabolical part was once someone went to the bathroom they had lost and were kicked out of the game. Since she and her brothers were—and still are—highly competitive with each other, no one wanted to go out. As the game wore on, squirming, wiggling, and sweating ensued. She was the youngest kid in the family and therefore had the smallest bladder. Added to that, she had the least amount of poker experience. As a result, she was usually the first one bounced. Still, it taught her to be a thoughtful, if not conservative, player.

Sitting at a poker table now, Quinn glanced up at the sign pointing toward the ladies' room. Giddiness rippled through her at the knowledge she could go use it and still rejoin the game. She smiled to herself. She loved her crazy brothers.

She rolled up the tops of her two hole cards with her thumb and stared at her pair of tens. With another ten and a pair of threes face up on the table in front of the dealer, she already had a full house. Had they not been at a table where each participant played against the dealer, she could have won a monster pot.

It would have been especially enjoyable to win a boatload of chips from the balding, fifty-ish man who, from his lobster-colored skin, had spent too much time in the sun. His serious losing streak had him dyspeptic. And, for some odd reason, he seemed to hold Quinn personally responsible for his run of bad luck. He openly glowered at her every time she won a hand. His increasingly red-faced animosity made no sense to her. They weren't playing head-to-head.

Balding Guy's wife had apparently seen it all before. She sat on the stool next to him and nursed her martini, impervious to his sour huffs and grumbles. Only an occasional eye roll altered her mask of boredom.

Devil horns practically sprouted from Quinn's head. If she was going to be the target of his unjustified ire, she was going to have some fun with it. And she could do it, too, with her full house.

Going the "dumb blonde" route, she blew out a sigh and said to James in an affected voice, "Can you help me, baby? I don't know if I'm doing this right. Should I make one of those bonus side-bet thingies?"

He rubbed her back and played along, eyes sparkling with humor. "You already did, darlin'. Before the cards were dealt."

"I did?" She looked down at the different stacks of chips on the table and giggled. "You're right, Jimmy baby. I did." She tossed a couple of chips into the ante pile. "I guess I'll keep playing then."

"If you want," James said. He vibrated with suppressed laughter. "We're just here to have fun."

As if his honor as a member of the He-Man Woman-Haters Club were at stake, Balding Guy added chips to stay in the hand.

With a thousand-yard stare, his wife took another sip of her martini.

The dealer turned over the last final two cards.

"I won, didn't I, baby?" Quinn asked, wide-eyed. She flipped over her hole cards, showing her full house.

"You sure did, sweet cheeks," he said with a megawatt grin. "You won three hundred dollars."

Sweet cheeks. It was all Quinn could do not to collapse to the floor overcome with laughter.

A vein in Balding Guy's forehead bulged like a thick rope. He turned a dangerous shade of purple and growled, "Come on, Barbara. Let's go hit the slots."

"Thank Gawd," Barbara drawled. She tossed back the rest of her drink, set her empty glass on the table, and snatched up her chips. Without another word, they bolted from their seats and were gone.

The dealer pushed Quinn's winnings toward her, retrieved the cards from around the table, and prepared to deal out the next hand.

As Quinn stacked her chips, James leaned over and kissed her cheek. "You make life fun."

"Thank you," she said. "So do you." With an impish smile, she slid a small stack of chips across the green felt and parked them in front of him. "Here's a little something for playing along. Go buy yourself something pretty."

This time, James didn't hold back his laughter.

When she finished tidying her chips, Quinn did a double take when she saw who had just filled the two seats vacated by Balding Guy and Barbara. It was none other than Rhys Townsend and Gibson Honeycutt IV. "Hey, fancy seeing you here," she said.

"Not really," Rhys replied. "We come here quite often. There's not a lot of nightlife on Provo." Provo was the name most commonly used for Providenciales, Turks and Caicos's most developed island.

"We noticed that, too," Quinn said.

James extended his hand across the table. "James Anderson, Quinn's husband."

Hearing him say those words sent a happy thrill hurtling through her.

Rhys shook James's hand. "Yes, I remember you from The Grove the other night. Rhys Townsend."

"Gibson Honeycutt," the younger man said and clasped James's hand. Quinn was glad to see Gibson looking clear eyed. She wasn't so sure he remembered her from The Grove, though. Given his state at the time, that wouldn't be much of a shock.

The woman on the other side of Quinn jolted when Rhys said his name. She clearly recognized it. Based on the furtive glances others around the table sent his way, everyone knew exactly who he was.

"So, James and Quinn Anderson," Rhys started as he tossed a chip into the pile as an ante. "I assume you're from the States."

"We are," James answered.

Rhys's eyes tracked the cards as the dealer distributed them. "What do you do for a living?"

"I'm a librarian," Quinn said.

Rhys chuckled and nodded. "That explains the book you had readily available."

"It does," she said with a smile.

"What about you, James?"

"I work for the government."

Gibson's head snapped up from where he'd lowered it to check his hole cards. "In D.C.?"

"Yes, actually."

"Do you know my dad? He's a senator."

His words set off a ripple of whispers around the table.

"Sorry, not personally. I'm just a drone. I'm way too far down the food chain to ever swim with the muckety-mucks on Capitol Hill."

"Eh," Gibson said dismissively. "You're not missing anything. Bunch of bores."

The poker hand got under way. Quinn chalked up the hush that descended over the table to the movie star in their midst. But as Quinn, James, Gibson, and Rhys chatted, others were drawn into the conversation. Before long, poker was secondary to the animated conversations taking place. Rhys had everyone howling with laughter when he told the story of a practical joke he'd pulled during the filming of *Waltzing with the Enemy*. The target of the prank—which had involved duct tape, cooked spaghetti, and a bicycle pump—had been a well-known actress, his costar, Jessica Santorini. Fortunately for Rhys, Ms. Santorini was a good sport and the threatened restraining order against him had turned out to be a joke of her own.

"It was also during that shoot Rhys and I became friends," Gibson said. "I was going out with the woman who played Edward Walker's dog walker. I used to hang out on the set."

"Right," Quinn said. "Samson the goofy pug. I love that dog." She frowned and her voice crackled with pique when she said, "I couldn't believe it when Manuela Guzman swiped him from Walker's flat in *One Death Away*. I got so mad when she threatened to turn him loose all alone in North York Moors if Walker didn't give her the location of the secret research lab."

Quinn caught the looks that passed between James and Rhys. Her chin jutted out. "I'm very passionate about the humane treatment of pets."

"I know," James said and pecked her cheek. "It's one of the things I love about you."

Mollified, Quinn turned her face to his and caught his lips in a quick kiss. Her face was only inches from his when she murmured, "I love you too." Neither of them moved. Was it her or had the room abruptly turned into a sauna?

The muscles in James's jaw worked. "What do you say? You ready to go?"

"I am," she said, holding his gaze.

They separated and began to gather their chips.

"Ah, the honeymooners are in need of some time alone," Rhys said with a knowing smile.

The heat rose in Quinn's cheeks when James gave him a sly look and replied, "Can you blame me?"

"Not in the least." Rhys turned to Gibson. "What do you say we invite the Andersons to our fundraiser on Saturday?" He returned his attention to James and Quinn. "We're having a bit of a soiree to raise funds for hurricane relief at Gibson's estate."

Her brows pulled together. "Was there one that came through recently we missed hearing about?"

Rhys swept his hand through the air as if swatting away a fly. "No, no. But there's always a nasty one blowing through the islands at some time or another. We've set up a fund and have these annual events to raise money beforehand."

In other words, a good excuse for throwing a party.

James shot her a questioning look. She responded with a noncommittal shrug. "That's a very kind offer, but—" James started.

Rhys held up his hand. "Yes, yes. I understand. Honey-mooning and all that." Quinn caught his meaning when he looked at her and mimed writing on his palm. She dug out a

piece of paper and a pen from her purse and handed them
over. "If you decide you'd like to attend, call this number,"
he said as he wrote. "Tell Grace I invited you personally.
She'll put you on the list."

Quinn took back the paper and pen and stuffed them in
her bag. "That's very kind. Thank you."

James and Quinn said their farewells and cashed out their
chips. A few dollars richer, they stepped out into the warm
night air and strolled hand in hand toward their rental car.

"I hope you don't mind us not accepting the party invite
right away," James said.

"No, it's fine. Although I do have to admit I'm curious
about what the inside of Gibson Honeycutt's estate looks
like."

"We can still go if you want."

"Why don't we sleep on it and see how we feel about it
tomorrow?"

He slipped his arm around her waist and pulled her to
him. He kissed her hair and rumbled, "Or we can not sleep
at all."

She smiled and rested her head on his shoulder. "That'll
work, too."

Warm trade winds caressed Quinn's skin as she reclined
in her lounge chair dug deep in the sand. An umbrella—and
a thick coat of sunscreen—protected her from the tropical
sun's scorching rays. She held her book open in her hands,
but her eyes gazed over the top of it. The latest escapade of
Edward Walker would have to wait.

Using her finger as a bookmark, she closed the book
and let her hand drop. With her other hand, she lifted her
aviator sunglasses from her face and set them atop her head.
She wanted nothing to alter the colors of the breathtaking
vista before her. A few yards in front of her, white sand met

impossibly clear, turquoise water. In the near distance, boats with brightly colored sails skimmed across the bay under white puffy clouds suspended in a vivid blue sky. She inhaled the scent of ocean and exhaled a sigh. This was paradise.

Her view only improved when James rose from the water like Poseidon, only without the beard and trident. It was as if a spell had been cast over her, altering the passage of time as she shamelessly ogled him. He seemed to move in slow motion as he plowed his way through the surf toward her. She licked her lips as he drew closer, his water-soaked board shorts clinging to his hips and thighs. When he slicked his wet hair back with his hands, she thought she might actually expire from sheer bliss.

Time returned to normal speed when he stood over her and shook his head like a wet dog. Droplets of water went flying, eliciting a squeal of laughter from Quinn. Truth be told, the cool spray felt heavenly on her warm skin.

James bent forward and gave her a salty kiss before re-claiming the lounge chair next to her. "You up for some snorkeling in a little while?" He swung up his long legs and slipped on his Ray-Bans. "The water's incredible."

Quinn watched two bikini-clad teenage girls walk by. They almost tumbled over each other openly staring at James as they passed. She smiled. Who could blame them?

"I'm ready when you are."

"Words a husband always likes to hear from his wife," James said with a salacious grin.

She laughed and whacked his arm with the back of her book.

Quinn lowered her sunglasses and deadpanned, "I'm afraid I'm going to have to put more sunblock on your back before we go in the water, though."

"That's a shame," he replied in a tone matching hers. "You know how much I dislike it when you rub your hands all over my back."

"Yeah. It's real drudgery for me, too."

From the corner of her eye, Quinn saw a figure sit on the empty lounge chair on her other side. Rather than stretching out, he sat facing her with his forearms on his knees and hands clasped as if waiting for her to notice him.

Quinn turned her head and sized him up in an instant. She put him at about forty years old. His short brown hair sported a few flecks of gray while the neatly trimmed beard covering his square jaw had none. Lean and fit, he wore khaki shorts, a T-shirt with the Turks and Caicos flag on the front, and black rubber flip-flops.

Puzzled, she looked into his hazel eyes and gave him a polite smile.

The man blinked once and said, "Aldous Meyers says hello."

Chapter Eight

Quinn stiffened, but managed to keep the pleasant smile plastered on her face even as alarm bells clanged in her head. How did this man know the name of her and James's supervising officer at the CIA? Until she knew what the hell was going on, she wasn't going to give him anything. "I'm sorry. You must have me confused with someone else."

James was already out of his chair and coming around the end of Quinn's lounger. She folded her legs up to make room for him. He sat next to her, his muscles rigid with tension.

"I don't believe I do, Quinn." The man's eyes darted to her husband. "Don't worry, James. I'm not going to hurt either of you." He sat straighter and smiled. "I understand congratulations are in order. Aldous tells me you two are on your honeymoon. May you enjoy a lifetime of love, joy, and happiness together." She caught a Texas twang in his words.

"Thank you," James said, his voice tight. The man's affability had in no way diminished the tautness in James's posture. He was coiled and ready to pounce on the interloper at the first sign of ill intent. "You have us at a disadvantage.

You seem to know all about us. We don't know anything about you. Care to share?"

"You bet. We should talk someplace a little more private."

The hair stood up on the back of Quinn's neck. "We're not going anywhere until we know who you are."

"The name's Dave Flores. I used to work with Aldous Meyers." He took his phone from his pocket and held it toward Quinn. "Go ahead and call him. Ask him about me."

Her nostrils twitched. "How do we know you aren't with some kind of cabal who kidnapped him and are just waiting for this call? He says you're his BFF only because he's got a gun to his head."

"Fine. Call him yourself," Flores said, returning his phone to his pocket.

James reached into Quinn's beach bag sitting on the sand between their lounge chairs. He retrieved his secure phone and touched the screen. "I'll call his office. If he's not there, his assistant should be able to verify his whereabouts."

James put the phone to his ear. After a brief pause, he said, "Good afternoon. Is Aldous Meyers in? This is James Anderson." He turned to Quinn and snapped a nod. "Thank you."

Internally, Quinn stepped down one DEFCON level.

From the look of concentration on James's face, Quinn knew Meyers was speaking.

"Yes," James said. "He just contacted us."

Meyers never was one for idle chitchat.

While James listened to their boss, Quinn kept her stare pinned on Dave Flores. To her surprise, his eyes never drifted lower than her face. She was wearing a bikini, after all, and an admittedly skimpy one at that. She always wore shorts and a T-shirt whenever she and James walked from their hotel room to the beach. Even then, she garnered open and long stares from the male population. And yet now, here she sat with very little fabric covering her and Dave Flores's gaze never dipped once.

"Yes, sir. We'll take it under advisement." A small smile formed on James's lips. "We're having a great time. Thank you."

And now Quinn lowered to DEFCON 3.

James ended the call, but kept the phone in his hand. Like her, James had relaxed some, but his undercurrent of wariness remained. "Meyers says we can trust you. He also said we have every right to remind you we're on our honeymoon and tell you to take a flying leap."

"He said that?" Flores asked.

James stared hard at him. "I embellished the last part. But the sentiment is the same."

"Fair enough. And I get you're on your honeymoon and all. I wouldn't be bothering you if this wasn't really important. Please"—his voice turned pleading—"give me a half hour. That's all I ask. If you can't or won't help me after you hear me out, that's fine. I'll go away and you won't see or hear from me again. I promise."

A wordless conversation comprised of raised eyebrows, shrugs, pursed lips, and nods took place between James and Quinn. After they'd exchanged winks confirming they had come to an understanding, James turned to Flores. "Whatever all this is about, it's not an imminent threat to national security. Otherwise, Meyers would have told us to drop everything and help you. So, we're not going to interrupt the rest of our day for you. Come to our hotel room tonight at twenty-one-hundred hours. We can talk freely there."

The relief from Flores was palpable. "Thank you."

James dipped his chin in acknowledgement. "And now if you'll excuse us, we have some important snorkeling to do."

Without another word, Dave Flores stood and strode off. Quinn watched his retreating form and let the tension leech from her muscles. "We had a normal honeymoon there for a little while."

"We did." James put his finger on her chin, turned her face to his and gave her a kiss. "But then again, with the way our first date went, would you expect anything less?"

She smiled. "It was a doozy, wasn't it?" After another kiss, she added, "What you're saying is normal is overrated."

"Exactly." After one more kiss, he stood and pulled Quinn to her feet. "Now come on, Mrs. Anderson. Let's go swim with the fishes."

James handed Quinn an unopened bottle of water and flopped down on the sofa next to her.

"Thanks." She twisted off the cap and took several long pulls. Being out in the sun and salt water all day gave her an epic thirst. Her cells soaked up the water like a dried-out sponge.

James guzzled down half his bottle in one breath. He set it on the table, angled his body toward her, and rested his arm across the top of the back cushions. "We have no idea what this guy wants from us. So if he asks us to do anything you're not okay with, that's good enough for me." He rubbed lazy circles on her shoulder with his fingertips. "I don't want this to ruin the rest of our time here."

"That goes for me, too. If you're not fully on board, we pass."

A knock sounded at the door.

Quinn glanced at her watch. "Nine o'clock straight up. The guy's prompt."

James went to the door and opened it.

Quinn stood when Dave Flores entered the room carrying a wine bottle with a red bow wrapped around the neck. After they exchanged greetings, he handed the bottle to Quinn.

"My wife insisted I bring you a gift since I'm crashing your honeymoon."

"Thank you," she said and took the bottle. "Is she here with you?"

"No, she's home with the kids. This is business, and she never travels with me for that. Most of the time I'm in parts of the world she's better off not being in." He breathed a quiet laugh. "When she found out I was coming to Turks and Caicos, though, it was a little harder for her to stay home."

"I'm sure. It's a beautiful place." Quinn indicated the armchair with her hand and set the wine on the table. "Have a seat."

"Thanks."

James and Quinn settled on the couch again. She nestled into his side when he draped his arm around her shoulders.

"What can we do for you, Mr. Flores?" Quinn asked.

"Please, call me Dave." He rubbed his hands together nervously. "I don't know exactly where to start, so I'll just dive right in. I'm former CIA. That's how I know Aldous Meyers."

"We kind of already had that part figured," Quinn said.

"Yeah, sorry. I left the agency a couple of years ago, after an op where . . ." He stopped and took a deep breath. "Where we ran across a human trafficking ring."

Quinn flinched. "That's awful."

"I left the agency and founded a non-governmental organization called Rescuing Lost Innocents. We work to rescue people caught in human trafficking. We also go undercover to compile evidence to bring down these rings and their exploitative customers."

"That's admirable work," James said, "but I'm not sure how we can help you."

Flores scooted forward in his chair and sat on the edge of the cushion. "Here's the thing. There's someone here on

Provo we believe uses the services of one of these rings. And you've met him."

"Rhys Townsend?" Quinn asked, her pitch rising.

Dave's head bobbed from side to side. "Maybe? We're not sure what his deal is."

"You're focused on Gibson Honeycutt," James stated.

"Yeah. He popped up on our radar recently. That's why I'm here in Turks and Caicos."

"You were at the casino the other night," James said. "That's how you knew we'd met Honeycutt."

"Yup."

"But how did you know we had a connection to Meyers?" Quinn asked. "You couldn't have looked at us at the casino and thought, 'Hey, I'll check in with my CIA buddy and see if they'll work with me.'"

"You're right. I had no idea. Before I came here, I talked to Aldous to get intel on local Provo police. Are they on the take? Would they be willing to help me if needed? He told me they're on the up and up. He also made this opaque statement that if I got into a jam while I was here, I should call him. He said he might be able to help me out."

Quinn craned her neck and looked up into James's face. "He must have been talking about us. He knew where and when we'd be here."

"Mm-hmm." James asked Dave, "Did he give you our names then?"

"No. I had no idea who or what he was talking about. I filed his offer away in my head and kept following Honeycutt around, trying to pick up any intel I could. Then I heard Townsend and Honeycutt invite you to that fundraiser at the estate. I figured that was a great way for me to get inside and scope things out. Perhaps the 'employees' on his estate aren't there willingly. If I couldn't get in as a guest, maybe I could as a bartender or something. I called Meyers again and told him I'd heard a young couple on their honeymoon get invited to a shindig inside Honeycutt's estate. I hoped he could pull some strings to get me to get into the party somehow. There was this long pause on his end of the phone. Then he described you both to a T. He only gave me your first names and permission for me to approach you if I needed to."

"I get why he told you about us, given he's helping you and all," Quinn said. "But why didn't he warn us?"

"He didn't want to intrude on your vacation if it turned out I wasn't going to need your help. I'm only talking to you now as an absolute last resort. The leads Meyers gave me didn't pan out. The party is strictly invite only. And the company catering the event only hires locals. That's obviously not me." The passion in Dave's voice grew. "Believe me, if I could do this myself, I would. But I don't want to let this chance at collecting some solid intel one way or the other slip away."

Quinn could certainly see why he felt like he needed to seize the opportunity.

"If we agree to help you, what exactly do you want us to do?" James asked.

"All I'm asking is for you to go to the party, scope things out, and report back. No secret audio or video recordings, nothing other than keeping your eyes and ears open." Dave's knee began to bounce.

Quinn said, "We don't have authority to do any of that other stuff anyway."

"Exactly," Dave replied. "Intel. That's all I want."

James looked from Quinn to Dave. "We may not find anything. Gibson might not be involved with a forced labor ring at all."

"You might not. No one would be happier than me to find out there's nothing hinky going on."

"And if we do find something?" Quinn asked.

"I figure out how to rescue whoever needs rescuing and take the bad guys down."

When Quinn gave James a questioning look, Dave leapt to his feet and headed for the door. "Let me give you some time to talk. I'll wait outside."

And they were alone.

She turned toward James and draped her legs over his thighs. Searching his eyes, she asked, "What do you think?"

"He's not asking for us to do much."

"No, he's not."

James brushed at the hair framing her face with a finger. "I can't walk away from this now that we know what might be at stake."

"I know. Neither can I."

"I guess that settles it."

"Good." She gave him a kiss and a hug before jumping up from the sofa and bounding to the door. She yanked it open and invited Dave back inside.

When the door was closed again, she said, "We'll help you, but on one condition."

She looked over at James and smiled at the adorable way his brow furrowed in confusion.

"Yeah? What's that?" Dave asked and regarded her with a wary eye.

"You promise to bring your wife here for a second honeymoon. And soon."

Dave grinned and blew out a breath. "You got yourself a deal."

Chapter Nine

A light breeze ruffled the skirt of Quinn's navy blue sundress the moment she stepped out of the rental car. Standing next to the water fountain at the center of the Honeycutt beachfront compound, she hooked the strap of her purse over her shoulder and glanced around to orient herself. She and James had already studied satellite images of the property situated on a promontory on the south side of Provo, so she already had its layout in her mind.

The massive main house stood before them. Smaller bungalows, presumably guesthouses and staff quarters, flanked the main house on either side. The tennis court was to their right. The turquoise ribbon of water that was the man-made marina where the Honeycutts moored their yacht shimmered on the far edge of the property.

Quinn's research had informed them the entire estate was worth a cool twenty-five million dollars, chump change to a family like the Honeycutts.

James handed the keys to the valet and came to stand next to her. Quinn laced her fingers with his.

The live ripsaw music drifting on the breeze grew louder as they strolled past burning tiki torches toward the entrance of the house. James looked over at her and asked, "So, honey, when are you going to buy me a spread like this?"

Without missing a beat, she answered, "As soon as I figure out where 'X marks the spot' on my map of buried treasure."

He barked a laugh. "Hot on the trail of some gold doubloons, huh? How's that going?"

"Pretty good," she said with an impish smile. "I've narrowed down the treasure being buried somewhere in the Caribbean, so I'm most of the way there."

"Clearly." They climbed the steps and entered the foyer. "Let me know when you find where to dig. I'll bring the shovel."

She grinned, rose up on her tiptoes, and kissed his lips. "Aw. Thanks, baby. I can always count on you."

They turned their attention to the young woman with a clipboard blocking their path into the rest of the house. More specifically, the two very large men behind her were the impediments.

"You must be the Andersons," the woman said in a lilting Bahamian accent. Her warm brown eyes were as dark as her onyx skin.

"We are," James said. "What gave us away?"

"Mr. Townsend mentioned you are here on your honeymoon." Her smile brightened. "We see many couples like you. You are easy to spot."

"Guilty as charged," Quinn said and returned the other woman's smile.

"I'm Grace," she said. She held the clipboard against her chest and offered a handshake. "We spoke on the phone."

Not much taller than Quinn, Grace wore a crisp white top and a navy skirt. Her hair, a mass of thin braids, was pulled back and held by a thick band.

"Thank you for adding us at the last minute," James said, shaking Grace's hand after Quinn.

"You're welcome. Thank you for supporting hurricane relief. Enjoy the party." Grace stepped to one side.

"Thanks. I'm sure we will," Quinn said.

As if she'd uttered the secret word, the two huge sentries stepped to either side like boulders rolling away from the entrance of a wizard's cave.

The scene before them, however, was nothing like the inside of a cave. In fact, it was the exact opposite. As was often the case in a home in a tropical clime, everything was white, including the walls, floors, and furniture. Splashes of color came from pillows on the couch.

They walked farther into the room and stopped. "Wow. What a view," Quinn said, completely awed. The entire back of the house was open to the ocean and sky. While waves crashed on the beach below, the setting sun painted the clouds above pink, violet, and orange.

The majority of the party was taking place at the back of the house, so James and Quinn stepped out onto the patio and walked along the lighted infinity pool. A bar was set up on one side of a large expanse of grass. The band, featuring a guitar, a hand accordion, drums, and a handsaw per- formed on a stage on the other side.

"Ripsaw music gets its name from the way the guy playing the handsaw scrapes the teeth of it with another implement, like a screwdriver, a nail, a fork, or a knife. It's said it sounds like paper ripping," Quinn said after watching him bend and scrape the saw for a few minutes.

James chuckled and slipped his arm around her waist. "Of course you know that."

She smiled at him unabashedly.

At the end of the lively song, the crowd of about fifty applauded.

"You want a drink?" James asked.

"I'd love one."

"Why don't you get us some food from the table over

there while I head to the bar?" He leaned down, kissed her cheek, and whispered in her ear, "Keep your eyes and ears open."

"Mm-hmm."

James moved off in the direction of the bar while Quinn sauntered toward the long table covered with food. As she went, her eyes darted from one beautiful face to the next. She even recognized a few. One was that of a well-known journalist who worked for a cable news channel. Another belonged to an actress who played a doctor on one of those weekly hospital TV dramas. The fact she seemed rather cozy with one of her costars—who wasn't her basketball star husband—made Quinn sigh. She wondered how long it would be before news of their interlude would go viral on the Internet. Her guess was before the end of the party.

While observing firsthand the indiscretions of the glitterati, so far, she hadn't detected anything that would indicate Gibson Honeycutt had any forced laborers on the premises. But then again, how would she even tell? It wasn't as if they'd wear signs, and Honeycutt likely kept them tucked away where they couldn't interact too much with visitors.

She picked up a plate and loaded it with a variety of fruits and some pieces of cracked conch, which was pounded, breaded, and fried gastropod. Just as she popped a piece into her mouth, she heard her name called from behind.

She spun around and saw a grinning Rhys Townsend closing in on her. "Quinn, it's great to see you. I was so pleased when Grace told me you'd accepted my invitation after all."

She held her finger up as she chewed as rapidly as possible. Once she swallowed, she said, "I'm a librarian. We rarely rub elbows with the rich and famous. And attending a swanky party at an island estate makes for a great honeymoon story."

"I'm sure it does." Rhys's gaze shifted to something over her shoulder. "Good evening, James. Good to see you again."

Since both hands held drinks, James raised one of the glasses in salute. "You too."

The three chatted for a few minutes. When Rhys left them to greet other guests, Quinn held a piece of watermelon up in front of James's mouth and asked in a hushed tone, "You see anything?"

"Not really. Gibson's already hammered. If he falls into the pool, someone's gonna have to fish him out before he drowns." He took the cube of fruit from her fingers with his teeth. "We're not going to get anything from him."

Quinn nodded. "This whole thing is like the setup of a murder mystery. Before the evening's over, someone will stumble across a dead body facedown on the beach and we'll all be suspects."

"Brick Cobalt novel? Or is it Chance Stryker?"

"Cat Rios, private detective."

"Of course," he said and shot her a wink. "How about you?"

"Other than Hollywood marital infidelity gossip fodder, not much." She lifted her drink from his hand and sipped. "All the workers I've seen circulating around the party appear to be members of the catering staff."

"Might not hurt to double-check," James said impassively. His gaze swept the area before returning to Quinn's face. "What do you say we take a tour of the house? Maybe the kitchen first?" Now that one of his hands was free, he picked up a bit of conch, dipped it in the sauce, and tossed it in his mouth. "Mmmmm. After we finish this plate of food, of course."

"Agreed."

Once their food and drinks had been consumed, they off-loaded their plate and glasses and sauntered into the house. Quinn noticed a constant stream of servers coming in and out of one area to their right. "Based on the noise and commotion, my guess is the kitchen's that way," she said, pointing.

James's eyes darted in that direction and he nodded.

They wandered into the impressively large kitchen with a massive marble-topped island at the center. Above it, copper pots and pans hung from a rectangular black wrought-iron frame attached to the ceiling. At one end of the island, a man poured champagne into glasses lined up on a giant silver serving tray. One woman stood at a fryer and lowered a basket of battered conch into a vat of bubbling oil. Another efficiently moved cut cubes of papaya, melons, and pineapple from storage containers to trays.

The man loading the divine spring rolls Quinn had munched on earlier onto a huge serving platter looked up and asked, "Can we help you?"

"Yes, I'm hoping you can answer a quick question for us. We're here on vacation and thinking of having a get-together for a few of our friends. We'd like to hire you to cater it for us, but my husband wants to know if we can save money if we bring some of our own workers to take the place of some of your staff. Serving the food, for instance."

"Money doesn't grow on trees, you know, sweetheart," James said without missing a beat.

"I'm sorry, madam, but that wouldn't be possible."

"What if we didn't cut down on your number of staff but still had extra helpers brought in?" James asked.

Spring Roll Man smiled politely and said, in a long-suffering tone, "That would not be possible either. It's imperative that our company vouch for the quality of all staff, in order to ensure your satisfaction."

Quinn bumped James with her hip. "See? Told you."

"Fine. You were right. It still doesn't hurt to ask."

"Unless they refuse to cater for us now." Quinn said to Spring Roll Man, "We'll get out of your hair. Be in touch."

"That answers that," James said as they left the kitchen.

"About the caterers, yeah. But it doesn't clear Gibson yet."

James steered them toward a hallway and pressed his ear to the first closed door they encountered. After a few seconds, he turned the knob and opened it partway. Quinn peeked through the gap and peered into a bedroom. The view through the floor-to-ceiling windows overlooking the ocean took her breath away. "What an amazing sight to wake up to every morning."

"It's not so great."

"What?" she said, incredulous. "Are you kidding?"

"I get to wake up and see you first thing every morning."

The sincerity in his eyes melted her heart. "Seeing you every morning is pretty great, too." She hooked her hand around the back of his neck, pulled his head down, and gave him a warm kiss.

He caught her up and kissed her deeper, leaving Quinn quivering and weak-kneed. "This gives me an idea in case someone spots us snooping around," James said. He pecked her nose and released her.

"Yeah?" Quinn followed him on wobbly legs to the next closed door. "What's that?"

He repeated his actions from outside the previous room. After he poked his head through the door, he shut it. "Everyone on Provo seems to know we're on our honeymoon. So nobody's gonna think it's weird for us to sneak off and look for a place where we can"—he looked at her with a twinkle in his eye—"know each other carnally."

Her hand flew up and clamped over her mouth to silence the giggle.

James stole down the corridor and approached yet another door.

She dropped her hand and followed him. "Hang on a minute. Are you saying we can't use it as an excuse once we're not on our honeymoon anymore?"

He pulled a face. "Not at all. It'll always be our go-to plan. And who says we can't sneak off looking for a dark corner for real? I plan on using it as a constant source of embarrassment for our grandkids." He affected a nasally whine. "'Ah, geez. Grandma and Grandpa are at it *again*.'"

If he kept that up, she really was going to be looking for a dark place to know him carnally. And soon. "Sounds like we'll need to set up a fund to pay for their therapy bills."

"Totally worth it." He opened up the last door. "This looks interesting." They stole into the small office and closed the door.

Quinn headed straight to the wall of windows and pulled the curtains closed.

James went to the desk, slid open a drawer, and rummaged through it. He pushed it closed and opened the next one down. "There's some official-looking Senator Gibson Honeycutt the Third stationery." James nudged the drawer shut with his knee and sat down in the chair. "A few pens. No files, no computer. Nothing," he said of the center drawer. He ran his hands along the underside of it. "I bet Gibson number four has never even stepped foot in here."

While James searched the desk, Quinn scanned the books on in the bookcase. "These books are nothing but decorations. This is an ancient encyclopedia set. And the volumes aren't even alphabetized." She stepped over one section and skimmed the books with blocks of black, tan, and red on the spines. "And these are a bunch of random case law books. *Supreme Court Reporter* number 121 is right next to *Federal Supplement* number 752. That's completely bogus. And then there's this old Martindale-Hubbell." She turned away and groused, "And those brass duck head bookends are worthless."

"I love it when you talk library," James said and stood. "There's nothing here. Let's go."

Quinn went to the window and waited while James

peeked through a crack in the door. "Clear," he said. Quinn flung open the curtains and sprinted across room. They were out the door and sauntering down the hallway again in seconds flat. If anyone noticed them, James and Quinn Anderson appeared to be leisurely touring the house.

Outside and part of the party again, Quinn asked, "Now where to?"

"That bungalow," he said with a dip of his head. He offered her his elbow. "Shall we?"

She hooked her hand into the crook of his arm and walked toward the smaller house to the east of the main one. A wall of heavy metal music blasting through the open front door greeted them. Quinn gritted her teeth and crossed the threshold.

At the center of the room was a pool table, around which Gibson and some of his dude-bro friends were clustered. The three women who had been at the restaurant with Gibson and Rhys now stood together at a bar and drank from red Solo cups. An unappetizing sludge of spilled alcohol and soggy tortilla chips coated the top of the counter. That explained the smell. Two guys spun the handles of their foosball players while the Ping-Pong and air hockey tables remained unused. With a baseball game playing on one huge TV and a basketball game on the other, it was like they'd entered Gibson's private sports bar.

Pool cue in hand, Gibson leaned over the green felt table and lined up his shot. He sent the cue ball smashing into the nine ball with a sharp clack. It missed the pocket by a mile, which didn't surprise Quinn, considering Gibson's drunken haze. The ball bounced off the bumper, hit two others, and came to a rest next to a third.

"Looks like we've stumbled onto a frat party," Quinn said into James's ear.

He shook his head. "Not enough puke on the floor."

Quinn stuck her tongue out between her teeth in disgust. "Gross."

As they watched the game, Quinn felt the stares of most of the men in the room fall on her. While it made her slightly uncomfortable, she wasn't about to cower. She'd already worked out in her mind how she'd use a pool cue like a kendo stick and lay out every last one of them if she needed to.

Gibson acknowledged Quinn and James's presence by jutting his chin in a silent "S'up."

James likewise responded.

"And thus the male greeting ritual is concluded," Quinn said in a sonorous, documentarian tone.

His side-eyed stare drilled into her, attempting to appear aggrieved. The tiny smile quirking on his lips told her he was anything but. He relented and took her hand. "Come on," he said, tugging her down the hall.

During their further exploration of the bungalow, they encountered a fully equipped fitness room and a small movie theater.

"What, no bowling alley?" Quinn asked as they left.

"Maybe the bowling pins are on back order."

Outside again, Quinn rested her hands on her hips and glanced around. A small, glowing orange dot in the distance caught her eye. She watched for a moment and noted when a second identical light arced up, brightened for a few seconds, and then lowered to its original position. The burning tips of lit cigarettes. "Remember the satellite photos? You can't see it very well, but there's a cottage on the other side of this big lawn." She indicated the general direction with the tip of her head.

James's eyes cut that way. "Maybe it's the *servants'* quarters."

"There are a couple of guys hanging out outside it. And all the lights are off."

"Maybe it's the valets having a smoke."

"No. That's them over there by the fountain," she said, squinting at the darkness. "Is it worth checking out?"

"I think so. We need to check out everything while we have the chance."

"Do we go up and start talking to them?"

"No." James took out his phone and turned it on. It cast a blue glow on his face as he pulled up the satellite image of the property. "Since it appears to be off-limits, we need to be stealthier in our approach." He swiped his thumb and finger across the screen and zoomed in on the cottage. "Here's what we're gonna do."

Chapter Ten

James and Quinn stayed in the shadows as they skirted along the security fence on the western edge of the Honeycutt property. Her sundress of navy blue had been a prescient color choice. Too bad she didn't have something to cover her blond hair, aglow in the moonlight.

They stopped fifteen yards from the cottage and hunkered down behind a hedge of shrubs.

Balancing on the balls of her feet, Quinn rose up only enough to peer over the top of the bush. Now that they were closer, she caught a better glimpse of the two men. Both were big. One was bald.

She sat back on her heels and whispered, "The slightly bigger guy was at The Grove the other night. I think he's a bodyguard." After a pause, she asked, "Why isn't he at the party guarding Gibson?"

"Maybe he's guarding something else." James cocked his head. "Listen. They're talking."

The music from the party made it difficult to hear the voices. Quinn dropped her gaze and stared, unseeing, at the dirt beneath her sandals and worked to filter out the noise. Frustrated that she still couldn't understand what they were saying, she squeezed her eyes shut and concentrated.

When she finally heard their words, her head snapped up. Wide-eyed, she stared at James and whispered, "Russian."

He nodded. Like a prairie dog, James popped up, looked around, and dropped down again. "There's light coming through an open window we couldn't see before."

"We need to see what's in there."

"We do. And we need a diversion to do it." He pointed toward the tennis court awash in fluorescent light. "I'll go over there a little ways and make some noise, see if I can draw them away from the bungalow. I'm thinking belligerent drunk dude will do it. When they come after me, you go to the window and peek in."

"Why not just tranq them?"

"It throws up a red flag that something nefarious is going on. I mean, I will if I have to. I hope leading them on a wild goose chase will do the trick instead."

"And once I text you I'm clear, your diversion ends and they go back to their post none the wiser."

"That's the plan. You got your Glock?"

She slid the hem of her skirt up her thigh to reveal the pistol held snugly in a lacy black holster.

"Sweet Moses, that's hot," he whispered.

Smiling, she flipped the skirt back in place. She sobered and ran her fingertips through his thick hair. "You be careful."

"I will. You too. If something goes sideways and you can't talk your way out of it, run like hell and find a place to hide. I'll find you," he said and wiggled his phone.

"The exact same goes for you." She leaned forward and kissed him, pouring into it the nerves and stress and emotions roiling in her gut. "I love you."

An internal light gleamed in his eyes when he looked into hers. "I love you, too." He squeezed her hand and gave her one more kiss. "See you soon." Still in a crouch, he duck walked to the end of the hedge and stopped. He peered around the edge toward the cottage and then sprinted toward the closest palm tree.

From her secreted position, she watched James's progress until he was swallowed by the darkness. Now all she could do was wait.

A bright yellow tennis ball arced through the air and bounced on the tennis court several times before coming to a rest against the net.

Both guards snapped to attention. Like bird dogs pointing at a quail, they stood stock-still and stared in the direction of the court.

Another ball sailed along the same trajectory as the first.

The bigger guy, the one Quinn had encountered at the restaurant, pointed toward the darkened area from where the ball had been launched. From his body language and tone of voice, Quinn deduced he'd ordered the other man to go investigate.

He dropped his cigarette to the ground, crushed it under his shoe, and trotted off in James's direction.

Quinn muttered a curse through clenched teeth. With the bigger guard staying behind, she still couldn't approach the house. Seconds passed. She rubbed her palms, now slick with perspiration, over her the fabric of her skirt. How would James force the bigger man to abandon his post?

A man's voice barked, sharp and demanding. A second voice, which Quinn recognized as her husband's, responded in a calm, conciliatory tone. That fired up the guard even more. James's response was more forceful. The volume and level of anger increased for both until they were engaged in a roaring, verbal brawl.

Quinn stared at the man left behind, silently willing him to join his comrade. She pumped a fist in silent celebration when he stalked off toward the ruckus.

The second he was out of sight, Quinn leapt up and hurdled the hedge. On the lookout for any new threats, her eyes darted left and right as she ran full steam toward the cottage. Hands outstretched, she crashed into the exterior wall next to the window, spun around, and pressed her back against it. The rough stucco scratched the skin of her exposed back and shoulders. Despite the residual cigarette smoke infiltrating her lungs, she drew deep breaths in through her nose to slow her galloping pulse.

Now that she had collected herself, she turned her attention to the room on the other side of the wall. She edged her head as close to the open window as she could, straining to hear any sound. Her head cocked to one side when she heard the beeps and burbles of a video game.

Quinn peeked around the edge of the window.

Atop one of two twin beds, a brown-haired boy in his early teens lay on his stomach, propped on his elbows. Brow furrowed in concentration, his thumbs furiously punched the buttons on the front of an ancient Game Boy.

A blond girl, about the same age as the boy, sat on the other reading a tattered paperback. She glanced up and froze in shock when her ice-blue eyes locked with Quinn's.

"I'm not going to hurt you," Quinn said. "I just want to talk. Can I come in and do that for a few minutes?"

The girl nodded.

Quinn dropped her purse onto the floor under the window and put her palms on the windowsill. With a jump, she pushed herself up, sat on the ledge, and swung her legs around. She slid down and snagged her purse. "Hi," she said with a smile. The last thing she wanted was to appear threatening, so she sat on the floor in front of them.

Before anything else happened, she had to warn James she would need a few minutes. She took her phone from her purse and held it up. "I need to let my husband know where I am." She sent him a message that read, Found something. Need more time.

The boy gave Quinn a curious look and then returned his attention to the Game Boy.

Her phone buzzed in her hand. James's reply text read, Copy. Bogies down. She wondered what that meant exactly. He'd have to fill her in on his adventures later. She looked up and said again, "I'm Quinn. I'd like to know your names."

The girl with the ice-blue eyes said in a perfect American accent, "I'm Mila. He's Pyotr." Quinn noted the many small, round scars marring Pyotr's bare arms.

"Such beautiful names," Quinn said. "Are they Russian?"

"Yes," Mila replied. Wariness sparked in those astounding blue eyes.

"I'm named after an American president." When Mila looked at her in confusion, Quinn clarified. "Quinn is short for Quincy. John Quincy Adams."

"Mila is short for Ludmila," she offered. "And I know about John Quincy Adams. He was the sixth president."

"I'm impressed," Quinn said. She was pleased Mila was engaging with her.

Mila shrugged. "I'm American, too."

"You are?" Quinn said. She couldn't hide her surprise. "Where are you from?"

"Washington, near the Canadian border. My parents moved there from Russia before I was born."

"Is Pyotr American, too? Is he your brother?"

"No, not my brother. He's Russian. His English isn't as good as mine. But it's getting better all the time. I'm teaching him."

Quinn took a deep breath. This was it. "If you don't mind telling me, how did you come to be here?"

"The big men fly Pyotr and me on a private airplane to different places to work at rich people's houses. We do laundry, clean the house, wash the cars, help in the kitchen, work in the yard. Tomorrow we'll clean up after the party. We run errands for them too. They give us packages to deliver to shops. Then people at the shops give us packages to take back."

"Who gives you the packages to take to the shops?"

"The people we come to work for. This time, it's Mr. Gibson and the man with the very white teeth, Mr. Rhys. They keep one of the packages we bring back from the shops. We take the rest back to Russia."

"Have you seen what's inside those packages you get?"

"Drugs," she said, without hesitation.

Quinn's eyebrows shot up. "Are you sure?"

Mila nodded. "Sometimes it's pills. Mostly, like from here, it's a white powder. When we get back to Russia, Pyotr and me and the other kids put it into smaller packages. And I saw Mr. Rhys snort some up his nose."

Quinn clenched her jaw to bite back an angry growl. Given Colombia's close proximity to the Caribbean, and by extension Turks and Caicos, it appeared Gibson and Rhys were part of a pipeline to smuggle cocaine into Russia. And they were using innocent children as drug mules. *Vile bastards*.

"Because Pyotr and I are the oldest, we're the ones who go all the places to bring whatever kinds of drugs back."

"How many times have you been here at Gibson Honey-cutt's house?"

"Five or six?" Mila said with a shrug.

"Do you do these things because you want to? Do you get paid?" Not that it mattered to Quinn if they were paid or not. They were just kids.

"They say we're paid with food and clothes."

Clearly not enough since both were rail thin and their clothes were faded and threadbare. She wanted to punch Gibson Honeycutt IV, Rhys Townsend, and whoever else was involved in this drug ring in their throats.

"And anyway, we have no choice."

Quinn's next question filled her with dread, but she had to ask. "Do the men, um, ever hurt you or do things to you they shouldn't?"

"I was hit and yelled at once when I accidentally dropped some drugs on the floor. That's the only time. I'm more careful now. They do the same to the others."

Pyotr spoke up for the first time. "I am hit more. Sometimes I am caught eating cookies from kitchen." He shot Quinn a sly smile. "I am not sorry."

Quinn chuckled, more than a little proud of Pyotr and his act of rebellion. It also relieved her to know their abuse wasn't as severe as she'd feared it might have been.

Mila sat up straighter. "Why are you here?"

"I'm here to help you escape. Both of you," Quinn said, her tone growing urgent. "Right now." She didn't care about catching ringleaders.

Quinn's head snapped toward the door when she heard footsteps in the hall.

Someone was coming.

Chapter Eleven

A burst of adrenaline had Quinn scrambling to her feet. She tiptoed to the closet and slid the door open. "Please don't tell them I'm here," she said as she stepped in amongst clothes hanging from the rod. Her eyes pleaded with Mila's. "Please. I only want to help you."

The interloper was right outside the door. Quinn had no choice but to slide the closet closed without knowing if she was about to be exposed. In the inky blackness, she withdrew her Glock from her thigh holster and held it at the ready.

She felt the blood drain from her face when she realized she'd left her phone and purse right in the middle of the floor.

Her grip on the pistol tightened when she heard the bedroom door open. A woman began to speak in a brusque, accusatory tone. The Russian Quinn had learned at the Farm was of little help. They spoke too low and too fast for her to catch any of the conversation.

Mila received what sounded like a terse admonition and then responded in a conciliatory tone. The bedroom door closed with a click and the footsteps faded down the hall. Quinn sagged against the back wall in relief.

"You can come out," Mila said softly.

Quinn stashed her pistol, slid open the door, and stepped out of the closet. She blinked against the light and looked at the empty spot where she'd left her belongings.

Mila twisted around, withdrew the purse and phone from under a pillow, and held them out toward Quinn.

"Quick thinking," Quinn said, taking them. She sat down again. "Thanks for covering for me."

"You're welcome." Mila's ice-blue stare froze Quinn in place. "Can you really help us?"

"Yes. Absolutely," Quinn said emphatically. "Climb out that window and go with me right now. We'll take both of you somewhere safe."

"We can't."

"Why not?"

"I have a younger sister and brother still in Russia. If I don't go back, they'll beat them. Pyotr's father abused him so he ran away. He has no family to return to."

"I'm sorry," Quinn whispered. As much as she wanted to rescue them right then and there, it couldn't happen. "I so much want to talk to you some more, but I don't dare stay much longer. Can you tell me the names of your minders? The people who take you places? Where you're kept in Russia? Anything at all that will help us find you again?"

"They don't think I know, but I do. It's Saint Petersburg," she said. "But I don't know which building. They make us stay inside and work."

How could she just leave them without a way to track them down? "I've got it," she said when inspiration hit. "Take my phone. It has a tracker that works all the time, even when the battery runs down." She sent a quick text to James telling him to meet her at the spot behind the shrubs. When she received his reply saying he would be there, she opened the Emergency Red Button app on her phone and tapped in her security code. The screen went gray and then an ominous black. Every byte of data had just been wiped from her phone.

She jumped to her feet and dropped the phone on the bed. "Keep it with you. It'll tell us exactly where you are. We'll come for you." Quinn's gaze burned into Mila's. "I promise."

The only sounds in the room were the digital beeps chirping from Pyotr's Game Boy as the seconds ticked by. "The woman who came in before," Mila said. "That's Mother Olga. She always comes with us when we go places. She and another woman, Zhanna, watch us all back in Saint Petersburg. They don't get along because Zhanna wants to travel, too, but Mother Olga always gets to go. The big bald man is Anatoly. The other guy is Viktor. They're pilots." She picked up Quinn's phone from the mattress and stuffed it under the pillow. "I don't know the name of the man who's in charge. Everyone only calls him Boss."

"That's great. Thank you." Quinn picked up her purse, looped the strap over her head, and sat on the windowsill. "Before I go, can you tell me your last name? I can get a message to your parents, let them know I've been in contact with you."

Mila's chin stuck out in defiance. "They don't care. They haven't done anything to try and find us." The hurt and betrayal in Mila's voice cut through Quinn like a knife.

"You don't know that. Relations between the US and Russia aren't always the best. They might be getting stonewalled. Either way, knowing your last name will help us. Please."

Quinn scarcely breathed as she waited.

"Semenov."

"Thank you." She swung her legs over and dangled them over the edge. "Take care and see you." She pushed off the ledge and landed on the ground with a soft thump.

She raced for the hedge and bit back a shout for joy when she spotted James crouched behind it waiting for her. He almost tumbled backward when she hurled herself at him and wrapped her arms around his neck. "People suck," she whispered.

James's arms cinched tighter. "I know." After another moment, he leaned back and searched her face. "Some of us less sucky people will make the suckier people pay for their suckiness."

She smiled at him, his words giving her hope. "I love you." After a quick kiss, she heaved a huge sigh and said, "Can we clear out? I don't want to be at this damn party anymore."

"We can, although we need to make a final appearance before we leave."

They stood, slipped into the shadows, and jogged toward the party. "Why?"

"I was being a belligerent drunk, right? I thought I could yell and bluster long enough for you to check things out. When I got your text, I had to go to plan B."

"You tranqed them."

"Yeah, but not in the way you think. I didn't want them to see me with a weapon, so I started a brawl. I threw a couple of good punches and flattened them both. While they were on the ground, I removed a couple of darts from the magazine and jabbed them. Only gave them a little juice. They were starting to stir when you texted me to meet you. In the end, they'll think I'm just this drunk who knocked them out."

"You need to be seen drunk at the party to back up your story."

"Yup."

They circled around to the back of the property and rejoined the party still in full swing. At the fully dressed man doing the backstroke in the swimming pool, Quinn said, "As my dad would say, this party is a real humdinger."

"It's exactly what we want. It makes my fracas with Thing

One and Thing Two even more plausible," he said as they headed straight for the bar.

"You mean Anatoly and Viktor. Excellent Dr. Seuss reference, by the way."

"Thank you. Hunter and I bonded over his books when you, your mom, and your sisters-in-law were getting manicures a few days before the wedding." He caught the bartender's attention. "Turk's Head, please." The man behind the bar opened a bottle of beer and handed it to James.

"I'm sorry I missed it. Maybe the next time you two read together, I can get in on the discussion regarding the deeper philosophical questions raised in *Green Eggs and Ham.*"

"We'll have to make sure Bailey and Wyatt are in on it too." He tipped up the bottle and guzzled. "Although Bailey will outthink us all."

"No doubt," Quinn said. When James raised the beer to his lips again, she noticed his red knuckles and hissed through her teeth. "Does it hurt?"

"Nothing a little ice won't fix." His gaze swept the area. "Townsend is at our two o'clock. You see Honeycutt?"

"No," she said, scanning faces. "We should say our goodbyes to Rhys. Gibson won't remember we were here in the first place."

"Astute observation, Mrs. Anderson." He slugged back the rest of his lager and set the empty bottle on a nearby table. His eyes went from sharp to unfocused and droopy in a split second. He slouched and draped his arm over her shoulder. Leaning heavily on her, he gave her a sloppy kiss. "How's my breath?" he asked, keeping his voice low.

A hoppy aroma filled her nose. "You could use a mint."

"Perfect." His right eye drifted closed in a lazy wink. If she didn't know better, she would have sworn he was honestly and truly blitzed.

"Okay, baby. Here we go." Quinn slid her arm around his waist. With a tight grip on his wrist, she half-walked, half-dragged her faux-drunk husband in Rhys Townsend's direction.

"I love it when you call me baaaaaaay-bee," he crooned.

A snorting chuckle sounded at the back of Quinn's throat. He was certainly having fun chewing the scenery.

Rhys's eyebrows rose in interest as they approached. "James, you seem to be having a good time."

"Great party," James said. His head wobbled as if he was having a difficult time balancing it on his shoulders. He drew in a deep breath and blew it through his lips like a motorboat.

Rhys choked back a cough.

Looking into Townsend's face, it took everything Quinn had not to grab a shrimp fork and stab it into the bastard's eye. She swallowed her fury and gave Rhys a rueful smile. "I need to get him back to the hotel. He had a couple too many bottles from the local brewery."

"Understandable," Rhys said. "My cohost has been in a similar condition most of the evening."

She studied him briefly, looking for clues as to whether or not he was coked up at the moment. She couldn't tell, so she forced herself to focus on getting them out of there. "It happens. Anyway, thank you again for inviting us. We had a great time. And we both apologize about that dust-up out by the tennis court." Her tone turned hopeful. "Bygones?"

Rhys opened his mouth to reply, but James cut him off. "I just wanted to play tennis," he slurred and scratched his nose. "But I couldn't find a racket." His face twisted into a dark scowl. "And those guys didn't like it when I started throwing around those balls I found." Like flipping a switch, his anger vanished. He guffawed and shot Quinn a rascally grin. "I said balls."

She snickered. "Yes, sweetie, you did." To an amused but puzzled Rhys, she explained, "He told me he was going to go use the bathroom. When he didn't come back, I went looking for him and found him out by the court in a scuffle with a couple of security guys. They'll be okay." She added an embarrassed, "You might want to send someone to check on them. They were kind of out cold when we left them."

"You knocked them out? Both of them?" Rhys asked, clearly shocked. "You don't have a scratch on you."

James puffed out his chest. "I'm scrappy."

"He also teaches Krav Maga on the weekends," Quinn said and gave James an indulgent look. "When he felt threatened, his instincts kicked in. So to speak."

"I'm sure everything will be fine," Rhys said.

Movement to her left drew Quinn's attention. Anatoly and Viktor shouldered their way through the crowd of party-goers. Their nostrils flared like angry bulls as they scanned the area.

Rhys looked toward them. "Ah, there they are now. As I said, everything will be fine."

Quinn felt James's muscles grow taut. When she saw the murderous rage in those men's eyes, Quinn's grip around her husband's wrist constricted like a boa. "They look like they're ready for round two. We don't want that. We have to go," she said to Rhys.

"I think that's wise. I'll calm them down," Rhys said and strode toward Anatoly and Viktor. "*Ciao*," he called out with a wave.

Despite James staying in character by dragging his feet and hanging on Quinn, they moved at a swift pace through the house. "Quinn. Sweetie, you're cutting the circulation off to my hand," James said as they stepped into the front courtyard.

"Sorry." She relaxed her hand. "I didn't even realize."

His fingers flexed and wiggled. "It's okay."

They stopped at the fountain. When one of the valets approached, Quinn said to her swaying husband, "I need the valet ticket."

"It's in my pocket." A lascivious grin bloomed. "You have to find it."

Quinn threw a feigned look of mild exasperation in the direction of the smirking valet. She stood in front of James, her front lightly pressed against his. With both hands, she reached around and plunged them into the back pockets of his linen slacks. She felt his wallet in one. Her fingertips brushed against the metal backplate of his phone in the other. After a little more exploring, she touched a slip of paper trapped between James's bum and the phone.

She pinched his butt before removing the ticket.

He shot her a scandalized look and murmured, "Cheeky."

"In more ways than one." She handed the paper to the valet. "Here you go."

From the backyard, she heard voices rise in anger. If she were to guess, Rhys was having a difficult time restraining the ego-bruised bodyguards bent on retribution. It wasn't smart on their part, really, to come after them since a "drunk" James had already given them a thorough beatdown.

Regardless, she and James needed to get out of there. "You don't have to get the car," she called when the valet unhooked the keys from the board. "Walking might do him some good." She fished a five-dollar bill from her wallet and held it out. "If you could just tell me where the car's parked, I'll take it from here."

"Yes, miss," the valet replied and hurried back. He happily exchanged money for keys. Pointing toward the road, he said, "Your car is fifth from the corner."

"Thanks," Quinn said. With her arm around James's waist again, she started them toward the front gate. "Come on, you."

James might have been hanging on her, but his stride was quick and sure-footed.

Behind them, furious voices echoed through the yard. Rhys had failed to persuade the raging bulls to stand down.

Quinn and James's pace picked up even as their body positions remained a wife helping her inebriated husband to their car.

They reached a metal security door next to the gate blocking the entrance to the driveway. She turned the knob and pushed it open. Once they were through, it closed behind them with a resounding clang.

Now clear of the property, Quinn spotted their car in the moonlight. They veered to the right and power walked across the gravel-covered road.

Headlights flashed and the car chirped when Quinn pressed the alarm button on the key fob.

She opened the passenger door. James dropped into the seat and said under his breath, "Hustle, baby."

The urgency in his tone had her glancing over the top of the car toward the gate. Anatoly and Viktor burst through the door and charged toward them. The light from inside the car drew them like bulls toward a red cape.

"Shit," Quinn hissed and slammed the door. She sprinted around the front of the car while James leaned across the center console and pushed the driver's side door open. She slid behind the steering wheel and jerked the door shut. The interior of the car was plunged into darkness. She jammed the key into the ignition and turned over the engine.

Quinn threw the car into reverse and cranked the wheel. She looked over her shoulder and backed up until the back bumper kissed the front of the car behind them.

Anatoly and Viktor closed in on them.

Quinn shifted the lever into drive and spun the steering wheel in the other direction. She glanced through the side window and yelped when Anatoly, his face thunderous, pointed a gun directly at her chest.

With her foot still on the brake, she twisted and threw herself on top of James, shielding him from the barrel leveled at them.

She squeezed her eyes shut and waited for the explosion of glass and the searing pain of bullets ripping into her back.

The bullets didn't come.

"Quinn! Their guns aren't loaded," James said. "I emptied their magazines while they were tranqed."

She sat up and spun around. Anatoly gaped at the inert pistol in his hand.

Before he got any bright ideas like pounding on the window with the grip of the gun, she lifted her foot from the brake. The car inched forward.

She sat up as straight as she could and stared at the front edge of the hood. "I can't see!" Perspiration spurted from every pore on her body. "Will I clear the car in front?"

"You got it. You got it." James gripped the dashboard. "Go! Go! Go!"

Viktor's fists pounded on the window behind her.

She gunned the engine.

Viktor bellowed when the car lurched into the road.

James looked out the back window as the car sped away. "I think you ran over his foot."

She flicked on the headlights. A cluster of palm trees rushed up on them. She yelped and spun the steering wheel. The car drifted as it made a violent right turn.

As the car streaked down the dirt road, she clipped on her seat belt. James did the same.

Her entire body buzzed as every synapse in her nervous system fired.

She checked the rearview mirror. No headlights followed them. There were only the receding lights of the accursed Honeycutt estate.

She slowed the car as they approached the end of the lane. She wheeled onto another dirt road, one that meandered along the coastline. Quinn drove as fast as she dared along the dark, unfamiliar drive. Keeping one hand on the wheel, she wiped the sweat from her palm on her skirt. She switched hands and dried the other.

Her eyes flicked to the rearview mirror again. There was only inky darkness.

It was only after she turned the car onto the paved, main highway she allowed herself the luxury of sucking in a lungful of air and blowing it out in a gust.

James was the first to break the silence. "You were going to take a bullet for me." His voice was subdued.

She peeked over at him. His jaw was set and his eyes were fixed on the blackness in front of them. "Yeah," she said and returned her attention to the patch of road illuminated by the headlights. "You would have done the same for me."

"Yeah, I would." He reached out, lifted her hand from the wheel, and kissed the back of it. He enveloped it in both of his and rested them on his thigh. "Don't ever do it again."

From the seriousness in his tone, she knew he wasn't kidding around. Neither was she when she answered with equal solemnity. "I can't promise you that, James, any more than you could promise me the same thing. We're partners. In everything. Forever." She looked over at him and then out the windshield again. "We have each other's backs. It's what we do."

From the corner of her eye, she saw his head fall back against the headrest. "You're right." After another stretch of silence, he picked up his head and turned his face toward her. She felt his intense gaze on her when he said in a thick voice, "Thank you."

She swallowed at the sudden lump in her throat. "You're welcome." Her lips twitched in a tiny smile. "Besides, it's what any CIA librarian spy wife would do for her CIA operative husband. Get used to it."

He squeezed her hand. "Yes, dear." She heard the smile in his voice.

They drove the rest of the way in easy silence. The time would come when Quinn would tell James all that she'd learned inside the cottage. But for now, they were content to decompress after the eventful evening.

Quinn turned the car into the hotel parking lot and parked near their suite. "I don't know if Anatoly and Viktor got good looks at our faces. It was pretty dark. But on the chance they scour Provo looking for us, how do you feel about not leaving the hotel property the rest of our honeymoon?"

James unbuckled his seat belt and kissed her cheek. "It's the perfect way to bookend it. Just the way it started."

She stole a kiss and opened her door. "My thoughts exactly."

Chapter Twelve

Quinn entered their darkened suite and flipped the switch on the wall, flooding with room with light. She lifted the strap over her head and tossed her purse on the sofa.

James closed the door. "You want to talk about it?"

She raked her fingers through her hair. "Yeah. Let me go change first." By the time she entered the bedroom, she was already shed of her dress, which she flung on the bed. She kicked off her sandals one at a time. They flew across the room, clunked against the wall, and dropped to the floor.

She turned on her heel and yelped at the sudden appearance of James filling the doorway. "You scared me." She pressed a hand to her chest and felt her heart galloping under it. "I guess I'm still a little jumpy."

He leaned his shoulder against the doorjamb, his hands stuffed in his front pockets. "Sorry. Just taking the opportunity to admire the view."

She *was* only wearing panties, bra, and thigh holster. All black. "You're forgiven." His open admiration of her was always appreciated.

He made no move toward her, although his eyes followed her as she moved about the room. "I gather you found some workers in the carriage house. Gibson is using them?"

"Yeah. A teenage girl and boy get flown around to do

domestic work for rich people. This time, it's Gibson." She withdrew her Baby Glock from its holster and set it on the nightstand. "Their primary function, though, is as drug mules."

James's eyebrows rose. "That's an unexpected twist."

"The girl, Mila, is around fourteen." She slid the holster off and tossed it on the bed. "My guess is Pyotr is about thirteen." Staring down at the holster but not really seeing it, she said, "He has cigarette burns all over his arms. Mila said he ran away from an abusive father."

Quinn shook the images of the round scars from her mind, turned, and slid open a drawer. She took out a pair of shorts and pulled them on. Her anger was ramping up again.

After pulling a shirt on over her head, she rammed the drawer closed with such force, the dresser back slammed against the wall.

"They're just kids!" Whirling around, she stalked over to her nightstand and grabbed her book. "Scumbags like Rhys Townsend and Gibson Honeycutt use them like slaves so they can snort coke!" She opened it to the page Rhys Townsend had autographed, ripped it out, and crumpled it into a wad. "Narcissistic bastard," she growled and hurled it like a fastball across the room. The novel was next to go flying. It made a spectacular racket when it smashed against the wall and clattered to the floor.

The next thing she knew, James's arms were around her, crushing her to him. They stood there, motionless, until she heaved a sigh when her anger subsided. He led her to the bed and said, "Sit."

She perched on the edge of it, her temples throbbing.

James retrieved a bottle of water from the mini fridge and held it out. "Drink."

She cracked it open and gulped down several swallows. The cold water soothed her parched throat, but couldn't extinguish the embers of anger still smoldering in her chest.

James walked on his knees across the mattress and

arranged the pillows against the headboard. Once they were sufficiently plumped, he propped himself against them. Legs outstretched and crossed at the ankles, he patted the spot next to him.

"You're so sweet," she said. She set the water on the nightstand and bounced across the bed. Stretching out, she mirrored his posture.

"It's what any CIA operative husband would do for his CIA librarian spy wife. Get used to it."

She chuckled.

"Tell me more about the kids you found," James said. "You said their names are Mila and Pyotr. I take it they're Russian."

"They are, although Mila told me she's American. I tend to believe her. She spoke perfect English."

"Really? American? Did she tell you how she got to be a drug mule?"

She deflated a little. "No. I did find out her full name is Ludmila Semenov. Her parents are Russian immigrants. She said she's from Washington state. She didn't say which city."

"Semenov? Not Semenova?"

"That's what she said. My guess is her parents went with the American style of last name. Less confusing."

James nodded. "Nice work. That's some great intel. We should be able to track down her parents without too much trouble." He paused for a moment, as if ordering his thoughts. He dipped his head and looked into her face. "You tried to get them to come with you, didn't you?"

"Yeah. I didn't care about bringing down human traffickers." She snorted a mirthless laugh. "And now drug traffickers, too. I just wanted to get them out of there."

"I don't blame you. It sounds like a harsh life." He entwined his fingers with hers. "Why didn't they go with you?"

"Mila has a younger sister and brother still in Russia

trapped in the same ring. The threat of their being beaten is plenty of incentive for her to stay compliant."

"Anatoly and Viktor came with them from Russia?"

"Mm-hmm. Both muscle and pilots. And there's a woman with them, too. Mother Olga. Almost had a run-in with her. I had to hide in the closet."

James's head clunked back against the headboard. "I know it's part of the job, but when you tell me things like that, it takes days off my life."

"Sorry." Her thumb drifted back and forth over his.

James lifted his head and looked down at his feet. "Where in Russia are they?"

"Saint Petersburg, but she didn't know where. They keep them locked up in a building where they process the drugs for distribution." When James groaned, she said, "It's okay. I gave Mila my phone."

"That's brilliant. The tracker will tell us exactly where they are."

"That's the idea anyway. And don't worry. I nuked it before I handed it off."

"Good. I took photos of Anatoly and Viktor while they were unconscious, so getting last names shouldn't be too hard. From there, we should be able to find some known associates." James took his phone from his pocket. "You okay with us meeting Dave sometime tomorrow?" he asked, his thumbs ready to type.

With exhaustion pressing in on her, she only could muster a quiet hum of assent in response. She scooted down the bed until she lay flat. Her eyelids drifted closed as her head sank deeper into the pillow.

A minute later, James's phone chimed. "Dave will be here tomorrow morning at eleven. He's excited we have actionable intel. It's the first real step in busting this open." He set his phone on his nightstand and switched off the lamp.

The mattress jostled as James slid down and turned onto

his side. Facing her, he curled an arm over her and pulled her toward him. She rolled onto her side and shimmied back into him.

As she lay there in the dark, lulled by the steady rise and fall of her husband's chest against her shoulders, Quinn was never more grateful for her truly charmed life. As drowsiness descended, her thoughts turned to Mila, Pyotr, and all people forced to work against their will. Her hope was that one day soon, they would feel a similar sense of love, freedom, and security. For Mila and Pyotr and the kids trapped in Saint Petersburg, she would do everything she could to make it to happen.

Quinn sat slouched in a padded chair with her bare feet propped against the metal railing surrounding their private veranda. Squeals of children's laughter floated on the breeze from the direction of the hotel's swimming pool. In her mind, she pictured Bailey, Wyatt, and Hunter splashing in the warm, sparkling water. Maybe someday she and James, her parents, grandparents, brothers, and their families could invade Provo for an Ellington family vacation.

She made a mental note to broach the subject with her mom sometime before returning her attention to her book.

It, and the crumpled page she'd ripped out of it the night before, had languished on the floor overnight and well into that morning. Every time she'd looked at them, they'd reminded her of that piece of human debris Rhys Townsend. A fresh wave of disgust and ire would wash over her.

When she couldn't ignore them any longer, she considered chucking both in the trash. *The Leopard's Claw* would be forever connected to Rhys. She'd stood over the trash can with the novel in one hand and the crumpled page in the other. The paper was a no-brainer. It went in the bin where it belonged.

The book was another matter. Edward Walker was a fictional mentor. He was suave, sophisticated, brave, and above all, resourceful. It had been Edward Walker who had inspired her to once use one of the hefty volumes of her *Compact Edition of the Oxford English Dictionary* as a weapon. She'd knocked two men out cold.

In the end, she'd kept the novel. She was determined not to allow Rhys Townsend to ruin Edward Walker for her. Of course, there was no way she'd ever watch another Edward Walker movie with him in it. It did give her an immense amount of pleasure to think when justice was served, Rhys Townsend's sorry ass would be in jail for trafficking both humans and drugs and the role of Edward Walker would be recast.

She returned her attention to the page. Villain Takudzwa Marufu had just locked Edward Walker in a cage with—unsurprisingly, given the title of the book—a leopard, when from inside their suite, she heard James say, "Quinn, Meyers is calling to video chat."

"Be right there." She stuck the bookmark between the pages, closed the book, and rolled to her feet. She slipped through the door and dropped *The Leopard's Claw* and her sunglasses on a nearby end table.

Dave Flores and James already sat on the couch in front of James's open laptop. Aldous Meyers's angular face filled the screen.

Quinn took her seat next to James. Meyers acknowledged her arrival with a dip of his chin. As was his usual modus operandi, he dispensed with pleasantries and got down to business.

"We verified the information you provided to us regarding Ludmila Semenov," Meyers said. "Her parents are Vasily and Ekaterina Semenov. They immigrated to the United States twenty years ago and reside in Peaceful Valley, Washington." Meyers shuffled some papers on his desk and picked up one piece in particular. "According to a State report, Ludmila, and her younger sister, Sasha and little brother, Ilya, traveled to Slavnoye, a small town in the Tver Oblast, two years ago to visit their maternal grandmother. According to said grandmother, an older cousin and the cousin's boyfriend took the three siblings on a day trip to Tver. They never returned to Slavnoye. None of them, including the cousin and boyfriend, have been seen or heard from since."

"I assume the grandmother reported all of them missing," James said.

"She did. She contacted the local authorities and the parents went to Russia to look for them. After an initial investigation, the whole thing was dropped. The parents reported their children's disappearances to authorities here in the US. The information eventually made its way to State. At this point, everything has stalled."

"What a nightmare," Quinn said. "Those poor parents. After all this time, they must think their kids are dead."

"A team has been dispatched to advise them of these recent developments."

"It's a real good news/bad news kind of thing," James said.

Meyers nodded. "Indeed."

"What about Quinn's phone?" Dave asked. "Is it still transmitting?"

James fielded that question. "Yes. It's still here on Providenciales."

That wasn't a huge surprise. The party had most likely continued until sunrise. She pictured an epically hungover Gibson only now prying open a gritty eye and cursing the brilliant sunlight.

"Have you got any hits on facial recognition for Anatoly and Viktor?" James asked.

"Not yet."

Dave rubbed his cheek. "So now what? How will all this work?"

Meyers folded his hands and set them on the desk in front of him. "Since the Semenov children are American citizens, the agency is in a position to assist in securing them. I've met with my superiors. They've given approval to use agency assets."

"What about my team? Are we sidelined?" From Dave's tone, he wasn't pleased at the prospect.

"No. This will be a joint operation."

Quinn looked at James. His nod was nearly imperceptible. "James and I request to be members of the task force," she said to Meyers. "The contacts he cultivated during his time in Russia might prove useful. And I promised Mila I'd see them again." Her eyes sharpened with a hint of defiance. "I keep my promises."

"I'm sure you do," Meyers said. "I assumed you and James would make this request. I've already attached you to what we've dubbed Operation Bear Trap. You will work with Dave and his organization to rescue and repatriate our citizens. You are also directed to assist him and his team in gathering evidence that will convict any and all individuals involved in this human trafficking ring. Disrupting the flow of cocaine and other drugs into Russia will be an added bonus."

"If we end up in Russia, that won't be easy," Quinn said. "Russia wasn't happy when the State Department's annual Trafficking in Persons Report listed them as a Tier Three country. The government's not even trying to comply with the Trafficking Victims Protection Act. We might not get much help." When Dave shot her a surprised look, she said, "What? I read it in the CIA *World Factbook*. The library produces it. It's a pretty great resource, if I do say so myself."

Meyers ignored her aside to Dave and plunged ahead. "It's true the Russians could do a lot more. Unfortunately, it doesn't look like that is going to happen anytime soon. Given the circumstances and the current political climate, we'll do the best we can."

"But at the very least, we get the Semenov kids home," James said.

"Absolutely. They are priority one," Meyers answered.

"What's next? Do we need to cut our honeymoon short?" Quinn asked. "Because we will if we need to, right, James?"

"For sure. We want all those kids safe as soon as possible."

"I appreciate the offer, but that won't be necessary," Dave said. "We don't know exactly where they'll be in Saint Petersburg or when they'll be back. We'll know more as we track Quinn's phone."

"Agreed. Enjoy the rest of your honeymoon and report back to Langley as previously scheduled. We will hopefully know more by then." Meyers paused. "Questions?"

The three on the sofa looked at each other.

"Andersons, see you Monday. Flores, I'll be in touch." The screen went black.

Quinn frowned. "I hate that we can't do something right now."

"I know it's frustrating," Dave replied, "but it takes time to do it right."

"I understand. It just sucks." Her ire flared. "What about Gibson Honeycutt and Rhys Townsend? Are they just going to go free?"

"Yup. For now." Dave's features hardened in resolve. "But now that we know what they're up to, we'll bust them eventually." He leapt to his feet as if solid rocket boosters had ignited in his back pockets. "I've invaded your honeymoon long enough. Adios." And he was gone.

"I guess we don't have to wonder what our next op will be," Quinn said.

"We don't." James stretched out his legs and laced his fingers behind his head. "And now we're just a couple of newlyweds on our honeymoon again."

"Who can't leave the hotel grounds because two very large, very angry Russians are looking to throttle us," she reminded him. She nestled into his side and tucked her feet up under her.

James dropped his arm behind her shoulders. "I'm not too worried about us finding ways to pass the time."

With two fingers on his jaw, she turned his face toward hers and rolled into him. She pressed her lips to his in a kiss that started off soft and easy. It didn't stay that way for long. As things heated up, Quinn broke the kiss and breathed, "Me neither."

He waited for her, with eyes closed and lips slightly parted.

She traced the tip of her tongue over his soft lips. He shuddered and strained to kiss her, but she backed away. When he relented and relaxed back, she caressed his face with a hand and feathered his lips with hers.

Desire for her radiated from him, sparking in her an urgent need. She crushed her mouth onto his in a smoldering kiss.

They had no trouble at all in passing the time.

Chapter Thirteen

Quinn slid the last piece of leftover chicken Parmesan off the spatula and into a plastic container. She snapped on the lid and set it on the shelf inside the refrigerator. "That'll make for some mean chicken Parm sandwiches for lunch tomorrow. I can hardly wait." The refrigerator door swung closed with a soft thump.

Next, she set the empty baking dish on the counter next to the sink. James rinsed off a dinner plate and placed it in the lower rack of the dishwasher. He shot her a playful smirk over his shoulder. "What makes you think you get any leftovers? I made it."

She crossed her arms and leaned her hip against the edge of the counter. "So that's how it's gonna be, huh?"

"When it comes to chicken Parmesan, I'm afraid so." James picked up the dish Quinn had set on the counter and stuck it under the faucet's stream of hot water.

Mesmerized, she watched the residual tomato sauce swirl down the drain. "I'm afraid the law doesn't back you up on that. Virginia is an equitable property state. Everything acquired in the marriage is divided equally."

"Should I be worried that you know that?"

She rolled her eyes. "Yes, because me spewing bits of trivia is a completely new thing."

He chuckled, turned off the water, and set the dish in the dishwasher.

"You're lucky I didn't ask you to sign a prenup before we got married," she said. "I mean, look at all the fabulous assets I brought into this marriage: my ancient and completely gross couch, my twenty-year-old car, my savings account bursting with a grand total of two thousand dollars." She glanced over at Rasputin, crouched over his food dish, chowing down on his dinner. "My cat."

"Yes, all are treasures," James said. "Although we've already ditched the couch." For Quinn, doing so had been bittersweet. Its better days had long past. But it was a part of Ellington family lore, having been used by each sibling and passed down the line until it came to her. As the youngest, she had no one to give it to when she and James combined households and moved into a new apartment. James had made a persuasive case to keep his sofa, pointing out he had been its sole owner and it wasn't stained as if it had been used in the performance of ritual sacrifices.

James rolled the rack into the dishwasher, squirted liquid detergent into the dispenser, and lifted the door. After shutting it tight and pressing the start button, he hooked his fingers through the belt loops at the front of her jeans and yanked her to him. "To be honest, I'm more interested in your other *assets*."

She grinned, looped an arm around his neck, and pulled him into a kiss. "My assets and I appreciate it."

"And I promise to share my chicken Parmesan with you. Not because it appears I'm legally bound, but because I love you."

"You're sweet. And I love you too." They shared another kiss, this one longer and a little more heated. When it ended, she said, "And thank you for making dinner."

"You're welcome." He laced his fingers together at the small of her back. "I got a movie for us to watch tonight."

"Only married a month and we're already staying home on Saturday nights," she teased.

"Okay, Miss Social Butterfly. Do you have another suggestion?"

"It's Mrs. Social Butterfly, thank you very much. And to be honest, I was thinking about writing out some more wedding present thank-you cards."

His expression turned sour. "That's no fun."

"I know, but that note thanking your Uncle Charlie for the chainsaw isn't going to write itself." Her nose wrinkled. "Seriously, what's the deal with that? I mean, I appreciate the thought, but we live in an apartment. What are we going to do with a chainsaw?"

He shook his head. "I got nothing. He's my mom's brother. Her side of the family tends to be"—he peered up at the ceiling as he searched for the right word—"unconventional." A devilish smile curled on his lips. "Can I write the thank-you for that black lacy number Nicole gave you? I owe her a tremendous debt of gratitude."

Quinn's eyes sparkled with delight. "I think we should both thank her." Every time she wore that sheer little nightie, some rafter-rattling sex ensued. "But you're right. I don't want to do that on a Saturday night. Besides, I want to keep enjoying my day off from Russian immersion. I'm only hours away from writing everything in Cyrillic."

A guilty look crossed his face.

She cut her eyes up at him. "What?"

"The movie is in Russian."

"Aw, James," she said, annoyed. "This is the first day all week we've spoken English at home." She shrugged out of his embrace, crossed the kitchen, and spun around. "I've been marinating in Russian twenty-four-seven since the day we went back to work. I spend all day, every day in that damn class at the agency. And then when I get home, I have to struggle and fight to come up with every word I want to say to you. I feel like a two-year-old, having to point at stuff and use one or two words at a time." She crossed her arms over her chest. "I'm sick of it."

"I know you are, and I know it's frustrating. But give yourself a break. You've only been at it for a couple of weeks. You're doing a lot better than you think."

Her shoulders lowered, but the scowl remained. "Really?"

"Yeah, really." She heard nothing but absolute sincerity in his tone. "Maybe you aren't quite ready to read *War and Peace* in the original Russian. But I'm sure you'll be rock solid when we get to Saint Petersburg."

She wasn't so sure about that.

He moved a shoulder in a slight shrug. "I thought a movie tonight would be a good compromise since we haven't spoken it at all today." He took a tentative step toward her. "It has English subtitles."

He was so incredibly sweet and patient. Her defenses began to crumble. "I guess it is important I do something with it every day."

He shoved his hands in his pockets and shuffled closer. "I'll make popcorn," he said with a smile that made her go all tingly.

Holy cow, he was sexy. And that smile of his always rendered her completely powerless to resist. Not that she ever wanted to. "Okay." She grabbed the front of his shirt and hauled him to her. "*Ya tebya lyublyu.*"

He stroked her cheek with the back of his fingers and responded to her declaration of love for him. "*Ya tozhe tebya lyublyu.*"

After they shared a tender kiss, she asked, "So which masterpiece of Russian cinema will we be watching?"

He went to the cupboard and removed a bag from the box of microwave popcorn. "You scoff, but it's considered an artistic tour de force." He removed the bag's outer cellophane layer, tossed it in the microwave, and pressed a button on the front panel. The oven began to hum.

"Artistic. Now I'm really worried." Quinn picked up her wineglass from the table and took a sip. "They can be hard to follow when you *do* speak the language."

A lone kernel popped in the oven. A few seconds later, several more exploded in rapid succession.

"I'm sure between the two of us we can get the main points figured out," he said.

With James's wineglass now in her other hand, she carried both into the living room and set them on the coffee table. The second she flopped onto the couch, Rasputin jumped up, sat on the cushion next to her, and began his after-dinner cleaning ritual. "You're a little more optimistic than I am." She watched Rasputin lick the back of his front paw and swipe it over his ear and face. "You still haven't told me the name of this cinematic wonder. From what you've said so far, I take it it's not *The SpongeBob SquarePants Movie*."

The explosions coming from the kitchen slowed until Quinn heard only an occasional staccato pop. James opened the microwave door, retrieved the now expanded bag, and pulled it open. He dumped the contents into a bowl and said, "That movie is a masterpiece of another kind. Tonight, our senses will be feasting on the black-and-white glory that is the 1938 classic *Alexander Nevsky*." Bowl in hand, he walked toward her. "And of course you're already searching the Internet about it."

She looked up from her phone and arched an eyebrow. "And this surprises you because . . ."

He set the popcorn next to the wineglasses. "I'm only

surprised by the fact you don't already know about it, oh Great Trivia Master."

She stuck her tongue out at him, garnering her a laugh. "I'm a librarian. I don't *know* everything. I just know how to *find out* about everything."

"Ah, your secret is out," he said and went to the DVD player.

While he pressed buttons on various remote controls and slid the disc into the machine, she skimmed the summary of the movie. "It says Alexander Nevsky was a thirteenth century prince who, among other things, waged war with an invading German army. Apparently it's a parallel to the Nazi threat to the Soviets." Her eyes followed James as he turned off the overhead lights and switched on a lamp. The room was illumined by a soft, yellow glow. "Sounds like a feel-good romp," she said, poker-faced.

He lowered himself onto the sofa next to her, lifted the bowl of popcorn, and settled back against the cushions. His feet propped on the table, he set the munchies between them, pointed the remote, and pressed play.

She burrowed into his side and tucked her feet under her when his arm curled around her back. "Oh, cool," she said, consulting her phone again. "The score was written by Sergei Prokofiev." They watched the opening credits, which featured no sound other than a hum and the occasional crackle of the original eighty-year-old recording. "Sergei must have had a no-opening-credits clause in his contract."

"Yeah, because the Soviets were all about fair compensation," James said before munching on a handful of popcorn.

Quinn clicked off her phone and dropped it on the cushion next to Rasputin. With front paws folded under his chest and tail wrapped around one side, the cat was the epitome of chill. He stared Zen-like through eyelids lowered to thin slits.

The movie opened with a shot of a battlefield strewn with

shields and swords. A bleached-white skull still wearing its helmet lay on a bleak, barren landscape.

"Cheery," James deadpanned.

At first, Quinn followed the story pretty well. Ragingly propagandist, noble, salt-of-the-earth Russians were forced to repel an invasion by the sinister, papist Germans who wore metal bucket-like helmets on their heads reminiscent of the Black Knight from *Monty Python and the Holy Grail*. Admittedly, she was more than a little excited when she understood random words here and there. Of course, the subtitles helped.

Eventually, though, her attention began to wane about the time the Germans who looked like the "Knights Who Say, 'Ni!'" sent their men to battle the Russian peasant army. It wasn't for lack of her trying to stay focused. The culprit was James. As they sat together—relaxed, easy, intimate—her body reacted to him. She throbbed. Her breathing grew shallow. Her mouth went dry. Her mind was hijacked by thoughts of jumping on him and kissing him senseless. And that was only for starters.

She wondered if James was afflicted by the same urges when he began to draw circles on her upper arm with his fingertips. Either way, it made her go utterly cross-eyed.

She shifted closer to him and drew in a deep breath. She was so fully consumed by him—his touch, his scent, the warmth his body emitted—she couldn't contain her desire any longer.

Fire burning in her belly, she twisted toward him and gently pressed her lips to his jaw.

He didn't react, at least overtly. She knew she had his attention, though, by the way the muscles in his abdomen quivered under her hand.

His eyelids fluttered as she continued to cover his jaw with delicate kisses. The more labored his breathing became, the higher her core temperature climbed.

Quinn picked up the popcorn bowl and blindly set it on the table. It clanked against a wine goblet that narrowly escaped tipping over. She rose up on her knees, straddled him, and settled on his lap.

His head dropped back against the wall. She lowered her mouth onto his awaiting lips. As they kissed, long and deep and sensual, his hands slithered under her top and caressed her back.

In the background, Prokofiev's stirring score played as an epic battle waged. Quinn sat back and peeled off her top. "You know? I'm enjoying this movie a lot more than I thought I would." She tossed it aside, sending Rasputin racing for the safety of the bedroom.

Captivated, James's eyes lingered on her, drinking her in. He threaded his fingers through her loose hair and drew her face toward his. Just before their lips met again, he rumbled, "Best. Movie. Ever."

Chapter Fourteen

The small air-conditioning unit mounted in the window rattled and wheezed as it pumped moderately cool air into a cramped hotel room in Saint Petersburg, Russia. It wasn't that the June weather was particularly unpleasant. Well north in latitude and perched on the eastern edge of the Baltic Sea, Saint Petersburg, one of the most beautiful cities in the world, was known to be humid but rarely oppressively hot. At that moment, had James and Quinn been the sole occupants of the room, the unit would have been more than adequate. But with the four additional members of Operation Bear Trap crowded into the tiny room, it couldn't overcome the stuffiness.

Two weeks had passed since James and Quinn had watched—and not watched—*Alexander Nevsky*. They'd learned exactly where in Russia's former imperial capital Quinn's phone had settled a few days later. Since then, the pieces of Operation Bear Trap had been put into place. Now, the team had assembled. It was time to execute.

Quinn stood in one corner of the room and watched Dave tap his fingertip on the screen of an iPad. The faces of two men in side-by-side photos appeared on a monitor. She recognized them immediately.

"These men are Anatoly Volodin and Viktor Rykov. They work for this man." Dave tapped the screen again and called up a surveillance photo. "Grigori Yefimov. He uses trafficked teens and younger kids to run drugs—cocaine for sure and likely heroin as well—here in Saint Petersburg. His legitimate business front is a strip club called the Bronze Monkey. It's located off Nevsky Prospekt, the city's main drag. The kids are in a different building a short distance away."

"And you didn't want to watch *Alexander Nevsky*," James whispered in her ear.

She poked him in the ribs with her elbow and bit her lip to suppress the smile.

"Yefimov operates the strip club and sells drugs on behalf of shadowy crime boss Konstantin Borovsky." Dave looked over to James and wordlessly asked him to pick up the narration.

James pushed away from the wall he'd been leaning against and straightened to his full height. "Very little is known about Borovsky other than he loves beautiful women and lives a life of luxury. He stays in the background and runs his empire through surrogates like Yefimov. It's safer for him that way. We don't know where he lives or where his base of operation is located. There aren't any decent photos of him, either. So it looks like the biggest fish of all is going to be outside this op's net."

That hadn't stopped Meyers from tasking James and Quinn to keep their eyes and ears open for any and all intel about Borovsky's person and location, though.

"What we *do* know," James said, "is that in addition to his human and drug trafficking, he has enterprises scattered throughout Russia featuring the mob's greatest hits: gambling, extortion, weapons smuggling, kidnapping, blackmail, money laundering, counterfeiting, fraud, murder. You get the picture."

All heads in the room nodded.

James continued. "Selling cocaine here in Russia is extremely lucrative. Since it's produced in South America, the distance to Russia makes it a scarcer, and therefore pricier, commodity. Gibson Honeycutt and Rhys Townsend in the Caribbean is a critical link in Borovsky's chain of distribution. Saint Petersburg's location on the Baltic allows for access to Scandinavia, as well as northern and eastern Europe."

The basso profundo voice of Larry Taylor, also known as LT, rumbled from the other side of the room. "How do the drugs fit in to our plan?" The former Navy Seal had the build of a linebacker and was handsome, with more than a passing resemblance to Idris Elba. He came off as the tough, no-nonsense sort. But when Quinn had asked him if he had kids when they'd first met, his face had lit up like a Christmas tree. By the time the conversation ended, Quinn had learned Kayla, age eight, was an orange belt in karate and Trey had won second prize at his middle school's science fair.

"The Russian government has done little to combat human trafficking and forced labor, so we'll try to get convictions on the drug angle," Reem Tabsh, the team's lawyer, responded. "They have a huge heroin/HIV problem here, and they take the infiltration of drugs a lot more seriously. The problem is, a number of local magistrates and police are paid off by Borovsky via Yefimov."

Dave nodded. "Reem will do everything she can to have Yefimov and crew arrested, tried, and convicted. But with the rampant corruption, it's not a slam dunk. Either way, our primary objective is getting the kids out of there. We can't just roll in blind with guns blazing. We have to get some intel and do this right.

"So here's the plan. James, you'll meet with Yefimov and tell him you want to buy some coke, but you insist you have to check out his product first and see his operation. Wave enough cash around until he has no choice but to agree. Once you're inside, you recon the building, scope out how many guards there are, entrances and exits and so forth. Then we'll come back here and develop a specific plan. One thing we already know is once we get the kids out, we'll take them to a safe house Yonatan has already secured." Dave tapped the tablet, and a map of the area popped up on the monitor.

Yonatan Litman, the team's tech and logistics wizard, pushed his wire-rimmed glasses up the bridge of his nose and peered at the map. He was a former member of the Israeli Defense Forces and likely former or current Mossad. Quinn wasn't about to ask. "The house is in Olgino, about eighteen kilometers from here. I checked it out yesterday. It's a big place with a lot of bedrooms. It will accommodate as many kids as we can spring. James, once you know how many work inside that building, I'll get the right number of vans lined up to drive them out there."

"Roger that," James said.

"We'll hammer out all the specifics when it gets closer," Dave said. "Reem's working on sniffing out non-corrupt local police to help with the raid."

LT rubbed his thumb over the goatee covering his chin. "Rehabilitation?"

"I've been in touch with a trafficking victims' assistance center here in Saint Petersburg. They'll have a counselor waiting at the house," Dave said. "They have a network of shelters throughout the region. We'll hand the kids off to them."

Quinn's nostrils flared. "Except for Mila and her siblings. They're American citizens."

A look passed between Dave and Reem. "We'll see what we can do," Reem said.

Quinn wasn't happy with the idea of the Semenov kids

having to stay in Russia for any longer than necessary. She was already trying to figure out which strings she needed to pull to get them safely back to the United States at the end of the op. Her grandfather came to mind. If anyone could make it happen, he could.

"Any questions?" Dave's gaze moved from face to face. "No? Okay then. Let's take a half-hour break before we go over the strategy for James's meet-up with Yefimov."

Reem made a beeline for Quinn. "Would you like to get some coffee with me? There's a cool, funky little place down the street from here."

"Sure," Quinn said with a cautious smile. She turned to James. "We'll be back in a little while. You want anything?"

"No, I'm good." He took her hand and gave it a squeeze. "Have fun."

During the walk to the coffee shop, the conversation remained superficial as they discussed the weather and their flights to Saint Petersburg.

The moment she stepped into the shop, Quinn was surrounded with the divine aroma of coffee. While she was a lover of all things coffee flavored, she had been, and always would be, a tea drinker.

Quinn gave the place a once-over, first scanning the faces of chatting customers and then locating exits. Once she and Reem had their drinks and had settled in at a small table near a window, she took a moment to check out the décor. The furniture and knickknacks were an eclectic mélange that looked like they'd been picked up at various yard sales and antique shops. The effect was utterly charming. "You're right. This place is funky. I like it."

"Right?" Reem stirred her coffee and set the spoon on the saucer with a clank. "I found it a couple of days ago. I can't function without caffeine."

"That pretty much sums it up for all of us." Reem had

been the one to instigate this little confab, so Quinn would let her take the lead. She sipped her tea, which had a heavenly smoky flavor, and waited.

An American of Middle Eastern descent, Reem's skin was flawless and her eyes were big and brown. She had a similarly slight frame to Quinn's and was only a few years older. "I know you want Mila and her siblings back in the United States as soon as possible. Everyone wants that. The thing is, these kids need time to deal with everything they've been through. Regardless of the kind of labor they've been forced to endure, it takes most young trafficking victims a lot of intensive therapy in a safe place before they're ready to be reunited with their families. Moving them too fast and too soon could be detrimental to their recovery. I've been involved in a number of rescues like the one we're planning. And I've followed up with a lot of the victims months after. The system we've set up works. Let it."

"I get it," Quinn said. "The last thing I want is to inflict more trauma. And I'm not advocating the Semenov kids fly back to the States with James and me only days after they're released."

A dubious eyebrow rose.

One corner of Quinn's mouth lifted. "Okay, maybe I do want that." She wasn't willing to give up completely, though. "Have you ever rescued American citizens trapped in a foreign country like this?"

Reem hesitated. "No."

"Like I said before, I don't want to do anything that will make things worse for them. And I'll defer to the professionals with regard to their treatment. I'm just thinking maybe their recovery would be aided by getting them out of Russia altogether."

"Perhaps." Reem didn't sound convinced.

Undeterred, Quinn continued. "I'm sure I don't have to tell you trafficking—*all* kinds—isn't only a problem here.

It happens in the United States, too. I read the other day the FBI rescued twenty underage girls and arrested their captors in Denver."

Reem stared into her cup and nodded tightly.

"Thankfully, that's not what we're dealing with here. But I'm sure there are treatment facilities in the US the kids could be placed in. I agree whisking them away the moment they're freed is probably a bad idea." Quinn tipped her head to one side and shrugged. "I am suggesting we keep it open as an option, though."

"We can move them there when they're ready."

Quinn held Reem's gaze. "When they're ready."

Now that the tension that had built between them had dissipated, Quinn exhaled a relieved breath. "If you don't mind telling me, how did you become a part of Dave's team?"

"Dave's wife and I are good friends and sorority sisters." Reem sipped her coffee and set the cup on the saucer again. "Two years ago, Dave was about to launch his first rescue operation in Cambodia and wanted legal advice on the kinds of evidence he'd need to secure convictions in child sex trafficking."

"Is that what you practice? Criminal law?"

She pulled a face. "No. I do corporate for a big firm in L.A. But not helping never even crossed my mind. So I found out what it took. I've helped him on about a half dozen rescues now. We've put away some real dregs of human society."

"That must be a fantastic feeling."

"It is." Reem's eyes flashed. "After the hell on earth those bastards put innocent children through, I sleep like a baby at night knowing they're in their own special hell now. There will never be a great enough punishment for exploiting those who should always be protected, but it's a start."

"I couldn't agree more. How does this work with your regular job?"

"There's always some downtime between rescue missions. My firm releases me to assist Dave pro bono. Not only does it give the firm a gold star for social activism, one of the senior partners is as committed to rescuing these kids as you and I are."

"Good for them, and you."

"Thanks. What about you and James? How did the Riordans get mixed up in this?"

James and Quinn were on a sanctioned CIA op and were therefore treating it like any other. But since the rest of the Operation Bear Trap team wasn't cleared to know their status as undercover CIA operatives, that fact had to be protected. To that end, James and Quinn were using the same cover name they'd used on other missions. While the other members of the team might suspect she and James had a connection to the CIA, it wouldn't be confirmed. "James and I were on our honeymoon and stumbled into it."

Reem's eyes grew huge. "Your *honeymoon*? How long have you two been married?"

"Six weeks. We happened to randomly meet the guys Dave was watching. He approached us and asked us to help him gather more information. That's when I met Mila and Pyotr."

"That was a pretty big imposition."

"When he explained it to us, we knew we had to help. You know the feeling."

"I do." Reem tilted her head. "And now you're both here. I take it James has experience in undercover work?"

"He does." Quinn wasn't going to elaborate, and Reem seemed to sense it wasn't something she should pursue.

"What do you do?"

"I'm a librarian."

Reem's head jerked back in shock. "And you came along? This is a dangerous business."

Quinn brushed off Reem's response with a laugh. "What can I say? We're newlyweds." A moment later, her mirth dropped away. She stared at the bits of tea leaves floating at the bottom of her cup. "I promised Mila we'd come for them." Quinn raised her gaze and looked Reem directly in the eyes. "I'll tell you the same thing I told Dave. I keep my promises."

Quinn watched Reem's face set with determination. "Then it's a good thing you're here."

Chapter Fifteen

A white surveillance van with VLAD'S PLUMBING in Cyrillic letters and a fake phone number emblazoned on the sides sat parked on a side street off Nevsky Prospekt. The wide boulevard lined with monuments, churches, shopping, a palace, and a cathedral was also the heart of the city's thriving nightlife.

Groups of young people on their way to bars and dance clubs paid not one iota of attention to James and Quinn standing face-to-face on the sidewalk next to the van.

It was ten o'clock in the evening, and yet the sun wouldn't set for another hour and a half. It allowed for plenty of sunlight for her to take in his disguise in all its glory. Earlier in the day, she'd helped him put a rinse in his dark blond hair. It was now, according to the box, espresso brown. And with it slicked straight back, a full fake beard applied, and brown contacts in place behind black-rimmed glasses, she hardly recognized him. Only his voice assured her the man was her husband.

She fiddled with the knot of his red necktie. Along with his dark blue suit and white dress shirt, he looked quite dapper. "I hate that I can't go in there with you."

"I know. But LT will be with me." He hooked a strand of

hair behind her ear. "And don't take this personally, but he's a little more believable as my bodyguard than you are."

"Yeah, well, that's only because he's twice my size. And a former Navy Seal." She smoothed a hand over his lapel and looked up into his face. "I could take them, you know. It's all about leverage."

"I know you could." He waggled an eyebrow. "For the record, you always have permission to put me on my back."

She shot him an arch smile.

"Besides, you don't want to go inside a strip club, do you?"

With a scrunched nose, she said, "No, although I'm sure the Bronze Monkey Nightclub and Massage Parlor is the classiest of establishments."

"I'm sure it is," he said, matching her droll tone. A mischievous look overtook his face. "If you did come in with me, you could pick up some pointers and finally do that stripper librarian routine you're always teasing me about."

"Hey! I've already got all the moves. Remember how Nicole had my bachelorette party at that pole-dancing place?"

"I do remember that. But sadly, I wasn't invited."

"What?" she said with a smirk. "You wanted to learn to pole dance, too?"

He beamed at her. "Who says I don't already know?"

"Maybe *you* should do the stripper librarian routine," she said with a laugh.

"Maybe I should."

"I so want to see that." Talking about her bachelorette party jogged a thought loose in her brain. "Oh, wait a sec." She grabbed his left hand, wiggled his gold wedding band over his knuckle, and slipped it over her thumb. Reaching up with both hands, she opened the clasp at the nape of her neck and unfastened her gold necklace. She transferred the ring from her thumb to the necklace. It now hung with her eagle pendant. "A married man shouldn't frequent strip clubs," she said and refastened the gold strand around her neck.

"Good catch." Thin lines crinkled around his eyes when he smiled. "And don't worry about this married man inside the Bronze Monkey. My only interest is in my stripper librarian wife."

"I guess I'd better fashion some pasties from colored book repair tape and buy a pair of stiletto heels," she said with a laugh. As she gazed into his handsome face, her smile waned. His beard felt strange on her palm when she rested her hand on his cheek. "You be careful."

"I will." He snaked an arm around her waist, pulled her to him, and gave her a quiver-inducing kiss.

From behind them, the sound of a throat clearing prompted them to part, albeit reluctantly.

"See you in a little while."

"I'll be here." Her smile might have appeared confident, but a current of nerves rippled under the surface.

James kissed her once more before releasing her. He spun on his heel and acknowledged LT with a nod. She watched the two men stride off together and disappear around the corner.

She pushed back at the worry creeping in on her by reminding herself James was a crack operative and had been on many dangerous missions long before she'd ever met him. Anyone who messed with him and LT would quickly find out they'd made a terrible mistake.

Confidence restored, she turned her mind to the mission at hand. She marched to the back of the van, grabbed the handle, and pulled open the door. She hauled herself up and closed it with a resounding bang.

Hunched, she duck walked to the empty chair next to Yonatan and sat in front of a panel of monitors. His eyes never rested on a screen for more than a couple of seconds.

He pushed one side of his headset off his ear and flipped up the microphone. "You know James's comm was open the entire time, right?"

A hand flew up and over her mouth. "No," she said through her fingers. "You heard all that?" She could practically feel the flames licking up from the tips of her burning ears. "Look, the stripper librarian stuff is a running gag with us. That's all."

Yonatan waited a beat before looking over at her. "I'm just messing with you. I didn't hear anything." A huge grin bloomed on his face. "But now I want to know more about this stripper librarian thing."

She groaned. She'd walked right into it. She smacked him on the arm with the back of her hand. "You're a jerk. You know that, right?"

His smile broadened. "That's what everyone tells me." He sounded inordinately proud of that particular accomplishment.

He sobered and pointed at the headset in front of Quinn. "Monitor One is James's feed." And just like that, they were down to business.

She settled the headphones over her ears and tugged the microphone down in front of her mouth. The video of people passing James on the street transmitted from the tiny camera secreted in his glasses was crystal clear.

Images on Monitor Two from LT's button camera were nearly identical.

Dave's feed showed him already inside the Bronze Monkey. On Monitor Three, a young woman in nothing but black skintight shorts and spikey heels danced on a raised platform made of thick, clear plastic. With her back pressed against a pole, she widened her stance, slid down, and swished her hips.

Quinn blinked and marveled at how uninhibited the

topless woman was. She would never be that uninhibited, at least not in public anyway.

She glanced at the remaining three screens. They showed the inside of the club from high angles and static positions. Yonatan had hacked into the Bronze Monkey's security cameras.

Yonatan brought his microphone to his lips and punched a key on his keyboard. "Comms are hot."

James and LT both responded with a muttered, "Copy."

Thanks to voice-activated technology, the music that would have otherwise blared into her ear through Dave's earpiece was filtered out. As a result, she clearly heard his cough of acknowledgement.

Quinn's gaze remained glued to the monitor showing James's feed. After walking another half block, he and LT turned right, opened a door, and climbed a set of stairs. Once they were inside the Bronze Monkey proper, her eyes flicked to one of the security camera monitors. As they were now in view, she watched them saunter across the room and sit on two of the stools lining the runway. The raised platform gave James and LT, as well as Quinn and Yonatan, quite a view of the dancers.

Quinn shoved her discomfort aside and concentrated on scrutinizing the inside of the club. The L-shaped stage was the center of everything, with poles installed at regular intervals.

The rest of the club was as Quinn expected. The walls were crimson and the decorative swags and floor-to-ceiling curtains hanging from a balcony were gold lamé. A statue of the eponymous primate sat like a Buddha in an alcove above the bar. To top it all off, the entire place was suffused with flashing blue and red lights.

A young woman with long black hair and makeup applied with a Spackle knife approached James and LT and asked them what they wanted to drink. In a short white dress, at least the waitress was fully clothed. Quinn wondered if to dress otherwise was a health code violation. Imagining herself in the same position, she decided it was more likely a matter of practicality.

"Sorry. *Po-angliyski?*" James said in a British accent. It was to his advantage that his cover didn't allow for him to speak fluent Russian. People tended to speak more freely in their native language if they thought others didn't understand.

"What do you drink?" Given her job in a cosmopolitan city like Saint Petersburg, it was a good bet she could ask that question in fifteen different languages.

"Ah. Yes." James held up two fingers. "Vodka, please."

She dipped her head and headed for the bar.

Quinn scoured the security camera feeds, studying the faces of the men scattered around the room. She spotted their target lounging on a cheetah-print sofa with a woman curled under each arm. "Yefimov is at your nine o'clock."

Movement on James's feed caught Quinn's eye. The entire screen was filled with the face of a bottle blonde with thin, penciled-in eyebrows, thick mascara, and glossy red lipstick. Her face moved in closer and abruptly disappeared. Quinn turned to the security monitor to take in the full scene. The woman had leaned in, showing off her ample cleavage, and had her lips next to James's ear. "I am Anya. I give you massage?" Her tone was as suggestive as it was sultry.

A tempest of fury raged behind Quinn's sternum when Anya slid a hand up James's thigh. Seething, she was seconds from smashing her fist through the screen to grab the woman by the throat. "Get your paw off my husband, you skank," she said, low and feral.

James choked and coughed into the back of his hand.

"Steady, Quinn," Yonatan said evenly.

James crossed one leg over the other, dislodging Anya's hand. "No, thank you."

Anya stuck her lower lip out in a pout. Her disappointment vanished the second she set her sights on LT. "Your friend, perhaps?" Her eyes lingered as she gave him the once-over. She licked her lips as if she were ready to devour him. "I show him very good time."

The placid look on LT's face never faltered, nor did he acknowledge the woman's solicitation in any way. He excelled at his role as the bodyguard.

"Actually, Anya, we're here to speak with Mr. Yefimov. I have a business proposition I'd like to discuss with him." James looked at the woman and cocked his head. "Do you know, is he here?"

She sat back and narrowed her eyes at him.

He retrieved a thick wad of euro notes from the front pocket of his slacks, peeled off a hundred, and tossed it on the bar.

She picked up the bill and clutched it in her hand. "He is there." She tipped her head in Yefimov's direction.

"Thank you," James said. He stuffed his billfold back in his pocket and turned his attention to the dancer in front of him.

Anya, apparently coming to the conclusion no additional funds would be forthcoming, took the hint. She stood and sauntered off. Her route was circuitous, but she eventually made her way to Yefimov. From the glances shot in their direction, James and LT were clearly the main topic of conversation.

The waitress returned with their drinks. James thanked her, paid the tab with a fifty-euro note, and told her to keep the change. Liberally handing out cash never failed to make friends and influence people.

James picked up his drink and tossed it back. He wheezed and managed to croak, "Tastes like kerosene."

"Really?" LT picked up his glass and stared down at the clear liquid. "Vodka here is supposed to be the best." As James had done, he downed it in a single gulp. He grimaced and said, "But not when it's distilled in a bathtub."

"Quality stuff." James cleared his throat. "Time to get this show on the road."

"Copy that." LT rose to his feet. Mountainous and intimidating, he scanned the room like a good bodyguard should. After an all-clear nod from LT, James stood and the two men started toward Yefimov's table. LT went first and cut through the crowd like the prow of a ship slicing through water. Seeing the way people gave them a wide berth helped alleviate much of Quinn's anxiety. She may have wanted to be there with James, but LT was the better choice.

Before they reached Yefimov, his bodyguard stepped in front of them and blocked further passage.

"Oh crap." She instantly recognized that scowl and bald head. It was Anatoly. James's disguise better hold. It was unclear whether or not Anatoly had seen James's face the night of their encounter on the Honeycutt estate. Either way, he would certainly recognize James from dinner at The Grove.

Anatoly glowered at James, their faces only inches apart. "No guns."

Tingling with nerves, Quinn pressed her fingertips to her temples and watched James stare him down. In a voice loud enough for Yefimov to hear over the thumping dance music, James said, "Tell your boss if he insists on retaining that policy my staggering amount of money and I are walking away."

Anatoly didn't move and continued to glare at James. At least there wasn't a glimmer of recognition on Anatoly's part. Quinn dropped her hands to her lap and blew out a breath.

"Let them pass," Yefimov ordered in Russian. When

Anatoly stepped to the side, Yefimov waved James and LT over. He pointed at two matching zebra-print chairs across the low, round table from him. "Come. Sit." He puffed on a cigar several times. A cloud of blue smoke shrouded his head. Quinn could almost smell the noxious odor through the monitor.

James sat. LT stood behind him with his hands clasped in front of him. The two stoic bodyguards stood motionless and engaged in a staring contest.

Quinn got a good look at Yefimov through James's feed. No more than forty, he had a wide face and a nose flattened by more than a few fists. His black hair was elaborately coiffed to camouflage his male pattern baldness. The bristly mustache sprouting under the busted-up nose held flecks of gray. She observed a shrewdness in his hazel eyes.

Exuding a relaxed and confident air, Yefimov leaned back and returned his arms to rest behind his two companions. Quinn hoped the young woman with the burning cigar embers inches from her head hadn't used a lot of hairspray. Otherwise, a spectacular conflagration was in the offing. "Anya tells me you have business proposition. I do not know what this could be."

"My employer will be arriving in Saint Petersburg in a few days. He'll be hosting a large number of friends at his summer home for a week and would like to procure a fairly substantial amount of a particular product for his and their enjoyment."

Yefimov gestured with a hand. The cigar moved precariously closer to the woman's hair. "Why come here to buy alcohol?"

"I'm referring to a substance not available from the Bronze Monkey's menu."

Yefimov took several puffs from his cigar and squinted at

James through the smoke curling up from his mouth. "Why do you come to me?"

"You come highly recommended by an acquaintance who has more than a passing interest in the use and distribution of your commodities."

"And who is this person?"

The more Yefimov dodged and parried, the more the acid in Quinn's stomach gurgled.

James crossed one leg over the other and brushed at something on his slacks. "It would be rather uncouth of me to name names, don't you think?" He laced his fingers together and dropped them on his lap. He stared at Yefimov with a bland look. "He is, after all, a well-known actor."

Yefimov's eye twitched. He knew exactly whom James meant. "Who is your employer?"

"I cannot tell you that either. Given that he is a minor member of a *very* prominent family in the UK, it is critical his identity remain anonymous. You understand."

"Of course." Yefimov filled the air with more smoke as he stared back at James with a steely gaze. "I can supply what he requests. How much does he want?"

"One kilo."

The Russian's head snapped up. "It will be expensive."

James batted away the comment with a hand.

"I can give to you tonight," Yefimov said.

"No, I would prefer it stay in your possession until my employer comes to town. We'll make arrangements to pick it up."

Yefimov took a puff from his cigar. "I want payment up front. One hundred eighty thousand euros."

"One hundred sixty thousand. You will get a down payment today, after I have checked the inventory at your distribution center for myself."

"No," Yefimov said with a frown.

"My employer will not tolerate inferior quality. No cutting it with baking soda or laundry detergent."

"My product is excellent quality," Yefimov said with an edge in his voice, clearly affronted at being suspected of anything else.

"As per the instructions from my employer, my inspection of the product and your premises is nonnegotiable. Take it or leave it."

Yefimov's nostrils twitched. "We will not go anywhere until you show me you have money with you."

James reached into the inside breast pocket of his jacket and removed an envelope thick with bills. "Twenty-five thousand." He lifted the flap and pulled the stack out partway before returning it to his pocket.

After a moment of quiet contemplation, Yefimov told the women he would be back soon and stood. He indicated a door at the back corner of the room with a jerk of his head. "Come."

Chapter Sixteen

Yefimov opened the door and stepped into a deserted alley behind the Bronze Monkey. James, LT, and Anatoly filed out behind him. Twilight was falling, but Quinn could still easily see the surroundings through James's and LT's cameras.

Yefimov spun around and rammed his fist into James's gut.

James doubled over and groaned in pain.

Quinn leapt to her feet. "Son of a bitch!" She threw off her headset and sprang for the back door of the van.

Yonatan clamped a hand around her wrist and yanked her back into her seat. "You rush in now, you'll blow up the whole op. Let it play out."

She conceded his point with a snarl, jammed her headset back on, and checked James's feed. It rose from his dress shoes to Yefimov's face. "What the hell?" James wheezed.

Yefimov grabbed James by the lapels and yanked him up straight. He expelled a loud grunt when the Russian smashed him against the wall.

Sharing James's point of view, she saw over Yefimov's shoulder that Anatoly had LT's arms pinned behind him.

Her cheeks flamed hot with fury. "I'm gonna kill that bastard if it's the last thing I do."

In a freakishly calm voice, Yonatan said, "Dave, be advised. Yefimov is flexing his muscles in the alley. We'll let you know if it gets out of hand."

"Copy," came his mumbled reply.

Yefimov's face filled the screen. Nose to nose with James, he spat, "You come to steal my drugs." He swung at James's face.

James raised an arm and blocked the punch. He broke Yefimov's grip on his lapel with the other and threw a right cross. Ycfimov's head snapped around when knuckles connected with jaw.

At the same time, LT spun out of Anatoly's grasp and put him in a chokehold. The more Anatoly struggled, the tighter LT's massive arm cinched around his throat. With his eyes bulging, Anatoly's red, blotchy head looked like it was about to explode like a squeezed balloon.

James stepped into Yefimov, put his shoulder into the other man's chest, and kicked Yefimov's leg out from under him. He landed flat on his back with a thud. Panic flashed in Yefimov's eyes as he stared down the barrel of James's Sig Sauer.

Panting, James asked, "Steal your drugs? What in blazes are you talking about?"

Yefimov held his hands up to shield his face, as if they would miraculously stop a fired bullet. "You are part of alliance between British and rival Russian syndicate come to take over my drug operation."

"I don't bloody know anything about that," James said. "I came to you with a simple business transaction, and I get punched in the gut. You know what, mate? Bugger off." James jammed his pistol back in his holster. "There are plenty of others in this city who will jump at the chance to take my money." He jerked at the front of his suit jacket and smoothed a hand over his hair. "I'm sure your boss will be very understanding when this business you run for him goes down the crapper after I tell my employer about this little run-in." His voice oozed sarcasm.

LT released Anatoly when James sent him a sharp nod. The big Russian dropped to his knees and gulped down mouthfuls of air.

Quinn pressed a palm to her forehead as James and LT stepped over the prostrate Yefimov and strode away.

"Come on, Yefimov," Quinn urged under her breath. "Stop them." She barely dared to breathe as she watched James and LT walk down the alley.

"Wait!" Yefimov shouted.

James and LT slowed their gait.

"Yes," Quinn whispered in victory.

"Wait," Yefimov said again. "One hundred fifty thousand euros. And you speak to no one about this misunderstanding."

James and LT stopped and slowly spun around. The Russians were now on their feet. "You sucker punched me, comrade," James said evenly. "One twenty-five."

Yefimov took a step. "One hundred thirty thousand."

James stared at him. "Against my better judgment," he said after what felt like an interminable pause, "you have a deal."

The Russians hurried forward and joined them.

"You touch me again and I will end you." The restrained yet menacing tone in James's voice sent a chill up Quinn's spine. He meant every word.

Yefimov's swagger returned as they exited the alley and proceeded down the sidewalk. It was clear he was trying to reassert equal status with James. The furtive, anxious glances he sent James's way belied his bluster.

Yonatan tapped at the keyboard of his laptop and pulled

up a street map. The red and green dots, James and LT, moved toward the blue one, the signal from Quinn's phone in Mila's possession.

"Dave," Quinn said, "James and LT are headed for the target."

"Roger that," Dave said in acknowledgement. On the map, his orange dot exited the Bronze Monkey and started for the building one block over, where the kids were held captive and drugs were processed.

The four men passed a building undergoing renovations, surrounded entirely by scaffolds and green netting, and turned onto a side street. They passed through a set of graffiti-tagged wooden double doors in a brick building discolored by layers of city grime and into a small, gloomy lobby. In its prime, the building would have been impressive, with its façade adorned by small statues and bas-reliefs. Now it was one of many suffering from decades of neglect and urban decay.

They climbed three flights of dingy stairs and walked down a poorly lit corridor lined with apartment doors. Halfway down the hall, Yefimov unlocked and opened a door on their left. They entered a room furnished with several ratty chairs and a sofa from when Saint Petersburg had been known as Leningrad. Two very large men sat on the sofa watching television. One was the burly and certainly armed Viktor. Quinn didn't recognize the other. But he was equally intimidating. They both rolled to their feet but then sat again when Yefimov informed them everything was fine.

A sturdy, middle-aged woman with hair the color of red bricks came into the parlor from a side door. Her face was pinched, with the corners her mouth turned down in a permanent frown. She warily eyed James and LT from under plucked and penciled-in eyebrows. Quinn recognized the voice and sharp tone when the woman spoke. Mother Olga.

Speaking in Russian, Yefimov informed Mother Olga James was there to check the quality of their drugs before purchasing a substantial quantity. Quinn rolled her eyes when Yefimov bragged he'd so masterfully negotiated the deal James was practically throwing money at him. "What a lying bag of flaming dog crap," she muttered under her breath.

LT choked and cleared his throat with a rumble.

James followed Yefimov through a different door from the one Olga had come. They walked into a bigger room crowded with three large, rickety tables. Three kids sat at each. From their size, she guessed them to be between the ages of ten and fourteen. Quinn couldn't tell which was Mila or Pyotr, mostly due to the disposable surgical masks each wore. At one table, three kids moved a variety of colored pills from open boxes into small zip-top plastic bags. At the other two, white powder was put on scales before going into the individual bags. Another large, scary-looking man sat at a desk stacked with currency. He scowled at James before running a pile of euro notes through a counting machine. A thin bottle blonde, presumably Zhanna, hovered over the kids and barked at them to work faster.

"We have high-quality heroin from Afghanistan," Yefimov said, pointing to one of the tables. "Perhaps your employer would like to offer it to his guests as well."

James sniffed. "No, thank you. It's a little too . . . street."

"As you wish." Yefimov stepped over to the center table. "Our cocaine."

James tapped the tip of his middle finger to the mound at the center of the table and rubbed the powder between his finger and thumb. Then he held it near his nose and sniffed. "Very good," he said and brushed it off his finger. He jutted his chin at the table. "How many workers do you have?"

"Why do you ask?"

"My employer might be interested in acquiring some domestic help. Perhaps we can purchase a couple of these."

"I have fifteen, but they are prized workers. I can sell you others."

Quinn hoped the six unaccounted for were asleep and hadn't been sold off.

"I'll take it up with him and let you know." James removed the envelope from his pocket and handed it to Yefimov. "Twenty-five thousand euros."

He snatched up the envelope and thumbed through the notes.

"You will receive the balance when I come to pick the product here Thursday at noon." He turned and walked toward the door. With his hand on the doorknob, he looked back over his shoulder. "A friendly warning, Mr. Yefimov. Do not cross me in any way. That would not end well for you." His words were as precise as they were chilling.

James opened the door and stepped into the hall, leaving an ashen Yefimov behind.

LT trailed James and shut the door behind them.

With long strides, they covered the distance to the stairs and bounded down them two steps at a time.

"Dave, what's your location?" James asked.

"Across the street from the building," came the reply. "I'll stay here until you're clear and make sure no one tails you."

"Much obliged," LT said. He took the lead and opened the doors to the street. Quinn heard a rusty creak behind his voice as he spoke.

Outside, it was now dark. From Dave's feed, James and LT were nothing more than shadowy figures striding purposefully down the sidewalk. When they disappeared into the darkness, Quinn studied the map on Yonatan's laptop. "You don't want to go past the Bronze Monkey again, so don't turn at this corner," Quinn said. "Go up another block and turn right."

"Copy that," James said.

Three minutes later, the back of the van opened. James and LT climbed in and sat on the floor. Yonatan scrambled into the driver's seat. He had the engine running by the time Dave hauled himself into the passenger seat.

Yonatan gunned the engine, and as he pulled the van away from the curb, Quinn took her place on the floor next to James. She laced their fingers together and rested both hands on her lap.

He took off his glasses and gazed into her eyes. In his, she saw flinty resolve. "We're gonna save them."

She cupped his face and stroked his fake whiskers with her thumb. "Yeah. We are."

Chapter Seventeen

Thursday arrived, the day Operation Bear Trap would be sprung. The members of the team gathered in their small hotel room headquarters for one final briefing. Preparations had been made, logistics had been studied, and every facet of the op had been checked and double-checked. Still, they needed to review everything one more time.

Excited and nervous, Quinn sat cross-legged on one of the beds. She pulled off a bit of pastry she'd bought at the coffee shop down the street with her fingers and popped it in her mouth. It was all she could do not to physically swoon at the flaky, buttery bun laden with chunks of semi-sweet chocolate. Nerves had her stomach twisted in a knot and yet she couldn't stop eating the little bit of carbohydrate heaven.

She pinched off another piece and held it up in front of James's faux beard-covered face.

Sitting next to her with legs stretched out, he opened his mouth. She deposited the morsel and after only one chew, his eyes widened. "Wow."

"I know, right? I'm gonna buy a bunch of these for Mila, Pyotr, and the rest to have for breakfast tomorrow."

"Pick up couple of extra for me while you're at it," James said.

As always, Dave stood at the front of the room. "If the newlyweds will quit feeding each other and quiet down," he said drily, "we can get started."

Had she not gotten to know Dave well over the last couple of days, her cheeks would have burned hot with embarrassment. Now, though, she made a show of peeling off a big chunk of the pastry and biting off half before defiantly stuffing the rest into her husband's mouth.

The room filled with chuckles from the other members of the team. Dave grinned and shook his head, then dove right in. "Reem is already coordinating with the police to arrest Yefimov and his crew on drug charges. Marina is at the house in Olgino ready to help get the kids settled once all the shouting is over."

Marina Khodyreva worked for an organization established specifically to assist liberated trafficking victims in making the transition from slavery to freedom.

"At eleven-thirty, James, Quinn, LT, and I will each drive one of the passenger vans Yonatan rented to where the kids are held. Let's not all park right next to each other. Too many vans in one place will draw attention. We don't want that."

Heads nodded in agreement.

"Job One is to get the kids out, into the vans, and to the house in Olgino. To do that, we neutralize Yefimov and his crew. Use the tranq guns if you can. We don't want any of the kids caught in potential cross fire."

"Everyone have your vests on?" Yonatan asked.

Each responded in the affirmative. Quinn tugged at the bottom of the bulletproof vest she wore under her blouse and business suit jacket. It was a little lighter weight than the ones she'd trained in. Yonatan had access to some excellent equipment.

"Once the kids are out of harm's way, Reem will call in an 'anonymous' tip to the local police already on board. They'll come in and arrest everyone and seize the drugs."

There was another chorus of nods. "Yonatan's running comms. Everyone plugged in? Eyes and ears?"

Quinn slipped on the tortoiseshell framed glasses with the hidden camera. Then she moved a strand of her long auburn wig over the communication device in her ear. "I'm set." With Anatoly lurking about, her disguise was a necessity.

James looked from Quinn to Dave. "Me, too."

"Affirmative," LT said.

"Good." Dave paused as if to let the importance of the moment sink in. "Saddle up."

Brimming with equal parts excitement, anticipation, and apprehension, Quinn jumped off the bed and helped stow the equipment scattered around the room. Once everything was secured, they left and took the lift to the ground floor.

Out the front door and onto the sidewalk, Yonatan crossed the street to the surveillance van, and LT turned left toward his vehicle. Dave turned right.

James took Quinn's hand. "Can I walk you to your car?" They started toward the vehicle parked across the street at their two o'clock.

Her smile was soft. "Sure."

A half-minute later, they stood next to the van's driver-side door. James took her left hand and slipped her wedding and engagement rings off her finger. "Don't want to tempt Yefimov and his crew. They'll steal these right off your hand if they get the chance."

She took off the necklace that still held his wedding band and threaded them onto the chain. Then he took it from her and held it by both ends. "Turn around."

She spun and swept her hair forward over her shoulder.

He settled their rings and eagle pendant on her chest, secured the clasp, and kissed the exposed nape of her neck. A shiver raced down her spine.

"See you there." He turned on his heel and hurried toward the van parked a short distance away.

She tugged at the front of her blouse and hid the rings under the material. The way they rested over her heart gave her an inordinate amount of joy.

Pushing all thoughts other than the mission out of her mind, she unlocked the door and climbed up into the driver's seat. "Time to go to work," she said aloud to the empty van. The engine roared to life, reminding her of her loud, rumbly 4Runner. She threw the vehicle in gear and pulled out into traffic.

She'd been warned repeatedly about dangerous drivers in Russia. Having successfully navigated through the dusty, congested streets of Amritsar, India, she figured she could handle anything. But unlike the crowded but somewhat controlled pandemonium of Amritsar, Russia had a reputation for criminally aggressive drivers, unsafe roads, and accident scams.

Just the day before, when Quinn and James were walking back to their hotel after touring the State Hermitage Museum, they'd witnessed one such scam. A man had stood on a sidewalk until a bus came into view. When it approached, he'd thrown himself at it. He'd bounced off the side in glancing blow, but it had still left him in a heap on the side of the road. Quinn and James had run over to assist him, but when the "victim" realized the bus had never even slowed down—let alone stopped—he'd climbed to his feet and brushed himself off. James and Quinn had left him standing on the sidewalk, uninjured and peering into the distance in search of the next vehicle at which to throw himself.

In the next hour, Quinn's sole goal was to get the kids to Olgino without a pedestrian bouncing off the side of her van or having an accident where the other driver might, in a fit of pique, smash a tire iron through a window. They had recently witnessed that, too.

She managed to travel the few blocks without incident and parked the van on a side street not far from the building.

From the chatter in her earpiece, she knew James and LT were waiting for her and Dave in the lobby. They would go up to the flat together.

Quinn entered the building and silently dipped her chin, acknowledging James and LT. Dave joined them a minute later.

Like train cars on a track, the four ascended the staircase in tandem. When they reached the appropriate level, they started down the corridor.

It was a different experience for Quinn, being in the hallway in person versus observing it through video cameras. She felt the full impact of its crushing oppressiveness now. The stale air was heavy with the stench of cigarettes and cooked cabbage. A television, its volume turned up as high as possible, blared inside an apartment they passed.

They stopped outside the flat's door. Dave looked into their faces in turn. "Ready?"

Heart thumping, Quinn's senses heightened. Colors intensified and lines turned razor sharp. She heard nothing but the muffled voices coming from the other side of the door. Her mind clear and focused, she squared her shoulders and said, "Ready."

Chapter Eighteen

James donned the mantel of leadership and opened the door. He entered the dingy front room first, followed by Quinn. LT and Dave waited in the hall for the signal to move in once the money and drugs had been recorded changing hands.

Yefimov and Anatoly stood waiting for them. A large, brightly painted *matryoshka* doll sat on one of the armchairs.

James pointed at the Russian nesting doll and said, "It appears my order is ready."

"Yes," Yefimov said. An icy chill ran through Quinn's veins when his gaze landed on her. "Who is she?"

"My personal assistant."

"I am sure she helps with many things." His suggestive tone and oily smile made Quinn's skin crawl.

James stared at Yefimov, stone-faced.

Yefimov's eyes traveled to the briefcase in Quinn's hand. "That is for me, yes?" The Russian seemed to be enjoying his perceived control over the situation.

Other than the steady rise and fall of his chest, James stood motionless with his arms hanging limply at his sides. Unblinking, he regarded Yefimov, as if trying to gauge how much longer he was willing to put up with his shenanigans.

The longer the uncomfortable silence stretched, the more Yefimov's nerves visibly strained. His smug smile turned sickly, and a thin sheen of perspiration sprang up on his forehead.

Quinn felt her own nerves begin to fray.

"Yes," James finally said. "Now, if we could dispense with any additional pleasantries. Show us what's inside the doll and we'll show you what's inside the briefcase."

Yefimov went over to the doll and pulled off the top half, revealing a two-pound brick of white powder wrapped in plastic.

James turned to Quinn and said, "Miss Riordan, if you will." She set the briefcase on the sofa and opened it. Bundles of one hundred euro notes were stacked across the bottom. Of course, only the top bill in each stack was real.

The phone in Yefimov's pocket rang. His brow furrowed when he looked at the screen. He put it to his ear and said, "*Da*."

Quinn tensed as she watched Yefimov listen. His face hardened and his eyes burned a hole in James with each passing second.

Busted.

"Now!" James shouted.

Anatoly went for his sidearm. Quinn flung the briefcase at him and knocked the gun from his hand as soon as it cleared his holster. She went for the tranquilizer pistol on her thigh.

Dave ran past her to secure whatever was on the other side of the door on the right.

Quinn pulled the pistol from her thigh holster.

The sharp clap of a gunshot ripped through the flat. Dave crumpled to the floor in the hall.

"Dave!" she screamed.

Anatoly lowered his shoulder, barreled into Quinn, and drove her back against the wall. Even with the protection of her vest, her chest exploded with pain and the breath in her lungs whooshed out in a gust.

Anatoly bounced off and raced out the front door.

Eyes watering and gasping for air, she was in no position to chase him. With the way her chest ached like she'd caught a cannonball, she had no choice but to let him escape. She couldn't dawdle, though. She pushed away from the wall and staggered toward the prostrate Dave.

She leaned a hand against the doorjamb and gulped down two mouthfuls of air. Seconds later, the pain in her chest abated and her vision cleared enough to peer through the opening and down the hall.

Viktor stormed toward her.

She raised her gun and readied to fire.

Her finger squeezed the trigger, but let up before firing when Viktor pitched forward and crashed to the floor.

Viktor's epic fall revealed a panting, grinning Pyotr with a chair gripped in his hands.

"Way to go, Pyotr!" Quinn shouted in Russian.

His eyes rounded with recognition when he heard her voice. "You were on island."

"I was. Are you okay?"

"*Da.*"

Movement behind Pyotr drew her attention. Quinn raised her pistol and yelled, "Get down!"

He dropped to the floor. Zhanna, her face contorted with fury and her fingers curled like talons, flew straight at them.

Quinn fired.

Zhanna stopped, wobbled, and then collapsed.

Quinn turned and knelt beside Dave.

Before she could speak, he wheezed, "I'll be okay. Took one in the vest."

Quinn's head snapped toward James when two more gun-shots sounded. The shots hadn't come from him. He was locked in a power struggle over Yefimov's gun.

Screaming and crying sounded from the other side of the flat.

Through her comms, she heard LT say, "The two guards in the drug room are down."

She leveled her pistol at Yefimov's back.

The men spun as she fired. She missed. The dart impaled the wall.

James smashed Yefimov's wrist against the top of the TV. His pistol clattered behind the stand.

Yefimov heaved at James, throwing him off, and then bolted out the door.

"Yefimov's running!" James yelled.

Quinn shouted, "Go after him!"

"What about you?"

"Viktor, Zhanna, and the other two guys are down," she replied. "I think Anatoly ran, too."

"James, go," LT said. "We've got this."

"Copy." He flew toward the door and careened into the hall.

There was still one of Yefimov's crew unaccounted for. "Pyotr, do you know where Mother Olga is?" she asked, forgetting to do so in Russian.

His arm swung up and he pointed to the opposite end of the hallway. "There is back way out. She took *tovarish*."

His comrades. Her fist clenched. "Is Mila one of them?"

"*Da*."

Quinn was already running. "Stay with LT and Dave. They'll get you all out of here to someplace safe," she said as he charged past him.

She flung open the door and stepped into a dark stairwell. Voices and footfalls echoed up the staircase from below. Mother Olga and the kids had a head start, but alone, Quinn could catch up to them fast.

Light from her phone's flashlight pierced the dimness, making her sure-footed as she scampered down the steps.

Bright sunlight filtered into the stairwell and then as quickly disappeared.

Mother Olga and the kids had just left the building.

Quinn sped up. She was close.

She burst out the door and onto the sidewalk. Blinking against the bright noonday summer sun, she scanned the sidewalk, left and right.

She glimpsed Mother Olga's ample backside just before it disappeared around the corner to her left. As she ran, Quinn stuffed her phone in one pocket and jammed her tranquilizer pistol in the other. She didn't dare brandish her weapon in public.

At the end of the block, she skidded around the corner. Mother Olga, along with two boys and two girls of varying sizes, was up ahead.

Quinn ran up on them like they were barely moving. She grabbed Mother Olga by the shoulder, spun her around, and punched her square in the face.

Stunned, Mother Olga stumbled backward and slid down a wall to the sidewalk.

A girl screamed.

She didn't have time to mess with Mother Olga and they were already garnering curious stares. It was time to move out. "Come with me," Quinn said in Russian. "We have to go."

Mila had the same reaction to her as Pyotr had only a few minutes before. "Quinn?"

"Yeah, it's me," she said in English. "We're here to rescue you. We have a safe place for you to go. Come on."

Mila nodded.

Dread jolted through Quinn when she saw only three faces looking into hers. "Where's the other girl?"

Eyes wide, Mila shook her head. "I don't know."

Quinn switched to Russian and asked the question again.

One of the boys pointed down the sidewalk. "She ran away."

"We can't leave her behind," Mila said, her voice pleading. She gripped a hand of each boy.

Quinn took the free hand of one of the boys and pulled the train down the sidewalk. "Don't worry. We won't."

Chapter Nineteen

Up ahead, a girl about ten years old zigzagged her way past startled pedestrians.

"Klara," Mila yelled. "Stop!"

At the end of the block, Klara ran left around the corner.

Mila let go of the boys' hands and sprinted down the street, calling Klara's name.

"Mila! Wait!" Quinn shouted. She and the two boys scampered after Mila. "James, are you okay?"

"Yeah," James panted through the comm. "Still chasing Yefimov."

"Copy that. Be careful."

"You too."

The boy on Quinn's left asked in Russian, "Mila knows you?"

"Yes. We are friends."

Apparently that was good enough for them. Their legs pumped faster.

They skidded around the corner. Halfway up the block, Quinn spotted Mila on her knees, holding Klara in a full embrace.

Quinn and her charges dropped to a jog. When they

reached the two, Quinn heard Mila comforting Klara in a soothing, gentle tone.

"Let's move out of the middle of the sidewalk," Quinn said. The five ducked into a nearby window alcove and stood in a tight cluster.

"You came for us," Mila said, her voice tinged with awe.

"I promised I would." Quinn smiled when Mila hugged her. As much as she wanted to slip into a shop with the kids and ply them with pastries and hot cocoa, they had to keep moving. "My Russian comprehension is way better than my speaking," Quinn said, releasing Mila. "Can you tell them I'm here to take you all someplace safe, away from the people who make them work?"

Mila repeated what Quinn had said. Mouths agape, they stared up at Quinn in stunned disbelief.

Before they moved from their hiding place, Quinn needed a better picture of the situation. "Guys, I need a sitrep."

"I'm tracking James in pursuit of Yefimov," Yonatan said.

"Dave, are you okay?" she asked.

"Yeah. Sore, but I'll survive." It relieved her to hear Dave's voice sounding strong. "LT and I have secured Viktor and his buddies and are getting the kids rounded up. We'll be in the vans and on our way in a few minutes. Pyotr's a great kid. He's explaining to them what's going on."

"Good deal. I'm with the four Mother Olga took off with. We're going to head for the van now."

"Copy that," Yonatan said.

When Quinn took a step to leave the niche they were hiding in, Mila clutched her arm and stopped her. "What about my sister and brother?" she asked. "And the others? What's happened to them?"

"Two of the men with us are getting all of them out."

Mila's ice-blue eyes gave Quinn a penetrating stare. "You're sure they're okay?"

"I'm sure." She stepped out of the alcove with four kids in tow. "We have to go back the way we came to get to the van."

Mila updated the other three as they walked.

They came to the end of the block and turned right. Quinn scanned the area. No sign of Anatoly or Mother Olga.

Fifty feet from the entrance to the building they'd fled, Mother Olga burst out onto the sidewalk like she'd been shot from a cannon. At the sight of Quinn and the kids, Mother Olga bellowed and barreled toward them like a charging rhinoceros.

"Crap!" Quinn yelped.

"What?" James shouted in her ear. Despite his heavy breathing, alarm colored his voice.

Quinn and the kids did a quick one-eighty, careened around the corner again, and raced up the street. Mila half dragged, half carried Klara along.

"Mother Olga's out for blood," Quinn said to whoever was listening.

Firing her tranquilizer gun in public was highly problematic. And she didn't want to throw another punch for fear passersby might see Quinn as the aggressor and come to Mother Olga's aid. She deemed it best not to engage the other woman and scanned the area for a place to hide. At her two o'clock, she saw a group of children and adults entering a building. "There," Quinn said. "Across the street."

Hands clasped, they stood between two parked cars and waited for a chance to cross the street. Visions of the guy she'd seen bounce off a bus flashed in her mind. That was the last thing she wanted to have happen.

At a gap in the traffic, she said, "Now!" They bolted across the street and reached the other side as an electric tram whooshed past.

"In here," Quinn said in a low tone as they strode toward the entrance. "Quick." They blended in with a knot of children and mothers and entered the building.

"What is this place?" the boy with brown hair asked as they walked past a kid-sized table displaying a number of picture books.

Quinn knew the Russian word. "*Biblioteka*." And from the small chairs and low shelves filled with tall books with thin spines, she knew it was, more specifically, a children's library. Too bad she would never be able to tell Nicole about this place.

"Let's get away from the door," Quinn said, using her librarian voice. She led them further into the library, all the while searching for a door through which they could escape.

In her comm, she heard a grunt and James say in a dangerous snarl, "Eat dirt, you son of a bitch." Apparently he had caught up with Yefimov.

Quinn tuned out the subsequent conversation between James and Yonatan as they discussed what next to do with Yefimov. Her mind was focused on her and the kids' precarious situation.

She herded them to an unoccupied corner and had them sit on the floor. "My name is Quinn," she said in Russian to the brown-haired boy. "What's yours?"

For the first time, the boy smiled, his mouth a jumble of partially grown-in adult teeth and empty spaces where baby teeth had fallen out. "Maksim."

Quinn smiled in return. "Hello, Maksim." She turned to the boy next to her. With black hair, tapered eyelids, and incredible cheekbones, he appeared more Asian than Caucasian. "And what is your name?" He looked to be just barely a teenager.

"Alikhan." He didn't smile, but Quinn observed deep curiosity lurking behind those guarded eyes.

Quinn turned to the younger girl. "And you are Klara." She was rewarded with a shy smile.

As much as Quinn wanted to continue to speak Russian, it would take ten minutes for her to formulate each sentence telling them what she wanted to say. They didn't have ten minutes. So she said to Mila, "Tell them I'm going to check things out. I'll come back and get you when I'm sure it's clear to leave."

Mila conveyed the message to the others.

Quinn noted their sudden anxiety. "I will be back," she said solemnly in Russian. "I promise."

She scanned the spines of the books on the shelves directly behind them. Most were picture books. These kids were too old for those. Eyes darting higher, she spied the perfect book to distract them while she was gone. Having run across a Hebrew translation of another book in the series in a youth hostel in Punjab, India, she wasn't the least bit surprised by her current find.

Quinn stood, slid the book from the shelf, and handed it to Mila. The teen's eyes lit up the second they fell on the boy wearing round glasses and flying on a broomstick. "*Garri Potter i filosofskii kamen*," Mila said.

Hearing his name pronounced "Garry" made Quinn smile.

The anxiety on the faces of the other kids was instantly replaced by awe. Quinn's smile widened. The Boy Who Lived really was magic.

Mila opened to the first page and began to read aloud in Russian of the Dursleys of Privet Drive. The listeners were so instantly enthralled they didn't notice when Quinn slipped away.

She walked toward the front of the library, her eyes never resting on a face for more than a split second. Alert and prepared for Mother Olga to descend on her like a shrieking raptor, she pushed through the front doors and outside again. No one pounced upon her. She heard no shrill curses or roars of anger. A sweep of the area told her Mother Olga was nowhere in sight.

On the other hand, the woman could have been secreted

in a nook or doorway, waiting for them to emerge from their hiding place.

Quinn took stock of their circumstances. She had to assume Mother Olga was still nearby and a threat. To do otherwise would be both foolish and dangerous. Given that, her options boiled down to two: wait Mother Olga out in hopes she would eventually abandon her vigil, or make a run for it. Escaping their current predicament without further traumatizing the kids by enduring an additional run-in with their former minder was the better choice. Quinn could think of no better place to hide for the rest of the day than in a library.

"Yonatan, Mother Olga might be lurking around," she said as she turned on her heel and reentered the library. "We're going to wait her out at our current location."

"Copy," Yonatan replied.

"We can come get you after Yonatan picks me and Yefimov up," James offered.

"Thanks, but I don't want the kids seeing that vile piece of human debris ever again."

"Good point," James said. "If you change your mind, say the word and we're there."

"Thanks. We're good."

Quinn was halfway back to the kids when a shout came from their direction. Her stomach dropped to her shoes.

She raced through the stacks and arrived to find Mother Olga with Alikhan's wrist in her grip, trying to haul him to his feet. Klara sat paralyzed with fear while Maksim crab-walked backward to get away. Mila was on her feet, whacking at Mother Olga with the Harry Potter book. Unfortunately, the paperback was ineffective.

Not wanting to brandish her pistol inside a children's library unless it was her last resort, Quinn glanced around for a bigger, heavier volume to wield. She knew, from prior experience, reference books could do a lot of damage.

None were nearby, but what she did spy sitting on the floor was even better. She ran over and picked up a wooden step stool. The rolling steel ones like she used in libraries back home would have done more damage, but she would make this one work.

She held the stool by two legs and cocked it back like a baseball bat. A fireball of fury burned in Quinn's chest when she charged at Mother Olga and growled, "Leave my kids alone, you hag."

At the sound of Quinn's voice, Mother Olga glanced over her shoulder.

With everything she had, Quinn swung the stool and clocked Mother Olga on the side of the head. The force caused the woman to spin around and crash face-first to the floor.

The urge to pound on Mother Olga until the stool was nothing but splinters was strong. The urge to get the kids to safety was stronger.

Quinn's clocking of Mother Olga was certain to draw the attention of library staff. The authorities would probably be called in as well. It was time to leave. And fast.

"We have to go," Quinn said, desperate to get away from the groaning Mother Olga. "Now."

Maksim and Alikhan scrambled to their feet and stood next to Mila. Klara, ashen and slack-jawed, remained motionless. Quinn scooped her up and ran for the exit, the other three at her heels.

They sped past the circulation desk and skidded around the corner. Quinn stretched out a hand, crashed into the door, and shoved it open. Behind them, the wail of a high-pitched alarm pierced the air as they tumbled out of the library. "Crap!"

"Quinn!" James shouted.

"Can't talk." Quinn threw a glance over her shoulder to make sure the kids were with her. When she saw the Harry

Potter book in Mila's hands, she understood why an alarm had sounded. The book had triggered the library's security gates. Usually, committing such an egregious violation of library protocol would have Quinn contemplating self-flagellation as a form of repentance. In this case, though, the accidental "unauthorized borrowing" of a library book was inconsequential when the freedom of four children hung in the balance. Even so, Quinn promised herself she would return the book to the library before she left Russia.

They ran down the street and rounded the corner. Three police cars, their lights flashing, were parked in front of the building where the kids had been kept.

With Klara still in her arms and the van in her sights, Quinn and the kids dropped to a walk and crossed the street. She set Klara on her feet when they reached the van, unlocked the side door, and slid it open. The three younger kids scrambled into the back seats while Mila climbed into the passenger seat.

Once they were clipped into their seat belts, Quinn hustled around to the driver's side. She checked the area once more before taking her place behind the wheel. No one paid them any attention. She turned over the engine, put the van in gear, and pulled out into traffic.

"James, Yonatan, we're good," she said.

James heaved a sigh. "Thank God."

"Is the house in Olgino secure?"

"It is," Yonatan said. "You're safe to head there now."

"Roger that."

The kids were finally on the road to freedom.

Chapter Twenty

Unlike the previous hour, the twenty-minute drive to the safe house in Olgino was blissfully uneventful. And at the beginning, they drove in complete silence. The kids were in shock, and understandably so. Their lives had been turned upside down. While it would ultimately be for the better, all the upheaval would take time to process. Quinn hoped the reigning quiet would act as a balm to soothe their confused and hurting souls.

They were crossing the Bolshaya Nevka, an arm of the Neva River, when Mila broke the silence. She gazed out the side window and asked in a subdued voice, "Where are you taking us?"

"To a safe house in Olgino." Now out of range, Quinn removed her earpiece and stuck it in a pocket.

"What will happen to us?"

For the fiftieth time in the last five minutes, Quinn checked the rearview mirror. "When we know it's safe, you all will go to a shelter set up especially to help kids like you."

"For how long?"

"As long as it takes until you're ready to return to your families."

A derisive snort came from the back of Mila's throat. "My brother and sister and I have no place to go. Our parents don't care that we're gone."

"That's not true," Quinn said. "In fact, it's the very opposite."

Mila's head snapped around.

"When you and your siblings disappeared, your parents went to Slavnoye and Tver looking for you. They also contacted authorities in the United States. Your case is still open at the State Department in Washington, D.C."

Quinn looked at Mila, who was openly gaping at her. Returning her eyes to the road, Quinn added, "Until we found you in Turks and Caicos, no one knew if you and your sister and brother were even alive. I wasn't there, but I was told when your parents learned you all are alive, they both broke down and wept with joy."

Mila turned her face toward the side window again. The hurt in her voice cut through Quinn like a knife. "They won't want anything to do with us when they find out what we were forced to do. They'll be ashamed of us."

"No, they won't. They already know. They also understand it wasn't your choice. They can't wait to see you again. It was all we could do to keep them from coming here and joining the rescue team."

A tiny smile flickered on Mila's lips when she looked at Quinn again. "I can't really picture my mom smashing Mother Olga in the head with a step stool."

"You'd be surprised," Quinn replied in all seriousness. "I bet she wouldn't think twice about it."

The interior of the van fell silent again.

Quinn steered off the dual carriageway and onto a smaller road that ran parallel to railroad tracks.

Mila's tone was soft when she spoke again. "My cousin

Yana and her boyfriend, Alexei, invited me and my sister and
brother to spend the day with them in Tver. She was twenty.
We thought she was so cool. We could hardly believe she
asked us to do something with them. We didn't think she even
liked us, being younger cousins and everything."

"I know what you mean, feeling like the tagalong. I have
five older brothers."

"That's how we felt, too. We were so excited to go to Tver.
Up 'til then it'd been pretty boring around my *babushka*'s
house."

"Hanging out with Grandma can be like that sometimes,"
Quinn said.

Mila sighed. "Yeah. We got to Tver and walked around
and saw some of the royal buildings Catherine the Great
had built. Stuff like that. Then Yana and Alexei told us they
were going to take us to see a movie. On the way, we stopped
off at a café. While we were sitting there eating, Alexei went
and talked to a man. A few minutes later, he came back and
sat down."

Quinn gritted her teeth. The next part of the story was
sure to be bad.

"We finished our food and then Alexei said, 'I didn't
want to say anything before in case it didn't work out, but
that man is a friend of mine. He owns horses. His farm isn't
far away. We're going to take you there so you can ride
them.' My sister Sasha was a horse freak. She almost came
unglued. So we all piled into Alexei's car and drove off."

Mila fingered the hem of her top.

"We came to a farm and went in the house. Then the man
gave Alexei some money and he and Yana left. I thought they
went out to Alexei's car for some reason. When they didn't
come back after a few minutes, I started to get really scared.
I asked the man to tell us where we were and what was going
on. He just sneered at me. Then I demanded he let me use the
phone so I could call my grandmother. He laughed at me."

"Was that man Grigori Yefimov, the man we just took you from?"

"No. I never knew this guy's name. He was the one who sold us to Boss—Yefimov—though." Mila's nose wrinkled. "His teeth were so brown and gross. And his house smelled like cigarettes and cat pee."

"Yuck."

"No kidding. Anyway, I still had no idea what was going on, but I knew we needed to get out of there. So I told my sister and brother we were leaving and I got up." Mila huffed a humorless laugh. "Like where were we going to go? I didn't even know where we were." She moved a shoulder. "I went for the door. He grabbed my arm and spun me around and backhanded me. Then he beat me half to death. We did what we were told after that."

Quinn gripped steering wheel so tight her knuckles turned white. "Barbarian," she muttered.

Mila fell silent.

The abuse those innocent kids had endured was unfathomable and the damage done profound. Quinn desperately wanted to make things better, but knew care and support and time would be what healed their deep wounds.

She maybe couldn't help them in the long run, but when she spotted a global icon on a sign along the road, an idea for an immediate indulgence sprang to mind.

Quinn angled the rearview mirror down and checked on the kids in the back. They gazed out the windows with faces filled with wonder. They deserved this.

She slid her phone from her pocket and placed a call.

The phone barely rang once before James answered. "Hey, baby. You okay?" His voice was thick with worry.

"We're fine." Connecting with him made her feel a thousand percent better. "Driving into Olgino now. How are you?"

"I'm good. Got Yefimov bound and gagged in the back of

my van. I'm waiting outside the police station for Reem. She and the police are bringing Viktor and the other two guys in from the flat."

"Yeah, I saw the police cars in front of the building. How much longer do you think you'll be?"

"Not very. Why? Can't wait to see me?" There was a smile in his voice.

"You know I can't. But that's not the only reason why I called." She slowed and turned onto a narrower street. They entered a residential area with large houses, security fences, and copses of maple, birch, spruce, and oak trees. "There's a McDonald's on the way to Olgino."

"I remember going by it when we went to check out the safe house the other day."

"I thought about stopping with my kids. But with everything that's happened, I didn't know if it was a good idea."

"You want me to stop and pick up some food on my way there?"

Quinn turned right again onto a one-car-width lane. The van jolted when a tire hit a deep pothole. "I do, but let me check with Marina first. I don't want to step on her lunch plans. We're almost to the house so I'll call you back one way or the other in a few minutes."

"Roger that."

They ended the call at the same time Quinn pulled up in front of the closed gate. After a call to LT, it slowly swung open. She maneuvered the vehicle through the gap and parked to one side of the courtyard.

The second Quinn turned off the engine, the three in the back began to chatter. Mila was the first out of the van. She opened the side door and reached in to get the others out.

"I got them," Quinn said. "Go. Find your sister and brother."

Mila didn't have to be told twice. She sprinted across

the courtyard and zipped past LT standing guard at the front door. "Sasha! Ilya!"

Maksim and Alikhan unclipped their seat belts and jumped out of the van. Klara needed a little help with hers. Once she joined the other two, Quinn slid the door closed. Klara slipped her hand into Quinn's as they walked together toward the front of the house.

When Quinn noticed the kids' steps grow more hesitant the closer they came to LT, she said in Russian, "This is my friend. His name is LT."

LT squatted down and greeted them with a wide smile. "*Privet.*"

Now at the kids' level, he was no longer the unapproachable giant. With shy smiles, they skirted past him and entered the house.

Inside, it was like a giant slumber party. Some kids explored the house, chatting excitedly and carrying the teddy bears Dave had provided for each to receive upon their arrival. A few of the more timid kids sat in chairs or on couches clutching their bears, bewildered.

Marina Khodyreva, the woman from the shelter, approached carrying three teddy bears in her arms. In her mid-fifties, she had a round, pleasant face and wore her dark hair short. She exuded warmth, comfort, and acceptance. "Welcome," she said in Russian. "My name is Marina." She asked them their names and handed each a bear. Klara took hers and tucked it under one arm while never letting go of Quinn's hand. Once the introductions were made, Marina said, "If you need anything, you can come to me."

All three nodded. Maksim and Alikhan wandered away. Klara stayed with Quinn.

"My husband and I thought it might be fun to treat all the kids to McDonald's for lunch," Quinn said to Marina in English. "He's on his way here now and could pick it up. We wanted to check with you first."

With a perceptive smile, Marina said, "It is extraordinary day. Why not eat extraordinary lunch?"

Thrilled to do this for the kids, Quinn bounced on her toes. She called James and said, "Operation Mickey D's is a go."

"Copy that. See you soon." From the excitement she heard in his voice, he sounded as if he had embarked on the most important mission of his career. In its own way, it kind of was.

Marina moved off, so Quinn looked down at Klara and squeezed her hand. "Come. I want to show you something." They walked to an empty spot on a couch and sat. "Anatoly saw me once before," Quinn said. "So I had to wear a disguise so he wouldn't recognize me." She was stretching the boundaries of her Russian vocabulary, so she asked, "Do you understand?"

Klara nodded slowly in rapt attention.

"I don't really wear glasses," Quinn said. She removed them and set them to the side. "And my hair isn't really red." She slipped her fingers under the hairline of the wig and lifted it off. Once the fishnet cap underneath was peeled off, she shook her head. Her blond hair tumbled down around her shoulders.

Mouth agape, Klara stared at her. Then she blinked several times and, with a sage nod, said, "It is a good disguise."

A smile erupted and Quinn dipped her head. "Thank you." She shot Klara an inquisitive look and held up the wig. "You want to try it?"

Her eyes like saucers, the girl scooted back in surprise. "Me?"

"Yes, you."

For the first time, a smile reached Klara's eyes when she gave Quinn a jerky nod.

Quinn slowly lowered the wig onto Klara's head as if it

were a coronation. The wig was too big, but it didn't matter. She grabbed her phone and took a picture.

Quinn lowered it so Klara could see the photo. The girl's hands flew up to her mouth, and the delighted giggle that burbled up had Quinn grinning along with her. A shaft of light had pierced the darkness of that precious girl's life. In the coming weeks, months, and even years, there would be times the seam of light would widen into a bright beam. And there would be moments when it would nearly be extinguished by the haunting shadows of her captivity. Quinn hoped for Klara, and each of the children, one day the light would overcome the darkness for good.

"I want to find Pyotr and say hello," Quinn said. "Would you like to come with me?" With the way Klara had become Quinn's shadow, she wasn't surprised when the girl gave her an enthusiastic nod.

Quinn plucked the wig from Klara's head and tossed it next to the glasses. They explored the house while they searched for Pyotr. It was big and bright and airy, with windows everywhere. And as Yonatan had said, with six bedrooms and plenty of couch space, it would easily accommodate all the kids and the adults sheltering them.

When she didn't spot Pyotr on the first floor, she climbed the stairs with Klara by her side. After peeking into a couple of empty bedrooms, she poked her head into the bonus room. Six kids sat piled together on a large sectional in the corner, their eyes glued to a flat-screen TV showing *Friends* dubbed in Russian.

"Pyotr," Quinn said.

At the sound of her voice, six heads turned toward Quinn. Five immediately returned their attention to the TV.

Pyotr slid off the couch, scampered across the room, and skidded to a stop in front of Quinn. For the first time, she realized he was almost as tall as she. He grinned at her.

"I didn't get a chance to thank you for your help at the flat earlier. You were very brave to hit Viktor with that chair like that," she said in Russian.

Pyotr squared his shoulders. "I was happy to hit back."

Quinn smiled. "I bet you were. He's in jail now."

"Good. He is a bad man." Pyotr's head tipped to one side. "You are speaking Russian."

"I've been learning so I could talk to you when I saw you again."

"It is not bad, but you need more practice."

"I will keep practicing," Quinn said with a laugh.

"I will practice English," he said, switching to that language.

She patted Pyotr's arm and beamed at him. "Deal." She said in Russian, "Are you hungry? We'll be having lunch soon."

"Always."

She imagined Pyotr, like any teenage boy, could down three cheeseburgers and call them appetizers. To Klara, she said, "Would you like to help me get it ready or stay with Pyotr and watch television?"

"Go with you," Klara said and took Quinn's hand again.

"We'll call you in a few minutes," Quinn said to Pyotr.

Hand in hand, Quinn and Klara bounded down the stairs, the steps creaking under their feet. They were headed for the kitchen when Mila and two younger children approached. One glance told Quinn who they were.

"This is my sister and brother," Mila said in English. She tipped her head toward the older, "Sasha," and then toward the younger, "And Ilya."

Other than being a boy of about ten, Ilya—with the same startling blue eyes and light blond hair—was Mila's clone. Sasha was clearly their sister, but her slightly darker hair and green eyes set her apart.

"I'm thrilled to finally meet you," Quinn said.

"You're American?" Sasha asked, her eyes challenging. In that way, she definitely took after her older sister.

"I am."

"Mila said you told her our parents looked for us. Is that true?"

"Yes."

"And they want us to come home?" Sasha's intense gaze probed Quinn's face, trying to discern any cracks of insincerity.

Quinn's candor never faltered. "Very much."

"Are we going back to America with you?"

That caught Quinn off guard. "I don't know. It's not up to me to decide." This time it was Quinn's turn to search Sasha's face. "Do you want to?"

Quinn's breath caught at the flash of fierce determination. "Yes. They can't find us there."

Ilya looked up at his sister. His huge, somber eyes turned on Quinn. The nod of agreement was almost imperceptible.

Quinn's gaze fell on Mila. There, she saw unwavering resolve.

The conversation with Reem had nearly extinguished the fire to get them to the U.S. as soon as possible. The tenacity she read in the faces before her now stirred the cool embers. They flared hot again when she said, "I'll do everything I can to get you back to the U.S. But I can't make any promises. Like I said before, I don't make the final decision."

"I know you'll do whatever you can," Mila said.

The front door flew open. James sauntered in, holding aloft large bags emblazoned with golden arches. With one of the biggest smiles Quinn had ever seen grace his face, he called out in Russian, "Lunch has arrived!" He winked at her when their eyes met.

His tie was gone, his pants had a rip in the knee, and his dress shirt was smudged with dirt. But he was safe and they were together. She blew out a sigh. That was all that mattered.

Quinn strode over to him. "You could be Santa Claus with these bags of goodies. All we need to do is turn that beard of yours white," she said and relieved him of two of the bags.

He slipped his arm around her waist and hugged her to his side. "You can shake my belly like a bowl full of jelly anytime."

She kissed his cheek and whispered a throaty, "I'd rather jingle your bells."

"Ho, ho, ho." His salacious tone and accompanying eyebrow waggle made her giggle.

Kids converged on them from all over the house, interrupting their tête-à-tête. The noise level grew to a roar when they realized the food had arrived from that mystical nirvana called McDonald's.

Marina clapped her hands and called for attention. While she gave them instructions, James and Quinn went to the kitchen and set the bags on the counter. Quinn found several serving plates in a cupboard while James made another trip to the van to retrieve the rest of the food.

Dave went straight for the refrigerator and began to haul out plastic bottles of Coke.

"Contraband," Quinn said in mock indignation. "Glad the police aren't here to witness us giving Russian minors fizzy drinks."

"They're only banned from buying it." He reached into the fridge and this time brought out two six-packs of Mountain Dew. "And only the caffeinated stuff, like this." Dr Pepper came out next. "After the hell of slavery those kids have endured, I'm totally okay with giving them something unexpected and wonderful to drink."

Quinn dumped the wrapped cheeseburgers out of the bag and began to stack them on a plate. "Amen."

James returned with another armload of bags and set to work unloading bags of French fries.

When the food was ready, they gave Marina the go-ahead.

The kitchen fell eerily quiet as the teens and children, now lined up, filed in. With awe and reverence, they approached the counter laden with food like an altar. One after another, they each picked up a paper plate and put on it a cheeseburger and a bag of fries.

The fact that fast food could trigger such sheer wonder had Quinn swallowing at the thickness in her throat. It was so easy to take the little things in life for granted. It was a stark and sobering reminder of how extraordinarily blessed she was.

Loaded down with food and drinks, they scattered throughout the house and sat down with their lunches. They ate like kings and queens at a feast.

Now that the kids were fully occupied with lunch, James and Quinn took the opportunity to make one more trip to James's van to get their overnight bags.

James opened the back door, but didn't reach in. Instead, he pulled Quinn into a kiss. His lips slid to her cheek. "I'm glad you're safe."

Her arms around him tightened. "I'm glad you're safe, too." After a long stretch of simply holding each other, Quinn leaned back and rested her palms on his chest. "What happened exactly? That phone call tipped Yefimov off, didn't it?"

"Yeah. We think it was someone in the police department. It's hard to keep an op like that on the low-down. Someone mentions Yefimov's name in passing and one of his inside guys gives him a heads-up. That's all it takes."

"I take it this"—she brushed at the dirt on his shirt—"is from when you took Yefimov down. How far did you have to run?"

"Several blocks. It was a magnificent open field tackle if I do say so myself."

She smiled. "I'm sure it was spectacular."

"I hauled him into an isolated corner of a random court-yard and used my tie to gag him."

"Did you go straight to the police station? I thought you'd have wanted to interrogate him, see what he knows about Borovsky."

He shook his head. "I asked him a few questions, but he wouldn't answer. I couldn't get too persuasive with him. Didn't want to risk blowing the case we built by having him show up with a black eye."

"So we won't be able to get any intel on Borovsky," she said with a frustrated sigh.

"Oh ye of little faith," he said with a twinkle in his eye. "I synced Yefimov's phone to my computer. Got every text, every call, every phone number. That's why I insisted Yonatan take us to my van. Pickpocketed it when I dumped him on the floorboard behind the front seats. Had it sync while we were in transit. Put it back when I hauled him out. He never knew it was gone."

"I guess I should start calling you the Artful Dodger." She rose up on her tiptoes and kissed him. "Sorry I doubted you."

"You are forgiven," he said, his tone magnanimous. Concern clouded his face when he asked, "What about you? What you were dealing with sounded pretty bad."

She recounted the events from chasing Mother Olga to flying through the library to fend her off. "We hightailed it out of there after I decked her with a wooden stool."

A grin bloomed on his face. "What, no OED?"

"Sadly, no." Her eyebrows shot up. "Oh! And we stole a library book."

He gaped at her, scandalized. "What would the Librarian Cabal say about such a treasonous act?"

"Given the circumstances, I think they'd give me a pass." She cut her eyes up to him. "Besides, you know I'll return it, even if it means mailing it back from the States."

"Of course you will." He kissed the tip of her nose and said, "We'd better get back inside before they send out a search party."

"You're right." They grabbed their bags, returned to the house, and stowed them in a downstairs bedroom. They removed their bulletproof vests and changed into more comfortable clothes. Their colored contacts were taken out, and James peeled off his fake beard.

"One more thing," Quinn said. She unclasped her necklace and let their wedding bands drop in her palm. They slid them on each other's fingers. "That's better," she said and admired her shiny gold rings.

"Sounds like lunch is over," James said at the increasing noise level.

They left the bedroom, and within a couple of minutes, Klara found them. "You are really her husband?"

"I am."

"You are also American?"

"Yes."

"Your Russian is very good," she said with approval.

His façade of solemnity never faltered. "Thank you."

Klara's eyes flicked to Quinn and then back to James. In a conspiratorial tone, she said, "Her Russian isn't as good. She promised Pyotr she would practice. You will help her?"

"Always."

"Good," Klara said, obviously pleased Quinn would receive desperately needed instruction. "Everyone should speak Russian." An amused look passed between James and Quinn when Klara took one of their hands in each of hers and tugged them toward the stairs. "Now we watch television."

And so they did.

Chapter Twenty-One

Barefoot, Quinn padded down the hallway and peeked through the half-closed bedroom door. Like the two rooms she had already checked, this one had six kids clad in brand-new pajamas crowded into beds or lying on cushions on the floor. There was plenty of room for them to sleep spread out throughout the house. None of them were remotely interested in that. In the face of the tremendous upheaval they'd endured that day, Quinn didn't blame them for craving the security of surrounding themselves with those they knew and trusted.

Unlike the other rooms, the kids in this room sat spellbound as Mila read aloud the Russian version of *Harry Potter and the Philosopher's Stone*. Quinn leaned her shoulder against the doorjamb and listened. She wasn't a hundred percent sure, but she thought it was the part where Hagrid made his smashing entrance into the miserable shack on the rock on Harry's eleventh birthday. She smiled to herself. Pyotr and Klara were right. Her Russian needed more practice.

She left them to their story and stole down the stairs, pondering the parallels between Harry's wretched existence under the Dursleys' staircase and the children's forced imprisonment and labor, before they were given abrupt and disorienting freedom.

It was an interesting premise that would have to be explored another time. All she longed for now was sleep. She slipped into their bedroom, where James was already stretched out on the bed. It took her less than a minute to strip down, throw on a tank top and a pair of boy shorts, and flop onto the mattress next to her husband.

"Bed check complete?" James asked.

"All present and accounted for." She stretched and gave in to a jaw-cracking yawn. "I think this has to be one of the most emotionally draining days of my life."

"It's right up there for me, too." James reached up and switched off the lamp on the nightstand. The last light of the long summer day filtered into the room through thin curtains.

"I can't imagine what it must be like for those kids," she said.

"It'll take some time for it all to sink in. They'll need a lot of support."

Quinn rolled onto her side and draped an arm over James's bare chest. "I want to take the Semenov kids back to the US with us when we leave."

"What about your conversation with Reem?"

"I agreed they shouldn't leave until they're ready. But they came to me earlier today and said they want to go where their captors will never find them. They *are* ready."

His fingertips lightly trailed back and forth over her forearm. "They may think they are, but are they really?"

Her head lifted off the pillow. "Why are you taking Reem's side?"

"I'm not. There aren't any sides in this," he said evenly, his gaze on the ceiling. "It's about what's best for the kids."

She levered up on her elbow and looked into his face. "But what if they don't want to stay here? Don't you think they'll be more receptive to therapy if they're in a place they want to be? Otherwise, we're just adding more layers of abandonment and resentment on top of the mountain of crap they already have to deal with."

When he didn't respond, she pressed on. "I've already done some research on places they could go to that do intensive therapy for kids and teens coming out of trafficking."

A smile danced on his lips. "Of course you have."

She nudged his thigh with her knee in response. The next part was sure to seal the deal. She moved closer and lowered her voice. "There's a rehabilitation center in Colorado."

His eyes snapped to hers at the mention of his home state.

"It's a ranch up in the mountains," she continued. "They have chickens and goats and horses and dogs. And it's super secure because they keep the exact location secret. The kids would live there until they're ready to go home to their parents."

"Okay, that does sound perfect for them. Say we get the go-ahead to take them back to the States. We can't take them on a commercial flight. They don't have passports."

"The grandmother in Slavnoye might still have them."

"Maybe. The parents could have taken them back, too."

She huffed in frustration. "You're right." Her brow knit as she thought. "What about the American consulate in Saint Petersburg? Or the embassy in Moscow?"

James chuckled and said, "How about we remember who we work for?"

"Of course." Quinn's head dropped back on her pillow. "They had a fake passport ready for me in just a few hours when we went to London."

"I blame exhaustion for not thinking of the agency first. I'll call Meyers in the morning. Who knows? Maybe he can wrangle a plane for us and I can fly us home."

"I'm all for that. You're so incredibly sexy, sitting in a cockpit, wearing your sunglasses and headset."

He flipped onto his side. When they were lying face-to-face, he said, "If you're good, I might let you handle my control stick."

She smiled. "What if I'm bad?"

"Then I'll definitely let you handle my control stick."

Snickering, she shifted forward and pressed her lips to his in a soft kiss. The connection they shared, the tender way he touched her face, drove the jumbled thoughts and emotions of the day from her mind.

Her fingers threaded into his hair. She opened her mouth and kissed him deeper.

His response was immediate and fervent. He rolled her onto her back and kissed her with a passion that had her moaning. His hand slipped under her tank top and massaged her breast. She hummed with pleasure as he stoked the fire in her belly.

Her heart pounding, she slid a hand under the waistband of his boxers and grabbed his butt.

He raised his head and whispered, "Just a sec." He gave her a kiss that left her seconds from combusting and scrambled out of bed. Her body hungered for him to return as she watched him tiptoe across the room and turn the lock on the door. "Don't want any of the kids walking in on us. They've had enough trauma."

"Now I know how my parents must have felt when all us kids were home," she said.

He dove over the end of the bed, crawled on top of her, and kissed her ravenously. The way he was settled between her legs, the weight of his body pressing down on hers, it filled her with searing desire. It was exquisite.

She grew more and more desperate for him. "What time are you supposed to relieve Dave from guard duty?"

"Not until four."

"Good. We've got plenty of time." Her hand slid under his waistband again, only this time down the front. "Now, about your control stick . . ."

Quinn jerked awake. Disoriented, she blinked itchy, dry eyes and took in her surroundings. It took a few seconds for her brain to process and come to the realization she was in a bedroom in the safe house in Olgino. James lay next to her, his face slack with sleep.

She flipped onto her other side and glanced at the clock on the nightstand. It was a little before one in the morning.

Her tongue was glued to the roof of her mouth and the annoying tickle in her throat conspired to ensure sleep would remain elusive until it was soothed. She sighed and sat up. A trip to the kitchen for a bottle of water was warranted.

Careful not to wake James, she eased out of bed, stole across the room, and slowly opened the door. She grimaced and shot a glance at him from over her shoulder when the hinges emitted a groaning creak. His steady breathing assured her he was still asleep.

In her tank top and shorts again—she and James had dressed and unlocked the door after their nocturnal activities in case any of the kids came looking for them—she ran her fingers through her tousled hair as she walked toward the kitchen.

Silhouetted shapes moving in the backyard caught her attention. It was likely Dave checking the perimeter, or perhaps trees swaying in a breeze. Regardless, it was prudent to investigate. She crept across the living room to a window and edged back the curtain. Three pajama-clad kids stood in the center of the yard.

Scowling with confusion, she hurried outside and closed

in on the three afflicted with nighttime wanderlust. Mila, Sasha, and Ilya stood with their heads tipped back and faces raised to the starry sky.

So as not to startle them, Quinn slowed and announced her presence by clearing her throat. When they looked her way, she asked, "What are you doing out here? Is everything okay?"

"We're sorry if we woke you," Mila said, sounding a little guilty. "Those stairs are really creaky."

"It's fine. Is everything okay?" Quinn asked again. At least now she knew why she'd awakened so suddenly.

"Mm-hmm. It's just that it's been a long time since Sasha and Ilya have gotten to see the stars. I've been on trips and have seen them, but they were always left behind." Mila hesitated before dropping her gaze to the ground and adding, "Inside."

Quinn stepped closer. Her tone was gentle when she said, "I understand." She raised her eyes and stared up at the pinpricks of sparkling light. "It's a beautiful, clear night. Perfect for stargazing."

They fell silent and beheld the expanse of stars. The only sound around them came from leaves rustling in the light breeze.

A light thump interrupted the peace. Instantly alert, Quinn's eyes darted toward the cluster of trees in front of the cement fence at the back of the yard. Her nerves jangled when she observed movement. "Go back in the house. Now." Her tone was sharp and insistent.

"They not move," a man's voice said in heavily accented English. A hulking figure stepped out from the shadows. He was big. And bald. The pistol he held was pointed directly at them.

Anatoly.

Careful to not make any sudden movements, Quinn

slowly stepped in front of the kids to shield them. "Leave them alone, Anatoly." Utterly defenseless, she scanned the area, looking for something, anything she could use as a weapon. All she saw was a patio table and chairs, and a folded umbrella upright in a stand. Unless she hurled a chair at him, everything around them was useless.

Not good.

"No. They belong to us. I take them back."

Quinn's mouth was so dry she couldn't even manufacture enough saliva to swallow. She held her hands up in front of her. "It's over, Anatoly. Viktor, Zhanna, your other buddies, and Yefimov are in custody. Olga is on the run. There's no one to take them back to. Your drug ring is busted."

Anatoly was unmoved by her speech. "They will go free soon. I take workers back. We pay money for them."

He must have gotten a message from Yefimov. No doubt the mole in the police department had somehow found out and supplied him with the exact location of the safe house.

"I can't let that happen, Anatoly. You'll have to go through me." She had one last card to play. If she could talk him into putting his pistol down, she might have a chance. "But at least make it fair. Do you really want to be known as the guy who shot an unarmed woman? That's not very manly."

He laughed, gravelly and derisive. His chest expanded when he asked, "You fight me?"

"Sure. I may be small, but I'm scrappy."

Quinn heard a whispered *whoosh* followed by a muted *thup*.

The scorn on Anatoly's face turned to shock. His eyes lowered to the knife handle sticking out of his chest. The gun slipped from his hand and he dropped to his knees. As he teetered, his lips moved, but no words came. His eyelids fluttered before he pitched forward and crashed to the ground like a felled pine.

Dave stalked past them and went straight for Anatoly. He kicked the pistol away and looked over at them. "Are you okay?"

"We're fine," Quinn said. At his questioning, if not slightly cross, expression, she said, "I found them out here enjoying the stars. Anatoly decided to crash the party."

His gaze fell on the kids and his features softened. "Ah. Well, it is a nice night for it." He squatted down and pressed his fingers to the prone man's throat.

Mila stared down at Anatoly, her face an impassive mask. Blood oozed from under him and spread over the patch of dirt where he lay. "Is he dead?"

"No." Dave gripped Anatoly's wrist and hauled him onto his back.

Anatoly's tattoo-covered arm flopped to the ground. His breaths had turned labored and gurgling as his chest cavity filled with blood.

"Not yet anyway," he added.

"Let's go back in the house," Quinn said and shepherded the kids toward it.

Each one shot a glance over his or her shoulder. As they looked back at one of the men who had robbed them of everything—their freedom, their dignity, their humanity—their expressions were mixed. Triumph. Contempt. Defiance. Peace. One thing was sure: None would lament the demise of that loathsome piece of human garbage.

James, dressed only in jeans, emerged from the house. "I woke up and you . . ." He switched to operative mode the second he observed the body on the ground. "Are you okay? What's going on?"

Quinn filled him in on everything that had transpired since she had left their bed.

His response was decisive. "I'm gonna help Dave figure

out what to do with Anatoly. You get on the phone with Meyers right now. Tell him what we talked about earlier."

Quinn nodded. She cast a glance at the dying man before looking at James again.

"Tell him to pull every damn string there is. We're leaving for the States as soon as possible." His eyes fell on each child's face in turn. "And you're coming with us."

Chapter Twenty-Two

Dave drove the van across the tarmac and brought it to a stop near a sleek Gulfstream G280 parked on the isolated airstrip one hundred kilometers outside Saint Petersburg. The jet's open hatch and deployed stairs reminded Quinn of a scene in the novel *The Hidden Scepter*. In it, Francesca Marucci, an unfathomably wealthy heiress, emerges from her stretch limo resplendent in oversized sunglasses and designer clothes. With a jewel-encrusted purse hooked over one arm and a fluffy Pomeranian tucked under the other, she glides up the steps and wings her way to Malta and the awaiting Brick Cobalt.

The three youngest passengers of the van may not have been fabulously wealthy, but they were indeed precious cargo. Their status as such was cemented by Aldous Meyers's response to Quinn's request to get the Semenovs out of Russia immediately. In the intervening eighteen hours, the man had moved heaven and earth to make exactly that happen.

Now, the seemingly impossible dream of three young, vulnerable souls was becoming a reality.

Quinn yanked on the inside handle, slid the van door open, and stepped out onto the concrete. The kids tumbled

out behind her. As their gazes traveled around the wide-open
landscape dotted with crumbling, Soviet-era buildings, their
faces displayed equal parts excitement and trepidation.

Their anxiety was understandable. In less than thirty-six
hours, they had gone from slavery to freedom, and witnessed one of their captors take a wooden stool to the head
and another bleed out in front of them with a knife impaled
in his chest. Quinn counted on the many hours of flying time
to help calm their frayed nerves.

Dave jerked open the back door, hauled out James's and
Quinn's suitcases and briefcases, and set them on the ground.
He placed the three small sacks that held the kids' scant belongings next to them. Sasha and Ilya had been able to
gather their and Mila's things before being whisked away
to the safe house. Sadly, it didn't amount to much. Mila currently wore a pair of shorts and a top excavated from Quinn's
luggage. Quinn was already planning on buying all three
new clothes once they were back in the States.

A figure emerged from the airplane's hatch, hopped down
the steps, and strode toward them. As the woman neared, she
grinned at James and opened her arms. "James. It's so good
to see you again."

"You, too, Lauren," he said and gave her a quick hug. "It
made my day when Meyers told me you'd be my copilot."

"When I heard the legendary Buckshot was a mover and
shaker behind this, I knew it was important. I volunteered
immediately."

Quinn smiled when she heard Lauren utter the name.
Buckshot was her grandfather's code name within the CIA.
Of course he was involved in clearing the way for the
Semenov kids to get home, even if Quinn hadn't directly
asked for his help.

Lauren's eyes darted to the three and then returned to
James. "I'm honored to be a part of it."

James rested his hand at the small of Quinn's back. "This is my wife—"

"Quinn," Lauren said. The two women shook hands. "It's nice to meet you." Lauren was taller and a little older than Quinn, with green eyes that were as sharp as a knife. "I feel like I know you." At the bemused look on Quinn's face, Lauren added, "James and I worked together in Moscow. When he came back after your adventures together, you were all he talked about."

Quinn was relieved to hear humor in her tone rather than annoyance. Still, she felt heat rise in her cheeks. "Sorry about that."

"Don't be," Lauren said. "We miss him in Moscow, but we're glad he found you and is so happy."

Quinn smiled, secretly thrilled by Lauren's comments.

Dave stepped forward and extended a hand. "Dave Flores." After a brief greeting, he turned toward the Semenovs. "And these three are your esteemed passengers." They lifted their hands in unsure waves as Dave said their names.

Lauren acknowledged each with a head bob. "What do you say, ladies and gentleman? Ready to get out of here?"

"Yes," they murmured in unison.

"Then let's roll," Lauren said in a way that was both kind and authoritative.

Dave smiled at the kids. "Take care."

Mila took a half step toward him. Her voice was filled with quiet dignity when she said, "Thank you for rescuing us."

A lump knotted in Quinn's throat when she saw the tears glisten in Dave's eyes. The muscles in his jaw pulsed twice before he rasped, "You're welcome." He swiped a hand over his eyes and cleared his throat. "Maybe when y'all are ready, you can come on down to Texas and visit me and my family. Have your folks bring you. We'll have barbecue."

Mila's smile lit up her face. "We will."

Quinn and James shared hasty farewells with Dave and promised to stay in touch. As the group walked toward the plane, Dave returned to the van and drove off with a final wave through the window.

"Is our flight plan all set?" James asked Lauren.

Ilya went up the steps first, followed by Sasha, then Mila.

With the kids' bags in her arms, Lauren's eyes followed each as they boarded. "Affirmative. You know how it is around here. Had to grease a few palms, but we're all good."

"I know exactly how it is," James replied.

He didn't elaborate, but Quinn knew he was referring to the disposition of Anatoly's remains after he'd assumed ambient temperature the night before. They had immediately called in Reem, who had then contacted her most trusted ally within the local police. Wads of cash had been freely distributed from the top police brass to the guys who hauled the tarp-wrapped body out of the back of the van. The inquiry into the unlamented departure of Anatoly Volodin from this earthly plane was opened and closed in record time.

A briefcase in each hand, Quinn followed Mila up the steps and ducked through the hatch into the interior of the jet. Its eight large leather seats, tables, monitors, and satellite phone screamed, "High-ranking intelligence officials use this aircraft." Her grandfather had ensured they traveled in style.

The kids had already chosen their seats, so Quinn took an open one in front of Mila and stashed the briefcases. Ilya literally bounced, excitement shining on his face. Sasha, on the other hand, was clearly tense and chewed on her lower lip.

Lauren boarded and stood in the space between the entrance of the cockpit and the rest of the cabin. With a tip of her head, she indicated the three passports sitting atop a shiny wood tabletop. "Compliments of the Unites States Department of State. They're already stamped with the same date you and James arrived in Saint Petersburg. If anyone asks when we stop in Reykjavik, the kids are your cousins and you're all on your way home from holiday." She opened the forward closet door to reveal three small suitcases. "We didn't want you young people returning to the U.S. without some new clothes and toiletries."

"I got a suitcase full of clothes from the same people once," Quinn said to a gaping Sasha across the narrow aisle. "They're like shopping ninjas. You'll love everything." She should have known the agency would supply clothes for the kids. That wouldn't stop her from buying more for them, though.

Lauren closed the closet door and slid into one of the two seats in the cockpit. After strapping in, she put on her headset. Seconds later, the engines began to hum.

James brought up the rear. He walked through the compartment and stowed his and Quinn's luggage in the aft closet. Then he returned to the front, pulled up the hatch, and secured it. He turned and faced them as Lauren had a moment before. James flashed a cheesy smile and said in a sonorous tone, "Welcome aboard. My name is James. I'll be your flight attendant and copilot as we wing our way across the globe. If the Rocky Mountain Regional Airport in beautiful Broomfield, Colorado, is not your final destination, too bad because that's where we're going."

Ilya clamped both hands over his mouth and giggled.

James shot Quinn a wink. He continued. "Our flight time is approximately thirteen hours, not counting fuel stops in Reykjavik and . . ."

He paused and his eyes widened to comic proportions. He spun around and ducked his front half into the cockpit. A few seconds later, he backed out and faced them again. He picked up his narration as if he'd never stopped. "Teterboro, New Jersey. I have no idea what time we'll be landing in Colorado because with all the flying and time changes and everything, the math is just too hard."

Side-eyed, Quinn peeked over at Sasha. The shoulders that had been scrunched up to her ears lowered, and her face relaxed into a genuine smile. Quinn breathed out a silent sigh of relief.

He pointed at the back of the cabin with both hands. "The lavatory is located at the back. For those of you who may not know, that's just a fancy word for bathroom. Also, I'll be coming through the cabin later to take your dinner orders." James waited a beat before barking a laugh and dropping his affectations. "Just kidding. You're on your own for dinner." He gestured at the counter to his left. "There's a little galley here, so feel free to pillage. There might be stuff to make a sandwich or something." Slipping back into his flight attendant voice, he finished with, "Sit back, relax, and enjoy your flight."

James dipped his head in acknowledgement of their rousing applause. "Thank you. Thank you. Now, please fasten your seat belts in preparation for takeoff."

Once all four passengers were clipped in, he took his place in the cockpit.

God, I love that man, Quinn thought as she watched him punch buttons and confer with Lauren.

The plane taxied into position, roared down the runway, jumped from the deck, and rocketed into the sky.

Other than the whine of the jet engines, the cabin was quiet as everyone stared out their windows. As Quinn watched the ground below race away, her thoughts were with those left behind. The good-byes with Klara and Pyotr had been particularly heart-wrenching. Klara's chin had quivered and giant tears had spilled out and traced down her cheeks. Pyotr had smiled, but his eyes were bright as they said good-bye. Quinn was sure they would never forgive her for leaving them, but the bone-crushing hugs they each gave her assured her she would always be in their hearts, just as they would always be in hers.

When they reached cruising altitude, Quinn got up and rummaged in the drawers until she found a deck of cards. They took turns playing game after game of Go Fish, Crazy Eights, Speed, gin rummy, and every game Quinn could think of. She considered teaching them Texas Hold'em, but when she noted their enthusiasm waning and fatigue setting in, she put the cards away and suggested sleep. All three curled up in their seats and used their teddy bears as pillows. They conked out in less than five minutes.

Quinn considered reading, but the cabin lights had been dimmed and she didn't want to wake their sleeping charges. Deciding to do some work, she retrieved her laptop from her briefcase as stealthily as possible and opened it. Thanks to onboard secure Wi-Fi, she checked her various email accounts. Among the messages from her parents, the library, Nicole, her brother Monroe, and her new sister-in-law Kelsey, there was one from James, including an attachment.

Curious as to why he would email her something, she clicked it open. Hey, Sexy. Thought you might like to check this out. She blinked. Was he sending her X-rated pictures of himself through their secure agency email accounts? That didn't seem like a very professional thing to do. Plus, why would he do that when she caught the live show every day? She peeked at the kids. Their eyes were still shut.

She faced forward again and, before she could change her mind, clicked on the link. A quiet chuckle escaped. To her simultaneous relief and disappointment, no racy photo of James appeared on her screen. He had forwarded the data he'd downloaded from Grigori Yefimov's cell phone. Events had unfolded at such lightning speed, they hadn't had a moment free to examine it.

Now that she had hours to kill and nothing to do, she decided to see exactly what kind of shenanigans Yefimov had been involved in. And if she uncovered any new information regarding the ever-elusive kingpin Konstantin Borovsky, all the better.

Her Russian had improved immensely during her time in Saint Petersburg, but she was in no way fluent. To make things easier on herself, she used an agency program to translate everything into English.

She opened the photos file first. Given the fact that Yefimov had run a strip club, his pictures had the potential to be more than a little awkward. It seemed prudent to go through those while the kids slept.

Her nose wrinkled at the many pictures of Yefimov with his scantily clad employees inside the Bronze Monkey. Whenever she ran across photos that featured Yefimov posing with non-employees, she took extra time to scrutinize each face. One with Rhys Townsend and/or Gibson Honeycutt might help to bust them someday in connection with either drug or human trafficking.

When she reached the end of the photos, she slumped back in her seat and huffed a breath in disappointment. She hadn't seen Rhys or Gibson, although there was a well-known CEO of an American tech company who would be getting scrutiny from the FBI in the very near future. Another face was vaguely familiar to her, but at that moment, she couldn't put her finger on who he was.

She rubbed her forehead with her fingertips and grappled with the fact she may have stared directly into the face of Konstantin Borovsky and not known it. The only pictures of him were grainy and taken from awkward angles. Undeterred, she sat forward and went back to work. She dumped every photo that included someone with Yefimov into a folder and flagged it for agency analysts to run each through facial recognition.

Next, she tackled Yefimov's email. Like with the photos, he had kept hundreds of messages from people she assumed were drug clients, most expressing their eagerness to visit the Bronze Monkey or thanking him afterward. Such innocuous-sounding messages were in no way incriminating. But now that there was proof he'd been running a drug ring and using child laborers, they turned much more sinister. The fact he'd kept them made her think he'd done so either for blackmail purposes or to guarantee his own protection.

Her breath caught when the name of a sender leapt at her from the screen: Dieter Ziegler. It was the same name as the doctor in Frankfurt from whom she and James had stolen the formula and prototype for a psychotropic drug.

"Wait a minute," she whispered aloud. She opened the folder marked for facial recognition and searched for the face that had niggled her earlier. When she found it, she pulled up an agency file and compared the two faces. They were the same. Ziegler and Yefimov had met.

She returned to Yefimov's email and read through the thread with Ziegler from several months earlier. The content was unremarkable, in that Ziegler informed Yefimov of his impending visit to Saint Petersburg to attend a pharmaceutical conference. While in town, Ziegler looked forward to visiting the Bronze Monkey. Yefimov's email to Ziegler in response was predictably solicitous.

It was the contemporaneous emails between Yefimov and someone only known as KB that had the hairs on the back of Quinn's neck prickling. Yefimov had informed KB, whom she assumed to be Konstantin Borovsky, of Ziegler's upcoming visit. Borovsky had told Yefimov to cater to the doctor's every whim in order to curry favor.

There was no reason for Ziegler to go to Yefimov and Borovsky to buy drugs. The guy had worked for a pharmaceutical company. The only thing that made sense was that Borovsky wanted to buy drugs from Ziegler. And while it was never expressly indicated in the messages, Quinn surmised Borovsky's goal was to get his hands on the drug she and James had liberated from Ziegler's office. She wondered if the agency had already uncovered the link.

She searched Yefimov's emails and retrieved only those between he and Borovsky. Most were about business at the Bronze Monkey. The one where Borovsky asked Yefimov to send some product, along with several kids, to his yacht for incoming guests was intriguing. She would ask Mila if she knew anything about a yacht. Given how little the agency knew about Borovsky, acquiring any firsthand knowledge would be akin to unearthing a gold nugget.

A thrill of satisfaction buzzed through her when she saw Yefimov had sent a follow-up email after Ziegler's visit to the Bronze Monkey asking if Borovsky had successfully secured the doctor's product. The curt response from Borovsky had informed him the drug was no longer available.

She knew why. After she and James had broken into Ziegler's office, an anonymous tip—from James—had been called in to German authorities alerting them to Ziegler's illegal drug peddling. He had been arrested soon thereafter. His computer, along with the formula, had been seized.

She looked up when James emerged from the cockpit and walked toward her. He braced a hand on the top of her seat back and bent forward.

She closed her computer, lifted her face, and received his warm kiss. "How's it going?" she asked quietly.

He didn't move. Instead, he hovered over her, the gap between their noses mere millimeters. "Good." He kissed her again. "Better."

She smiled up at him when he still didn't move away.

The heat behind the next kiss had her melting into her seat.

"Much better." He gave her one of those crooked smiles that caused her heart to bounce inside her chest like a rubber ball. After one final kiss, he dropped into the seat across the table from her and stretched his long legs down the aisle. "We'll be landing in Reykjavik in about thirty minutes. How are you?"

"Good. I've been going through Yefimov's phone." One corner of her mouth lifted. "I must confess I thought the email attachment might be something of a more personal nature."

His smile was slow and sexy. "Sorry to disappoint. Maybe next time."

His smolder completely derailed her. Her mind careened into dangerous territory with visions of her and James doing all kinds of things to each other in the tiny lavatory. She bounced an eyebrow. "Since our joining the Mile High Club would be wildly inappropriate under the circumstances, why don't I tell you what I found on Yefimov's phone instead?"

His voice rumbled from deep in his chest. "That's probably a good idea."

She battled the increasingly vivid thoughts of her and James together by raking her fingers through her hair and saying, "I think Borovsky wanted to buy Dieter Ziegler's psychotropic drug."

His interest clearly piqued, he cocked his head and said, "Really." James seemed to hang on her every word as she relayed the contents of the correspondence on the matter.

When she finished, James said, "There's a list of names that downloaded along with Ziegler's formula. We assumed they were potential buyers."

She sank back, deflated. "So this isn't new intel at all. You already knew Borovsky wanted to buy Ziegler's drug." She frowned and asked, "And why don't I know about this list?"

"Well, when the files were first analyzed, you were busy getting married and going on your honeymoon with this stud." He jerked his thumb at his chest.

She smirked and rolled her eyes.

"And I only found out about it while you were neck deep in learning Russian."

"Fine. I get why I didn't hear about it, but what's the hold-up on using the list to set up a sting to draw them out or something?"

"Ziegler gave all the buyers code names. We have no idea who they are. In this case, the names are of dead national heroes. We can guess at their nationalities, but don't have any actual names. There's Qin Shi Huang for China and Mohammed Ali Jinnah for Pakistan and Omar Mukhtar for Libya." He shot her a knowing look. "Guess the name he used for his Russian buyer."

One name immediately popped into her head. "Alexander Nevsky."

"Ding, ding, ding."

"Okay, so finding out Borovsky wanted to buy the drug is a big deal after all." Growing excited, she sat up higher in her seat. "We can use the formula as bait to draw him out. Maybe we can't bust him for his drug and forced labor racket," she said, snapping her head toward the slumbering Semenovs, "but we can nab him when he tries to buy Ziegler's drug."

James slouched and rested his head on the back of his seat. With fingers laced and resting on his chest, he considered her. The pressure behind her sternum built as she waited, watching the gears turn in his head. "You and I stole the prototype. We're right there on the security cameras."

"Exactly," she said as softly as her eagerness would allow. She pitched forward, her words coming in a torrent. "We could come out now and say after we swiped the formula, we called the cops on Ziegler to get him out of the picture. With him in custody, he couldn't reconstruct it."

He pushed himself up, leaned on his elbows, and tilted in until their foreheads nearly touched. "Giving us exclusive control. No competition."

"With your contacts in Moscow, I bet we can get a message to Borovsky informing him the formula is for sale again."

"We'd have to meet in person. Given his penchant for staying hidden, he might not agree."

"We'll figure something out. If he wants Ziegler's drug as much as it seems he does, we don't give him a choice. No meet, no sale."

"We need to meet with Meyers about all this as soon as we get back to Langley." Even in the faint light of the cabin, his eyes gleamed bright blue. "You ready for another adventure, Mrs. Anderson?"

"With you, Mr. Anderson?" She rolled forward until their lips met in a tender kiss. "Always."

Chapter Twenty-Three

James, Quinn, and the Semenov kids had flown countless hours and traveled thousands of miles, crossing both ocean and continent. Yet it was the final fifteen miles of their journey up the steep, twisting, narrow ribbon of road perched on the side of a mountain that had Quinn's stomach flopping like she'd swallowed a live trout.

James shifted the black SUV that had been waiting for them when they landed in Colorado into a lower gear and cranked the steering wheel. The engine whined as James took on a particularly nasty hairpin turn.

Quinn blew out a nervous breath and rubbed her sweaty palms over the thighs of her jeans.

James's eyes never left the road when he asked, "You okay?"

"Yeah. At least this road isn't icy and snow packed like when we drove down from the cabin in Arrowhead. *That* was scary."

He smiled at the memory. "That was a fun drive. I was already crazy about you. By the time we got to the airport, I was a goner."

"I was head over heels for you before that." Her stomach stilled as she recalled the beginning of their first op together.

She shot him a sly look. "Admit it. You only fell in love with me because I kept feeding you In-N-Out."

"You found me out." His tone was as dry as the dirt clinging to the hood of the SUV.

"I thought so," she said, sounding as wry as he.

Quinn twisted around and checked on the siblings. Ilya sat between his sisters, the stuffed puffin James had bought him at the Reykjavik airport firmly in his lap. Sasha clutched the jackalope plush, complete with antlers and cottontail, purchased in the gift shop of the hotel in Boulder they'd stayed at the night before.

Their faces showed no sign of the nerves the perilous road induced in Quinn. In fact, they were fully engaged in watching the scenery roll past. There were times when Quinn's side of the car came so close to the wall of jagged rocks and boulders, a hand extended out the window would touch them. On the other side of the road, the terrain sloped down so precipitously they drove amongst the tops of pine trees. And still the vehicle climbed.

Ilya leaned forward and peered out Mila's window. The sky was an impossible shade of blue. "We're so high up, we can almost touch the clouds," he said.

Mila's gaze rose. "They look like piles of cotton balls."

Quinn turned forward again and looked out. They were just below where mountaintops met sky.

The knot in her stomach loosened further when terrain on either side of the road flattened and the asphalt gave way to dirt. A dozen mailboxes of various shapes and colors sat in a row along one side of the road. They passed the occasional dirt driveway that disappeared into the forest.

They emerged from the trees and drove along the edge of an expansive meadow. At its center stood a small pond. Beyond, the Rockies loomed in colored layers: the closest, green; the middle, slate; and the furthest, hazy gray. "Wow," Quinn breathed.

The SUV bounced over the rough washboard surface, the tires losing traction and sliding even in the gentlest bends.

Quinn checked the GPS. "It's about another quarter mile. The turnoff will be on the right."

As they neared the entrance, James slowed the vehicle.

Most of the fences along the road demarcating property lines were of the rustic split-rail variety. The fence Quinn spotted just beyond the tree line was high and chain-link. Of this, she approved immensely.

James drove at a snail's pace as they approached where the map indicated the entrance should be. Quinn spotted the unmarked driveway and pointed. "There it is."

He wheeled into the drive and stopped in front of a metal gate. While James put his window down and pressed the button on the intercom, Quinn observed the security cameras installed on tall wooden poles. The people at Elkhorn Ridge Ranch were serious about the protection of their residents.

James gave their names to the gatekeeper at the other end of the intercom. After a pause, they were told to drive forward as the gate slid open.

They drove another quarter mile through a dense forest of pine, birch, and aspen trees before arriving at the compound. The front of the large, ranch-style house made heavy use of wood, rock, and glass. There were two other buildings on the property. One was obviously a barn. The purpose of the other was yet to be determined. A dozen chickens strutted around a pen while five horses munched on grass in a paddock.

James stopped the SUV at the end of a line of parked cars and shut off the engine. Before Quinn had her seat belt unfastened, Sasha asked, "You're not going to leave us right away, are you?" The anxiety in her tone cut through Quinn like a knife.

"No way. We'd like to meet the people here and tour the place." She craned her neck and smiled. "And maybe pet the horses." The uncertain faces she beheld brightened at the prospect.

A small cloud of dust blossomed up around Quinn's feet when she jumped down from her seat. The air was warm and dry and carried the scents of wood, dried pine needles, and horse. Chickens clucked, birds chirped, bugs and grass-hoppers buzzed.

A woman, her long brown hair in a single braid down her back, hopped down the front steps and strode toward them. "Welcome to Elkhorn Ridge Ranch. My name is Katie," she said with a welcoming smile. "I'm on staff here and part of the welcoming committee." In her jeans, boots, and loose, flowing top, she looked like a bohemian cowgirl.

Quinn shook Katie's hand. "I'm Quinn, and the beast of burden unloading the bags back there is my husband, James."

He poked his head out and waved.

Katie acknowledged him with a wave of her own before turning her attention to the three kids. "You must be Mila and Sasha and Ilya. We're glad you've come here to be with us for a while. If you need anything, you can always come to me." The woman exuded genuine warmth and compassion.

Three heads nodded while gazes were pinned to the ground.

"Let's go in the house and put your things in your bed-room. We have new clothes and personal items available, but it looks like you're pretty well set," Katie said.

The group started for the house. Ilya and Sasha slipped their hands in Quinn's. James wrangled two rolling suitcases while Mila pulled the third.

"An agency we work with got some things together for them before we left Russia," Quinn said. "Their sponsors, if you will."

"That's so great," Katie said. "Most of our residents come to us with next to nothing. We give them new clothes not only as provision, but to show them how valued they are to us. We're here to restore their humanity."

"It sounds like this will be a great fit," Quinn said.

They climbed the front steps and entered the house. They were still in the entryway when a sleek, black Labrador retriever trotted toward them. His thick otter-like tail furiously whipped back and forth.

Katie rubbed his side. "This is Bear. He's the most enthusiastic member of our welcoming committee."

The dog greeted each person with a polite sniff. He received chin scratches and ear rubs in return. When he completed his rounds, he circled back and sat on his haunches next to Sasha. He looked up at Katie expectantly.

From the interest Quinn read on Katie's face, Bear's action was significant. No doubt a therapy dog, she guessed he was signaling something of importance to Katie. Quinn doubted it was a coincidence he'd picked out the most vulnerable of the three to sit by. Her esteem for the ranch grew with each passing moment.

"Let's drop your bags in your room and then I'll show you around," Katie said.

They walked straight down a hall and stopped outside a doorway. "This will be your room. We usually have two per room, but we brought in bunk beds so you can be together. If that doesn't suit you, we can make some adjustments."

Quinn peered into the room. The walls were painted a soothing blue. Patchwork quilts covered the three beds. A thick pillow and a stuffed lamb sat atop each. It was homey and inviting. And perfect.

"No," the siblings said as one. Mila spoke for all after they exchanged glances. "We want to stay together."

"Well, then we guessed right, didn't we?" Katie said with a bright smile.

While the kids, with Bear's assistance, sorted out who would take which bed, Quinn, James, and Katie stood outside the room in the hallway. "Thank you for taking them in on such short notice," Quinn said.

"We're glad we're able to help." Katie's voice lowered when she said, "Especially when we got a phone call from the State Department asking us to take in three American citizens arriving from Russia."

"We didn't take someone else's place, did we?" Quinn wanted the best for the kids, but not at the expense of others equally in need.

"No, not at all." Katie slipped her hands in her pockets. "It was perfect timing. Two girls just left us a couple of days ago. We usually have only girls stay with us, but under the circumstances we're happy to make an exception. If anything, because of social stigmas, boys and young men coming out of trafficking don't get the kind of help and attention they need. We're glad to be here to help Ilya."

"How long do your residents typically stay?" James asked.

"It's hard to say. Every victim has different issues, different needs. The shortest we've ever had was six weeks. The longest anyone can stay is two years. Those are usually cases where it's not safe to return them to the home because it's where the abuse started in the first place. So often, these kids run away from home and then end up being trafficked. Sometimes they're lured away from home by online predators promising modeling or acting jobs. All that to say, when they leave, we make sure each one is placed into a safe, stable environment."

"That shouldn't be an issue here," Quinn said and gave Katie a summary of how the Semenovs had ended up being sold to work for a drug dealer. "Their parents had no idea what happened to them until recently. They're more than ready for their children to come home."

Katie nodded. "A liaison at the State Department put us in contact with them. They're completely on board and have already signed the paperwork. And we'll certainly keep them in the loop. They'll need counseling and support as well." She smiled at the kids as they walked out of the bedroom. "Let's take a walk and I'll show you around."

Katie led them through a sitting room, complete with leather chairs and stone fireplace; the dining room with a long table at the center; and the kitchen. Quinn noted everywhere they went, Bear stayed glued to Sasha's side.

They descended a set of stairs and stood in the doorway of a large, open room. The many windows installed in one wall afforded an incredible view of the ranch's open acreage. Soothing music played as six girls around Mila's age stretched on mats. At the direction of the instructor at the front of the room, they changed positions.

"Have you ever done yoga?" Katie asked in a voice just above a whisper.

Three heads shook.

"We'll teach you. You'll love it." Katie pointed at the glass door. "Let's sneak out the back."

Single file, they quietly skimmed the wall as they headed for the door. Only Bear's jingling tags and toenails tapping the hardwood floor announced their presence.

Outside again, they walked to the building the purpose of which Quinn had yet to divine. "This is our school," Katie said. "We have several teachers on staff."

Mila's head snapped toward Katie. "We get to go to school?"

"Yes. Absolutely." They entered the classroom filled with tables, chairs, books, and computers. A whiteboard attached to one wall was covered with algebra written with black marker. "We'll find out where you are and go from there."

Ilya's shoulders drooped. Chin near his chest, he mumbled, "I can't read very well."

"That's okay," Katie said gently. "Our teachers are really good at teaching that."

"Science, too?" Mila asked.

"Absolutely. It's fully accredited. Everything you learn here in our school will be accepted by the school you'll attend when you go home."

They left the school and crossed the yard. In the distance, a tan and black Rottweiler loped toward them. Quinn could have sworn the big, solid dog had a smile on its face.

"Hey, Buttercup. The back forty secure?" Katie called out. Buttercup came at them with such speed and exuberance, Quinn was afraid she'd knock them over like bowling pins. She stepped in front of Ilya and bent her knees, ready to take the brunt of Buttercup's mass hurtling toward them.

The dog skidded to a stop in front of Katie. "You come to say hi to our new residents?" She thumped Buttercup's side.

Much like Bear, Buttercup inspected each visitor with her nose. She was in the middle of sniffing James's shoes when a ruckus sounded from the goat pen. Her head snapped up and her entire body stiffened. The Rottie's nostrils flared and relaxed repeatedly as she sniffed the breeze. Apparently, the goats' issues required further investigation. Filled with a new sense of purpose, she trotted off.

Katie's eyes remained on the retreating dog. Her affection for Buttercup was obvious when she said, "As you've likely figured out, Buttercup is an important member of ranch security." She started the group toward the chicken coop. "We'll check on the chickens and let her sort out the goats."

When they reached the pen, Katie picked up a metal bucket by the handle and held it toward Ilya. "Could you do me a huge favor and feed the chickens?" When the boy hesitated, Katie said, "Come. I'll show you." The two scooted through the gate. The chickens converged when Katie took a handful of feed and tossed it about. Ilya copied the action. The birds pecked at the ground.

"I have an important job for you, Ilya," Katie said, her voice turning almost conspiratorial. "Every day, you'll need to find the eggs these chickens lay. If you go into the henhouse right now, I bet you'll find one or two."

Ilya's eyes rounded and he nodded solemnly. He disappeared into the wooden coop. A moment later, he reappeared cradling a single brown egg. He cupped it in both hands as if it were the most precious thing in the universe.

Ilya grinned at Quinn with unbridled joy. She smiled back and blinked at the sudden wetness in her eyes. It was true the kids had a ways to go. But in that moment, and for the first time, Quinn truly believed they were going to be okay.

James sidled up and put his arm around her. She sighed and rested her head on his shoulder. Without having to utter a word, she knew. He believed they would be okay, too.

"Nicely done, Ilya," Katie said enthusiastically. "Do you like eggs? If you do, we can have Danielle fix it for your lunch if you want. If not, that's okay, too. We have lots of food, and Danielle is an amazing cook."

Ilya gaped at Katie, clearly astounded by being asked if he would like something or not. "I'd like to have it for lunch."

"Super," Katie said. "Come on out and take it to Danielle in the kitchen. Mila, can you go with your brother?"

"Sure," Mila said. "Come on, *bratishka*."

"Meet us at the goat pen," Katie said as they walked toward the house.

The remaining group ambled toward the goats. Sasha, with Katie on one side and Bear on the other, walked in front of James and Quinn. Katie talked to Sasha about how she would be helping tend the goats, just as Ilya was now an egg wrangler.

Quinn held back from engaging in the conversation. She was aware the kids had grown attached to her, and for obvious reason. But she and James couldn't stay. And it was important for them, especially Sasha, to trust the ranch staff and feel safe in their new environment. James and Quinn stepping back was part of that transition.

Toward the end of Sasha's goat orientation, Mila and Ilya rejoined the group. They moved on to greet the horses and learned all would get a chance to care for and ride them. And just as Ilya and Sasha had specific duties, Mila was given additional grooming responsibilities the younger and smaller kids couldn't perform.

Now that the tour was complete, they returned to the house. Katie said, "Why don't you go unpack while James and Quinn and I go over some paperwork?"

The siblings, and Bear, trundled off while the three adults headed for the room with the fireplace. Once seated, Quinn said, "It's time for us to leave, isn't it?"

Katie's smile was sympathetic. "I'm afraid so." She folded her hands and rested them on her lap. "I can see how fond you are of them and how they've bonded to both of you. That's a good sign."

"They're very special young people," James said, his voice tight with emotion.

"I can tell," Katie said. "I'm confident we can help them heal."

Quinn slipped her hand into James's. "If it's possible, we'd appreciate it if you could keep us updated on how they're doing."

"Oh, for sure. If you want, we can also let you know when you can contact them directly."

"We'd like that," James answered.

"Good." Katie handed Quinn a clipboard with a number of documents to sign. When the final paperwork was finished, Katie stood. "I'll go get them and give you a few minutes to say good-bye."

Katie got up and disappeared down the hall. A moment later, the kids shuffled in alone. From their downcast expressions, they knew what was coming.

Quinn put on a smile, even with the boulder of sorrow lodged in her chest. "It's time for James and me to go."

Ilya's eyes flooded with tears. "I don't want you to."

"I know, sweetie." Quinn ruffled Ilya's golden hair. "But we have to go back to work."

"And those chickens look like they'll be laying lots of eggs," James added. "You'll be busy every day."

"Will we ever see you again?" Sasha's voice was nothing more than a croaking whisper.

"Of course you will," Quinn said. "We'll make sure of it, won't we, James?"

"You bet."

The tears Quinn fought broke free as she gave first Ilya, then Sasha, a final hug. As she embraced Mila, Quinn whispered, "You are one of the bravest, strongest, and most courageous people I've ever known."

"We can never thank you enough for what you've done for us. All of us." Mila stepped back and grinned as she wiped her cheeks. "And for the copy of *Harry Potter* you hid in my suitcase."

"I didn't want you all missing out on the rest of the story just because we had to return the Russian one," she said with a watery laugh.

After watching them hug James, Quinn gazed into each face one last time. They were exactly where they needed to be. It didn't make it any easier to leave them, though. As if to cement the idea in everyone's minds they would all see each other again, she left with, "See you later."

After a final wave, she and James turned and walked across the room and out the front door. Quinn blew out a breath and swiped her forearm across her wet eyes. "It's a good thing I'm not wearing makeup. I'd be a complete mess."

James laced his fingers with hers as they strolled across the dirt toward the SUV. "You're beautiful even when you look like a raccoon."

"Thanks. I know you mean it since you've seen me that way more than once."

He shrugged. Her red, drippy nose and smeared makeup had never bothered him. "Like I've said, I'm always happy to be your Kleenex." He opened her door, and as she heaved herself up into the seat, he asked, "Now that the kids are safe, you ready to go after Borovsky?"

A renewed sense of purpose flamed in her chest. "Hell, yeah," she growled. Her thirst for justice overcame her sadness. It felt good. "Let's go nail that son of a bitch."

Chapter Twenty-Four

Quinn stared at the computer screen and frowned. She'd hit another dead end. She shifted in her butt-numbing chair at her desk inside the CIA library, closed her eyes, and rubbed her temples. There just wasn't enough information. She was never going to figure it out.

Soft footfalls approached from behind. Before she swiveled around in her chair, she knew it was James.

"Hey." He kissed her cheek. "You ready to meet up with Sydney in the lab?"

She drew a deep breath in through her nose. Her mood lightened as she reveled in his scent. She heartily approved of the Viking cologne he'd purchased duty-free in Reykjavik. "Yeah."

"What's the matter?"

Apparently her mood hadn't sufficiently lightened.

The raspberry she blew might not have been particularly professional, but it perfectly encapsulated her frustration. "I still can't find Borovsky's yacht. You would think one as big as Mila said it was wouldn't be that hard to find."

"Too bad she couldn't remember the name."

"It is. But she was just a scared kid. I can't blame her for not remembering every detail. Frankly, I'm surprised she didn't block it all out of her mind."

"True. What about Reem? Was she able to get any intel from Yefimov or Viktor?" He sat in the chair next to her desk. "Get one of them to roll on Borovsky?"

"Not yet, but let me check again." She clicked open her email. Two new messages sat in her inbox. "Oh, good. Got one from Katie and one from Reem. Which one first?"

"How are the kids?"

Quinn opened the email and scanned it. "They had a good first week and are all settled in. The hope is their parents will be able to visit them in a few weeks."

"Great. And what's Reem got to say?"

Her breath caught as she scrolled through Reem's message. "Yefimov is dead."

James bolted up. "What?"

"He was found dead in his cell with a sheet wrapped around his neck. Russian authorities are calling it a suicide."

"Suicide my ass," James said. "Borovsky ordered the hit because Yefimov knew too much and Borovsky was afraid he'd roll."

"Which was exactly what we were trying to get him to do."

"What about Viktor?"

Her shoulders sagged as she read Reem's email further. "He's been released. All the evidence against him was miraculously misplaced. Payment for taking Yefimov out?"

"Maybe. Probably. Either way, Borovsky got his money's worth out of his people inside that police department. Dave has to have copies of the video recordings we made inside the drug den. Reem can give them to the police again."

"She already did, but not before Viktor was released. He's gone with the wind." She slumped in her chair. "Crap. We're back to square one."

"Not exactly. We don't have to worry about Yefimov and Anatoly anymore."

"Silver lining." She usually felt sympathy at the passing of a fellow human being. But given the devastated young lives those two had left behind, their ultimate and eternal disposition didn't faze her.

"And now, with Ziegler's formula, we have a shot at coaxing Borovsky from his hidey-hole."

"Good point." She locked her computer and stood. "Let's go see what that green goo of Ziegler's does exactly."

They left the library and proceeded to the Directorate of Science and Technology wing. They badged through a set of locked double doors and strode down a long hallway. Stark white walls and harsh, fluorescent lights gave off a cold, sterile vibe. The faint astringent odor didn't help lessen the unnerving feeling that made goose bumps sprout over Quinn's skin.

"It gives me the creeps down here," she said. Her voice bounced off the walls. "I hope we don't accidentally walk into a secret lab with specimens of alien life forms pickled and floating in jars."

"You mean in that gross, murky yellow liquid?"

"Yes! Exactly."

"Then don't go in there," James said and pointed to a door as they passed.

A glance at a tag on the wall indicated the room was filled with cleaning supplies. Smirking, she asked, "A janitor's closet?"

"See, that's what they *want* you to think it is." They came to a stop in front of another locked door.

"I get it," she said. "It's actually the Langley version of Area Fifty-one." Quinn swiped her badge, activating a retinal scanner. She positioned her eye in front of the lens. Blue light filled her vision.

"Yup," James said.

When she'd appeased the security gods, the lock clicked. She pulled the handle and swung open the door. "I'm glad this lab won't have anything like that in it."

"Nah. All the weird stuff is back there. They're just working on reanimating the dead in here."

She chuckled. As James swiped his badge, she surveyed the lab. Long, waist-high counters were covered with computer monitors, microscopes, beakers, test tubes, and various pieces of research equipment. Quinn could only guess at their uses and had no intention of touching anything. She had no desire to accidentally trigger some sort of biohazard emergency that would quarantine parts of two states and end with her glowing in the dark.

She was a little disappointed she didn't see any contraptions with flasks and tubes and Bunsen burners, where blue liquid bubbled and sinister vapor trickled down the sides of beakers. On the plus side, body parts in need of reanimation were nowhere in sight.

James rested his hand on the small of her back. Together, they headed toward Sydney's workstation.

A couple of techs dressed in white lab coats glanced up as they passed. Most continued working, ignoring them completely.

They found Sydney Pettigrew at her station, her head down and absorbed in her work. It was clear she hadn't heard them approach and remained oblivious to their presence. Quinn politely cleared her throat.

Sydney flailed and almost toppled off her stool.

"I'm sorry," Quinn said. "I didn't mean to startle you."

Sydney steadied herself and stood. "No, no. Not your fault. I get so wrapped up." In her late thirties, she was slight and barely taller than Quinn. Her light brown hair was pulled back in a messy ponytail.

"I know how that is." Quinn had met Sydney once before,

when they'd deposited with her the vials they'd stolen from Ziegler's office.

"You're here to see what *Herr Doktor* was up to," Sydney stated.

"Yes," James said. "We want to use the drug as bait."

"We need to know what it does and hope it's sufficiently enticing for our elusive target to crawl out from under his rock," Quinn added.

"Oh, it's definitely that," Sydney said. The conviction in her tone was intriguing.

"So it's more than some kind of psychoactive drug?"

A wary expression overtook Sydney's features as she glanced at something over Quinn's shoulder. Quinn turned to see who or what had caused the disruption. She smiled when her eyes met those of the spry, gray-haired man coming toward them.

Grandpa.

She wanted to kiss his cheek in greeting, but refrained. The goal was to keep their familial connection under the radar. "What are you doing here?" Her tone was a mixture of delight and surprise.

"Curiosity, mostly. I heard some interesting things about Ziegler's drug and want to learn more about it." He and James shook hands.

"I'm sorry," Sydney said, guarded. "You are . . ."

"Where are my manners?" Grandpa said. "Please forgive me. You can call me Buckshot."

The hum of activity in the room abruptly ceased, like when the principal walks into an elementary school classroom.

Sydney paled, audibly gulped, and started to fidget with the buttons of her lab coat. Tongue-tied, all she could get out was a strangled, "Right. Yeah. Okay."

Quinn felt bad for the woman. To her, he was her sweet, generous grandfather whom she adored. During her growing-up years, he had stoked her fire for adventure with his stories of exotic, faraway places he'd visited as an importer/exporter.

It was only a year and a half ago she'd learned of his true occupation. He'd been part of the CIA for fifty years. Now officially retired, he still consulted on ops and recruited new officers. It was he who had drafted Quinn in the first place. Because of his longevity and preference to remain mostly in the background, he had gained legendary, if not mythical, status. Now that his granddaughter was there, though, he took a more active interest in her ops.

"Sorry for the interruption," Grandpa said, ignoring the fact that every set of eyeballs inside the lab was on him. He grasped his hands behind his back. "Carry on."

Quinn detected a ripple of furtive whispers as the noise level in the room returned to normal.

Sydney had regained her composure. "The answer to your question, Quinn, about it being more than a psycho-active drug is yes and no. Have you ever heard of scopo-lamine, also known as the Devil's Breath?"

"It's said to be a mind-control drug," Grandpa said. "It's derived from nightshade plants in Colombia and Ecuador. The myth is all one has to do is blow some of the white powder into a victim's face and they will do anything you tell them to. They have no control over their thoughts or actions."

"Can it do that?" Quinn asked.

Sydney shrugged. "There are all kinds of stories, mostly from South America, about people who had the drug slipped into their drink or food. While they were under its influence, they cleaned out their bank accounts and apartments and handed everything over to the person who drugged them. Some victims claim they knew what they were doing but couldn't stop themselves. Others say they don't remember any of it and wake up on a park bench the next day. They only know what happened after piecing it all together later."

"If true, that's terrifying," James said.

"Synthesized scopolamine in extremely low doses isn't terrible. It's used to treat motion sickness and nausea, stuff like that," Sydney said.

Quinn folded her arms. "That doesn't sound so bad. I assume higher doses are the problem."

"Yeah, it's definitcly nasty stuff. It has an amnesiac effect. Some pharmacologists think that's what makes victims believe they were under mind control. They don't remember."

"So Ziegler did something with scopolamine?" James asked.

"Sort of. He took what some people believe the Devil's Breath does and synthesized a way to actually do it."

"Oh boy," Quinn mumbled.

Grandpa's head tipped to one side. "Ziegler created a new drug?"

"Yeah. He calls it Zieglopam," Sydney said with a roll of her eyes. "But it's not just the drug, it's the delivery of it that's crazy brilliant." When Quinn's eyebrows shot up, Sydney added quickly, "Not that I condone what he did. Because, you know, mind control . . ."

"You have a professional appreciation for Dr. Ziegler's achievement," Grandpa said diplomatically.

"Yes. Thank you. That's what I'm trying to say." Sydney blinked at him as if rebooting. A quick headshake and she was back on track. "Ziegler figured out a way to use nano-technology to control minds."

Quinn's eyes widened. "What?"

"You mean like nanobots?" James asked.

"Sort of? More like a nanoshell. Hang on. I brought a visual aid." Sydney picked up a box of malted milk balls from the counter. She fished one of the round candies from the box and held it up between her thumb and forefinger.

"Obviously a nanoshell is a lot smaller 'cause, you know, this isn't really the definition of nano, you know what I mean?" She smiled and waited for a response.

"Got it," Quinn said. "Smaller than a Whopper."

Sydney held the box out toward them. "Anybody want one?"

The men declined. Quinn, however, was always up for chocolate. "Sure. Thanks." Sydney handed her the box.

James sighed in mild exasperation and shifted from one foot to the other.

Sydney bit the Whopper in half with her front teeth and held it up again. "The biopolymer shell is like the outside chocolate layer of this malted milk ball. Instead of the crunchy part in the center, it's hollow."

Quinn tossed a Whopper into her mouth as she listened.

"Each nanoshell carries a tiny amount of Zieglopam. Millions of these nanoshells are suspended in the green solution you liberated from Ziegler's safe."

"What do these nanoshells have to do with scopolamine?" James asked.

"It's the delivery system for the Zieglopam. The main difference is Zieglopam suppresses the part of the brain in charge of moral reasoning." Sydney popped the other half of the Whopper in her mouth.

"Why don't you start at the beginning," Grandpa said patiently. "Say someone has been injected with Ziegler's solution. What happens?"

"The nanoshells are filled with Zieglopam, right? But instead of the Zieglopam working on the brain as soon as it's injected, it stays inside the shell. So it's just circulating around the body in the bloodstream with the red and white blood cells, platelets, and stuff until it's released."

"And when is that?" Quinn asked before eating another malted milk ball.

"Whenever the person who injected the nanoshells triggers

it to. The nanoshell has a biochemical fuse that's activated when it's hit by a low-power radio pulse set at a very specific frequency. That fuse causes the nanoshell to break down. The drug is released into the bloodstream and carried to the brain. Moral reasoning is compromised and the person will do any heinous thing they're told to do. They don't even try to control themselves because they don't care."

"So these nanoshells could be in a person for hours before the Zieglopam is released?" James asked.

"Sure. Days. Weeks even. There's no reason to believe it couldn't be indefinite."

Grandpa scratched his cheek. "The injected person effectively becomes a sleeper agent. Like *The Manchurian Candidate*."

Sydney nodded. "I think that's the idea. You inject the solution with the nanoshells into a person. Before you release them back into the wild, bomb them with a drug like Versed to induce short-term amnesia. They wouldn't even remember you shot them up with anything in the first place," Sydney said. "They go on with their lives. At the appropriate time and/or place, the Zieglopam's released, they're told what to do, and they do it. No questions. No hesitations."

"Truly mind control," Quinn said.

"What about these radio frequency pulses?" James asked. "Can they travel far?"

"Not really." Sydney pushed a pile of papers, a couple of journals, and an open comic book to the side as she rummaged for something. "Here we go." She picked up her phone. "We fabricated a microchip based on a schematic on Ziegler's thumb drive. It's attached to the SIM card in the victim's cell phone. It emits a pulse when it receives a signal from a phone call. The victim's phone needs to be nearby, but the person making the call can do it from anywhere. Once the Zieglopam takes effect, the person in control can call again and give voice commands over the phone."

"The applications are endless," Grandpa said.

Quinn looked at her grandfather. "Some high-level government official could be kidnapped and pumped full of this stuff. He's released, not remembering any of it. At some time down the road, he's in a meeting or something, gets triggered, and kills everyone in the room."

"Ordinary people could become murderers or armed robbers or suicide bombers or extortionists or whatever." James blew out a breath. "Not good."

"Does it work?" Quinn asked and tipped her head toward the phone in Sydney's hand. "You said you fabricated the chip. Have you synthesized the nanoshells and drug, too?"

"Yes. We used the formula and studied the prototype you swiped from Ziegler's facility in Frankfurt. We've tested it on mice to make sure the nanoshells don't cause problems like embolisms or trigger the immune system. So far, so good. We know the drug releases into the bloodstream, but we can't exactly test mind control on a mouse. We're not ready to use human subjects yet. Don't want to fry somebody's brain, or have them never come out of it or something if it doesn't work the way it's supposed to."

"And we all thank you for that," Grandpa said.

Sydney acknowledged him with a tip of her head. "We found some video of a test Ziegler did, though." She went to her computer and tapped at the keyboard. The four clustered around the monitor. A video, with a date and time stamp from six months earlier, began to play.

A camera mounted in an upper corner looked down into a waiting room. Half of the chairs lining the walls were occupied. Most of the people stared at their phones. An elderly gentleman flipped through a magazine.

A young woman, clearly bored, brushed her thumb over the screen of her phone. When it rang in her hand, she answered, paused, and asked if anyone was there. She shrugged, ended the call, and went back to scrolling.

"Nothing interesting happens now," Sydney said and advanced the recording, "other than the guy over there on the left who gets a piece of gum from his pocket. I couldn't tell if it was spearmint or Juicy Fruit. I don't think it was bubble gum since he doesn't blow . . . any. . ." She glanced over her shoulder. "That's not important," she mumbled and turned back around.

The time stamp indicated ten minutes had passed when the recording returned to regular speed. The young woman's phone rang again. She answered and, this time, remained silent as she listened intently. Without an acknowledgement or farewell, she ended the call and put the phone in her purse. Then she stood, turned around, and grabbed the chair she'd been sitting in by the armrests. She lifted it over her head and charged at the elderly man with the magazine.

Abject terror contorted his face as she brought the chair down on him. Unable to raise his arms in time, it caught him on the head. He crashed to the floor. Blood gushed from the gash the metal chair had opened on his forehead.

She stood over him and raised the chair again. He curled into a ball and moaned when she smashed him with it.

Quinn clamped a hand over her mouth as she watched in horror.

"Dear God," Grandpa whispered.

At the same time several people jumped to their feet to intervene, two large men sprinted into the room. They disarmed the woman of her chair and hustled her out through the door from which they'd entered.

A man in a white lab coat and a woman in scrubs flew into the room. Quinn recognized him immediately. "That's Ziegler."

Ziegler dropped to his knees beside the battered, unmoving man on the floor.

The screen went black.

They remained silent, stunned by the act of brutality they'd just witnessed.

"I hope he's okay," James said finally.

"Me, too. And I hope she came out of it without any long-term effects," Quinn added.

Sydney snatched a clipboard from the counter and flipped through several pages. After consulting one particular page, she said, "According to Ziegler's notes, the older guy had busted ribs, a collapsed lung, and a concussion. The test subject was given midazolam, which, among other things, produces short-term amnesia. When she 'woke up,' they told her she fainted in the waiting room. Other than saying she didn't know why she'd fainted in the first place, she never questioned what happened. They monitored her for a little while, gave her some juice, and sent her on her merry way. Ziegler doesn't say what happened to her after that."

"My guess is he would probably have followed up, but was arrested before he could," James said.

"It's a good thing he was, too." Grandpa's expression was grave when he said, "Think of the devastation this would bring if it fell into the wrong hands."

Quinn shivered at the prospect.

"The drug should do the trick and draw Borovsky out." James turned to Grandpa. "Are you still okay with us using it as bait?"

"Yes. We control both the prototype and the formula. And we're working with the Germans. Ziegler is currently being held at a remote, highly secure undisclosed location. There's no danger of him reconstructing and distributing it."

Quinn imagined Ziegler's "undisclosed location" wasn't exactly a resort.

"Now that we know exactly what this stuff does, we can get the message to Borovsky that it's for sale," James said. "I'll call my contact and get it rolling."

"Thanks for the Whoppers, Sydney," Quinn said and set

the box on the open comic book. Her gaze drifted over the colorful drawings and she did a double take when something caught her eye. She picked up the comic book and held it closer to her face. "Who's this guy?" she asked. "That's not Thor, is it?" He was huge and muscled, a red cape billowing out behind him. Curly ram horns stuck out of the sides of his helmet.

"No, that's Perun the god of thunder and lightning. He's like a Russian Thor." Sydney's words began to pour out. "He first appeared in *Captain America* in 1989. He was originally part of the Supreme Soviets who go after—"

"That's great, Sydney, but what I'm interested in is that," Quinn said and pointed at the double-headed battle axe Perun held in his massive, meaty hand.

"Yeah, Thor has his hammer. Perun has his axe. Later, he has a hammer and sickle, too, you know, as an obvious reference to the Soviet—"

"Anatoly had a tattoo on his forearm almost exactly like that axe," James said as he peered at the page from over Quinn's shoulder.

"Exactly!" Quinn said, excited that James had made the same observation. She wasn't sure if Perun and the axe tattoo on Anatoly's arm had anything to do with anything, but her brain was already buzzing with possibilities.

"Uh-oh," James said. "I've seen that face before."

"As have I, my boy," Grandpa said. "The best thing to do is sit her down at a computer and let her release her inner bloodhound on an unsuspecting Internet."

Quinn shrugged and set the comic book down where she'd found it. "He's not wrong."

"Agreed," James said. "What are you thinking, Quinn?"

The vague impressions swirling in her mind coalesced into a tangible thought. "What if Anatoly, Viktor, and Yefimov all had the same tattoo?"

"Like a gang tattoo," James said.

Grandpa nodded. "Displaying their membership and loyalty."

"Exactly," Quinn said. "If we find out all three have the same tattoo, maybe we can uncover some connections that give us more intel on Borovsky."

"Like Borovsky sees himself as Perun, Russian god of thunder?" James asked.

Quinn lifted a shoulder. "You never know. Maybe we'll find out Borovsky's studied Slavic mythology. Maybe Anatoly's tattoo has nothing to do with Perun or Borovsky and he's just really into axes."

"All are possibilities. I have every confidence you will discover the true meaning of Anatoly's tattoo," Grandpa said, his eyes shining with pride.

"Me too," James added with a smile. Turning his attention to Sydney, he said, "Thanks for bringing us up to speed on Ziegler's research. We'll be in touch."

"You're welcome and okay," Sydney stammered, clearly perplexed by the strange and sudden turn the briefing had taken.

"You've done an excellent job with all of this," Grandpa said. "Really. Well done. You are a credit to the DS and T."

Relief overtook Sydney's features as she heaved a huge sigh. "Thank you, sir."

Grandpa dipped his head. "Carry on."

Quinn had to force her steps to remain steady and measured as they walked for the door. Once outside the lab, they stopped. A bundle of nervous energy, she bounced on the balls of her feet.

James grinned at her. "You're about to explode."

"I am. I gotta go." She rose up on her tiptoes and kissed James on the lips. Then she pecked her grandfather's cheek, spun on her heel, and race-walked down the corridor.

Grandpa's voice echoed when he called out, "Happy hunting, angel."

She turned around and walked backward long enough to wave and say, "Thanks." Facing forward again, she made quick time returning to the library. She had research to do.

Chapter Twenty-Five

Quinn sat down at her desk and ordered her thoughts.

She would first pursue the thing that had caused her brain to itch in the first place: Anatoly's tattoo. Pen in hand, she sketched a crude outline of the double-headed battle axe on a yellow legal pad. She eyed her rendering and snorted. It would never be mistaken for a da Vinci.

Under the axe, she wrote the word *Perun* using both Latin and Cyrillic characters.

Next, she composed an email to Reem asking if there were any photos of the three men's tattoos available for her to examine. In the U.S., tattoos could be photographed when a person was arrested and booked. She hoped the police in Russia had a similar procedure in place.

Email sent, she set off on a quest to learn more about Perun. Some sources indicated the storm god sported silver hair and a golden mustache. In addition to his axe, he was also associated with arrows of thunder and lightning, fire, eagles, horses and carts, and hammers. It came as no surprise to read that, like Thor's hammer Mjölnir, Perun's axe always returned to his hand after smiting evildoers.

The archeological evidence pointing toward an ancient cult of Perun grounded the mythology in real life. The ruins of a shrine to Perun had been discovered on the island of Peryn not far from Novgorod in the 1950s. It consisted of a circular ditch in the ground with eight round fire pits positioned at equidistant points corresponding to points on the compass. A tall oak idol was likely erected in the hole at the center of the circle. She copied the diagram of the site on her legal pad and jotted a note indicating the layout was similar to symbols of Perun called "thunder marks." Ancient devotees had hewn such marks on wooden beams of their homes to protect them from lightning strikes.

While new bits of trivia about Perun were now and forever lodged in her brain, it still didn't get her any closer to Borovsky. Her research path was blocked until she heard back from Reem, so she spent the next hour reviewing books for possible inclusion in the library's collection.

Duty performed, she checked her email and whispered a quiet "yay" when Reem's response included photos of the three men's tattoos. Viktor's and Yefimov's had been taken at the time of their arrests. Anatoly's tattoos had been documented posthumously.

Quinn studied each tattoo. Her disappointment at not finding Perun's axe on Yefimov or Viktor was short-lived when she recognized a different tattoo on all three. It was the circular thunder mark she'd run across earlier.

They *were* linked to each other—and to Perun.

Were they modern-day devotees of an ancient Slavic god? Perhaps. Given their associations and occupations, it was more likely they were declaring loyalty to their crime syndicate and its boss, Konstantin Borovsky. Why Perun? Was Borovsky the modern-day devotee? Had he grown up hearing the stories of Perun's exploits? Maybe he'd lived near Peryn at some point in his life. Maybe he still did. For all she knew, Borovsky was an egomaniac who considered himself akin to the supreme deity in the Slavic pantheon.

She pictured him as a burly, cape-wearing axe-wielder who lived in an underground lair alit by flaming torches.

Borovsky probably hadn't achieved peak Bond villain status, but what if Perun was his "brand"? She searched the Russian State Registration Chamber to see if any foreign or domestic corporations included Perun or Peryn in their names.

A corporation with the generic-sounding name of Perun Industries popped up.

"Interesting," she said to herself. She blew a soft raspberry when she noted corporate officer and director information would have to be requested in person. Half the people in the building she worked in could hack into the database, but triggering an international incident was not on the day's agenda. She would be good and go through the channels. Someone from the Moscow station could make the request on her behalf.

She dropped her pursuit of corporate information for the time being and decided to tug at the yacht thread again. She went to the Cayman Islands shipping registry, where half of the world's super yachts were registered.

There was no singular list of yacht names she could peruse, but there was an option of searching vessel name availability. If she typed in a name and it wasn't available, that meant there was a boat with that name. Grabbing her pen again, she wrote a list of twenty names with Perun in them, including Perun's Axe, Perun's Hammer, and Thunder of Perun.

She worked through the list and came up empty. Frustrated, she chucked her pen at the notepad. Her quest really was quixotic. The rational part of her brain told her to stop. Their best chance of drawing Borovsky out was with Ziegler's drug. Finding out the name of his yacht wouldn't be a bad thing, but it wasn't mission critical.

But the bloodhound librarian in her wouldn't let go that easily. She reviewed her notes and made another list. When it was exhausted, she'd call it a day.

Name after name came back available.

Until one didn't.

Her eyebrows knotted as she stared at the screen. What just happened? Had she made a mistake? She typed **Perun's Chariot** again. The response came back as it had before: unavailable.

She tried not to get too excited. Her finding was based on supposition. She had exactly zero proof that a vessel called *Perun's Chariot* registered in the Cayman Islands had any connection to Borovsky whatsoever. That wasn't going to stop her from presenting everything she'd uncovered to Aldous Meyers. If he believed it actionable, he could coordinate with various international maritime agencies and track down *Perun's Chariot*. There might even be a satellite or two involved in the hunt.

She typed up a report and attached it along with the tattoo photos to an email to Meyers. Her empty stomach rumbled as she clicked **send**. She checked her watch and was surprised at how late it was. No wonder she was starving.

James had to be waiting for her in his office. Quinn locked her computer, secured her work papers in her desk, and snatched her bag from a drawer. She bid good night to her coworkers and swept out the library door.

She spotted James halfway down the hall. His eyes lit up when he saw her. "Hey. I was just on my way to see if I could drag you away from your research. I'm hungry and it's your turn to make dinner."

When they met, he turned around and walked with her. She looked up at him, side-eyed. "The thrill is already gone, huh? All I am to you now is a cook?"

He heaved a faux sigh of resignation. "It was bound to happen."

She lowered her voice and said, "And here I was planning on making fajitas wearing nothing but an apron and a smile."

Her hand shot out and grabbed his arm when he stumbled. Once he was steady again, he gave her a dumbfounded look. "You're pure evil, you know that, right?"

The expression she wore was the picture of innocence. "I have no idea what you're talking about."

"Uh-huh." He gazed down at her. "I know what you're up to. You're trying to distract me. We get home and, you know"—he waved his hands around—"do stuff. The next thing we know, it's too late for you to cook and we're ordering takeout."

Alone in front of the elevators, Quinn pressed the down button. "Would eating Chinese naked in bed together be such a bad thing?"

His eyes crossed a little. "No. Not a bad thing. At all. Ever."

"So my plan worked."

His enthusiastic grin was infectious.

"Absolutely."

Chapter Twenty-Six

Several days later, James's ringing phone awoke Quinn from a sound sleep. While he fumbled with his phone and cleared his throat, she blinked and squinted against the morning light filtering into their apartment bedroom. Clearly irritated by the commotion, Rasputin leaped off the bed and stalked out.

"Hello." James sat up and, after a brief pause, replied to the caller in Russian.

Her addled state didn't allow her to catch much of what James was saying.

He swung his legs over the side of the bed, grabbed the pen that lived on his nightstand, and began to write. As he did, he made the kind of monosyllabic grunting noises people make to let the other person know they're furiously writing down every detail of imparted information.

Curiosity piqued, Quinn was now fully awake and caught bits and pieces of what James said. He thanked the caller and offered to buy him a drink the next time he was in town. The call ended.

"I take it that was your Moscow contact," she said.

"Mm-hmm. Just as we suspected, there's no way for us

to contact Borovsky directly." Their conversation stalled when James got up and used the bathroom. "Got the info on one of his lieutenants, a guy named Ivan Ovechkin," he said as he exited. "We'll start with him."

"Good. Now that we know *Perun's Chariot* belongs to Borovsky and assuming he's on it, we can start planning the op to meet up with him in person."

James headed for the kitchen while Quinn took her turn in the bathroom. While she washed her hands, inspiration struck. Excited by her idea, she hurried from the bathroom and found James at the sink, filling the coffeepot with water.

"Let me take point," Quinn said.

James looked at her with a puzzled expression.

"On the op. I should be the one to meet with Borovsky."

"No, you shouldn't."

Her lips pressed together in a deep frown. "Not this again," she said through clenched teeth.

"Not what again?"

"Your overprotective streak." Her aggravation burned hot. "I'm a trained operative, the same as you."

He slapped the faucet off. "I'm fully aware of that."

"And yet you still treat me like I'm the librarian you met at the Westside Library a year and a half ago."

"That's a load of crap." He dumped the water into the coffeemaker and jabbed at the start button. Then he whirled on her, his eyes blazing. "And completely unfair. Did I say you weren't ready when we were tasked to break into Ziegler's office? No. I was thrilled to have you by my side. And what about Saint Petersburg? Never once did I even *hint* you shouldn't go in with the rest of us."

"That doesn't mean it hasn't come back now." Her volume had risen to equal his.

Still clad in only his boxers, he crossed his arms over his bare chest and widened his stance in defiance. "It hasn't."

"So you have some other reason why I shouldn't take point?"

"As a matter of fact, I do. Borovsky is a Russian man. He's never going to give a woman the time of day. We've got to go at him from a position of strength and respect. And that means man to man. That means me. I take point."

Quinn shook her head. "No. That's exactly the opposite of what I think we should do."

"So now you're an expert on Russia? After being there once? I lived there, you know."

She rocketed so beyond livid, her vision went wonky before an eerie calm settled over her. In a dispassionate tone, she said, "I know I'm not an expert on Russia. And you don't have to remind me you lived there. I missed you every stinkin' day you were gone."

He opened his mouth, but she cut him off before he could utter a sound.

"So you don't think I know enough about anything to have a good reason why I should take point, huh? Well, I do because I know men. You said it yourself. Borovsky loves beautiful women. I'm no supermodel, but I like to think I clean up pretty good."

James's shoulders lowered a fraction.

"And I agree with you that a super-rich, super-powerful man like Borovsky won't respect me because I'm a woman. That's the entire point. We use his machismo to our advantage. He'll assume I'm just some weak-willed woman he can overpower with his animal magnetism. If I bait it so he thinks he can get the formula *and* I'll succumb to his charms, he'll be begging me to meet *him* in person."

Now it was Quinn's turn to stand with her feet set apart and arms folded in front of her.

James blew out a long breath and his gaze lowered to the floor. His arms now hanging limply at his sides, his voice was soft when he said, "The day of our wedding, right after

I finished getting ready, your dad took me aside. He said he wanted to talk to me about something. I thought it was going to be a reprise of his 'You hurt my daughter, I hurt you' speech. It wasn't that at all."

Quinn cocked her head, baffled by the abrupt change in topic.

His focus moved from the floor to his hands, where the thumb of one rubbed into the palm of the other. "He said marriage wasn't always going to be tickle fights and fireworks."

Quinn's ill humor ebbed. "He used those exact words?"

"Mm-hmm."

"I don't know if I should laugh or gag at the idea of my parents having tickle fights." She let loose with an exaggerated shudder.

He chuckled and took a step toward her. "Anyway, he told me when we engage in 'verbal combat'—his words again—and I hurt your feelings, I need to apologize and ask for forgiveness."

"My mom told me pretty much the same thing," she said and shuffled closer to him. "Now I see it was all a conspiracy."

"For our benefit."

"Yeah." At the same time, they each took a final step that bridged the distance between them. James laced his fingers behind her back while her hands rested on his bare shoulders. "It's hard to argue with a couple who've been married for almost forty years," she said.

"It is, so I'm going to take their advice and apologize. Your reason for wanting to take point is brilliant. I'm sorry I dismissed it before I even heard it. And I'm sorry I made that snarky comment about you and Russia and stuff. It's not true and I was out of line." In his face, she saw nothing but absolute sincerity when he said, "Please forgive me."

"I do." As she stared at a spot on his chest, her mother's

words about both sides saying hurtful things echoed in her mind. "And I'm sorry I jumped down your throat about you still being overprotective. You're right. You've never tried to keep me from being a full team member. If anything, you've been incredibly supportive. I apologize." She cut her eyes up to his face again. "Forgive me?"

He dipped his head and caught her up in a tender kiss. "Of course."

She brought his mouth down on hers again and gave him a scorching one of her own. Her belly clenched as every cell in her body seemed to pulsate. She broke the kiss long enough to whisper, "I think this is the part where we make up."

James lifted her and set her bare bottom on the kitchen counter. "The best part."

Quinn wrapped her legs around his waist and kissed him with abandon, reveling in the erasure of their height difference. It was delicious, being at his level: eye to eye, face to face, chest to chest. When she took his lower lip between her teeth and sucked, he gripped her hips and slid her to the edge of the counter. She threw her head back and gasped when he moved into her, writhing and bucking against him as her pleasure built.

He released a feral growl when she raked her fingernails across his bare back. He leaned her back and thrust deeper. She grew more frantic until she arched and nearly blacked out as she expelled a long, lusty moan.

James tensed, called out to a higher being, and then relaxed.

Quinn panted for breath, her teeth tingling, and her every nerve buzzing. In the background, three long beeps pierced through her warm, happy haze. "Coffee's ready," she murmured.

"Caffeine is good in the morning." He kissed the tip of her nose. "But *you* are better."

"Ditto." She breathed a quiet laugh. "I'm not sure I'll be

able to slice mushrooms on this section of the counter ever again without getting hot and bothered, though."

"We have lots of other counter space."

"What happens when we've done this on every inch of it?"

"We move."

She laughed and kissed his neck. "Sounds good to me." She slapped his butt and said, "Come on. We need to get to work. We have an op to plan."

A week later, Quinn sat on the sofa of their apartment and eyed the phone lying on the coffee table. It belonged to her recently conceived alter ego, Victoria Chamberlain. She wiped her palms over her thighs to dry the nervous perspiration and reminded herself that slipping into a new persona was something she'd been trained to do. Plus, James and her grandfather were always insisting she was a natural at it. Still, butterflies swooped in her gut as she readied to call Borovsky's lieutenant, Ivan Ovechkin.

The thing was, the stakes were incredibly high and she didn't want to blow it. They wanted to bust Borovsky before he could reestablish his Saint Petersburg ring.

Quinn pictured the faces of all the children who had been trapped in that terrible life. Her resolve steeled, she picked up the phone. She tapped the numbers on the screen and put the phone to her ear. As she listened to the ring tone, she locked eyes with James sitting on the edge of his armchair. His steady gaze and encouraging nod imbued her with confidence.

The moment she heard a voice at the other end of the line, she became Victoria Chamberlain.

"Hello. I'm trying to reach Mr. Ivan Ovechkin." She lowered the register of her voice a touch, making it warmer. Richer. Smoother. "I was told I could reach him at this number." Her words were refined and unhurried.

"Who is this?" The man's voice snapped with annoyance.

"Oh, good. You speak English." She released a relieved, throaty chuckle. "My Russian is abysmal."

"Who is this?" He was growing more aggravated with each passing second.

"Forgive me. Where are my manners? My name is Victoria Chamberlain. I have an item for sale I believe Mr. Konstantin Borovsky is interested in purchasing. I was told Mr. Ovechkin could relay a message to him on my behalf." She paused and waited for him to confirm his identity. When the silence dragged on, she said, "Am I speaking with Mr. Ovechkin?"

"What is this item?"

Whomever she spoke with was trying to keep the upper hand.

Allowing real irritation seep through, Quinn said, "I'm not going to have the same conversation with every lackey on the food chain. Either I speak with Mr. Ovechkin right now, or you get to explain to Mr. Borovsky how you let the chance to purchase sole control of a newly developed drug slip through your fingers because you were too busy playing games." She let her verbal barrage hang between them before adding a caustic, "Good luck with that."

"I am Ivan Ovechkin." He still sounded grumpy, but the interest that had crept into his voice was unmistakable.

Her tone turned silky again. "Now that wasn't so hard, was it?" Channeling her inner Victoria, Quinn crossed one leg over the other and continued. "The drug was developed by Dr. Dieter Ziegler. I believe Mr. Borovsky was at one time one of the parties interested in purchasing it."

"Perhaps."

"Let's not start that again," she said with a sigh. "I'm not going to play this idiotic cat-and-mouse game with you. Good-bye, Mr.—"

"Wait," he said with a panicked edge in his tone. "A mind-control drug?"

"Yes."

"Mr. Borovsky is interested."

"Good. When can I meet with him?"

"It is not so simple. I must have proof drug works."

"That's fair. I can send you a video of Ziegler's own tests."

"No. That will not prove what you say you have is real drug."

"Are you accusing me of trying to sell you a fake?"

"No. But I will not waste Mr. Borovsky's time if it does not work as promised." Real fear colored his words when he added, "That would be bad for me."

They had prepared for this scenario. "I see your point. I already have appointments to meet with several other potential buyers over the course of the next week. After that, I know I'll be exhausted from all that traveling, so I'll be going on holiday in Monaco."

Maritime authorities had tracked *Perun's Chariot* to the Mediterranean. Monaco was a magnet for super yachts like Borovsky's. The belief was he would be willing to go there since he could hide in plain sight.

"I adore sunbathing at their topless beaches," she purred. "No tan lines."

Her eyes landed on James, who gaped at her. From the sharp intake of air she heard on the phone, she imagined Ovechkin to be similarly slack-jawed. She shot James a wink. It was just too easy.

"Perhaps you can meet me there?" After a brief pause, as if consulting her calendar, Quinn said, "I can see you a week from Friday."

"That is acceptable."

"Wonderful," she cooed. "I'll be in touch regarding the exact when and where. *Ciao.*"

She touched the screen and tossed the phone on the cushion. Relief and excitement rippled through her.

"Nicely done," James said.

"Thank you." She rose from the sofa, moved to his lap, and slipped an arm behind his shoulders. "How's your French?"

"Language? Passable. Kiss? You tell me." He threaded his fingers into her hair and drew her into a deep, open-mouthed kiss that left her twitchy and throbbing.

"I'm not sure." Their breaths mingled as she gazed into his eyes and rubbed his nose with hers. "I'm gonna need a *lot* more data. You know. For science."

His lips curled up in a tiny smile. "If you insist," he said and gave her a kiss that dissolved her bones. "You know. For science."

Chapter Twenty-Seven

Quinn stood on the balcony of their opulent suite at the Hôtel de Paris in Monte Carlo and looked out at the bright, white yachts dotting the Mediterrancan. Some cruised the water, leaving a wake of white foam behind them. Others were anchored and unmoving, like gleaming pearls scattcred across a pillow of bluc velvet.

Various intelligence sources confirmed one of the yachts crowding the coast of Monaco was *Perun's Chariot*. And although those same sources couldn't definitively confirm Borovsky was on board, she knew he was. She could feel it.

James stepped out onto the veranda and stood next to her. "Ovechkin will be here in a few minutes."

A ball of nerves and excitement knotted in her chest. She turned and looked at his profile, his eyes fixed on a point in the distance. His jaw and cheeks were covered with stubble. The several days of growth gave him a rougher edge, commensurate with his role as Cade Burton, Victoria Chamberlain's bodyguard and right-hand man. "Darius and Sydney are in position?"

"Mm-hmm. Sydney has the fake Zieglopam ready to go. And Darius is down the hall with his room service cart."

"Good." She patted the French twist at the back of her head. "And I look okay?"

His gaze lingered over her white formfitting blouse, black pencil skirt, and black high heels. "You look great. Just the right balance of professional, polished, and sexy." His tone turned snooty. "Very Victoria Chamberlain."

"Victoria thanks you ever so much," she said, mimicking him.

James held his arms out to the side. "How about me?"

She cast a critical eye over his shiny blue suit and open-collared shirt. "Mostly hit man with a little lounge singer thrown in for good measure."

"So perfect for Cade the bodyguard."

"Absolutely. But if that suit ever shows up in James Anderson's closet, his wife will promptly remove it and kill it with fire."

His smile was lopsided. "Noted."

They turned and went inside. "Hey, Sydney," Quinn said, leaving the door open to allow the warm sea air fill the room. "James says you're all set."

Sydney futzed with the vials and hypodermic needles on the table, adjusting them until they lined up in a tidy row. She glanced over her shoulder and said, "Oh, hey, Quinn. Yeah. I'm ready." With an embarrassed, unsure smile, she added, "I hope I don't blow it. I don't get out in the field very often."

Oddly enough, knowing someone was more nervous than she helped calm Quinn. She looked Sydney directly in the eye. "You'll be great. You know more about Zieglopam than anyone. Just answer Ovechkin's questions and he won't have any other choice but to believe we're in possession of Ziegler's formula."

At the knock on the door, the tension in the room ratcheted up. Quinn watched James as he went to the door. Before her eyes, his features hardened and gaze sharpened as he morphed into Cade Burton. At the same time, she felt her back stiffen and her chin rise. She took her place at the center of the room and clasped her hands.

James clutched the doorknob and looked at Quinn. In his eyes, she only saw Victoria's bodyguard silently waiting for her to signal when to open the door.

Quinn's nerves gave way as Victoria took over. She dipped her chin.

James opened the door.

Three men stood in the hallway. She assessed them instantly and came to the rapid conclusion the man in the center was Ivan Ovechkin. The two huge, beefy men of similar size and body style to Viktor and Anatoly were obviously the bodyguards.

Quinn smiled and took two steps forward. "Mr. Ovechkin, thank you for coming. You're welcome to have your friends join you, although I must insist they surrender their weapons to Cade until our business is concluded. I wouldn't want you getting any ideas about forcing me to give up the formula at gunpoint."

Ovechkin nodded at his men. He walked into the room and the bodyguards filed in behind him. They removed their pistols from the holsters at their hips and handed them to James.

Quinn arched an eyebrow and said in a mildly scolding tone, "You too, Mr. Ovechkin."

He stared at her for a moment, as if testing her resolve. When she returned it without a single blink, he slid a pistol from a shoulder holster and handed it over. With a suppressor attached to the muzzle, it was the most impressive and disturbing of the lot.

"Wonderful," Quinn said and swept her hand toward the ornate light blue sofa. "Now, with that unpleasantness over, please have a seat."

While Ovechkin moved to the sofa and sat, James carried

the handful of weapons to where Sydney was set up. He removed the magazines and ejected the chambered round from each pistol. Then he meticulously lined up weapons and ammunition on the table.

"Cade, if you could call room service and tell them we're ready for our refreshments, please."

"Yes, ma'am."

James went to the room's telephone and picked up the receiver. As he murmured into it, Quinn perched on the edge of the sofa's matching chair, angled her legs to one side, and crossed her ankles. Queen Elizabeth had nothing on her.

Quinn studied Ivan Ovechkin. The man didn't look like a Russia mafia lieutenant. His sandy blond hair was parted on one side, cut shorter on the sides and a little longer on the top. His features were boyish, but the telltale squint lines radiating from the corners of his gray eyes suggested he was a little older than it seemed at first glance. Dressed in khaki pants, a white dress shirt, and a blue blazer, he looked like a wealthy businessman on holiday.

Ovechkin's eyes strayed over to Sydney and her paraphernalia. "I am ready for demonstration to begin."

"Of course," Quinn said. "I've already secured a subject. He'll be here momentarily."

"Is it real mind-control drug?"

"Yes. When the drug is activated, the person will do anything you ask of them regardless of how distasteful, evil, or immoral they find it. There is no free will."

After a knock, James held the door open while Darius, dressed in the hotel's room service livery, pushed in a cart. Arranged atop it was a bottle of champagne in a silver ice bucket, accompanying crystal flutes, and a tray laden with crackers, fruits, and cheeses.

Quinn stood and gestured toward Darius. "This is

Philippe. He has agreed to be our test subject, for which he will be compensated handsomely. Isn't that right, Philippe?"

Darius offered her a stiff bow from the waist and murmured a deferential, "*Oui, madame.*"

"*Nyet*," Ovechkin barked.

Quinn's eyebrows rose. "I beg your pardon?"

"How do I know he does not pretend and we pay money for drug that does not work?"

"Because I am not a liar." Quinn gave the Russian an icy glare.

Unmoved by her feigned pique, he crossed his arms over his chest and scowled at her.

Their first choice was to get through the op without having to inject anyone with the real Zieglopam. Sydney still didn't know what the long-term effects on the brain were. But Ovechkin was forcing their hand. Fortunately, they had prepared for this exact objection.

She wasn't about to abdicate control of the demonstration by negotiating with Ovechkin, so she went for a position of strength. "Fine. We'll use one of your men here." Neither flinched. "They would never pretend the drug worked if it did not, would they?"

Ovechkin's glower ebbed as he contemplated her proposal.

She held his gaze and waited with a façade of cool indifference. This was in stark contrast to her internal strain, as evinced by the drop of nervous perspiration trickling between her shoulder blades.

"*Da*," he said finally. The tension that had built whooshed from the room. Ovechkin pointed at the taller of the two thugs. "Dmitri. You will take drug."

James slipped Darius a tip and sent him on his way with a surreptitious nod while Sydney sprang into action.

"Okay, Dmitri. Can I call you Dmitri?" Perspiration sprouted on Sydney's forehead when a stone-faced Dmitri mutely stared at her. "Never mind. And don't worry. You'll be fine." Her next words were muttered under her breath. "I think." In a louder voice, she said. "If you could take off your jacket, please."

Dmitri did as instructed, revealing a muscular upper body reminiscent of the comic book Perun.

Sydney put her hands on Dmitri's arm to guide him toward the designated treatment chair. She jerked them away like she'd touched a red-hot stove. "Wow. Okay. Muscles like granite." She stabbed a finger toward the chair. "I just need you to sit down right there. *Setzen Sie sich bitte*." Wide-eyed, she looked at Quinn and said, "I only know German."

She gave Sydney a smile and said in a calming tone, "It's fine, Marie." Sydney had asked to use the cover name in honor of the two-time Nobel Prize winner Madam Curie. "I'm pretty sure he's getting the gist of it."

Sydney huffed out a breath. "Ah. Okay. Good."

Dmitri sat and shot Sydney a dark look that said, *You hurt me, I'll kill you*.

Quinn just hoped Sydney didn't faint dead away on the spot.

To her credit, Sydney did not. If anything, the threat of bodily harm seemed to help her focus. She held up a thin rubber strip. "I'm going to tie this tight around your arm to get a vein in your elbow to pop. Then I'm going to inject the drug into the biggest one. It won't feel any different than if you were having a blood test done. *Verstehen Sie?*" Sydney slapped a hand to her forehead and muttered, "Ah, crap. I did it again."

Dmitri's lips twitched, as if fighting off a smile. "*Da*." He straightened his arm, rolled it, and braced it on the chair's armrest.

A tattoo of Perun's thunder mark was prominent on Dmitri's forearm.

Sydney snapped on a pair of latex gloves and tied the

tourniquet around Dmitri's bicep. She hunched over the exposed inner elbow and poked at it with a finger. "Wow. Your veins are like ropes. I know people who would give their right arm, no pun intended, to have—"

Quinn cleared her throat.

"Sorry." Sydney cleaned the target area with an alcohol wipe and picked up the syringe filled with the green solution. Holding it up in front of Dmitri, she asked, "Ready?"

"Yes."

Sydney removed the cover from the needle and positioned the sharp tip just above Dmitri's skin. "Okay. Here we go."

Dmitri's impassive expression never changed when Sydney jabbed the needle into his vein. The guy was a badass.

Quinn watched Sydney depress the plunger and snap off the tourniquet. As nanoshells filled with a mind-control drug invaded Dmitri's circulatory system, she wondered if he believed he could beat its effects. Did his nonchalance stem from the idea that his sheer size would overcome it? Their play had turned into an actual test of Zieglopam's efficacy. If Dmitri beat the drug, they'd have to get out of Dodge. Fast.

When the syringe was empty, Sydney removed the needle, pressed a cotton ball to the injection site, and folded Dmitri's arm back to hold it in place. "The next part is the trickiest," Sydney said. She pressed the tip of her finger to a small paper square and held it up. "You have to stick this little doodad onto the SIM card in the person's cell phone. It's kind of like an RFID tag that transmits and receives. Ziegler was a genius at nanotechnology. The stuff he was able to get onto this tiny—"

"Marie, if you could show Mr. Ovechkin where to put it on the phone, that would be great," Quinn prompted. She didn't mind having to refocus Sydney when she occasionally derailed. Because Sydney's nerves were both genuine and appropriate, they served to lend credence to her being nothing more than a scientist, not a smooth con artist or covert operative.

"Right. Sorry."

Sydney took Dmitri's iPhone and pointed at one side edge. "See this? That's where the SIM card lives. All you have to do is pop it out and stick the tag to it." She poked the end of a bent paper clip into the small hole and ejected the tray holding the SIM card. She attached the tag to the card and returned it to the slot. "No one will ever know it's there." She handed the phone back to Dmitri and picked up her own. After a few taps on her screen, she said, "The tag just sent me Dmitri's phone number. Isn't that cool?" Sydney held up her phone and grinned. "There's an app for that."

"Very impressive," Quinn said. "Are we ready to proceed?"

"Yes, ma'am. I put the app on your phone, too, so you have Dmitri's number stored as well."

"Excellent. Thank you, Marie." Quinn handed her phone to James. He took it and left the suite. "I've asked Cade to leave the room so as not to influence the test in any way, and to show how it works remotely."

Thirty seconds later, Dmitri's phone rang. He didn't get a chance to answer since it chimed only once.

"Would you like some champagne while we wait?" Quinn asked Ovechkin. "Some fruit, perhaps?" She wiggled her fingers in a wave at the second bodyguard. "Something for your friend?"

"I will have fruit," Ovechkin said. "Nothing for Yuri."

Thankful for something to do, Quinn busied herself with serving him food and drink. She tried to engage him in small talk, but his uninterested grunts ended it quickly.

The silence stretched until Ovechkin spoke unexpectedly.

"If the drug is working on Dmitri, can I make him do something now?"

"Let's find out," Quinn said. "Dmitri, I want you to hit Mr. Ovechkin in the face with your fists so hard, you break his jaw."

Dmitri crossed his arms over his chest and stared at her in defiance.

Ovechkin frowned. "It does not work."

"If I may," Sydney said. "The tag on the SIM card has to be engaged by a phone with the app for it to work."

That exchange fed into Ovechkin's obvious and growing skepticism. As time dragged on, he grew more fidgety and the strain in the room grew almost to be unbearable.

Through it all, Dmitri showed no outward signs he was affected by the drug in any way.

Quinn's adrenaline spiked when Dmitri's phone finally rang. If the drug didn't work, the whole thing was about to get ugly. The steps of their contingency plan raced through her mind as Dmitri put the phone to his ear.

Just as the young woman in Ziegler's video had done, Dmitri listened in silence. Then he set the phone down on the table, stood, and picked up Ovechkin's pistol.

All eyes watched with fascination as he slapped the magazine into the grip, and pulled back on the slide.

He whirled around, pointed the pistol directly at Ovechkin's chest, and pulled the trigger three times in rapid succession.

Eyes wide with terror, Ovechkin jerked with each spit of the gun.

Yuri lunged for Dmitri.

Quinn leapt up and stopped him with a knee to the groin. His face turned the color of an eggplant as he clutched his nuggets and gurgled.

"I'm so sorry about that, Yuri. But I can't let you interfere with the demonstration," she said.

By the time Quinn returned her attention to Dmitri, he sat unperturbed in his chair with his fingers laced together and resting on his lap.

The shock on Ovechkin's face transformed to confusion when he glanced down and frantically patted his chest. There were no bullet holes in his blazer, no spots of dark blood blooming on his white shirt.

"In preparation for our little demonstration, Cade swapped out your magazine with one loaded with blanks. He's quite the magician." During their various run-ins, James had noted all of Borovsky's henchmen carried the same kind of nine-millimeter pistol, one used by Russian military. When the time came, he was well prepared to make the swap.

Ovechkin leapt to his feet, his face mottled with rage. "You bitch!" Spittle flew from his mouth as he advanced toward her.

She snatched a pistol from the table, inserted a magazine, and chambered a round. "That's far enough." She leveled it at his chest and cocked the hammer with her thumb. "Cade didn't touch the bullets in this gun."

The door to the suite swung open. James was by Quinn's side in an instant, having covered the distance in three strides. His voice cracked like a whip when he asked, "What seems to be the problem?"

"Apparently Mr. Ovechkin didn't take too kindly to his unexpected participation in our demonstration. I'm not sure why, since we've clearly shown the drug works." She angled her head to one side and asked, "Or do you believe Dmitri would willingly put three bullets in your chest?"

Ovechkin's eyes darted from Quinn to James to her finger on the gun's trigger.

Her tone turned steely. "Sit. Down."

When he didn't move, her jaw clenched in frustration. "I can assure you if you don't sit your stupid ass down, I will fire this gun. Or are you waiting for Dmitri to jump to your defense?"

Ovechkin looked over at Dmitri. The big man watched the goings-on in absolute disinterest.

James spoke up. "The drug is still active in his system. I told him he was not to come to your aid under any circumstance." He glanced at Yuri. He was clearly unsure what to do now that he had sufficiently recovered. "Or your buddy's. You should also know he will snap your necks with his bare hands if either of you lay a finger on Ms. Chamberlain."

One of Ovechkin's eyes twitched closed and winced as if in pain. He raised his hands in surrender and backed up. Once he was seated again, Quinn decocked the hammer and lowered her arm.

From the corner of her eye, she saw Sydney slump and drag her sleeve across her forehead.

"Mr. Borovsky will pay double highest bid from competitors," Ovechkin said.

The demonstration had been a smashing success. But it still surprised her that Ovechkin made the offer without checking with his boss first. "He should know it's currently at fifteen million euros." Ziegler's documentation indicated he was originally asking ten million, so fifteen wasn't that big of a stretch.

Ovechkin paused, looked down at the floor, and then raised his gaze to her face. "He will pay thirty million euros now. He will wire transfer money to any account you wish. I take formula and drug with me."

Holy crap. They hadn't expected it to happen this quickly. "Let's not get ahead of ourselves," Quinn said. "I haven't agreed to sell it to him yet." The whole point was to meet with Borovsky in person. "My father taught me to never do business with minions. I meet with Mr. Borovsky in the flesh and hammer out a deal, or it doesn't happen at all."

"Mr. Borovsky only makes deals through his—" Ovechkin broke off.

Quinn's brow lowered, puzzled by his midsentence stoppage. She cut her eyes toward James, who squinted at Ovechkin. Something was up.

She reviewed their interactions with Ovechkin since the moment he'd walked in: the prolonged pauses, the sudden questions, the distant stares.

She stifled an "aha!" when the answer came to her.

Borovsky was there. Somewhere. If they thoroughly searched Ovechkin, they would likely find he wore an earpiece and perhaps even a minuscule hidden camera.

"Do you gamble, Miss Chamberlain?" Ovechkin asked.

That was an odd question. "I've been known to play a few hands of Texas Hold'em."

Now that she understood what was going on between Borovsky and Ovechkin, the hesitation before Ovechkin spoke made perfect sense. "Mr. Borovsky invites you to the private poker game he is hosting tomorrow night at Casino de Monte-Carlo."

"I'm not going to gamble with Ziegler's formula." He had to be caught buying it, not winning it.

"No. You asked to meet in person. He agrees."

"To negotiate the deal, not play poker."

"You intrigue him. He wants to know you better."

She bit back a snort. *I bet he does.*

"He also offers you gift of buy-in of fifty thousand euros. No strings attached."

There are always strings attached, she thought. A man like Borovsky always wanted to be in a position of power. What better way than to have her in his debt? Plus, he probably thought she would succumb to his charms and beg him to allow her to sell him the formula for next to nothing.

And beg him for other things as well.

Gross.

If playing poker meant they would finally bust Borovsky, make him pay for his crimes, and dismantle his empire, then she would jump through whatever flaming hoops necessary. Except one. Leading him to believe she would fall into his bed was an entirely different matter.

"That's very generous. Tell Mr. Borovsky I accept his invitation and look forward to meeting him."

Ovechkin rose to his feet and buttoned his jacket. "Nine o'clock tomorrow evening." He looked at Dmitri and asked, "How much longer?"

Sydney stepped forward. "It should be completely out of his system in about four hours."

"Cade, the phone please," Quinn said.

James placed it in her upturned palm.

She called Dmitri's phone. When he answered, she touched the screen once and said, "You will now go with Mr. Ovechkin. He will take you directly to Le Bar Américain here in this hotel. There, he will ply you with drinks and food until the effect of the drug wears off. If you leave without stopping at the bar, you will break both of his arms." Her gaze fell on the other guard. "And you will share all food and drink with Yuri." She ended the call and said to Ovechkin, "I think they both deserve treats, don't you?"

Dmitri stood from his chair and looked at Ovechkin expectantly. Yuri blinked at Quinn in astonishment.

From the nasty sneer he shot her, it was clear she'd not made a friend in Ivan Ovechkin. So be it. If things went the way they were supposed to, his ass would be in jail, along with Borovsky and the rest of his crew, within a few days.

Ovechkin and Yuri silently gathered their pistols and

magazines. As the three men filed out the door, Quinn called out, "*Ciao!*"

An acknowledgement of her farewell was not forthcoming.

Once the door shut, Quinn dropped into a chair and stretched out her legs. Arms hung loose over the armrests, she rested her head back and said, "That was exhausting."

James replied with a formal sounding, "Yes, miss. May I pour you some champagne as refreshment?"

She gave James a funny look.

He touched his index finger to his lips, informing her and Sydney to stay quiet. James lowered to his knees beside Quinn and put a cheek against hers. "I need to sweep the room to make sure they didn't leave any bugs," he whispered in her ear.

She nodded. "Thank you, Cade. Champagne would be lovely." It made sense. If Borovsky was willing to spy on her via Ovechkin, what was to say he wouldn't keep trying once he was gone?

James rose and headed for the bedroom to get the listening device detector.

Quinn went to an obviously befuddled Sydney and relayed to her James's concern in a whisper.

Sydney's mouth made an O, and she nodded slowly. "I'll get started cleaning up."

"That would be great," Quinn said. She went the cart and made a point of clinking the bottle to the glass as she poured the champagne.

James returned to the sitting room and began to sweep it with a handheld device.

Keeping a conversational tone, Quinn said, "I think the demonstration went well, don't you, Marie?"

"Yes, ma'am, other than the hiccup at the beginning where we had to change test subjects." Sydney carefully returned everything she'd laid out back into the appropriate slots cut into the gray foam inside a hard-sided protective case.

"If anything, it made it all the more compelling," Quinn said, keeping her eyes glued to James as he worked.

James moved the detector along the couch where Ovechkin had sat. He stopped and left it hovering in front of the end table. He went down on all fours, poked his head under the table, and craned his neck to get a look at the underside. He backed out, sat on the floor, and pointed at the front edge of the table.

Quinn nodded and said, "Cade, I'm going to go use the powder room. I'll be back in a moment." She crooked her finger asking him to follow.

"Yes, ma'am." He climbed to his feet and trailed her to the bathroom.

Safely away from prying ears, Quinn asked, "What do we do? Do we bust it, jam it, or play along?"

He ran his fingers through his hair and scratched the back of his head. "If we play along, we could use it to feed him bad intel."

"Like what? We're playing this straight until we bust him when he pays us for the drug."

"Good point. We could hedge our bets and jam it. He would just think it's not transmitting for some reason."

"True," she said doubtfully. "What if the jammer fails and he hears the real us by accident? That blows everything."

He rested his hands on his hips. "But if we bust it, he'll know we went looking for it and found it."

"Is that a bad thing? If I'm a criminal selling a mind-control drug I stole from another criminal, he might actually think more of me if we do find it and crush it. It gives me street cred."

"I love it when you get all gangsta," he said with a grin.

"But yeah, I get it. It'll make you a worthy opponent and not some naïve pushover."

She gave him a coy look. "Some guys like a challenge."

"This guy sure does." He leaned in and gave her a quick kiss. "Let's hope Borovsky does, too."

They left the bathroom and Quinn headed straight for the bug. She reached under the table and felt around until her fingers touched the small electronic component. She pried it loose and held it up to her lips. "See you tomorrow night, Mr. Borovsky." She dropped it on the floor. It popped and snapped when she crushed it under the heel of her pump.

"That should get his attention," James said.

"Speaking of attention, Victoria needs a kickass dress." She chucked him under his chin and said, "Come on, Cade. We're going shopping."

Chapter Twenty-Eight

"Hey, babe? You about ready to go?" James's voice drifted from the sitting room of their suite to where she stood in front of the bathroom mirror.

"Yeah. Just a minute." Quinn swiped her lipstick over her lower lip, slid it back into the tube, and dropped it in her silver clutch. After snatching a tissue from the box and blotting her lips, she checked her face in the mirror one more time. She wore more makeup than usual, a lot more actually. It looked pretty good if she did say so herself.

In her final act of primping, she adjusted the soft, blond curls that brushed her bare shoulders with her fingers. Satisfied there was nothing left to do, she grabbed her purse, flicked off the light, walked through the bedroom, and came to a stop just beyond the doorway.

Hands deep in the trouser pockets of his blue pinstripe suit, James stood with his back to her and gazed out the window.

When he didn't turn around, she cleared her throat and asked, "What do you think?" She bent a knee and struck a pose.

He spun around. The moment his eyes landed on her, his

jaw dropped and he openly gawped at her. He looked like he'd been beaned in the cranium with a two-by-four.

Ruby red and tight, the off-the-shoulder taffeta dress hugged her curves, showing off her hourglass figure. A cascade of diamonds hung from her neck. Large teardrop rubies hung from each ear. The dress stopped mid-thigh and in her high red heels, her legs looked longer than she had ever seen.

Earlier, when she'd tried it on in the shop, she had convinced herself that while Victoria Chamberlain would wear a killer dress like that, Quinn Ellington Anderson never would. Given the thrill she felt at observing her gobsmacked husband, though, it was time to reconsider.

"You . . . I . . . You . . ." James clamped his mouth shut, scrunched his eyes closed, and drew in a deep breath as if trying to clear cobwebs from his brain. Once he collected himself, he opened his eyes and said, "You're gorgeous. Absolutely gorgeous." He went to her and slipped his arms around her waist. "Is it wrong that I want to keep you to myself? I don't want to share you with a lech like Borovsky."

"You're sweet," she said and pecked him on the lips. "Unfortunately, that's not in the cards tonight. No pun intended." She wiped at the stain of lipstick she'd left on his lips with her thumb. "Although when we get back here tonight, you *will* have me all to yourself."

"I'm looking forward to it." His eyes clouded. "I know you can handle yourself, but trust me. One look at you and Borovsky won't want to let you go tonight."

"Then Victoria will teach him he can't always have what he wants."

"I'm serious, Quinn. Powerful men like him don't always take no for an answer."

"I know. But we'll be in a public place the entire time. And you'll be with me. He wouldn't dare try anything."

His eyes flashed fiery blue. "If he does, I can't promise I won't kill him right there on the spot."

She was equally serious when she said, "I can't promise I won't have already killed him myself." Her eyes bored into his. "He's not going to take me away from you."

The muscles that had grown taut under her hands loosened and his face relaxed into a sheepish smile. "I'm sorry. I get a little overprotective."

"Really?" she teased, relieved that the tension had dissipated. "I've never noticed."

He gazed down at her from under hooded eyelids. "Very funny."

"I thought so." Her smile softened as her eyes roamed his handsome face. "I love you."

"I love you, too," he said and gave her a kiss.

She swiped at his lipstick-covered lips again and picked up her purse. They left their suite, strolled through the elegant hotel lobby, and swept out the door.

The casino was a short walk across the Place du Casino, the grassy square the casino and hotel shared. It wasn't an easy walk though. They had to snake their way through the bumper-to-bumper supercars clogging the drive that circumnavigated the square.

They passed a low, sleek red Ferrari, its engine growling and whining as it crawled along. James nearly tripped over his own feet when he spun around to ogle it.

"Did you see that? That's a 458 Spider."

"I know, sweetie. Your dream car." She loved how animated he got whenever he came across an amazing, high-performance machine. And they were everywhere in Monaco. He was like a kid in a candy shop.

"You'd look smokin' hot in that car," he said.

"How about me in *this* dress in *that* car?"

He released a low, tortured groan. "Oh my God, baby. That's just not even fair."

"Aw, geez," Quinn heard Darius grumble through her earpiece. "Are you two at it again?"

"Again?" James said in faux offense. "I can assure you, my good man, it never stops." Like flicking a switch, his tone turned serious. "Except now. We're coming up on the front steps. You in position?"

"Affirmative. I'm in the room directly across from where Borovsky's set up camp."

"Copy," James replied.

"Sydney, how's my feed?" Quinn touched the necklace with a tiny camera secreted in one of the stones resting on her chest.

"Better than cable."

"Roger that." She slipped her hand into the crook of James's arm and held on as they climbed the steps. At the top, they passed through one of the arched doorways. With the interior's intricate designs and lush, golden opulence surrounding them, she felt like she'd instantly been transported back in time one hundred fifty years.

They traversed the black and white marble tiled floor and entered an atrium lined with light brown marble columns. Quinn's eyes were drawn upward to the wrought iron and frosted-glass skylight. It was simply breathtaking.

Her focus was pulled away from the décor when they turned left and stopped at one of the podiums at the entrance to the gaming rooms. "*Bonsoir. Bienvenue au Casino de Monte-Carlo,*" said the tuxedoed man staffing it.

"*Merci,*" Quinn said, making eye contact. "And now I've pretty much exhausted my French."

"Not to worry," he replied. She detected a slight sniff in his tone. "May I see your passport please?"

She retrieved it from her clutch and passed it over.

He glanced at the booklet and in a flash, his mild boredom evaporated. Now solicitous, he handed her passport back and said, "Mademoiselle Chamberlain, Monsieur

Borovsky has been eagerly awaiting your arrival." He raised a hand and waved over a steward. "Claude will show you to Monsieur Borovsky's table."

Quinn stepped to the side and indicated James with a hand. "My associate will be accompanying me," she stated.

The man's façade faltered. She read real fear in his eyes, as if he were terrified of the consequences of allowing James to go with her when he shouldn't.

She gave the man a disarming smile. "I'm sure Mr. Borovsky won't mind. If he does, his issue will be with me."

He seemed to relax at her willingness to take any heat, although the dots of perspiration that had sprung up above his upper lip remained. "Of course."

James handed him his passport. After a cursory glance, he returned it and said, "Thank you, Monsieur Burton."

Claude gave them a stiff bow from the waist. "Follow me, please."

Quinn fell in step behind Claude, with James by her side. Under normal circumstances, she would have slipped her hand into his, or taken his arm. But their covers wouldn't allow it, so she grudgingly kept her hands to herself.

They walked through a room filled with video slot machines. Their bright, flashing garishness was a jarring juxtaposition to the crystal chandeliers, gilded décor, and large paintings depicting eighteenth-century aristocratic life.

They left the pings and chimes of the slots behind and continued into a room dominated by gold and red. Scores of gamers played at blackjack and craps tables, their chips clattering as they made their bets.

A wide wooden desk loomed ahead with patrons queued up at it. A quick glance at a sign informed Quinn admission had to be paid to enter through the golden door. Following Claude, she and James didn't stop and sailed through. Apparently being a guest of Konstantin Borovsky had its perks.

The lounge they entered had Quinn stopping dead in her

tracks. Her breath caught as she beheld the rich blue and gold hues of the stained-glass panel in the ceiling above.

"Exquisite, is it not?" Claude said, speaking for the first time.

"Absolutely stunning," she breathed. For a moment, she completely lost herself in the paintings, reliefs, mirrors, and cartouches decorating the room.

James touched her elbow. "Miss Chamberlain?"

She blinked and gave him an apologetic smile. "Sorry. I got a little swept up."

"Perfectly understandable," Claude said. He gestured toward the middle of three sets of double doors to their left. "We have arrived."

Her mind snapped into focus when she recognized the two bulky, stone-faced men standing guard. Dmitri and Yuri. She slipped a twenty-euro note from her clutch and handed it to Claude. "*Merci.*"

"*À votre service,*" he said with a smart bow. "*Bon chance.*" He turned on his heel and retraced their steps.

Before approaching Dmitri and Yuri, Quinn made a show of once again looking up, down, and all around the room. It was during that inspection she spotted Darius playing poker at a table in a nearby room.

She sauntered over to the two sentries. "Hello, again. How are you feeling, Dmitri? No ill effects from yesterday, I hope."

He blinked, as if startled that she would ask about his health. "I am well. Thank you." His accent was heavy, but she understood every word.

"Good." She dipped her chin and gave him a sly smile. Getting on the good side of big men with guns was never a bad thing. "Did Mr. Ovechkin do what he was told?"

He grinned, something she had the feeling didn't happen very often. "*Da.* We ate and drank much."

"Perfect," she cooed. She turned and shot Yuri a wink.

"Sorry again about that incident yesterday. I hope there are no hard feelings." When his cheeks pinked and a tiny smile played on his lips, she knew she had him—both of them—wrapped around her little finger.

She waited for them to move out of the way so she could enter the room. When they didn't, she asked, "Is there a problem?"

Dmitri licked his lips. "Mr. Borovsky say no cell phones."

Her exasperated huff wasn't only for show. "Very well." She took her phone from her purse and handed it over. Turning to James, she said, "Cade, hand Dmitri your phone."

The big man looked suddenly contrite and slightly constipated. "He may not go in room."

Her eyes flashed. "What? Why?"

"Mr. Borovsky say no one but you."

It was all part of Borovsky's constant game to gain and keep the upper hand. He may have thought he was making her feel weak and vulnerable. In truth, it just pissed her off.

James gave her a tight nod. "I'll be right here."

"Thank you, Cade." She turned back to Dmitri, who tugged at the collar of his shirt with a finger. Narrowing her eyes at him, she asked, "Now what?"

"I must search purse."

She rolled her eyes and opened the bag. Dmitri peered down into it, but didn't touch any of the contents. She snapped it shut and held out her arms. "Are you going to frisk me, too?" She rotated three hundred sixty degrees. "Like I could hide a gun under a dress this tight."

In fact, she was hiding a gun under that tight dress. But by making a preemptive stink about it, she hoped it would prevent them from actually searching her. And with James being excluded from the room, she needed the Baby Glock secured to her inner thigh more than ever.

The pink in Yuri's cheeks deepened to crimson and engulfed his entire head. She found his bashfulness rather endearing.

"You go in." Dmitri put a massive hand on the doorknob and pushed open the door.

"Thank you, Dmitri." She shot James a here-goes-nothing look. "Wish me luck."

"You don't need it," James said. The electricity arcing between them was palpable. "You'll be great."

The urge to crush him in a fierce hug almost propelled her into his arms. The promise of falling asleep in them later would have to satisfy her for now.

She strolled under swags of gold-trimmed maroon velvet hanging above the doorway and entered the room.

A sixty-ish-year-old man leapt from his chair and hurried to greet her. "Miss Chamberlain. Welcome. I am Konstantin Borovsky." He took her hand, lifted it to his lips, and kissed the back of it.

She had been expecting to see a ponderous, balding man with sagging jowls and massive eyebrows. The man before her was nothing like that. His gray hair was short but thick. The light eyebrows above blue, wide-set eyes indicated that in his youth, his hair had likely been blond.

Surprisingly trim, his tuxedo fit him perfectly. In fact, all of the five men milling about the room were dressed for a night at the opera. There wasn't a tracksuit or tacky gold chain to be found.

"It's a pleasure to meet you, Mr. Borovsky," Quinn said. "Thank you for inviting me to play poker with you and your colleagues." She glanced at the men in the room and swallowed her snarky "This is quite the sausage fest" comment before it could escape. Instead, she said, "I hope my skills aren't too much of a disappointment."

He continued to clasp her hand in both of his. "Not at all. It will be a fair game since your dazzling beauty and charm have dulled our wits." From the way his face shone as his gaze traveled over her, he was pleased with what he saw.

He released her hand and turned toward the men milling about. "These are my associates."

She had the feeling that if she were to look, she would find a tattoo of Perun's thunder mark under each tuxedo sleeve.

"You know Ivan."

"Yes, of course. Nice to see you again, Mr. Ovechkin." They shook hands, although his pinched expression made it clear he didn't feel the same. He was probably still sore about what had happened the day before, not that she blamed him. She understood how having a gun fired at your chest at point-blank range could to leave one grumpy and holding a grudge.

"This is Nikolai, Pasha, Mikhail, and Steve," Borovsky said, introducing the rest of his guests.

"Steve?" she asked with a bemused smile.

"My mother was big Steve McQueen fan," Steve said.

"Ah. Of course," Quinn said.

Sydney said in Quinn's ear, "Hold as still as you can when you shake their hands. I want to get pictures to put faces and names together." This was the first time an outsider had infiltrated this deeply into Borovsky's organization. They had to make the most of the opportunity.

"Come. You will sit next to me so we can chat."

Borovsky held her chair as she took her seat at the semicircular table covered in burnt-orange felt. As she did, she scanned the room and located the two sets of doors on either side of the one she just entered through. There were also two windows that led to the outside. Whether they could be used for escape was unclear—it was likely a nasty drop.

"Thank you." She eyed the colorful chips stacked at her station. "I hope I don't go bust in the first ten minutes."

"If you do, then I will obtain more chips for you," Borovsky said. He lifted a finger. At his signal, the croupier began distributing the cards. "Unlike the rest of the tables in the casino, we will not be playing against the dealer. The management has approved, and has been compensated handsomely, I might add, for us to play a friendly game amongst ourselves."

"Sounds like fun," she said, and tossed her ante into the pot. "Your English is impeccable, by the way, Mr. Borovsky."

"Thank you. I owe it to my three decades in international business."

A young woman slipped into the room to take drink orders. She looked at Quinn expectantly.

"I'd like an unopened bottle of still water and a glass, please," Quinn said.

"Unopened," Borovsky said, sounding amused. "You are afraid something nefarious might befall your drink?"

She shrugged and shot him a disarming smile. "Just being cautious."

"Perhaps I should be offended that you do not trust me."

"You did plant a bug in my hotel suite."

He chuckled and ordered a bottle of champagne, the cost of which probably equaled her annual salary when she worked at the Westside Library. "One must do what is necessary to gain an advantage in any negotiation," he said without a hint of regret.

"Hence my caution." She peeked at her hole cards—the two of diamonds and the five of hearts—and folded.

"Excellent point. However, had I been able to find out more about you, Miss Chamberlain, I would not have had to rely on subterfuge. Why is there so little information about you available?"

"I could ask the same question about you." To her surprise, Borovsky folded his hand without a glance at his cards. The action made it abundantly clear she was his primary interest that evening, not poker.

"Touché." He angled himself toward her and rested an

elbow on the table. "Tell me how you came to be a part of such an unseemly business as selling a mind-control drug."

"Nothing is free, Mr. Borovsky." She dropped her chin and said in a husky tone, "I'll show you mine if you show me yours."

His smile turned wolfish. "I do not usually engage in *quid pro quo*. But since you intrigue me so, I will play. You answer my question, and I will answer yours."

"Fair enough." She launched into her story, keeping in mind that the best course of action was to remain as close to the truth as possible. "I was working as a reference librarian in California when a handsome patron came in looking to learn more about certain pieces of an art collection. He told me he worked for the insurance company covering the items and needed to get valuations."

"You are a librarian?"

"I used to be."

"I cannot wait to hear how a librarian became a thief."

"As we researched the pieces together, I started to grow suspicious. I had the feeling he didn't work for an insurance company, but was actually getting ready to steal the pieces we were researching. When I confronted him, he admitted I was right."

"But you did not turn him over to the authorities."

"No. He asked me to help him for a cut of the take."

"And you did this?"

She lifted a shoulder. "Librarians don't get paid very well. It was my chance to pay off my student loans and have some left over."

"You stole the pieces and sold them?"

"We did. It was quite the rush. We then successfully pulled off a number of similar jobs."

"This man. Is he the one with you now?"

She pulled a face and shook her head. "Oh no. I had to split from him. He'd fallen in love with me," she said with a sigh.

"It got way too complicated and I don't like entanglements. Plus, I was tired of splitting the money when I was doing most of the work. I invented Victoria Chamberlain, hired my own crew, and struck out on my own."

"Victoria Chamberlain is not your real name?"

"No."

"Then you are not entangled with Cade, was it?"

"No, although he's an *excellent* stress reliever." With a flirty wink, she added, "If you know what I mean."

James's response in her ear was a gruff, "I'll show you stress relief."

Quinn guessed the uncomfortable choke was Sydney's while the deep chuckle came from Darius. She schooled her features and didn't react to the goings-on in her ear. "Okay, Mr. Borovsky, your turn. How did you get your start?"

"I began my career as a *fartsovshchik*."

"I'm sorry. I'm not familiar with that term."

"As a young man in the 1970s and 80s, I sold goods from the West to my fellow Soviets yearning to be fashionable and trendy."

"You mean like Levi jeans?"

"Yes. Levi's, Lee, Wrangler. Young Soviets craved anything from the West: leather jackets, boots, Marlboro cigarettes, Japanese radios, tape players. I once sold a recording of Pink Floyd's *The Wall* for twenty rubles. That does not sound like much now, but for a common Soviet, it was almost a week's salary. It was very lucrative."

"And then everything changed when the Iron Curtain fell and the Soviet Union dissolved."

"Yes. My business model changed. I diversified. Now I own many legitimate businesses."

And a bunch that aren't, she thought.

The server returned with their drink orders and set a bottle and empty glass on the table. As requested, Quinn's bottle was unopened.

Borovsky poured champagne into the two flutes the server set out. It didn't escape her notice that they would be drinking from the same bottle, so the idea that it was somehow spiked was debunked. Regardless, she needed her head clear and her mind sharp. The glass would remain untouched.

That didn't go unnoticed. "You can soothe my disappointment at not drinking my champagne by telling me how you came to be in possession of an illicit mind-control drug."

"I suppose I could—"

"Dammit," James spat, stopping her cold. "We might have a problem. Viktor's here."

Chapter Twenty-Nine

Quinn coughed into her hand to disguise her sudden midsentence stoppage.

"Are you unwell?" Borovsky asked with concern.

She needed a few seconds to sort out the jumbled thoughts triggered by James's warning her of Viktor's presence. She unscrewed the top of her water bottle and took a sip.

"He's coming this way," James said barely above a whisper. "We don't know if he'll recognize you or not. Excuse yourself and hide out in the ladies' room until it's clear."

The memory of Anatoly pointing a gun at her through the car window flashed in her mind. From her reckoning, Viktor had only seen her back, not her face. And she'd been a redhead with glasses when she almost shot him with a tranquilizer dart at the drug flat in Saint Petersburg.

She couldn't bolt. How long would Viktor stay? She couldn't hole up in the bathroom forever. She'd have to take her chances.

"Dammit, Quinn," James hissed. "Get out of there."

"I'm fine," she croaked. Her response was as much to James as it was to Borovsky. She made a show of patting her chest and gave the Russian an embarrassed smile. "Frog in my throat."

"Viktor is talking to Yuri and Dmitri," James said.

Borovsky rested a hand on her arm. "Are you in need of assistance?"

She stopped herself from slapping his hand away. "No, thank you."

"Here he comes," James said.

Viktor stepped into the room.

Quinn lowered her chin and slowly poured her water into the empty glass, keeping her head down.

Viktor passed behind her.

James's voice teetered on the edge of desperation. "You can still bail if you need to."

"Say the word and we'll come bust you out," Darius said.

It must have been torture for them, forced to remain frozen in place in the face of her necessary silence. She quietly cleared her throat, hoping they grasped her tacit acknowledgement.

The glass filled, she had no choice but to stop pouring. As she sipped from her glass, she turned her head a little and pegged her eyes to the side to see what was going on.

Viktor bent and spoke in a hushed tone directly into Borovsky's ear.

Much like how James, Darius, and Sydney must have felt, not knowing was the worst. Had Viktor recognized her or James, and was he at that very moment ratting them out? Was she about to be exposed as an impostor to a notorious Russian mob boss? That would not turn out well.

She set her glass down and crossed her legs so the thigh with her Glock strapped to it rested atop the other. She laced her fingers together and placed them on her lap, presenting herself as merely waiting for the interruption to end. In truth, she was tense and alert, ready to draw her weapon and fire at the first sign of trouble.

Her senses heightened when Borovsky shoved away from the table and rose to his feet. He went to the man named Mikhail and gripped him by the hair. Borovsky reared Mikhail's head back and propelled it forward, smashing Mikhail's face against the top of the poker table.

"How dare you?" Borovsky growled in Russian. "You have no right to sample my product without permission."

Quinn watched in horror as Borovsky lifted Mikhail's head and rammed it onto the table. Again. And again. And again. Stacked poker chips bounced and clattered with each blow.

The other men sat stoically, their eyes downcast, as Mikhail received his epic beatdown.

The dealer trembled as the color drained from her face.

And then it ended. Borovsky stepped away from Mikhail, whose head was tilted forward and lolling to one side. One eyebrow sported a nasty, oozing gash. Blood dripped from his nose and onto his white shirt. Red splotches marred the orange felt covering the table.

Borovsky snapped his fingers and flicked a hand through the air. "Viktor, you and Pasha will remove Mikhail from my presence."

Neither spoke as they slung Mikhail's limp arms around their necks and lifted him from his chair. His legs moved under him as they carried him away, but at half speed and with no weight on them.

"Holy hell!" James said in a strangled whisper the second the men passed through the doorway. "Quinn! Are you okay?"

Borovsky tugged at his cuffs and smoothed a hand over his hair. "I apologize for the interruption. One must deal with problem employees immediately."

"It's fine." Quinn's smile felt weak and wonky. "I'm fine," she added for James's benefit.

He returned to his seat and gestured to the dealer. Hands still quaking, she slowly dealt out the cards for another round of play. To Quinn, Borovsky said, "You were about to tell me how you came to be in possession of the item I will be purchasing."

She took a sip of water and peered at her hole cards, buying herself some time to reset and refocus. She bottled up the fear and anxiety and let Victoria Chamberlain take over. "Call," she said and tossed a chip into the pot.

Once again, Borovsky pushed his cards into the muck pile without a glance. His eyes were glued to her.

"I had a student from Germany for a roommate one semester in college. Sabine. We've stayed in touch. Not long ago, she told me she was the personal assistant to this super-smart scientist who had developed an amazing drug. Like any good reference librarian, I was able to ask a bunch of questions and get more information from her about it."

Borovsky shot her a knowing look. "Personal assistant?"

The auditory memories of the doctor and Sabine doing the wild monkey dance on his couch flooded her brain. The panting. The moaning. The spanking. "*Very* personal," Quinn said.

"I see."

Quinn could see she had Borovsky completely enthralled. "Please continue."

"One second." She checked the community cards the dealer had lined face-up on the table. Nothing there was helpful, but she decided to stick it out with her pair of eights. She tossed another couple of chips into the pot. "Anyway, after I talked to Sabine, I decided to find out more about Ziegler and this drug of his. One thing about librarians is we're good at digging up information that might be otherwise hard to find."

"What kind of information?"

She shrugged and answered in a voice that made it seem like it was no big deal. "Scientific journal articles and books he'd published, transcripts of his symposium lectures, grants he'd received, honors, awards, degrees. Things like that."

"It was then you decided it was worth stealing?"

She looked past Borovsky to Nikolai, her opponent in the hand. Even with the final community card showing on the table, she still only had a pair. He pushed in a large bet. "I fold," she said and flicked her cards across the table toward the dealer.

"Yes, putting all of his disparate interests together with what Sabine had told me, I felt like he was on to something big. So I obtained schematics of the building, photos of their security badges, protocols, uniforms, schedules."

"Impressive. Did Sabine help you acquire this information?"

"No. To this day she has no idea I had anything to do with the theft." Quinn wrinkled her nose. "I do feel kind of bad she lost her job when I called the authorities on Ziegler."

"You could not have him remaking his formula," Borovsky said.

"Exactly. Once she was cleared from any wrongdoing, Sabine got a new job. I'm glad about that."

"When did you realize you had, as you Americans say, 'struck gold'?"

At that moment, Pasha slipped back into the room and returned to his seat.

"I found Ziegler's list of interested buyers—every single one very rich and very powerful. And when I learned exactly what the drug does, I knew I had hit the big time. I have to say, though, even with all my skills, I found next to nothing on you."

"And yet with so little information, here you are."

"What can I say?" Her eyes followed the cards being passed out by the dealer. "I'm good at my job."

"I can see that you are." He folded his hand and asked, "What will you do once you have millions of my euros?"

"I'm not sure. I can't decide if I want to use it to expand my business, or retire forever."

"Two very different options."

"Yes."

"Perhaps I should offer you a job within my organization," he said, his voice turning velvety. "Your talents and skills would be of great value to me. I would pay you handsomely."

She smiled and moved a shoulder. "Maybe." Glancing at him side-eyed, she said, "What would your wife think of you offering me a job?"

Borovsky started. "How do you know about her?"

It had been a stab in the dark, but she wasn't about to tell him that. "I'm good at uncovering hard-to-get information, remember?"

He leaned toward her and said rather urgently, "You have made it so I cannot forget anything about you." His tone lightened when he sat back. "My wife and I have a mutually beneficial arrangement. I live happily on my yacht and she lives happily in Russia spending my money."

She masked her revulsion and cooed, "Sounds like a win-win situation."

"It is," he said proudly.

Their conversation moved on to other topics as they returned to the poker game. She lost more hands than she won, but that was insignificant.

By midnight, Quinn was antsy and ready to leave. Their time of meet and greet had come and gone, and now she was wasting her time. Her intentions to take off remained unspoken, but as soon as she had a decent hand, she would go big and, win or lose, go home. Fifteen minutes later, she rolled up the tops of her two hole cards with her thumb and took a peek. The ace and king of hearts.

This was it.

Everyone stayed in the hand long enough to see the flop. Her ace and king didn't pair, but the two and jack of hearts put her on a potential flush. Had she not already decided this was her last hand, she probably would have folded when Ovechkin made a substantial bet. In this case, losing wouldn't be a bad thing. She pushed a tall stack of chips forward. "Call."

The dealer flipped over the turn card. The nine of spades did her no good. Ovechkin kept pushing with bigger bets. She kept calling.

All she needed was another heart on the river, the final community card, and she'd get her flush. If not, she'd at least need to pair one of her hole cards to keep from ending up with a garbage hand. She was okay with losing because it would mean she had a good excuse to leave. But winning a big hand would be a lot more fun.

The dealer flipped over the last card.

Boom.

She drew her heart.

The moment she saw that sweet, innocuous four of hearts, she used her training to stay cool and not react. None of the community cards had paired, taking away the possibility of a full house or four of a kind. A straight flush was also impossible. And her ace ensured a win on the chance Ovechkin caught a flush, too.

She peered over at Ovechkin, who sat as still as a statue with his eyes pinned on an indiscriminate spot on the table as he ruminated. Eventually, he announced his all-in and pushed the entirety of his chips toward the center of the table.

Reading his bets, she figured he had something, probably three jacks. If he had nothing and was trying to bluff, he'd chosen poorly.

She already had Borovsky eating out of the palm of her hand. But to really seal the deal, she decided to have Victoria add a little drama to the proceedings. She stared down Ovechkin and absently played with a chip as if wrestling with a difficult decision. Finally, she sighed and said, "You only live once. Call."

Ovechkin jumped from his chair like a fire had been lit under it. With an air of supreme confidence, he turned over his cards. He had exactly what she'd suspected, a pocket pair of jacks. He stretched out his arms, ready to rake in the chips.

"I believe my hearts beat your jacks." She flipped over her cards, revealing her flush.

"God, you're hot," she heard James say through her earpiece.

Ovechkin glared at her, trying to incincrate her with his eyeballs. It appeared she had cultivated in him a lifelong enemy.

Borovsky beamed at her with approval. "You are a shrewd foe who is to be taken seriously."

"It would be wise for you to remember that," she said as she leaned over to retrieve her purse. "And on that winning note, I'm going to take my leave."

"So soon?" Borovsky glanced at his watch. "It is only one o'clock. At least allow Ivan a chance to win back his chips."

She flicked a hand through the air. "Oh, he can have them all back. This was never about the money. But I really would like to get some sleep." Now on her feet, she offered Borovsky a hand. "Thank you for a lovely evening. I enjoyed getting to know you. And now I'd like to set up a time when we can conclude our transaction tomorrow."

As he had done when she'd first arrived, he clutched her hand in both of his. "You will sell me the drug?"

"I can't say no to thirty million euros."

"Wonderful." He led her away from the table and pressed her hand against his chest. She willed herself to not to pull it away. Anyone other than James touching her that way was the worst part of her job. "Please come back with me to my yacht. Tonight. I cannot bear to spend the night without you sharing my bed."

"I have a very strict rule of business before pleasure. It's part of my dislike of entanglements." *Also, ew,* Quinn thought.

"Then we complete the deal tonight, right now," he pleaded.

Her mind spun. The team wasn't ready for that. "I'm not going to do a thirty-million-euro deal in the middle of night," she said firmly. When she noted his mood darkening—the man didn't like being told no—she turned flirty again. She stepped into him and pressed her body against his. "There will be plenty of time for pleasure after our business is concluded," she purred in his ear. "I promise you. I'm worth the wait."

Borovsky shivered. His grip on her hand tightened. "What if I take you back to my ship like a pirate kidnapping a fair maiden?" he said in a playful tone.

It took every ounce of self-control not to go CIA badass on him like she had on the douchebag at the karaoke bar the night before her wedding. But ending up with a half dozen guns pointed at her wasn't especially appealing.

Still, Victoria Chamberlain—and Quinn Ellington, for that matter—would have none of it. She stiffened, took a step back, and gave Borovsky a frigid stare. "I know you think you're teasing, but threatening violence against a woman is never funny." Her eyes snapped to the spots of blood on the table.

For the first time, she saw his confidence waver. She doubted a woman had ever stood up to him before.

She also hoped she hadn't just blown the op. And that she wasn't about to get punched in the mouth.

"I apologize. I would never hurt a woman. I was only trying to convey how much I want you." Borovsky's tone grew ardent. "I have never met a woman who makes me flame with passion the way you do."

Blech.

"Come to my yacht tomorrow and bring the drug. We can complete our business and at the same time, you will taste the life of luxury you can have if you stay with me."

"I don't want to put anyone out." She glanced over at the men still sitting at the table. "It looks like you have a literal boatload of friends staying with you."

"Not all stay with me on the yacht. I have arranged accommodations for them here in Monte Carlo."

Or if they were staying on the yacht, they wouldn't be anymore.

Doing the deal on the yacht could make the logistics of taking him into custody a little more complicated. But he was insistent and the primary objective was to bust him on the drug sale. Victoria Chamberlain had no good reason to say no.

James must have come to the same conclusion. In her ear, she heard him say, "He's not going to budge on this yacht thing. Accept his offer. We can make it work."

"All right, Mr. Borovsky," she said. "I would love to finalize our transaction on your yacht. I look forward to it."

His eyes flashed in triumph. "Be at Port Hercule tomorrow afternoon at four o'clock. Ivan will text you the details of where to meet."

"I'll be there. Thank you again for a lovely evening." She tried to pull her hand away.

Rather than releasing it, he lifted it and pressed his lips to the back of it. The way he lingered over it made her stomach churn.

She tugged again, and this time successfully extracted it. "Good night."

It was all she could do to keep from flinging open the door and sprinting through the casino as if a rabid badger snapped at her heels. But Victoria Chamberlain didn't sprint. She sauntered.

Which was exactly how Quinn walked to the door. She opened the door and tossed a glance over her shoulder. "Bye, boys." She turned and strolled out, leaving them frozen in place with wide eyes and hanging jaws.

She locked eyes with James. So near to him now, she ached to be held in his arms. But with a better than even chance Borovsky would have them followed, their embrace would have to wait until they were in the privacy of their hotel suite.

She stopped in front of Dmitri and cut her eyes up at him. She rolled out her hand and held it there. A coquettish smile danced on her lips.

One corner of his mouth lifted. He retrieved her phone from his pocket and set it on her awaiting palm.

She waved the phone in farewell and chirped, "See you." She spun on her heel and strode away. James fell in step beside her.

Neither said a word as they made their way through the casino. Only when they were outside and hurrying down the front steps did James say, "Darius, we're clear. You're good to go."

"As soon as I catch my gutshot straight draw on the river." Ten seconds later, he muttered, "Crap."

"Sounds like it's time to cash out," Quinn said.

"Yup. I'm out of here."

"I'll keep comms open until everyone is back," Sydney said. "I mean, if that's okay. Is that okay? I'm not usually in the van, although it's really not a van. A hotel room isn't a van."

"It's okay," James said. "We'll let you know when to shut them down."

"Ah. Okay. Good," Sydney said.

Quinn drew in a deep breath and let the night air fill her lungs.

"You okay?" James asked.

"Yeah," she sighed and expelled the air with a gust. "It feels good to be outside."

"I'm just glad you're away from Admiral Lecherous."

Using descriptive names for bad guys was something she often did. James doing so now had her laughing out loud. It was a wonderful release after the stress she'd endured over the past few hours. "Admiral Lecherous. Is he the evil twin of Captain Sanctimonious?" She was referring to a Sikh extremist they had dealt with during their op in India.

"He is." James wasn't laughing, though. "I could live with Captain Sanctimonious judging our lusty public behavior. It's not easy for me to listen to a smarmy bastard like Borovsky drool all over you."

"I know. It's not any fun on my end either. But it's part of the job."

They wove their way through the surprisingly crowded sidewalk and started up the steps of the hotel. "I'm not going to be sandbagged again. Come hell or high water, I'm going to be on that yacht with you tomorrow. I don't care what Borovsky says. I'm not going to let you be dropped into a pit of vipers alone."

"What if he stomps his foot and says absolutely not? If I don't go, it blows the whole op."

"I don't think he'll do that. I heard it in his voice. He'll do whatever it takes to have you. And if it means having your bodyguard tag along, so be it. He'll figure he can deal with me if needed."

"I don't like that sound of that. He's a violent son of a bitch. You saw what he did to that poor guy Mikhail."

"That's one of the reasons you're not going on that yacht alone."

They passed through the lobby and rode the lift in silence.

Back in their suite, the first thing Quinn did was to pull the blackout curtains closed to frustrate prying eyes. James also did a quick sweep of the room in case Borovsky had decided to have more bugs planted while they were out.

"Sydney, Darius. Quinn and I will call Meyers and get him up to speed. We'll need him to coordinate with Monegasque authorities," James said after he'd deemed the room to be clean. He slipped off his jacket and tossed it on over the back of a chair. "You two get a few hours of shut-eye. We'll meet in here at oh-eight hundred to work out logistics for tomorrow afternoon."

"I'll bring the coffee and croissants," Darius said.

"Sounds good," James said. "Sydney, we're taking out our comms. Be sure to shut down the necklace video feed, too, please."

"Roger that. Good night."

"Good night," Quinn said.

They removed their earpieces and set them on the coffee table. Quinn went into the bedroom, closed the curtains, and hummed with relief when she stepped out of her shoes.

James followed her into the bedroom. "I know you can take care of yourself," he said, picking up the dangling thread of their conversation. He sidled up behind her, swept her hair forward over her shoulder, and worked the clasp of her necklace. "And I'm not saying any of this as your husband, but as a fellow operative."

When the necklace was lifted away, she spun around and gave him a dubious, if not amused, look.

He returned it with a roll of his eyes. "Humor me, okay?

Put aside the fact the guy's a violent whack job. Just look at the sheer numbers. No one person can take down Borovsky and his entire crew alone."

Starting at the top, she unfastened a button of his shirt and began to work her way down. "But the two of us can?"

"If we have a solid plan, yeah. For sure. Darius and Sydney will be part of it, too."

"What about Viktor? Won't he recognize you?"

"I don't think so. It was dark when we scrabbled at the Honeycutt estate. He never got a good look at my face. And I wore a disguise in Saint Petersburg. If he didn't know you, he shouldn't know me either. Maybe I'll wear a hat and sunglasses just in case."

"Now I'm picturing you in aviators and a sea captain's hat."

"I'll make sure it has lots of gold leaf on the bill. You know. Inconspicuous and understated."

"Exactly," she said with a chuckle. Finished with his buttons, she turned around. James lowered her zipper. The dress dropped to the floor. She picked it up and tossed it on the bed.

Now in nothing but bra, panties, and lace thigh holster, she lifted her bare foot and braced it on the edge of the bed.

James's gaze never left her as she slid the Baby Glock from the holster and set it on the mattress. "I know you don't want to do this, but if Borovsky won't back down and refuses to do the deal unless you go to his yacht without me, are you ready to walk away? Can you live with that?"

"I won't like it, but yeah, I can because I know you're right." She tugged off the holster and tossed it next to the pistol. "I can't do it by myself. Nobody could." With her foot still on the edge of the bed, she rubbed both hands over where the tight holster had been to soothe the minor itch.

"Here. Let me." His arms slipped around her sides from behind.

A blissful hum escaped when his hands slowly slid up and down her thigh.

"Like I said before, I don't think it will come to that." His voice in her ear was deep and seductive. The more he spoke, the higher his hand drifted up her inner thigh. "You and a case full of a mind-control drug is an irresistible combination." His words barely penetrated her pleasurable fog.

Her head dropped back on his shoulder. The words she spoke sounded thick and dreamy. "What about calling Meyers?"

"It's still early evening in DC. It can wait a little while." There was a smile in his voice when he added, "I thought you might enjoy a little stress relief first."

"Oh. God," she gasped when his hand slipped under the waistband of her panties and slid lower.

"Besides, Cade wants to remind Victoria of what she'd miss if she left with Borovsky on his yacht."

She tried to respond and tell him that would never happen, but the fingers massaging her made speech impossible. All she could manage was a long, guttural moan.

"I'll take that as you're not going anywhere without me." Her feet left the floor when he swept her up and laid her in the middle of the bed. Seconds later, he was atop her, his delicious weight pressing her into the mattress.

The searing, sensual kiss she gave him told him he was right.

She had no intention of going anywhere without him.

Chapter Thirty

James and Quinn walked single file down a narrow pier toward the assigned location. There, they would board the yacht tender, the motorboat that would ferry them to *Perun's Chariot*. As they passed boat after boat moored in their slips, they were surrounded by a symphony of maritime sounds: the screech of seagulls, the clang of ropes against aluminum masts, the hollow pop of water slapping against fiberglass hulls.

The figure of a large man loomed ahead at the end of the causeway.

"Borovsky and his crew sure are punctual, aren't they?" James said from behind.

"I'm okay with that," Quinn said. "At least we don't have to wait around and wonder if we're being stood up."

"Yeah," he drawled, his tone heavy with sarcasm. "Because Borovsky would suddenly lose interest in trying to seduce a gorgeous blonde."

Quinn twisted around, dipped her chin, and lowered her sunglasses. With a wicked glint, she said, "You never know. Maybe his stash of Viagra fell overboard."

James barked a sharp laugh.

"Oh, snap!" Darius said exuberantly through her earpiece.

"How do you . . ." Sydney sputtered. Quinn pictured her face the color of a ripe tomato.

Quinn spun forward, added a shoulder shimmy to her walk, and turned on a megawatt smile. "Hello again, Dmitri," she said as they neared. "*Kak dela?*"

He blinked in surprise. He obviously wasn't prepared for her to ask how he was in Russian. "*Spasibo, horošo.*"

"I'll assume that means you're fine," she said. Her smile never faded when she peeked around Dmitri and waggled her fingers at the young man in the navy blue polo shirt and khaki pants. Given his uniform and the fact he was positioned behind the steering wheel, it was clear he was a member of the yacht's crew. Whether he and his fellow crew members were part of Borovsky's nefarious squad or simply doing a job remained to be seen.

The crewman lifted a hand and called back, "G'day, miss." From his youth, his uniform, his Australian accent, his tan, and his sun-bleached blond hair, she tended to believe he was simply a guy who worked on a yacht. Still, they would have to account for him and all the crew when the time came to take Borovsky into custody.

Quinn looked up at Dmitri. "Shall we?"

His apologetic grimace told her everything.

"He doesn't want Cade coming with me, does he?" Quinn ripped off her sunglasses and poked them into Dmitri's chest. Her tone was biting when she said, "You call your boss and tell him if Cade isn't allowed to come with me, I'm out of here. There are plenty of people who will pay me an obscene amount of money *and* treat me with respect."

Dmitri gulped, took his phone from his pocket, and made a call. He would have been surprised to know she and James understood every word he spoke in Russian. She appreciated the fact he conveyed Quinn's words verbatim. She also felt more than a little satisfaction when Dmitri described her ire and opined his belief she would follow through with her threat.

She tapped her foot as they waited for the call to end. Would Borovsky draw a line in the sand and send her packing? James didn't think he would, but she wasn't so sure. What if she'd bruised his ego by standing up to him? They would have to formulate a whole new plan.

Dmitri lowered his phone and returned it to his pocket.

The suspense was excruciating. Had Borovsky's ego or libido won out?

"Mr. Borovsky say he may come, but he must give up gun." Score one for libido.

"That seems fair," she said and spun around. "Cade?"

If James balked, she would trust his judgment and reject Borovsky's counteroffer.

His expression never changed as he set the case full of fake Zieglopam on the wooden slats, reached around, and tugged his Sig Sauer from the holster in his waistband. He handed it to Quinn, who turned and gave it to Dmitri. She gave the big man a withering stare, as if challenging him to ask from her further concessions.

Based on her interactions with Dmitri the night before, she was confident he wouldn't be checking the thigh where her tranquilizer gun currently resided under her sundress. And with her Baby Glock secreted in a pocket in her purse designed specifically for concealed carry, she was well armed.

What she didn't want was for James to be frisked.

His Baby Glock was strapped to one ankle while his tranquilizer gun was holstered at the other. If he had to give those up, too, James would pull the plug on the op. Tranquilizing Borovsky's men, and possibly yacht crew, was an integral part of their plan. Otherwise, they would be outnumbered.

If Dmitri had an order to search them, he ignored it. He

tucked James's Sig into his front waistband and hopped into the yacht tender. Carrying an unholstered weapon in such a fashion was a good way to accidentally shoot off the family jewels. Quinn chose to keep that tidbit to herself.

She lightly touched the crewman's proffered hand as she stepped onto the tender. As she did so, she noted the absence of tattoos on his arms, Perun's thunder mark in particular. That made her think it was even less likely he was a Borovsky acolyte.

James hopped on with the case of fake Zieglopam in hand. They sat on the cushioned seats and watched Dmitri and the cute Aussie unwind the ropes from the cleats tethering the boat to the pier. Dmitri shoved the boat away from the dock while the crewman started the motor. Seconds later, they were slowly cruising toward the port's exit.

They motored past a cruise ship docked at the entrance of the harbor and out onto the open water. The crewman pushed the throttle forward and sped up. As they skimmed over the waves, Quinn couldn't help but marvel at the breathtaking beauty of the Côte d'Azur. The buildings and houses climbed the mountains until it grew too steep and the sheer rock won.

It was moments like that where she sometimes had a hard time wrapping her head around the fact it wasn't all a dream. She was on the French Riviera, with an incredibly handsome and sexy covert operative who had somehow fallen in love with her. And married her, no less. Now they were a jet-setting couple who traveled the world trying to make it a safer place. Never in a million years, as she sat in a library school classroom learning the correct way to catalog a DVD, would she have believed such things were possible.

She sighed, wishing she could snuggle into James's side and share with him all the things flashing through her mind. The stolen moment of squeezing his hand while Dmitri's head was turned would have to suffice.

She dragged her attention away from the coast, pushed her existential musings aside, and scanned the area, hoping to catch a glimpse of *Perun's Chariot*. From satellite images, she knew it would be one of the larger boats they would encounter, but not so large that it would attract attention, something Borovsky eschewed. The monstrous yachts half the size of the *Titanic* with swimming pools and helicopter pads tended to end up on lists on the Internet.

The Aussie angled the tender directly toward a sleek, modern yacht gleaming in the bright afternoon summer sun. It was about two hundred feet long with three discernable levels. A couple of Jet Skis tied at the back of the yacht were dwarfed by its size.

Quinn tore her eyes away from *Perun's Chariot* and surveyed the proximity of the other boats anchored nearby. They were, after all, off the coast of a playground for the rich and famous. It only made sense the area was teeming with pleasure vessels. Still, Borovsky stayed true to his penchant for secrecy. *Perun's Chariot* was anchored farther away from the rest.

The helmsman steered toward the aft swimming platform, where Borovsky stood waiting. Next to him, two crew members dressed identically to the tender's Aussie pilot stood ready to spring into action and secure it. Ivan Ovechkin, Borovsky's ever-present shadow, stood behind his boss.

The Aussie expertly guided the boat into place and cut the motor. His crewmates had it tied to the platform in no time. Their efficiency was impressive.

Borovsky beamed at Quinn and extended a hand to help her out of the tender. "Welcome aboard my humble boat. You look lovely."

Touching Borovsky wasn't her favorite thing, but to not accept his offer of help would be impolitic. She took his hand and stepped up onto the platform. "Thank you. And you're being too modest. This magnificent yacht is hardly humble."

Her compliment clearly pleased him. "I call it home."

James bounded out of the tender like a sure-footed mountain goat and took his place beside Quinn.

Borovsky's lips pursed with disdain when he laid eyes on James for the first time.

James stretched to his full height, a good four inches taller than Borovsky, and stared him down.

It wouldn't have surprised her if, at any second, the two men engaged in a measuring contest. She was certain who would win that contest, not that she was biased or anything.

Borovsky's gaze traveled to the case James carried. "I assume that is my drug your lackey has there."

On the inside, she bristled at Borovsky's overt slight. Outwardly, she smiled and said sweetly, "Until your money is transferred into my account, my associate is holding my drug."

"Then we should get down to business. Afterward, we will dine alfresco and enjoy the view of the coast. My chef has created a delightful menu for us to enjoy."

"That sounds wonderful," Quinn said with as sincere a smile as she could muster. She was more than happy to get their business out of the way first. The sooner the money was transferred into Victoria Chamberlain's Swiss bank account, the sooner they could put their plan of capturing Borovsky into motion and get off that "rust bucket," as her dad would call it.

To that end, Quinn kept a running total of people on *Perun's Chariot*. So far, in addition to Borovsky, Ovechkin, and Dmitri, she counted four crew members.

"I am glad you approve." Borovsky started up a steep set of steps. "Follow me." He led the way, with Quinn, James, and Ovechkin following. Dmitri brought up the rear.

"So, *Perun's Chariot*," Quinn said as they went up one level. "Are you a modern-day fan of an ancient Slavic god?"

"You certainly have been checking up on me." From the grin Borovsky shot her, he obviously took her question to mean she was enthralled by him and thirsted to know everything about him. In truth, she was simply compelled to search out the answer to the question she'd pondered while tracking him down. "I grew up near Peryn. As a boy, I was fascinated by the shrine discovered there and learned all I could. One day, the grandmother who raised me showed me a carving in a doorframe of our house. It was a thunder mark. Do you know it?"

"I do. It must have worked since the house hadn't burned down."

"Indeed. As for the yacht name, I cannot ride in a chariot of fire as Perun did, but I can in a chariot that takes me across water."

"You're so sweet to honor your grandmother."

Borovsky preened at her ego strokes as they walked past an informal outdoor sitting area, through an open sliding glass door, and into a living room. With a gray, white, and black color scheme, the room was sophisticated and expertly decorated.

Yuri sat on a couch and watched a soccer match on the TV attached to the wall at the opposite end of the room. He leapt to his feet when the group entered.

"Margarita, we will take appetizers and drinks on the sundeck," Borovsky said in Russian to a teenager about the same age as Mila positioned behind a bar to their left.

"Yes, sir."

"Dmitri, Ivan will accompany me. You may join Yuri and watch the match if you wish."

Dmitri accepted and offered his thanks.

Quinn now knew where Yuri and Dmitri would be planted for an indefinite chunk of time.

The group skirted along the end of a formal black lacquer dining table and ten chairs. "Will the men we played poker with last night be joining us for dinner?" Quinn asked.

"No," Borovsky said. "I believe they will be visiting one of the other casinos tonight."

She wanted to account for Viktor, but asking too many questions could raise suspicion. "I'm sure they'll have fun."

"My master suite is ahead." Borovsky indicated with a wave of his hand. "Perhaps I can give you a private tour after our business is concluded."

Quinn managed to not throw up.

"Perhaps," she said with a smile she hoped conveyed flirtation, not revulsion.

They climbed another narrow staircase, this one circular, and arrived in yet another parlor dominated by black and white.

A shock of brick-red hair caught Quinn's eye. She did a double take.

Mother Olga lounged on the couch with her feet tucked up under her, reading a book.

Quinn's stomach dropped.

Quinn had worn an auburn wig and glasses during the raid in Saint Petersburg. She'd also run off with four of Olga's kids and clocked her in the head with a library stool. Would she recognize Quinn's face?

Thankfully, Mother Olga was so absorbed in her book she gave them only a cursory glance as they trooped through the room.

"Olga is my cousin," Borovsky said, as if he wanted to assure Quinn she didn't have any competition. That, of course, was inconsequential to Quinn. It made sense that Mother Olga had a new gig, so to speak. She not only worked for her cousin, she was there supervising the kids forced to work on the yacht. Quinn's jaw clenched when she realized the raid in Saint Petersburg had apparently only been a minor inconvenience to Borovsky's organization. She hadn't thought it possible, but the desire to shut down Borovsky and his empire became even stronger.

Borovsky pointed at another dining table, this one only slightly less formal than the previous one. "We will be dining here tonight."

No, we won't, she thought with no small amount of satisfaction.

They ascended one more set of stairs and arrived on the uppermost level of the boat.

Furniture had been arranged into a sitting area in the middle of the sundeck. Quinn took the seat on the couch Borovsky indicated and he immediately claimed the spot beside her. James sank into the low armchair on Quinn's end of the couch and set the case on the deck at his feet. Ovechkin sat in an identical chair directly opposite him.

"Wow," Quinn said, glancing around at the amenities. "Another bar and a hot tub, too. *Perun's Chariot* is incredible. It's like a floating mansion."

"I enjoy it." Borovsky rested his arm atop of the back cushions and scooted closer to her. "I am hoping you will join me for an extended holiday once our business is concluded."

She smiled, even as she swallowed her disgust. "Speaking of business, shall we get started? Then we can discuss other things."

Margarita appeared with a tray and set it on the low, square table at the center of the seating area. The plate was covered with a variety of fruits, cheeses, and crackers. Two small cut crystal bowls were filled with two different kinds of caviar.

She had no desire to try either, especially the slightly larger orange eggs. They looked like the salmon eggs she used as bait to catch rainbow trout on family fishing trips in California's Sierra Nevada mountains. She'd had no desire to eat them then. A fancier presentation didn't make them any more appealing now.

"Both vodka and champagne, Margarita," Borovsky said. To Quinn, he said, "Many people drink champagne with caviar. I think good vodka is better. If you have not tried it, you should."

She preferred her fish eggs baited on a hook. "I'll take it under advisement," she said in an easy tone.

While Margarita went behind the bar and gathered bottles, glasses, and flutes, Borovsky looked at the case on the deck. "May I see?"

"Of course," Quinn said. "Cade?"

James set the case on his thighs and opened the top so that the contents faced them.

"This is the remainder of Zieglopam we synthesized," Quinn said, "along with a cell phone tag we assembled. The complete formula and schematics are on the thumb drive."

"And you have not retained any of this information for yourself?"

"I didn't say that." When his brows pulled together in a frown, she asked, "You wouldn't give up your one and only copy, would you?"

He turned thoughtful. "I must admit I would not."

"You have my word. I won't sell it to anyone else."

"Very well." Ovechkin handed Borovsky an electronic tablet. "If you will give me your account number, I will transfer the thirty million euros right now."

This was it. She reached into her purse, took out a piece of paper with the account number on it, and handed it to Borovsky.

Heart thumping, she watched him tap the screen. A moment later, he said, "It is done."

Through her earpiece, Sydney said, "The money is in the account. We got him."

Now came the dangerous part.

"Ready to move on your signal," Darius said.

Borovsky's tone was merry when he said, "Now we celebrate with vodka, champagne, and caviar." He picked up the bottle of champagne Margarita had brought to the table a moment before and filled two flutes.

James closed the case and secured the clasps. Resting his arms on top of the case, he said, "If you will excuse me, I think I'll go watch the match with Dmitri and Yuri."

What James was actually going to do was tranquilize and secure them—and anyone else who needed to be subdued—before returning to her so they could take down Borovsky together.

"That is an excellent idea, Cade," Borovsky said. The man looked like he was seconds from strutting around the deck like a peacock. "You will accompany him, Ivan."

Even better, Quinn thought. While James was busy with the three bodyguards, she could take Borovsky out by herself with one shot from her tranquilizer pistol.

Movement at the top of the stairs drew her attention. Quinn glanced over to see a middle-aged man in a thick bathrobe and flip-flops walk toward them. Since he had a beach towel slung over his shoulder, Quinn assumed he was on his way to the hot tub.

Her blue eyes locked with the man's emerald-green ones.

The world tilted.

The man was Rhys Townsend.

Chapter Thirty-One

"I apologize, Konstantin. I didn't realize you—" Townsend stopped and blinked in surprise and confusion. "Quinn. James. I didn't expect to see you here."

Borovsky's relaxed posture vanished. He bolted up in his seat and snapped, "Do you know these people?"

"Yes," Rhys said, clearly perplexed. "I met Quinn and James in Turks and Caicos a couple of months ago. They were on their honeymoon."

Borovsky turned and eyed her with suspicion. "Explain this."

"It was our cover," James said without missing a beat. "We were doing a job."

Equilibrium regained, Quinn said, "That's right. We've used a number of aliases. I've already admitted Victoria isn't my real name." Her muscles grew taut.

"You weren't really on your honeymoon? You had me fooled." Rhys looked at Borovsky with raised eyebrows. "They were *very* convincing."

A malignant energy radiated from Borovsky.

"Was Gibson Honeycutt's estate your target?" Rhys asked. A light bulb practically blinked on over his head.

"Anatoly and Viktor caught you reconnoitering the grounds. That's why you got into that fight."

"No," James said. He may have appeared at ease, but Quinn knew he was as tense as she. "We were casing the casino the night you invited us to the estate."

Borovsky ignored James and Townsend. He rose to his feet and seethed at Quinn. "My operation in Saint Petersburg was raided soon after that by, among others, a handsome man and attractive young woman." A malevolent calm settled over him. He didn't know it all. But he knew enough. His eyes burned with rancor when he snarled, "Kill them."

Ovechkin leapt up and whipped out his weapon.

James heaved the case at Ovechkin and knocked the gun from his hand. He launched across the table and drove his shoulder into Ovechkin's gut. They tumbled over the chair and crashed to the deck.

Quinn went for the tranquilizer gun in her thigh holster. Borovsky smashed the side of her face with his fist, knocking her sideways. She fell off the couch and dropped to her hands and knees. Stars sparkled at the edges of her vision.

Borovsky grabbed her arm and hauled her to her feet. She blinked and her vision cleared in time to see him rear back his hand. He drove the knockout punch forward, his face twisted with unmitigated rage.

She ducked, grabbed his arm, and pivoted. With a mighty yank, she flipped him over her shoulder.

His back hit the deck with a solid thump.

Quinn ripped her tranquilizer pistol from its holster and took aim.

Before she could pull the trigger, Borovsky rolled away. He grabbed a chair cushion and flung it at her, knocking her off balance. He scrambled to his feet, sprinted to the back edge of the deck, and hurdled over the railing.

She dashed forward and leaned over the rail. He crawled

off the cushions of the outdoor lounge one level below. He bellowed for Dmitri and Yuri.

Quinn whirled around. James and Ovechkin scrabbled on the deck in battle.

She raised her pistol. The second she had a clear shot at Ovechkin's back, she squeezed the trigger. The dart impaled Ovechkin below the shoulder blade. He arched, roared a string of expletives, and went limp.

"Nice shot," James said and pushed off the unconscious bag of bones.

Quinn hurried over and helped James to his feet. "Thanks. You okay?"

"Yeah. You?"

"Yeah. Borovsky jumped over the rail and landed one deck down." She went to the bar and peered behind it. Margarita crouched with the wine bottle gripped in both hands, ready to wield it as a club. The bottle shook and her breaths came in short, gasping bursts.

"It's okay. We're not going to hurt you," she said in Russian. "We're United States federal officers here to take Konstantin Borovsky into custody." Margarita didn't respond and looked to be on the verge of hyperventilating. "Take a long, deep breath, hold it, and then blow it out." Quinn demonstrated.

Margarita did as instructed.

"Good." Relief swept over Quinn when Margarita's panic began to subside. "Do that a few more times."

While Margarita performed her breathing exercises, Quinn glanced over her shoulder to see James lifting a set of plastic zip-tie handcuffs from her purse. "Townsend isn't back here," she said. "He must have bolted during the ruckus."

"He can't have gone far," James replied. He stepped over Ovechkin, tugged the Russian's wet noodle arms behind his back, and tightened the cuffs around his wrists. "Probably holed up somewhere." James relieved Ovechkin of his gun, checked the magazine, and slapped it back in place. He straightened and slid the pistol in the empty holster at his hip. "Let's find him and Borovsky."

Quinn turned to Margarita. "Stay hidden until things settle down. Hang on to that bottle just in case." Margarita gulped and nodded. Quinn gave the teen a confidence-boosting smile before pushing away from the bar.

"I'll take point," James said. He hustled to the top of the steps with his tranquilizer pistol level in front of him.

Quinn grabbed her purse from the sofa, tossed the strap over her head, and settled it across her chest. She fell in behind James.

They stealthily descended the steps and stopped at the bottom. James peeked into the salon where Olga had been reading. "Clear."

They stole through the lounge and came to an open doorway.

James poked his head around.

A gunshot exploded. A bullet hole blossomed in the wood above them.

He snapped his head back. "Olga's guarding a door."

"I bet that's where she stashed the kids working on this tub." Quinn gripped her pistol tighter. "That woman pisses me off." She stuck her arm around the edge of the wall and pulled the trigger. She yanked her arm back, looked into James's eyes, and waited. A few seconds later, as expected, she heard the unmistakable clunk of a body collapsing on the floor. "Knocking that woman out never gets old."

"She deserves it," James said. They hurried down the hall. "Borovsky might be hiding in there, too." He stepped over the unconscious woman and tried the doorknob. "Locked."

"She's gotta have a key." Quinn rifled through Olga's pockets. Her fingers touched metal in a front pocket of the other woman's slacks. She handed a key to James. "Try this one." Olga's pistol went into Quinn's purse.

James slid the key into the lock. It turned. He put his hand on the doorknob and pointed his gun at the door.

She stood and readied her pistol.

He held her gaze. "Three, two, one."

He shoved the door open. They barreled into the room. Their shouts of "United States federal officers!" could barely be heard over the screams of the three early teens huddled together at the center of a king-size bed.

James checked the closet while Quinn tried the knob on the bathroom door. Locked. "Over here," she called to James and indicated the door with a tip of her head.

He raised a foot and smashed it against the door. The jamb splintered as the door slammed open.

Quinn rushed into the bathroom and found Rhys Townsend cowering in the shower stall.

She grabbed him by the lapels of his bathrobe and hauled him to his feet. Her fury uncontained, she yanked him forward, and smashed him back against the granite shower wall.

"You bastard!" she thundered. "Using innocent kids to fuel your coke habit!" After another hard shove, she spun him around and pushed his chest against the wall. Blood trickled from a cut on the back of Townsend's head.

James stepped into the shower and helped Quinn secure plastic cuffs around Townsend's wrists. They hauled him into the hall and pushed him onto his knees next to Olga.

When Quinn cocked the hammer of her pistol, he sputtered, "Don't shoot me. I'll give you money. Drugs. Anything."

"The only thing I want from you is the years you stole from innocent children," Quinn spat. "Oh, right. You can't do that. You lose." She squeezed the trigger and put a dart in Townsend's back.

He crashed face-first to the floor.

While James cuffed Olga, Quinn returned to the bedroom. Ashen and clinging to each other, the two boys and a girl were clearly petrified.

Making her tone as gentle as possible, she asked, "Do any of you speak English? *Russkiy?*"

One of the boys whispered, "I speak little."

Hearing the thick Russian accent, Quinn switched to Russian. "I know you're scared. It's going to be okay. As soon as we tie up all the bad people on this boat, you'll be taken somewhere safe. You won't have to stay with Mother Olga anymore."

"You know Mother Olga?" the girl asked.

"Sort of. We've run into each other a couple of times." With a small smile, she added, "Mother Olga doesn't like me very much."

Quinn released a relieved breath when the three kids seemed to relax, if only a little.

"In the meantime, we need you to stay safe right here in this room. We're going to lock the door and keep the key with us. Don't open it for anyone. Do you understand?"

Three heads nodded.

Darius's voice came through her earpiece. "Hey, you two," he shouted. "You'd better hustle. Borovsky and one of his thugs are getting ready to jump ship."

Quinn cocked her head and detected the faint *thwup* of Darius's helicopter overhead.

"Copy," James said. He leaned into the room. "Babe, we gotta go."

"Roger that." She didn't want to promise them she'd see them again. Given the fluidity of the situation, she wasn't sure she would. Instead, she smiled and said, "Take care." She stepped out of the room and locked the door.

"We gotta head for the aft platform," James said.

They backtracked toward the staircase.

"The yacht tender?" she asked.

"Yeah."

"If Borovsky's got either Dmitri or Yuri with him, where's the other?"

"Between us and them would be my guess."

They stole down the stairs to the level above the platform. They skirted past the formal dining table and took up a position behind the partition between it and the room where Yuri and Dmitri had watched television.

The motor of the tender revved.

James peeked around the partition. A burst of automatic gunfire had him dropping to the floor, pulling Quinn down with him. "Every. Time," he hissed.

Quinn drew in a breath. The smell of gunpowder hung in the air. She glanced up at the wall above their heads. Splinters of wood stuck out at wonky angles where the bullets had blasted clean through. "Whoever it is, he's carrying a serious caliber," she whispered. "Did you see where he's positioned?"

"Behind the bar. You keep him busy. I'll skirt around behind the furniture and take him out from the other side."

"You be careful."

"I will. You too."

To cover James, Quinn needed more firepower. She took her Glock from the secret pocket in her bag and gripped it.

James counted down from three on his fingers.

He power crawled across the gap and hid behind the closest armchair while she stuck the gun around the divider, aimed toward the bar, and fired three times.

She whipped the gun back and called out in Russian, "Give yourself up."

"You speak Russian after all."

Yuri.

The growl of the motor grew faint as Borovsky and Dmitri sped away.

"I do. Some," she said. James gave her the signal to keep

talking. "Come on, Yuri. Let's not do this. I don't want to hurt you. Borovsky just left you behind to fight us off by yourself." James scrambled from the armchair to behind the couch. "Is he really worth taking a bullet for?"

"Without him, I would have nothing." He popped up and fired off another burst of bullets, shredding an upper section of the partition.

She winced at the rifle's concussion.

"I must protect him."

Time to take a different tact. "Do you have a family, Yuri? A wife? Children?"

"I have a wife, a daughter, and a son."

She peered around the edge of the divider and spotted James. He'd commando crawled along the front of the couch and taken up a position at the end nearest the bar.

"You know why these kids are here, Yuri. Would you want your children taken away from you and sold into slavery?"

"I cannot leave. I do not care if they kill me. They will torture my family."

Quinn knew he was right. She peered around the corner. Yuri duck walked from behind the bar toward the partition, his AK-47 gripped in front of him.

"I bet if you give up information that will help take down Borovsky's organization, the United States government will be very grateful."

James rose up and fired.

Yuri never saw the dart coming. He looked down at it, jabbed into his upper arm, with an expression of shock. Seconds later, he crashed to the floor like a bag of wet sand.

"Clear!" James called.

She popped out from behind the wall.

"Cuff him and meet me on the platform," James said. "We can catch them on one of the Jet Skis."

"Copy." She headed for Yuri while James strode for the stairs.

"Darius, you got eyes on the tender?" James asked as he descended the steps.

"Affirmative. I'm right overhead."

"Copy," she heard James say.

Quinn listened to James identify himself to the crew on the platform and explain the situation while she restrained Yuri's hands behind his back. She picked up the Kalashnikov, flicked on the safety, and released the iconic curved magazine. A yank on the charging handle ejected the chambered round and sent it arcing through the air. She stuck the magazine behind a throw pillow on the couch and hid the rifle behind the bar.

Now that Yuri and his weapon had been secured, she trotted to the top of the steps. His back to her, James watched two crewmen tug the Jet Ski into position at the platform.

She was halfway down the steps. A metallic click from above and behind caught her attention. She craned her neck and spotted an unaccounted-for crewman standing at the back rail two decks up. He pointed a pistol directly at James's back. The tattoo on the inside of his arm was Perun's thunder mark.

She raised her Glock and squeezed off three shots.

Chapter Thirty-Two

James whirled around.

The gun dropped from the man's hand and hit the platform with a clatter. He reeled backward and out of sight.

Body buzzing, Quinn bounded down the last few steps and took her place beside James.

"Thanks," he said and kissed her.

"Always." She heaved a breath in relief.

The two crewmen goggled at her.

James chuckled as he bounded onto the Jet Ski and straddled the seat. "I've guess they've never seen a quick-draw librarian before." He punched the ignition and started the engine.

Quinn hopped on, sat directly behind him, and wrapped her arms around his waist. "Now they have. From the looks of things, they won't forget."

"Nope. You're kind of unforgettable." He gripped the handlebars and yelled, "Hang on."

She cinched her arms around him, crushing her front to his back.

The Jet Ski leapt forward with such violence, she would have somersaulted backward into the Mediterranean had she not been holding on for dear life.

James hunched over the handlebars and slalomed the watercraft through seagoing traffic. The fine spray kicked up by the wake at their feet dampened Quinn's legs. "Darius!" he shouted over the rushing air and engine noise. "I can't see the yacht tender. Are you above Borovsky?" The helicopter hovered in the distance a couple hundred feet above the water.

"Affirmative." After a beat, Darius said, "I see you. You're a half mile out and closing fast."

"Can you strafe the water in front of them? Slow them down?" James asked.

"Negative. Too many boats."

The section of the motorcycle-like seat Quinn straddled was higher than James's, giving her a good vantage point to search the area from over his shoulder. They were headed straight for a stretch of coastline where it was nothing but breakwaters protecting waterfront hotels. "Where are they going? The port's that way," she shouted and pointed to her left. Crashing into a wall of rocks didn't seem like a very solid getaway plan.

James steered behind a yacht they were rapidly closing in on. They both lifted from the seat to let their legs work as shock absorbers as the watercraft bounced over the yacht's trailing wake.

Once the yacht no longer blocked their view, Quinn spotted the tender only three hundred yards ahead. The wind swept away her whispered, "Oh crap."

They were speeding directly toward a beach crowded with holiday sun worshipers. A line of small buoys bobbed in the water, demarcating an area for swimmers to enjoy the warm water.

"They could drown someone," she yelled.

James had no choice but to slow the Jet Ski as they closed in on the swimming area. The beach was lined with cabanas, umbrellas, and lounges.

At the last second, Dmitri, who Quinn could now clearly see standing at the wheel, veered the tender away from swimmers bobbing in the water and toward a small dock.

The bow of the tender dropped when Dmitri cut the throttle. He spun the wheel and the boat swerved. It didn't plow into the dock, but it came in hard enough that Borovsky tumbled out of his seat. Dmitri rushed to the side of the boat and gripped a cleat to keep them from drifting.

Borovsky clambered to his feet and scrambled off the tender, leaving Dmitri to act as a human mooring line.

James steered the Jet Ski directly at the tender. Quinn's eyes stayed pinned on Borovsky, carrying a briefcase in one hand and a pistol in the other. His hands had been empty when he jumped over the railing when all hell broke loose. In the time before he escaped from *Perun's Chariot*, he'd apparently sought out and grabbed a briefcase. That led Quinn to believe it was crammed with incriminating evidence he needed to keep from the authorities who would inevitably swarm the yacht. The kingpin sprinted across the short, narrow causeway toward a small boathouse.

"Darius, you got eyes on Borovsky? He's about to go inside that little building," Quinn said.

James cut the engine and let the Jet Ski drift forward. He already had his Baby Glock trained on Dmitri, who was now lashing the tender to the dock.

"Yeah, I see him," Darius said. "He's through and headed for the main building."

"Main building of what?"

"A beach resort."

They were barreling headlong into a hostage situation. Or worse.

The front of the watercraft drifted forward and gently kissed the tender's aft. James didn't bother tethering the Jet Ski. He hopped onto the dock, his pistol never wavering from the center of Dmitri's chest. He took Quinn's hand and swung her up. She sailed through the air and alit lightly next to him.

Dmitri stood stock-still. A pistol lay on a nearby seat cushion.

Like his gun, James's eyes never left Dmitri as he spoke. "I think it's fair to say we've developed a bit of a soft spot for you. Please don't do anything stupid. I don't want to have to shoot you."

Uncertainty crossed Dmitri's face as he weighed his options. His eyes flicked from James to the pistol on the seat and then to Quinn.

"Please, Dmitri," Quinn said. "Don't." She considered pulling her tranq pistol and ending the standoff. Fearful her movements might precipitate a shootout, she remained motionless instead.

Quinn swallowed and braced herself for what was to come.

Chapter Thirty-Three

Dmitri's shoulders slumped in defeat and his hands rose in surrender.

Relief washed over Quinn as she dug yet another pair of plastic cuffs from her bag. While James kept his pistol trained on Dmitri, Quinn hopped into the tender and searched him. Between the Sig Sauer Dmitri had taken from James earlier, his own nine-millimeter GSh-18 pistol, and the nasty seven-inch knife sheathed at his ankle, the man was a walking armory.

Quinn directed Dmitri to sit. "You made the right choice," she said and cuffed his wrists together through the steering wheel. "You play nice with the authorities and maybe it won't turn out terrible for you."

"Darius, where's Borovsky?" James asked.

"I don't see him. I think he's inside the building." A few seconds later, Darius said, "Oh, nope. I see him. Looks like he couldn't get in. He's still on your side of the building. Headed toward the big pile of rocks to your left."

"Sydney, send a team to our current location to pick up Dmitri," Quinn said. "No need to come in hot. He's unarmed and secure."

"Roger that," Sydney said.

James scanned the rocks and then pointed. "There he is." He took Quinn's hand and hauled her onto the dock. "We gotta go."

"Bye, Dmitri."

Weapons lowered but ready, they loped across the board-walk, through the boathouse, and past the stunned employee behind a desk. Out the front, they pivoted left and hurried along the path. Borovsky was already halfway up the bank, picking his way over the rocks at a diagonal.

"Sydney, we need you to scrub all security camera footage for this location," Quinn said. "And send the police out to Borovsky's yacht. Tell them four bogies are tranqed and cuffed, one's been shot—condition unknown—and there are three trafficking victims locked in a stateroom and one hiding behind a bar on the top deck."

"Roger that."

Quinn heard computer keys furiously clicking.

"Darius," James said. They came to the end of the path and followed Borovsky onto the rock pile. "What's at the top of this bank?"

"Avenue Princesse Grace."

Borovsky stopped unexpectedly and swung his pistol around.

They dove for cover behind a palm tree.

Borovsky fired. Bits of rock flew up in the air like tiny volcanic eruptions.

Quinn lay still and tried to ignore the rock jabbing her rib cage.

When the bullets stopped coming, she poked her head around the tree. Borovsky had disappeared.

James trained his pistol on the top of the ridge. "Darius. Sitrep." They couldn't move until they were sure Borovsky wasn't waiting to pick them off once they were in the open.

"Borovsky's standing in the middle of the street with his gun pointed at an oncoming car," Darius said.

James and Quinn were on the move. They scrabbled over the rocks as fast as they could.

As they neared the top of the bank, Borovsky's shouts tumbled down from above.

Darius continued his play-by-play. "He's pulled the guy out and dumped him on the street."

An engine roared and tires screeched. Quinn didn't have to be told what happened.

"And he's off," Darius said.

Quinn and James cleared the rocks and ran across the dirt to the street. The man who had just been carjacked stood in the middle of the road, unhurt and extremely pissed. Red faced, his neck veins bulged as he screamed in Italian and shook a fist in the direction Borovsky had escaped.

Predictably, the spectacle had brought traffic going both directions to a halt.

"Darius, what kind of car?" James asked.

"I can't tell exactly. It's a black supercar. Ferrari, maybe. I'm too high to see the badge."

James went to speak to the incensed victim still in the throes in his epic diatribe. James shouted a question at him in Italian. He received a dizzying, spittle-infused torrent of words in response.

Long, angry car horn blasts failed to remove them from the middle of the avenue.

Returning to Quinn's side, he said, "No wonder he's furious. He was driving a Pagani."

Quinn's eyes grew wide. "Holy crap. A Huayra?"

"Thankfully not. A Zonda."

"Still super expensive. What do we do now?"

The driver at the front of the long line of traffic leapt out of his car. Face twisted with rage, he charged toward them, clearly intent on physically removing the human blockade. He seemed completely indifferent to the fact both Quinn and James were armed.

"We chase him," James said. He grabbed Quinn's hand and sprinted for the now driverless car. As it turned out, it was the same red Ferrari 458 Spider James had lusted over the night before.

James headed for the driver's side while Quinn raced for the passenger's. She gripped the latch and used momentum to pull the door open. She slingshot around and threw herself into the seat.

The second her door closed, the car rocketed forward. The Ferrari's owner clawed at the door handle as it sped past.

Quinn swiveled around and watched the man run after them. After about twenty yards, he stopped and stood helpless with his arms limp at his sides. He disappeared from sight when the car made a violent left.

Once she was no longer pressed against the door by the force of the turn, she yanked the seat belt across her body and jammed the buckle into the slot.

"Darius, where's Borovsky?" James asked.

Quinn pulled up a map on her phone. Their quarry had at least a three-minute head start. Even in a Ferrari, she wasn't sure they could catch him.

"Working his way up the mountain, west on Avenue du Président Kennedy."

Quinn scrutinized the map. "Got it." She set a course and said, "Stay on this until we loop to the right. I'll let you know when to turn again." She scanned the sky and spotted Darius's helicopter following Borovsky in the distance. "And, babe? If we're going to catch him, you need to channel your inner Formula One driver."

"I thought you'd never ask." He grinned and revved the engine. With the Spider's top down, the screaming, powerful growl filled the air like a sonic perfume. It was intoxicating. "Oh, baby," he rumbled.

She shot him an amused look. "I think I'm offended. I've only ever heard you make a noise like that when we're in bed together." Her elbows, pressed into the seat, stabilized her as they careened around the loop. The tires squealed in protest.

The road narrowed and grew steeper. James downshifted accordingly. "I could say the same thing about you and Double-Doubles."

She shrugged. "True." She checked the map and said, "Hang a left at the end of this road." As the car climbed higher, her eyes were drawn to the impossibly blue Mediterranean. "Oooo. I know. We should eat Double-Doubles in a Ferrari."

"Now you're talking." A smile curled on his lips. "If the time we ate them in a town car is any indication, it'll be really fun."

"TMI, people," Darius grumbled. "Sheesh."

"Sorry," Quinn said even though she wasn't.

At the end of the road, James made the left. Now that the road was wider, he opened up the engine. He swerved the Ferrari in and out of traffic, blowing past every car ahead of them as if they were standing still.

They steadily climbed and left Monaco behind. Looking down, Quinn took in the entire principality nestled against the mountains at the edge of the sea.

She was well aware they were on a desperate chase to apprehend a powerful Russian crime boss. And it wasn't exactly what she should be thinking about given their current situation. But she couldn't get over how incredibly hot James looked as he maneuvered the Ferrari through the winding, twisting roads of the French Riviera. With the wind tousling his hair and the way his body was fully engaged in handling the precision machine—it all made her heart rate skyrocket.

She wrangled her inappropriate thoughts, returned her focus to their task, and checked their progress on the map. Unless Borovsky was as good of a driver as James, which she severely doubted, they had to be getting close. Plus, they were practically under the helicopter. "Darius, we're in the red Ferrari. How far behind are we?"

"Less than a mile. You're gaining on him, and fast."

James barely slowed as they raced up on a nasty hairpin turn. Quinn swallowed a yelp when the back end of the Ferrari wiggled as he accelerated out of the turn. A glance into his face told her he was having the time of his life.

Quinn's palms, on the other hand, were sweaty. Only the short guardrail flashing past her side of the car stood between them and a steep drop down the mountain.

"He hit traffic and turned onto another road," Darius said and told them where to turn.

"Is it a dead end, I hope?" James asked.

Quinn checked the map. "No. Sorry. It leads to a major road." She slipped the phone under her thigh and searched for the back of the black Pagani. "I wonder if he knows that or took a wild-ass guess."

"Don't know. All I know is this needs to end before he gets on that main road."

The Ferrari went faster than she'd thought possible.

As they tore around a curve and on the short straightaway, Quinn caught a glimpse of the Pagani. "There it is," she said. "Nice driving."

"Thanks. Now we need to get him to pull over."

"Maybe we can give him a little encouragement." Quinn pulled out her Glock and held it out the window. "I hate the idea of putting a bullet hole in a quarter-of-a-million-dollar car."

"More like a half million. At least."

She groaned. "Not helping." With the engine behind the driver, the back of the car was substantial and there wasn't much of a back window. She pulled the gun back inside the Ferrari. "He probably wouldn't even realize a bullet hit it. I'd just be wasting ammunition."

"The road curves too much for us to pull up next to him. I can't see oncoming traffic."

Quinn surveyed the road ahead. "At that next right-handed bend, I'll see if I can get a shot at the passenger side." A car passed them going in the other direction. "As long as it's clear." With both hands on her Glock, she rested her forearms on the top of the car door and trained her sights on the Zonda.

James adjusted the Ferrari's speed so she could have a clean shot as the Zonda came out of the bend. It went into the turn and was obscured by the top of a tree.

It flashed into the open.

Quinn fired three quick shots.

The passenger-side window shattered.

The Pagani swerved toward the sheer face of rock on the other side of the road.

A delivery truck came around the blind corner from the other direction. The driver blasted the horn and slammed on the brakes.

The Pagani swung across the road and missed the truck. Borovsky overcorrected and ran out of road. The supercar crashed through the low stone wall and sailed over the edge.

James brought the Ferrari to a stop.

The sickening sound of a massive crunch and shattering glass came from below.

And then there was silence.

Chapter Thirty-Four

Quinn leapt from the Ferrari and inched toward the edge of the pavement. Standing at the brink, she cautiously peered over the precipitous drop and beheld the grotesque scene one hundred feet below. The Zonda lay on the road below, its doors gone and its front crumpled. Borovsky had been thrown from the car and now lay unmoving and in a contorted and unnatural position ten feet from it.

James stepped over next to her. "This is why you should always wear your seat belt."

"No kidding." Quinn turned her head toward the sound of sirens in the distance. They were faint at first, but growing louder with each passing second. "We need to get out of here." While the U.S. and Monegasque governments were coordinating efforts, the CIA covert operatives preferred not to become embroiled with local authorities.

James turned his attention to the helicopter hovering overhead. "Darius, is there someplace we can drive to where you can land and pick us up? Ditching a stolen Ferrari that was just involved in a high-speed chase is at the top of our list of things to do."

"Copy that. Scanning the area now." The helicopter went higher and drifted north. After another minute, he said,

"There's a golf course not far from your position as the crow flies. I can land there."

Quinn and James were already sprinting toward the Ferrari. She slid into her seat, strapped in, and studied the map on her phone. "Got it."

"Meet you on the fairway of the dogleg north of the clubhouse."

Quinn zoomed in on the satellite image while James eased the Ferrari back onto the road. "We'll be there in about twenty minutes."

"Roger that. I'll keep circling until you're in position."

Quinn played navigator and directed James along the twisting, winding roads.

Fifteen minutes later, they turned onto a narrow road that went right through the center of the course. They cruised into the clubhouse parking lot and parked the Ferrari near a line of empty golf carts awaiting their club-wielding drivers.

James cut the engine and used the hem of his shirt to wipe down the steering wheel. Quinn copied him by swiping her skirt over her door handle and seat. Once their fingerprints were at least smudged enough to make them unidentifiable, they hopped out of the Ferrari one last time.

James hustled to the back of the car and took a picture of it with his phone.

"You want me to take one of the two of you together?" Quinn asked with a crooked smile.

After a beat, he looked at her sheepishly and asked, "Would you mind?"

Quinn chuckled and took a picture of him leaning his hip against the car. One glance at the photo of her super-sexy man next to that super-sexy car told her it would become her phone's wallpaper the second she got the chance to change it.

She fell in step with James as they strode toward the entrance to the clubhouse.

"I want the Ferrari to get back to its owner," James said. He swung open the door and they headed for the man behind a counter.

When they arrived, James asked him, in Russian, if he spoke English.

The man shook his head and wafted his hands through the air, clearly having not understood a word James said.

James repeated the question, this time in English but with a prominent Russian accent.

Quinn appreciated her husband's subterfuge. When the authorities arrived later and asked the man to identify the couple who'd left the Ferrari, his first response would be, "They were Russian."

James held the Ferrari's key up for the man to see. "We borrowed red sports car. We leave in car park." He set the key on the counter and wrote the car's license plate number on an unused scorecard. "Please call police to have car go back to owner."

With that, they turned on their heels and hurried outside, leaving the dumbstruck man in their wake. "Darius, we're on our way," James said and broke into a jog.

Trotting next to him, Quinn checked her phone and pointed her right. "That way."

"I see you," Darius said. "Heads-up."

They hopped a chain-link fence, cut between two sand traps, and loped across a fairway. Quinn felt bad for distracting the guy in his putting stance on a nearby green, but it couldn't be helped. Not that his, or anyone else's, concentration would return anytime soon now that a helicopter was descending onto a fairway from right above their heads.

The second the copter's skids touched grass, Quinn and James bent their heads and pushed through the turbulent air churned up by the whirling blades.

Quinn scrambled into the copter first, threw herself into the back seat, and strapped in. James swung himself up into the empty seat in front of her. She jammed her headset on while James hauled the door closed. Darius pulled up on a lever and the helicopter lifted off the ground.

As they ascended, Quinn looked down at the statue-like golfers gaping up at them. They stared up at the sky like they were watching an alien spacecraft lift off.

James settled his headset on his ears and said into the microphone, "Thanks for the ride."

"Any time. Where to?"

"Let's check out what's happening on Borovsky's yacht," Quinn said.

"On it." Darius turned the helicopter back toward the coast.

Quinn glimpsed the scene of the car crash as they flew over it. She spotted a police car, fire engine, and ambulance. Her eyes were drawn to the spot on the road where Borovsky had landed. "How much you want to bet Borovsky's body is under that tarp?"

James looked down. "Not gonna take that bet. I'd lose."

A moment later, they were racing over the Mediterranean.

Darius flew them over *Perun's Chariot*. Two red police boats were tied to either side of the yacht. Uniformed officers swarmed the boat. Peering down at the place where their meeting with Borovsky had gone sideways, she hoped the police approached Margarita and her wine bottle-cum-weapon with caution.

"It looks like local LEOs have the situation under control," James said. "I don't think there's anything else for us to do."

"In that case, I'm gonna get us on the ground," Darius said.

While Darius communicated with the heliport, Quinn said to James, "I know why we can't, but I wish we could be in on bringing Olga and Townsend and the rest in."

"I know. Me too." James twisted at his waist and faced her. "The boats will have to dock at the port to offload them. Is there someplace nearby there where we can hang out and watch? Where we can blend in with a crowd?"

Quinn had her phone out before he could finish asking his question. "There are several restaurants with tables outside right along the edge of the port. Depending on where they dock, we might be able to see some of it."

"Restaurants, huh?" James said with a smile. "I could eat. Darius?"

He landed the helicopter and cut the engine. "I won't say no to dinner."

"Hey, Sydney," Quinn said as they strode across the helipad. "Want to meet us at the brasserie at Port Hercule in about fifteen minutes?"

"I thought you'd never ask."

Darius completed the necessary paperwork, and the three took a taxi to the port. They spotted Sydney already sitting at a table in the outdoor seating area and joined her.

Quinn sat and was powerless to do anything other than simply stare out at the tall, gently swaying sailboat masts. In the previous three hours, she had met with a Russian crime boss, engaged in a gun battle on a super yacht, chased said crime boss by both Jet Ski and supercar, witnessed him plunge over a cliff to his death, and then been whisked away via helicopter from a mountaintop golf course. To now be sitting in a restaurant where the sounds of normal life surrounded her—the hum of voices, the occasional eruption of laughter, the thumping beat of music—it was jarring.

James's hand rubbing her shoulder pulled her from her reverie. "Quinn, you okay?"

She smiled and fingered the menu on the table in front of her. "Yeah. It's been quite the day."

"It always takes me some time to regain my equilibrium once a job is over," James said. "It's weird to suddenly be normal again." He was always so perceptive to her emotional state, especially when it came to all things spy.

"Oh good," Sydney said. "It's not just me. I mean, you guys were the ones out there dodging bullets and zooming around on a Jet Ski and driving a Ferrari and flying a helicopter and stuff—which was super badass, by the way. I was only running comms, and I feel weird."

"You handled yourself really well, Sydney, especially injecting the Zieglopam and all that," James said. "The next time we need a scientist on an op, we'll be calling you."

Her eyes grew to the size of saucers. "Really? I'm just a lab rat."

"So?" Quinn said and lifted a shoulder. "I'm a librarian."

Sydney tipped her head and looked at Quinn with a thoughtful expression. "Good point."

Their server arrived, and a minute after they ordered, a police boat drove toward the dock. While the view from the brasscrie allowed Quinn to observe it cruise through the port, she wouldn't be able to see the boat's occupants disembark from her current vantage point.

"I'll be back in a few minutes," she said and jumped from her chair. She skirted between two potted plants and hustled down the street toward the two police cars awaiting the boat's arrival. Spying the ambulance made her stomach drop. Had one or more of the kids been injured? She slowed her steps to a stroll as she approached.

So as not to be too obvious, she'd planned to walk past the police boat, albeit slowly, and watch as the passengers were offloaded. That plan was quickly discarded since the commotion on and around Borovsky's yacht had drawn a crowd of curious onlookers. She joined them at the back and stood on her tiptoes.

A minute later, four young teens, Margarita and the three Quinn and James had left locked in a bedroom, were escorted off the boat surrounded by police. Despite the warm summer air, the kids clutched at the blankets draped over their shoulders. They wore the same dazed and confused expressions as the kids had in Saint Petersburg. At least they were all walking under their own power. It relieved her mind further when she watched the kids climb into the ambulance. The gesture made her feel fairly confident the authorities would treat them as the victims they were.

The ambulance had barely pulled out of the parking lot when the second police boat pulled into a slip. The first passenger escorted off was a scowling Mother Olga, her hands secured behind her back. Quinn hoped the cuffs around Olga's wrists were the ones she'd cinched on earlier. It seemed appropriate, as Olga had become a bit of a nemesis.

Next off was Yuri, followed by Ivan Ovechkin. Their perp walks garnered only a ripple of murmurs from the crowd and one cell phone raised to record the event. All that changed the second Rhys Townsend stepped into view. A loud gasp rose, followed by his name flying from every mouth. An entire crop of cell phones popped up, snapping pictures and recording him as he walked with his head down and face turned away. That would do little to mitigate the news of his arrest crisscrossing the globe in a matter of seconds.

Once the suspects were loaded into police cars and whisked away, the crowd dispersed. Quinn turned and rejoined her husband and coworkers at their table. She sipped the ale delivered to the table during her absence and reported what she'd witnessed. She ended her account with, "If people think Rhys Townsend being arrested is a scandal, I can't even imagine how crazy it will get when the full story comes out." She lowered her voice so only her tablemates could hear. "Drug running, a Russian crime boss, and human trafficking? It's a cable channel docudrama just waiting to happen."

Sydney snickered and said in an equally low tone, "*Rhys Townsend: The Shocking Story of a Fallen Star.*"

"Perfect. You should write the screenplay," Darius said with a laugh.

She grinned. "Even better. I'll put it into comic book form. I'll make us all superheroes."

"As long as you don't make my cape a cardigan sweater buttoned at the neck, I'm all for it," Quinn said.

"I've wondered about that," Sydney said with a sly look. "You're a librarian *and* you go into the field?"

"Mm-hmm. As needed."

"Do the other librarians know?"

"They might have their suspicions, but no one has said anything to me about it. You know how it is." A common phrase uttered at the agency was "need to know."

"The people back at the lab think I'm on vacation." Sydney slumped back and sighed. "I wish I really were here on vacation. I mean, I'm in *Monte Carlo.*" She shoved herself higher and stammered, "Of course you know I'm in Monte Carlo because you're here with me in Monte Carlo. I didn't mean to imply—"

"We got it," James said with a smile.

"Okay, good. It's just that I'm thinking, what are the chances of me ever being here again? How cool would it be to do all the touristy things, like hit the beach or go parasailing or tour the palace—" She rocketed forward, her eyes dancing with unbridled excitement. "Oh! The aquarium!"

Quinn looked over at James, whose eyes were already on her. Neither said a word. A single flick of his eyebrow told her he was thinking the same thing she was.

She pushed back her chair and stood. "Excuse me for a minute. I need to make a phone call."

Clearly baffled by Quinn's abrupt actions, Sydney mumbled, "Oh, okay." Darius wore an only slightly less perplexed expression.

Quinn took up a position next to a planter at the edge of the patio and placed her call.

"Hello, angel," her grandfather said. "It appears congratulations are in order. Borovsky's dead, several of his people—as well as Rhys Townsend—are in custody, and four innocents have been freed from trafficking. Well done."

"Thank you, Grandpa. I can't wait to tell you about it when we get back. It was pretty wild."

"I look forward to hearing your tales of adventure. The members of your team made it through unscathed? You're okay? James is well?"

"He is. We're all good."

"Excellent. I'll be sure to congratulate Darius and Sydney personally upon their return."

"I know they'll appreciate it. Actually, Sydney is one of the reasons I'm calling. I was wondering if you could extend her assignment here in Monte Carlo for a few more days."

Chapter Thirty-Five

Summer faded and transitioned to fall. For James and Quinn, most of the season was consumed by their task to thwart an assassin hired to kill a high-ranking Montenegrin government official. Fortunately, they were able to expose the nefarious plot, take down the would-be assassin and her benefactors, and still make it to San Diego in time to spend Thanksgiving with Quinn's family.

Now December had arrived, and James and Quinn were on yet another mission. This one, though, was of a more personal nature. And while a light drizzle fell from the ceiling of low, gray clouds overhead, the less-than-cheery weather failed to dampen Quinn's soaring spirits.

"Happy anniversary." Her cheeks were pink and stung with cold, but the hand laced with James's and buried deep in the pocket of his overcoat was toasty warm.

He shot her brilliant smile. "Happy anniversary."

"You know what I'm talking about?"

"You wound me deeply, madam," James said. The twinkle in his eyes belied his outrage. "Of course I know. Exactly two years ago today, I walked into the Westside Library and asked you to help me find out more about a Celtic brooch."

"I'll always have a soft spot in my heart for Ragnar's

brooch," she said affectionately. "And please accept my deepest apologies for questioning your romantic integrity."

He stopped them halfway up the steps that led to the entrance of the Washington State Legislative Building and turned toward her. He wrapped his free arm around her waist and pulled her to him. He gave her a kiss that sent heat rolling through her extremities. The kiss ended, but he held her firmly in his embrace. "Apology accepted."

"Thank you." She smiled at him and brushed her fingers through the wavy, damp hair at his temple. "I gotta say, you make apologizing extremely enjoyable."

He puffed out his chest. "I am pretty magnanimous, aren't I?"

She snorted and bumped his shoulder with a wry smile. "Come on, you."

They mounted the rest of the steps and entered the building. After flashing their federal identifications at security, they followed the rest of the guests toward the rotunda. Quinn glanced up at the impressively high dome soaring overhead as they ascended the marble steps. A massive bronze Tiffany chandelier hung from the center of the dome. She would never tire of visiting places of such stateliness and beauty.

James and Quinn arrived at the designated area where rows of chairs were lined up facing a wooden podium. Half the seats were already taken. Guests who chose not to sit yet milled around the edges of the seating area. A reporter and cameraman from a local news station were busy setting up at the back.

Quinn's gaze swept the space, locating exits and uniformed security personnel. She was also searching for familiar faces. She spotted one a short distance away and touched James's arm. "I see Dave. He's right over there."

Dave sent them a low-key wave. She returned a similar one in response. "Emily's here, too."

They joined Dave and his wife. After greetings, hand-shakes, and small talk, James asked, "Now that the trafficking ring run by our dearly departed Russian friend has been dismantled, what's next?"

Intel critical to taking down Borovsky's empire had come not only from his laptop inside the briefcase recovered from the demolished Pagani, but from Yuri and Dmitri. They'd rolled on everyone they could inside the organization. Quinn wasn't privy to all the details regarding the deals they'd struck. She was fairly confident if they served any time for their involvement, their families would be protected. For all she knew, the lot of them had been relocated outside of Russia. Odds were good she would never know.

"I've been hearing whispers about a small town in Cambodia that forces children to cater to men with deviant proclivities. We're fixing to check into it sooner than later."

Quinn swallowed her revulsion and turned to Emily. "It must be hard to have Dave out of the country so much."

"It is. But knowing what he does and who he helps, it's worth it." Emily's face beamed with excitement. "And thanks to you, he's taking me to Turks and Caicos this summer."

Quinn grinned along with her. "I'm so happy for you." She knew from personal experience growing up as the daughter of a Marine, the sacrifices families made when loved ones were deployed. It gave her an immense amount of pleasure to know Emily would be honored for her unsung role. "Give the conch a try." Quinn wrinkled her nose and added, "Just not raw."

"Dave already warned me about that," Emily said with a quiet laugh. "I think I'll stick to something a little less exotic."

"A wise choice," Quinn said.

A voice over the portable speakers asked guests to take

their seats. The two couples sat together. When the sound of feet shuffling and chairs scraping the floor ceased, a man stepped behind the podium and said, "Thank you for coming today and supporting our effort to shine a light on the evil that is human trafficking. We are here to talk about not only what happens in other parts of the world, but what takes place right here in this country."

The speaker went on to discuss how men, women, and children are stolen, bought, and sold. How they are lured into modern-day slavery and forced into hard labor, child pornography, or prostitution where they are never freed from their "debt." The statistics were dizzying, and by the time he neared the end of his talk, Quinn wished for a meteor to crash into Earth and destroy them all.

"I know it sounds like the world is nothing but a raging garbage fire," the speaker said. "And sadly, it seems like the dark, horrible news is all we ever hear. Today, we want you to hear a story of survival, of courage, of selflessness, of compassion, and ultimately, of hope. We are honored to have a remarkable young woman speak to us today. Please welcome Mila Semenov."

The rotunda echoed with the sound of polite applause. Quinn sat up as straight as possible to get a clear view of Mila as she approached the podium. A lump formed in her throat the second her eyes landed on the teenager. She hadn't seen her since she and James left her and her siblings at the rehabilitation ranch in Colorado months before.

Mila was beautiful.

Her hair was longer and the color in her face gave her a vitality that had been absent before. And while Mila was obviously nervous, the quiet strength Quinn noted from their first encounter was present.

Eyes glued to the paper on the lectern, Mila hooked a strand of hair behind her ear and said, "My name is Mila and I just turned fifteen." Her voice was clear, but hesitant. "I've never talked in front of a big group of people like this before. But if me telling my story can help others like me and my brother and sister, I'll do my best."

Several people in the audience shifted nervously in their seats.

Quinn's palms turned sweaty with empathic anxiety as she silently cheered Mila on.

Mila's gaze rose from the podium to the front row before her. A soft, affectionate smile formed. "These are my siblings, Sasha and Ilya." As she looked at them, Quinn watched Mila's confidence grow. Her shoulders squared and her startling, clear blue eyes met with those in the audience. "Up until a few months ago, we worked as slaves for a drug dealer in Saint Petersburg, Russia. We worked all day, every day, putting cocaine, heroin, and different kinds of pills in bags for sale on the street. I was also a drug mule, although I didn't know that was the term at the time. My sister and brother and I were trapped there for two years."

With a clear, measured voice, Mila told the story of how she and her siblings had been tricked, betrayed, and sold by their cousin and her boyfriend. The room grew as silent as a tomb as she spoke of the fear and despair they'd endured.

Throughout the room, throats gruffly cleared and fingers swiped at watery eyes.

Mila cast a spell over the audience as she told of how she and Pyotr would be sent all over the world to work as domestics and carry drugs back to Russia. She spoke of the guilt she felt for occasionally getting away from the horrible existence in Saint Petersburg while others were stuck inside the dreary flat. "And then, one day, a miracle happened."

The air seemed to be sucked out of the room as the audience waited.

Mila's eyes landed on Quinn and locked with hers. "Our guardian angel crawled through a window and promised to rescue us."

Quinn's eyes flooded with tears. James covered her hand with his.

Mila's gaze shifted from Quinn to James to Dave. "It wasn't right away and it was more like an army of angels, but if it wasn't for them, my brother, sister, and I wouldn't be here now."

She broke eye contact and held the crowd in the palm of her hand as she, without naming names, told the story of the people who'd risked their lives to free them from their captors. She seemed to know instinctively not to speak of the extraordinary flight back to the United States. Instead, she easily moved the story along by talking about Elkhorn Ridge Ranch and its importance to their journey of healing.

Mila smiled at those in the front row again. "We're back home with our mom and dad now. I don't think they're going to let us out of their sight ever again." A current of quiet laughter rolled through the crowd. Mila paused to listen to a member of the honored front row. She grinned and reported, "Ilya just said, 'I'm okay with that.'"

Quinn joined the swell of laughter and dabbed her knuckle under her eyes.

When a hush fell over the audience again, Mila shrugged a shoulder. "I don't know if anything I said today was helpful to anybody. I guess I'd just like to say if you can't climb through windows or go places to save kids like us, support the people who can. Maybe you can help get a ranch or a house set up here in Washington that can help kids once they're free but still kind of broken. If you can't, tell other people about what you've heard today. You might get them interested in doing something. People won't know there's a problem to fix if nobody tells them about it." She looked around the room and after a beat said, "I guess that's it. Thanks for listening."

The room went still, the air charged with electricity. Then, like a clap of thunder, it exploded with applause. As one, the audience rose to their feet.

Mila stepped back from the lectern and gave a little wave to no one in particular before returning to her seat.

The applause eventually subsided and everyone sat. Two more speakers made short speeches, one about policy and funding and the other about fair trade. Both were interesting and informative, but, for obvious reasons, failed to pack the emotional punch of Mila's.

When the event was over, it was all Quinn could do not to barrel her way through the crowd like a running back to get to Mila, Sasha, and Ilya. But a crush of people surrounded them and Quinn craved quality time. Thirty seconds snatched between well-wishers and the reporter with a microphone wouldn't do.

James, Quinn, Dave, and Emily stood off to one side and chatted while they waited for the crowd to clear. Amongst their varying topics, Quinn spoke of her recent research regarding the whereabouts of the kids' cousin, Yana. Her intel indicated that, ironically, Yana was stripping at a club in Moscow. None voiced disappointment to hear the boyfriend, Alexei, was currently incarcerated in Siberia for drug trafficking.

Thirty minutes later, Mila came at Quinn like a heat-seeking missile. They enveloped each other in a crushing embrace.

"I'm so glad to see you," Mila whispered. "Thank you for coming."

"We wouldn't have missed this for anything. I'm so proud of you."

"I want a hug, too," Sasha said, tugging at her older sister.

Ilya hadn't bothered asking. He shoved an arm between Mila and Quinn and squeezed.

With a watery laugh, Quinn released Mila and gave first Ilya and then Sasha proper hugs.

Quinn nearly dissolved into a puddle as she watched them greet James with shorter, but no less heartfelt hugs. James's glassy eyes made the grip on her emotions even more tenuous.

While the kids hugged Dave and smiled at Emily, their parents, Vasily and Ekaterina, shook hands with James and Quinn.

"We can never repay you for what you did to help bring our children home," Vasily said, his voice thick and raspy. He wasn't as tall as Quinn's father, but the broad build and steely eyes reminded her of him. Vasily cleared his throat in a struggle to maintain his composure.

Ekaterina wasn't as restrained. Plump tears of gratitude coursed down her face.

"Seeing them here with you is the best repayment possible," James said.

Quinn lowered her voice. "How are they doing?"

"Still adjusting," Ekaterina said. "They have only been home for a month. But they are doing well. Katie from Elkhorn Ridge Ranch connected us with a wonderful therapist here. They might even be able to start back to school next fall."

"I'm so glad to hear that," Quinn said. At the tug on her sleeve, she looked down to see Ilya's face gazing up at her.

"Can I ask a question?"

Quinn chucked a finger under the boy's chin. "Of course."

"Where's Mother Olga?"

"She's in prison."

Ilya's brow lowered. "Good. She deserves it."

"And Boss?" Sasha asked, referring to Grigori Yefimov.

"He's dead."

Their expressions reminded Quinn of when the three had watched Anatoly expire in the safe house's backyard. No tears would be shed over their captor's death.

"What about Gibson Honeycutt and Rhys Townsend?" Mila asked.

Quinn's eyes slid from Mila to her parents, silently questioning whether or not she should answer. The kids apparently had not seen the tabloids and celebrity websites that had been plastered with headlines and photos covering Townsend's arrest and subsequent charges. The last thing Quinn wanted to do was open wounds that were now beginning to heal.

Ekaterina nodded.

"Gibson's father has managed to shield him, so far anyway. Townsend is in jail in Monaco awaiting trial. The investigating magistrate considered him a flight risk, so he was denied bail."

"What happens to him if he's found guilty?"

"Since he's not a citizen of Monaco, he'll be sent to a French prison to serve his time."

Mila's body went rigid with tension. "What happens if he gets away with it?"

"I don't think that will happen," Quinn said. She and James were aware of the physical evidence and testimony that had been collected against Townsend. The chances of him being found not guilty were low. "But if it docs, he can be charged with drug smuggling in Turks and Caicos. A request to have him extradited has already been filed."

Mila's arms crossed in defiance. "I'll testify against him," she said without hesitation. "And Gibson Honeycutt, too, if they arrest him."

Quinn met Mila's resolute gaze. "So will I."

After a beat, Dave said, "From the looks on your faces, Townsend had better hope he's convicted in Monaco. He doesn't want to come up against you two."

"As long as he ends up in jail, I don't care where it is," Mila said.

Full-throated agreement sounded from everyone.

"Hey, with it so cold and rainy outside," James said, lightening the mood, "I could go for some warm pie and hot coffee. Who's with me?"

The positive response was loud and enthusiastic.

Sasha's face was incandescent with excitement. "Can I have coffee too?" she asked James breathlessly.

James raised his hands as if in surrender. "That's up to your mom and dad."

"We'll get you some hot cocoa," her mother said.

Vasily winked at his younger daughter and said conspiratorially, "You can have a sip of mine."

Quinn chuckled and shook her head as the Semenov family hurried off to collect their belongings. When it came to daughters, most dads were complete pushovers. She would know.

The phone in Quinn's pocket buzzed. She pulled it out far enough to check the caller ID. "Excuse me. I need to answer this."

James's forehead creased in silent question.

Quinn squeezed his hand before stepping away and putting the phone to her ear. "Hi, Grandpa. What's up?"